DEATH IS A REAL KILLER

BY

RANDALL J. FUNK

<u>ALSO BY RANDALL J. FUNK</u>

Death is a Clingy Ex

Death Lives Across the Hall

Death Wears a Big Hat

Death is Sleeping with My Wife

Death Stole My Ride

Death and the Fanboy

Death Will Be Brief: Joe Davis Mystery Tales

Published in the United States by Ghost Light Press, LLC

www.randalljfunk.com

ISBN: 978-1-7351-016-3-7

Cover design by Ann McMan

First edition

Special Thanks to:

Samantha Papke, for her help in preparing the manuscript.

Ann McMan, for her usual awesome work on the cover.

Everyone who has bought the previous Joe Davis books and helped me along on this adventure.

For my mother, who has gone home

and

for Alice Tibbetts,

"Small time, but in that small most greatly lived"

CHAPTER ONE

The hardest part of dealing with any violent change in your life is letting go of the past and embracing the New Normal. Because the New Normal wasn't what we signed up for. Life pulled a bait-and-switch. (That's essentially what prayer is: an attempt to get through to Life's Consumer Affairs Division.)

The moment you have to work toward is accepting that the Old Situation is gone and will not be coming back. When life first takes a violent lurch, we tend to think, 'No, it's okay. I'll just get the Old Situation back right away. It's no big deal. I just have to close my eyes, tap my ruby slippers together and say, 'There's no place like home.' That will work. Right? Right?"

We focus all our attention on the impossible ways in which we'll get the Old Situation back. The Twin Towers are gone? We'll just rebuild them. My husband left me? He'll come back. I've been thrown out of my house? I'll buy it back. I just need to think of a product America really needs. We use up energy best spent on adjusting to the New Normal. It's like going to back to sleep and trying to resume an interrupted dream.

How long it takes to finally lose the dream of the old life and accept the new way of things depends on the individual's personal makeup. And the amount of pot they have available.

My name's Joe Davis. I get paid to write stuff like that.

Personally, I haven't had too many violent changes to my life. At least, not in recent years. I live a comfortable life as a thrice-weekly columnist for *The Daily Bugle*, an indie newspaper that ditched the newspaper portion a few years ago and has since functioned strictly as a website. My column, *Cup o' Joe*, covers all manner of topics: pop culture, sports, entertainment, politics, social mores, what have you. The same stuff with which I've bored many a friend and ex-girlfriend, and now use to (barely) make a living. But hey, I've got a nice one-bedroom apartment, a couple of cats, and a bit of spending money. It's been that way for a while now. I've got no complaints.

My friend Mike, on the other hand, has had nothing but upheaval for the last several months. But he seems to have landed on his feet. "I think this job is going to work out," he says, waving a hand at our surroundings, "It's a little blue collar, but that's okay."

Our friend Carol holds a potsticker in a pair of chopsticks just below her mouth. "Whatever happened with that temp job?"

Mike runs a hand through the brush of brown hair on top of his big bulldog head. "I had to leave. There was an…incident."

Carol and I pause in our eating. *Incident* is Mike's favorite euphemism. It usually means he's committed some insane act that he'll now justify with the kind of logic only Abbott and Costello could appreciate.

We're hanging out at Fong's Wok, which for my money (and I've given them plenty of it) is the best restaurant on St. Paul's Grand Avenue. The restaurant itself is a simple affair. It's small and square. There are four rows of plain white tables from the window to the wall. The kitchen area is slightly open, allowing customers to see and hear the employees. A large counter dominates one wall. Japanese lanterns and a few nameless prints provide the decoration. A bistro in every way. Since it's February and the temps outside begin with a minus sign, we've made sure to get a table along the wall rather than along the windows. Mike reaches for one of my cream cheese wontons. I whap him with my fork, backing him off.

He clutches his hand as if I've done real damage. "Hey, what the fuck, man?"

"You know the rules," I say, "Once it's on the plate, no sharesies."

"Would it kill you to give up a wonton?" he asks.

"No, but it might kill *you*," I say.

He frowns and sits back in his chair. This dinner was originally supposed to be just Carol and me, but Mike has joined us, waiting for his next delivery. It's hard to believe that less than a year ago, he was working a comfortable real estate job, a gig that ended when he was caught in an affair with his boss's daughter. (It was as sordid as it sounds.) Since then, he's worked a string of temp jobs and tried to keep the bill collectors at bay. He left his most recent temp job about three weeks back but hasn't yet expounded on the circumstances.

I dip a wonton in some sweet 'n' sour sauce and try to keep said sauce from spilling on my black dress shirt. "What happened with the temp job?"

Mike pats his hands on his lap. "All right, the best part of that job was the individual restroom on the first floor. It was like a sanctuary. I'd go in there, lock the door and let loose. Best part of my day, next to going home."

Carol power-rolls her blue eyes, but I give Mike my undivided attention (more as a matter of protocol than anything). "Covers the basics," I say.

"All right, one morning, I stopped down there, and it was occupied. No big deal. I figured I'd just come back later. Except I came back, like, five times that hour and it was *still* occupied. I was getting pissed. I'm thinking, 'What the fuck?

Did somebody die in there?' Anyway, it turned out somebody died in there."

Carol nearly chokes on her potsticker. "Wait, what? Seriously?"

"Seriously," Mike says, "Some poor dude had a coronary on the throne."

"Holy shit," I say.

"Literally," Mike says, "Poor bastard's meeting St. Peter with his pants around his ankles."

A chill goes around the table (not that it takes much with the temps outside). Mike *does* tend to overstate situations, but in this case, the facts speak for themselves. I set down my fork, temporarily ignoring my orange peel beef (best in the city, by the way).

"That is not the way I want to go," I say, sipping my beer, "How about you guys?"

Mike strokes his goatee. "I'd rather not go at all. But if I had a choice, having an infarction while forcing out a gnarly turd would not be high on the list."

I shiver. "I hate that word. Infarction. If that's what takes me, tell everyone I had a heart attack. *Infarction* sounds like I farted myself to death."

"Which this guy more or less did," Mike says.

"Makes you think," I say,

"Makes you think."

Carol lowers her head and tries to keep her gold necklace out of her kung pao chicken. Disgust with us is not a new thing for her. Particularly with Mike. The two of them dated for about a year. It's been over for a while now, but Mike's capacity to disgust Carol has not diminished. Hard to believe those two crazy kids couldn't make it work.

"Obviously, I had to quit that job," Mike says.

"Because of that?" Carol asks.

"Absolutely," Mike says, "Follow the chain. The only thing I liked about that job was the first-floor restroom. I couldn't use it after that."

"Why not?" I ask, "The guy wasn't still in there, was he?"

"No."

"Was the shitter, in fact, haunted?" I ask.

Mike smacks the table. "No, Richard—or perhaps Dick—it wasn't haunted. But it might as well have been. You need to relax when you're on the crapper. Otherwise—"

"I'm aware of the process," I say.

"Then you'll understand how I'd never be able to relax knowing some guy *died* in there."

Carol waves her hand, as if erasing a blackboard. "Oh my God, can we drop this subject? I'm trying to eat."

Can't blame Carol, given that I have a weak stomach myself. Furthermore, I can't blame Mike for quitting the temp gig. I'm abnormally susceptible to the heebie-jeebies. And a reluctance to share a bathroom could be one of the reasons I'm still single. Mike, though, has recovered nicely. At first, he wasn't thrilled about working at Fong's. But rent was due, and he needed the infusion of tip money. Beyond one incident in which an angry customer referred to him as a *broke-ass delivery man* (which may or may not have become a nickname we hung on him for a few weeks), things have worked out swimmingly. He *does* look resplendent in his black slacks, black dress shirt and stocking cap (the last two of which have *Fong's* stenciled in red). He can even wear his black leather jacket and heavy boots on the job. A win all around.

Fong himself interrupts our chat, appearing at the front counter. He's a short, wiry man with thick eyebrows and a head of graying black hair. When he speaks, his voice booms out over the restaurant.

"Mike! Delivery up!"

Mike slides out of his seat and swaggers to the front, pulling on his gloves as he goes. He gets a hero's welcome from the kitchen and responds with a little bow of his head. Fong positively beams at him.

"You be back soon?" Fong asks.

"Always," Mike says.

That gets another round of applause from the kitchen. Mike holds his head high and sashays out the front door. One of Fong's daughters, Biyu, is working at the front counter. She's a slim, attractive girl with beautiful dark eyes. Her hair is up, held in place by chopsticks. A tight-fitting rust-colored dress with a gold pattern hugs her body. Her eyes focus on Mike as he walks out. Her full lips twitch in appreciation. Oh boy, this might get interesting. Fong works his way over to our table.

"Joe Davis!" he says, spreading his arms wide, "How are you? Everything okay with your food?"

"Great as always, Mr. Fong," I say.

"That good, that good," Fong says, sounding genuinely pleased.

I introduce him to Carol, who compliments him on the kung pao chicken. Fong is gracious but takes it in his stride. He's used to compliments on his food. Carol looks toward the door, where Mike just left.

"Is Mike working out as a delivery person?" she asks.

Fong throws his hands out. "He's the greatest. Fast and friendly. Business up the last few weeks because we get food there so fast. Best delivery man we ever had. We love him!"

Fong's voice rises so that everyone in the kitchen (and the greater St. Paul area) can hear him. A chorus of agreement comes from the kitchen, most of them cheers and then, as the cheers fade, a voice in the background says, "We love Mike!"

"Glad to hear it," I say, before finishing off my wanton.

I'll be honest: I'm shocked. Mike is not only surviving, he's thriving. Still, I can't help wondering if this is going to turn out like most of Mike's relationships: promising at first, followed by the inevitable disillusionment.

Fong looks toward the front. Someone from the kitchen has placed a couple to-go bags on the front counter. Fong excuses himself and goes to the front. He grabs the to-go order off the kitchen counter and calls out, "Ron." He's looking at a kid of Asian descent sitting at a nearby table and staring at his phone. The kid doesn't respond, so Fong is a little more forceful. "Ron!" This time, Ron hops to his feet so fast he nearly drops the phone. I half-expect him to salute.

"Yes, Mr. Fong," Ron says, his voice sounding a bit like Bullwinkle Moose, "I'm sorry."

"I don't care about sorry," Fong says, "Delivery up. You go."

"Yes, sir."

Ron grabs the bags, struggling with them until he realizes they'd be easier to handle if he put his phone away. He fumbles for the door. Fong's voice follows him.

"You want to learn, you watch Mike," Fong says, "Do what he do. Mike the best delivery man we ever had."

"Got it, Mr. Fong."

Ron scurries out the front door, nearly crashing into someone as he goes. A blast of cold air hits us in the ankles. Carol and I wait it out (like an Ice Cream Brain Freeze) then go back to our food. I close my eyes, savoring the feeling of my orange peel beef melting in my mouth. Carol expertly wields her chopsticks, (I'm too clumsy to use them myself) making short work of the kung pao chicken.

"I can't believe Mike found something he can excel at," Carol says.

"We should probably take a wait-and-see attitude," I say, trying to avoid looking toward Biyu.

Carol looks around, as if someone who gives two shits might be listening. "I don't know if I should get on my high horse about work. I snuck out of the office yesterday and did some day drinking."

Thankfully, I've just swallowed my food, or I might have choked on it. *Carol* was goofing off? She's supposed to be the best of us. Even now, at dinner, she looks professional and adult. Her dark hair falls perfectly to her shoulders, brushing her white sweater. She wears only a hint of makeup, though she doesn't really need it. Her normally cool blue eyes have a mischievous gleam in them. This is the diamond in our own particular rough. And yet, she was playing hooky from work.

"What happened there?" I ask.

Carol dabs at her lips with her napkin. "I got a call from my friend Evie. We knew each other in college. She lives in the Cities. We hang out from time to time. Anyway, she was doing some day drinking and wanted me to join her. So, I slipped out of the office for some barhopping."

It takes a second to form the words. "That doesn't sound like the sort of thing you'd do."

She greets that with a flip of her hand. "Evie always had that kind of influence on me. Besides, I'm allowed to have fun from time to time, aren't I?"

I'm not going to argue. Carol *should* be allowed to play hooky when the mood strikes. But it's so far out of her normal scope. Carol's an ad writer, one of the better ones you'll find, and is never shy about reminding me that she does serious work while I write my column and goof off. And now *she's* goofing off? It's like coming home and finding your mother lying on the living room floor, surrounded by empty Stoli bottles and singing *Tubthumping*. (Come to think of it, that's so far out of my mom's scope I can't even picture it. And don't want to. Let's, let's move on.) I adjust the napkin in my lap.

"You get any blowback from your boss?" I ask.

"I'll find out on Monday," Carol says, "I doubt it. There wasn't anything important on the agenda. That's one of the reasons I snuck out."

Ah, that's our Carol. Wild and crazy and out of control…after she's cleared her schedule. At least it's nice to know she has this side. Yes, she got herself in some trouble last fall at a bachelorette party, but that was alcohol-induced. *This* was a decision made in the cold, sober light of day…to induce alcohol. I raise my glass of beer in a toast.

"Here's to goofing off," I say.

Carol picks up her red wine and joins me. Something gets her attention, over my shoulder. I turn to see our buddy Lars, wearing a ski jacket and a hat with flap ears, gliding up to the table. He whips off the hat and stuffs it in the pocket of his coat. A beautiful woman with dark hair, thick eyebrows and a full mouth stands a few feet behind him. Her cold eyes study the picture windows. Lars attempts to fluff up his quasi-pompadour.

"Greetings and salutations and stuff and things," he says, giving us a slight bow, "Are we enjoying the evening?"

"We are, indeed," I say, "Feel free to pull up a chair."

Lars gives us a nervous laugh and turns to the beautiful woman. She says nothing, but one eyebrow rises ever so slightly. Lars spins back to the table.

"No can do, I'm afraid. Iris and I, uh, have plans for the evening."

We turn toward Iris. We weren't entirely sure she was with Lars, given her unwillingness to approach the table. I have to say, she's breathtaking. Perfect cheekbones, alabaster skin, full lips. I'm not sure what quality is in her eyes, intensity or coolness or both, but it turns my guts to Jell-O. She slips off her thick overcoat and reveals a blue sweater and jeans clinging to her shapely body. She's not enough of a twig to be a model, but she could certainly pass for a movie star or a Fox News bubblehead. Lars starts to step away from the table, then stops.

"We need to talk about the fundraiser," he says to Carol.

"We do," Carol says, "Let's get together for coffee or something."

"Done deal, sister." He throws out a flipper-like hand to the table. "You two have a good evening."

He slips away from the table and offers his arm to Iris. She tosses her coat over the arm and strides toward a corner table. Lars slinks after her. I give a small whistle.

"Holy mother…" I say, "*She* is dating Lars?"

Carol tilts her head. "So it would appear."

"Wow," I say, "Lars has dated some good-looking women, but this Iris is a whole other story."

"Different author altogether," Carol says.

"Not even the same language." I turn back toward Carol. "What's the fundraiser Lars was talking about?"

"We're raising funds to rebuild the Kellen Community Center," she says.

"The Kellen neighborhood. That's over by Frogtown, right?"

"It is," Carol says, "The community center closed a handful of years ago. Lack of funding. The city is willing to put some money into it, but only if the bulk of the cost comes from private donors. Lars is trying to raise the money."

"Seriously?"

"Yep. He's holding a big fundraiser at the center in a few weeks. I agreed to help him out."

I'm surprised. Lars fancies himself an entrepreneur, but a community center sounds altogether too altruistic to be within his purview. Yes, he went through a growth phase a few months back where he was concerned with the community. But that went away when the mentor who led him down that path turned out to be a weirdo of the highest order. Maybe more of that stuck to Lars than I realized.

"A community center?" I say, "What's in it for Lars?"

"I don't know," Carol says, "I'm just helping him out with the copywriting and the organization." She taps a chopstick on my plate. "He might be asking you to help, too."

"Me? What could I do?"

"Publicity. You're a…a…" She mumbles into her eggroll. "A celebrity. Kind of."

I sip my beer, covering my smile (although I'm sure Carol knows it's there). My column affords me a weenie bit of celebrity which never fails to annoy my friends (Carol particularly) and amuse me. I set my beer down and assume a self-important air.

"It sounds like a lovely idea," I say, "I'll have to take it up with my advisors, of course. See if it's the right project for me. I have my reputation to think of, you know."

"Don't think too hard," Carol says, "I'm not pushing you to do it. The exact opposite, really."

Carol and I finish our meal and chitchat a little while longer. Beyond the fundraiser, there isn't a lot we're up to these days. Just experiencing the midwinter blahs. The news is on the HD TV in the corner. I can't hear it, but the headlines are all depressing. Terrorist attack overseas, tough talk from menacing countries, a CEO killed out in Excelsior (wow, that's different), a woman attacked at a light rail station, partisan wrangling at both the federal and state level, the Wild on another losing streak. And my father wonders why I rarely watch the news.

As we're leaving, I notice Lars and his girlfriend in conversation. Apparently, Iris *does* talk. In fact, she's doing all the talking. Lars looks like he's in the principal's office. He tugs at his scarf and is sweating, despite the cold. He doesn't look up or acknowledge us as we leave. Once we're on the snow-covered sidewalk, Carol offers me a ride home. I decline.

"It's just a few blocks," I say, huddling into my peacoat and tucking in my scarf, "I can walk it."

"Joe, it's below zero out here," Carol says.

"I'm from northern Minnesota," I tell her, "We get weather like this in July."

Carol rolls her eyes. She's heard my *I'm from northern Minnesota* schtick enough times to know she won't talk me out of walking home. She simply bids me a hasty goodnight and jumps into her car. I power-walk east on Grand Avenue, safe in the knowledge I'll probably be home by the time Carol's car warms up.

It's only about six blocks back to my building, but it doesn't take long to get chilled in this kind of weather. It's February and we're in the middle of a cold snap. Daytime highs have been in the single digits and overnight lows have had a minus sign in front of them. It's only been this way for a week, but when the temps are this extreme, it seems like years. You start to wonder if it's ever going to be warm again.

Nothing moves. Even the air is still. It feels clean, but not refreshing.

I round on to Dale Street and move toward Summit Avenue, an old-school artery in St. Paul, lined with mansions that F. Scott Fitzgerald once called a "museum of architectural failures." (Scott was a bit of a spoilsport…in addition to being a brilliant novelist and a raging alcoholic.) My building sits near the corner of Summit and Dale. It's a converted brownstone. My apartment is on the third floor. The snow crunches underfoot. The cold sends needles up my arms and legs. My face is frozen and heavy. I regret wearing dress shoes instead of boots. My feet are two blocks of ice. I duck down the alley to the parking lot at the back of the building, then sprint up the erector set of decks and stairs that were attached (poorly) to the building somewhere in its history. I tuck my chin deeper and deeper into my scarf. Once on my deck, I fumble with my keys before finally getting through the backdoor and into the thankful warmth of the apartment. I flex my fingers, the blood flow returning painfully to my extremities. Next time, I should just accept the damn ride home. I don't even live in northern Minnesota anymore.

I lean against the backdoor, enjoying the warmth. My apartment is fairly simple. The hallway from the backdoor leads past the single bathroom and single bedroom. After that is a thin kitchen with a breakfast bar, then the living room, with arch windows facing Summit and a desk in the corner. It's not much, but it's everything I need.

The lights are off, but that's not unusual. What *is* unusual is that my cats, Lenny and Squiggy, are not here to greet me. They always seem to sense my approach from miles away and are standing in kitty formation whenever I come through the door, be it the front or the back. But there's no sign of them. Maybe they went to bed early. I walk down the hall, looking for the light switch by the front door. Just as I reach it, a voice stops me.

"Good evening, Joe Davis."

There's nothing unpleasant about the voice. It's clear, lilting and feminine. Yet it sends a chill down my already frozen spine. I forget about the light switch and slowly turn toward the breakfast bar separating my kitchen from my living room.

A woman sits at my breakfast bar. Her tall body lounges, cat-like, on the counter. Honey-colored hair flows past her shoulders. Her large eyes are focused on me, and a smirk plays at one corner of her full mouth. She's dressed completely in black: coat, sweater, cargo pants, boots, the works. I don't *know* that a gun is hiding in the folds of her leather trench coat, but I suspect it is and that she can get to it and blow me away before I'm aware of what's happening. I freeze in position. We stand there in the dark.

"Hello, Deirdre," I say, "Good to see you again."

But we both know that's a lie.

CHAPTER TWO

The first rule of staying safe is: never think you're safe. Similar to the old just because you're not paranoid doesn't mean people aren't out to get you *adage, just because you feel safe doesn't mean you aren't, ultimately, screwed. Just when you think the collection agency has given up on you, the subpoena arrives. Just when you think your ex has finally moved on, you get the forty-five drunken text messages. Just when you think the boss doesn't know you've been coming in late for a year and half, you get called into their office to explain. You can't let your guard down, practically, defensively or karmically. Only bad stuff will follow.*

Of course, you could live your life in such a way as to avoid someone coming after you, but where's the fun in that?

I had hoped Deirdre had forgotten about me. *Why* I thought I would have that kind of luck is perhaps more a mystery.

Deirdre and I met a little more than a year ago. We didn't exactly hit it off, but then it wasn't the kind of occasion that lends itself to bonding. Deirdre had been hired to kill my friend Carol. By the end of the evening, she not only hadn't killed Carol, she actually saved my life. But she also let me know she wasn't happy with my interference and could reconsider her goodwill at any time. She's crossed my mind now and again, but after a while, I figured she had forgotten about me.

First time I've been bummed out someone *didn't* forget about me.

I stand with one hand on the doorknob and one just below the light switch. (Best to keep my hands where Deirdre can see them.) For some reason, I don't want to turn on the lights. Maybe that will make Deirdre's presence here real. I'm not breathing. The only sound in the room is the hiss of the radiator. Deirdre studies me for a few long moments. She uncoils herself and slides away from the stool, effortlessly getting to her feet. Her eyes glide around the apartment.

"I wondered what the *inside* of this place looked like," she says.

"How many times have you seen it from the outside?" I ask.

A corner of Deirdre's mouth rises. "You probably don't want to know that."

She's right on that one. I've got another question I don't want answered but it seems the most relevant one to ask.

"What brings you by?" I say.

Deirdre wanders around the living room, her back to me. "You don't watch the news, do you?"

"Nobody watches the news. I get that stuff from the internet."

"Then you haven't looked at the internet."

I could sit here and play Twenty Questions, but that's not going to get Deirdre out of my apartment any sooner. Or keep her from killing me. I jog my short-term memory. What's gone on lately that might involve Deirdre? I run through the headlines I saw on the TV at Fong's. She probably has nothing to do with the Wild's losing streak or the crappy weather. The terrorist attack is in the ballpark, but still probably not Deirdre. Then it hits me.

"The guy who was killed out in Excelsior," I say, "The CEO or something."

Deirdre turns toward me, the smirk fading slightly. "Alex Hollins. Very good."

"You killed him?"

There's a long pause. Deirdre doesn't even move the muscles in her face. But I get the feeling she's weighing some kind of decision. When she finally makes it, her head tilts back, almost imperceptibly.

"No, I didn't," she says, "That's why I'm here."

My first thought is that she wants to kill me as a replacement for this Alex Hollins guy. I remind myself that Deirdre is a contract killer. She doesn't work for free. (One has professional pride to consider.)

"I'm not quite following you," I tell her.

Deirdre perches on to the arm of my futon. Her mouth is tight as she forces out the words. "I need your help."

The idea is laughable, of course. And I would laugh, but I'd probably get shot. Instead, I go with the other thing I'm feeling: confusion.

"You need *my* help?" I ask, "With what?"

Deirdre's mouth flattens. She looks around the darkened room. "You have anything to drink around here?"

"The liquor shelf is in the corner," I say, "Otherwise, I have beer in the fridge."

"Whiskey will do."

"I'll get you a glass."

I step into the thin kitchen and fetch a highball glass. Deirdre declines ice. As long as I'm in the kitchen, I get a beer out of the fridge. While I'm pouring her whiskey, Deirdre avoids the arch windows at the front. I should probably take off my coat but it gives me a strange feeling of security. Drink in hand, Deirdre settles herself on the arm of the comfy chair in the middle of the room. I stand behind the futon, figuring I need to keep *something* between her and I.

"You're nervous," she says, her cold eyes twinkling.

"You come home and find a contract killer in your apartment, it doesn't exactly take the edge *off.*" Deirdre doesn't say anything. "What do you need my help with?" I ask.

Deirdre takes a healthy drink of whisky. "I was hired to eliminate Alex Hollins. I went to his house to do it. But someone had gotten to him already."

There doesn't seem to be anything to say other than, "Who?"

Deirdre doesn't raise her voice, but the look on her face conveys her sense of bewilderment. "I don't know. But the police are going to think I did it."

Wow. This is not where I expected the evening to go. Sure, my being confused isn't new, particularly after a couple of beers. But that the confusion regards the killing of a CEO? That's a new one. I step around the futon and sit on the arm.

"Maybe you should give me the whole story," I say.

Deirdre drains the rest of her whiskey, looks to the liquor shelf, considering another, then sets the glass on the coffee table. "Alex Hollins is CEO of Hankerson-William. Some company here in Minnesota. You ever heard of it?"

I have. Hankerson-William is one of those multi-billion-dollar companies that gives grants to public broadcasting and sponsors charitable events and local sports teams and has its hands in so many interests, you aren't entirely sure what it is they do. But you've certainly heard of them.

"Who hired you?" I ask.

"I don't ask those questions. I have someone who arranges my work. They give me the assignment and I carry it out. Pure and simple."

A chill, one that has nothing to do with the cold, rolls through me. Deirdre might as well be talking about a trip to the grocery store. ("I need eggs, bread, soup, and the head of Alfredo Garcia.") I try not to let her see me shiver.

"Then what happened?" I ask.

"I went to his house. It's a great big place out beyond the suburbs. The security system was going to be turned off. I was told the guy would be home, working in his study. The house is secluded. The servants leave at a certain hour. The wife would be out. There shouldn't have been any problem." Deirdre goes to the liquor shelf and pours herself two fingers of whiskey. "The study is on the first floor. When I got there,

Alex Hollins was already dead. Lying right in the middle of the floor. Stabbed in the chest and the abdomen."

I set my beer down. "And nobody else was in the house?"

"Nobody that I could see. I didn't hear anything when I was approaching the house. Then the police showed up. A lot of them." Deirdre sips her whiskey, "They had the place surrounded. There's a path through the woods on the back of the property. I got there just before the police closed it off. But I'm pretty certain they saw me. There's a motion sensor light in the backyard. Looked like a damn floodlight. There's a chance they got a good enough look to identify me." She drains the glass. "If you'll pardon the expression, it was a clusterfuck of the highest order."

I sit back on the arm of the futon and think about the blurb on Alex Hollins's murder that I saw on the news. I don't remember them mentioning a suspect, but then the sound was off on the TV, and I wasn't paying a great deal of attention in the first place.

"What do you think happened?" I ask.

It's a stupid question, one that popped out of my mouth before I thought about it. Deirdre gives it a lighter version of the *Are you an idiot?* look I get from Carol every now and again.

"It was a set up," she says, "Someone arranged for me to eliminate Alex Hollins, then did the job themselves. They left me to take the fall for it."

"Why?"

"I don't know. But it was a set up. I know that much."

This brings us to another question I don't particularly want to ask. "What do you want my help with?"

Deirdre sets her glass on the coffee table. "I need to be cleared of this. I can't afford to have my face plastered all over TV and the internet. That happens and my career is over. I need a place to hide and to find out who set me up. I want you to help me."

I try not to choke on my beer, but it's an effort. Deirdre isn't the first person to ask for my help with a thing like this (she's the most dangerous, but not the first). Usually, I'm moved to help because it's a friend of mine. But Deirdre and I aren't friends. And she can't exactly appeal to my sense of justice. Deirdre might not be guilty of Alex Hollins's murder, but she's guilty of plenty of others, I imagine. It doesn't exactly stir the Dudley Do-Right in me.

"I don't think this is a good place to hide," I say, "Its small. I've got people coming and going at all hours. You'd be discovered."

"I'll stay out of sight. I know how to do it." Deirdre senses my hesitation. "You owe me. I saved your life."

"And I saved *your* life," I say, "Twice, as I recall."

"Twice?"

"I gave you the keys when you were handcuffed to the lamppost," I say.

"The lamppost you and your friends handcuffed me to?"

"Still, I didn't have to give you the keys. I did it to save you. That puts me ahead, two to one."

"All right." Deirdre gets to her feet. Unconsciously, I get to mine as well. "We'll have to even those odds," she says, "I can save your life…" A pistol appears in her hand. "By choosing not to kill you. Because if you don't help me, Joe Davis, that's exactly what I'm going to do."

Remember what I said about getting too comfortable? I let myself get so drawn into this conversation, I'd gotten numb to the ever-present danger of Deirdre's, well, presence. I back up, again putting the futon between us. (It won't stop a bullet, but it makes me feel better.) My heart beats in my ears.

"I've got to tell you," I say, "You're a hell of a shrewd negotiator. You've got a deal."

Deirdre lowers the weapon. It disappears into the black coat. I lower my hands. My breath comes back. Huh.

Never thought a deal with the devil would be quite
so…calming. Deirdre looks around the apartment.

"I'd like to turn in," she says, "We can figure
everything else out in the morning."

"Fine by me. You can sleep in my bedroom if you
want. I'll take the—"

"The couch will be fine for me."

That's a relief, really. I hate giving up my bed. Deirdre
takes off her trench coat and drapes it over the back of the
futon. (Instead of the coat tree by the door. I wonder if this
partnership is going to work.) I edge toward the hallway.

"You have anything with you?" I ask, "Change of
clothes? Toiletries?"

Deirdre shakes her head. "I travel light. I'll figure
something out."

"I've got an extra toothbrush," I say, "And a pillow
and an extra blanket."

She laughs, but it's completely internal. "You look like
the kind of guy who has an extra pillow and blankets."

I start toward the bedroom, then stop. "I haven't seen
my cats. Are they…?"

"They're fine. They ran into the bedroom as soon as
they saw me."

Typical. There's no way the cowardly bastards would
warn me there was an intruder. Not when presented with an

opportunity to save their own asses. Going to make cuddling with them tonight an awkward experience.

But then this whole night has been an awkward experience, right?

***

I do love my apartment, but it's indifferently heated. The radiator in the living room keeps things nice and cozy. But the bedroom doesn't get the same warmth. I generally keep the door open at night in order to warm the room. However, it didn't feel right to have the bedroom door open with a guest sleeping in the living room. When I wake up in the morning, I'm buried under a comforter and two blankets. The cats are plastered against either side of me. I have an old sweater wrapped around my head. I'm wearing a Batman sweatshirt, flannel pajama bottoms and my warmest socks. And it's still cold as hell.

Two cats, littermates, run my household: Lenny, a butterscotch tabby who constantly demands food and attention (like Julius Caesar with less cunning and more appetite), and Squiggy, the nervous former runt of the litter, whose black-and-white coloring and obsequious manner reminds me of a butler. Squiggy notifies me of the need for breakfast by gently tapping me with his front paw. Lenny notifies me by sitting on my face.

I open the bedroom door and step cautiously into the hallway. My feet feel brittle against the hardwood floor (possibly the legacy of all the running I do). Already I feel warmer. I'm not sure if Deirdre is awake yet, so I try to be quiet. The cats speed down the hallway and into the kitchen. I peek into the living room. Deirdre is still asleep on the futon. The blanket is wrapped around her, her black bra visible. Her honey-colored is splayed across the pillow. She looks peaceful. I didn't know killers could look peaceful. There's your fun fact for the day.

I put a mix of wet and dry food into the cats' bowls and get a pot of coffee started. (I try to never confuse those two activities.) While the coffee brews, I make my way over to the desk in the corner. Deirdre's clothes are flung about the room, causing me a pain. My apartment is normally as neat as an operating room. Orderly room, orderly mind. Needed for writing. I pick the clothes up, fold them and pile them on the coffee table. That done, I carefully slide into the desk chair and get on the internet to do some research. The arch windows are ringed with frost. The radiator hisses and pops. (I should talk to management about that.)

I start by looking up Alex Hollins. Not surprisingly, all the immediate articles are about the murder. They don't tell me much I don't already know. There is mention of a suspect fleeing the scene, but no details are provided.

The research on Hankerson-William tells me a little more. They're essentially an umbrella company with a lot of subdivisions. They have their hands in retail, oil refining, mining, medical research, etc. The website has glowing biographies of its upper management, Alex Hollins chief among them.

I dig a little deeper into Alex Hollins himself. A lot of the articles are from public events. The guy certainly wasn't camera shy. Whether the camera loved him is a matter of more debate. Yes, he's got bright blue eyes, swept back blonde hair and an engaging smile. But the face is a little fat, the chin a little weak. In several photos, his appearance is accentuated by a tall blond with porcelain features and a tight mouth. If I'm reading the captions right, the woman is Chelsea Hollins, Alex's wife. In the few pictures where Alex is not smiling, there's an intensity, even a coldness in his eyes, something matched by his wife. I'll have to do some research on her.

I dig into Alex Hollins's biography. He was ambitious, that much is obvious. Master's degree in business. Top of his class at the University of Minnesota. A mid-level management position right out of college. CFO at Hankerson-William within ten years, COO a few years after that, then CEO (E-I-E-I-O). Since then, Hankerson-William's profits have grown by a hundred-and-fifty percent. Most of the diversifying they've done has happened at Alex Hollins' behest. Even in dry print, it's an impressive biography. What it doesn't tell me is who might have wanted him dead. I note the writer of one of the articles. Alberto Castillo. Ah, that presents some possibilities.

There is a stirring on the futon. I spin around in the desk chair. Deirdre sits up, pulling the blanket over her. She brushes the hair out of her eyes and looks around. She has no reaction upon spotting me. I wonder if anything ever startles her. I gesture toward the kitchen.

"Cup of coffee?" I say.

"Please," she says.

I go into the kitchen, get my *Writers Do It Between the Covers* and *Porter's Bay* coffee mugs out of the cupboard and pour two cups of java. I'm about to move back to the breakfast bar when Deirdre's voice comes from the next room.

"Stay in there for a minute," she says, "And turn around. I'm getting dressed."

"If I'm in here, why do I have to turn around?"

"That hall mirror doesn't reflect into the living room?"

She's right. It does. There's a ninety-five-percent chance I wouldn't look into it. Still, if I were Deirdre, I wouldn't trust that other five percent. I turn around and wait for the all-clear. Once I get it, I join Deirdre at the breakfast bar. She pulls her hair into a ponytail as I set the *Porter's Bay* mug in front of her. She takes a sip, then closes her eyes and hunches her shoulders slightly, as if the coffee contains a life-giving force, (which it absolutely does). Her eyes are glassy from sleep, but that's the only difference from last night. I get the feeling she can immediately go from asleep to alert. I place the sugar bowl, the cup with the collection of sweetener packets, and the cream pitcher in front of her. They're accompanied by a saucer holding a coffee spoon. Deirdre looks down, trying (and failing) to cover her amusement. I gesture toward the toaster.

"I could make us some English muffins," I say.

"Let me guess," Deirdre says, "You have jelly and butter right here as well."

"Of course. Unless you prefer peanut butter. I've got some of that in the—"

"Coffee's fine." She picks up the mug. "What's a Porter's Bay?"

"My hometown," I say, "It's up on the North Shore."

"Sounds cold."

"It can be. But it's nice. Full of tourists in the summer." I gesture toward the futon. "Did you sleep okay?"

"Fine. I've had worse. I'm just glad your radiator works." She looks back toward the arch windows. "Is this state *ever* warm?"

"In February? No. But some years, thanks to our friends at Global Warming, spring starts right after New Year's."

Deirdre looks at me over her coffee cup, one corner of her mouth twitching. The cats, breakfast finished, stroll past Deirdre, paying no attention to her. They curl up on the futon, taking advantage of the warmth she left behind, and begin their morning nap (which will precede Second Breakfast).

"We need to come up with a plan," Deirdre says.

Strangely, getting down to business relaxes me. It's less awkward than casually having a contract killer to coffee.

"Okay, first, regarding you being on the run," I say, "is there anything you left behind that the cops might use to identify you? Cell phone? ID? Anything like that?"

"No," Deirdre says, her tone a little edgy, as if I've insulted her professionalism, "I have my ID and a cell phone on me, but that wouldn't do them any good. The cell phone's a burner and the ID is fake."

As if to emphasize, she fetches the phone and the ID out of her trench coat, carefully avoiding the window as she goes. She sets them on the breakfast bar. I view each of them with a cursory eye. The ID is from Missouri and has the name *Deirdre Park* on it.

"The name on the ID is fake?" I say, "Then, Deirdre's not your real name?"

"No, it's not."

"What *is* your real name?" I ask.

Deirdre sets her coffee cup down. "That's on a need-to-know basis."

"And I don't need to know."

"Exactly."

Well, this partnership is off to a flying start. Still, it was probably a dumb question. Deirdre hasn't made a living at what she does by giving every Tom, Dick and Joe her background information. I toy with my coffee cup.

"I need to know about how you work," I say, "I'm not being nosy. I just need to know what kind of information you do and don't have access to."

"Fine."

I take a shallow breath. "Okay, so you're hanging out…wherever it is that you live. And you're contacted about doing a job. How does that work?"

"I have someone who answers my calls and makes arrangements. We'll call her Emily."

"Not her real name?"

"Correct." Deirdre slides her coffee cup aside. "Emily contacts me and we work out an itinerary. Once the money's deposited, I go to work. Emily makes travel arrangements, works out burner phones or IDs or anything that I need. Then the job begins."

"That's how it worked this time?" I ask.

"It did."

"Is there any way to contact Emily?"

"No. I have a code I send her. It tells her I'm in trouble and she should cut off contact. Then she disappears."

"Disappears where? Actually, forget it. You won't tell me, right?"

"Right."

That's a pity. This "Emily" probably knows the contact information for the person who hired Deirdre and is therefore the person who likely set her up. We're still at Square One.

"Okay, we're thinking someone hired you and set you up," I say, "But we don't know who that is."

"Whoever it was probably worked through another person anyway," Deirdre says, "That's how we do this. Put as many layers as possible between the client and me. Keeps everyone safe."

"Except this time."

"Except this time."

I pinch the bridge of my nose. I can't really pursue this by knowing what Deirdre knows. Too many layers of secrecy. Besides, she's here for my help. I need to bring something different to the table. (And if I'm one thing in this area, it's *different*.) Still, I'm uneasy. I've got a life. Not much of one, granted, but I've got friends that come and go and people who call on me from time to time. I don't know how long I can have Deirdre staying here.

As if on cue, the front door opens and Lars barges in.

CHAPTER THREE

In my hometown of Porter's Bay, there's a large park near the edge of town called Bennett Park. It has baseball fields, softball fields, tennis courts, an amphitheater, a gazebo, rolling lawns, the whole shooting match. When I was a kid, the playground was home to a kickass rocket ship slide, containing numerous stairs, slides, secret passages, and such. To a kid, it was the Garden of Eden. I was twenty-five and living in the Cities when they tore down the rocket ship slide and I damn near cried when I got the news. But I did have a checkered history with the park.

You see, every year I was at Cobb-Cook Elementary School, the teachers planned a big picnic at Bennett Park, near the end of the school year. The idea was to take the kids over at lunch and let them play all afternoon, returning just in time for final bell (thus allowing the teachers to take rotating smoke breaks behind the gazebo). It sounded so promising. And yet, nearly every year between grades one and six, it f'n rained on the day of the Bennett Park trip. It got to the point where I didn't even look forward to the trip. Even the one day we managed to make it, I couldn't entirely enjoy it. I kept waiting for the skies to open up and the monsoon to start.

The result, I think, is that I've grown up with the point of view that if anything can go wrong, it most certainly will. Even the best, most noble plans will ultimately fall before the whims of fate.

It's probably good I don't get that many wedding invitations.

Then again, you didn't need to be Nostradamus to see this situation was going to blow up in our faces. In fact, whoever had *The Next Morning* in the *When Will the Fecal Matter Hit the Cooling Unit* pool just came up a big winner.

At first, everything seems fine. The front door closes with a gentle click. Lars starts toward the kitchen, his bathrobe billowing around bony frame. Then he stops when he sees Deirdre. He doesn't seem to recognize her. He smooths the long-sleeved tee under his robe and tips a hat he's not actually wearing.

"Why, hello, madame," he says, his voice taking on the closest thing it's got to a suave tone, "I didn't realize Joe had a visitor. Allow me to introduce myself. My name is Lars. And you are…someone I've met before."

My whole body tenses. My brain drums out the same thing. *Please think you know her from someplace else, please think you know her from someplace else, please think you know her from someplace else.* He raises a finger and slowly points at Deirdre.

"Oh, I met you when…" Lars's eyes get wide. "Oh." Then he adds: "Merde."

Several things happen before I can make a move. Lars backs toward the front door. Deirdre grabs Lars's robe, and throws him over the futon. Lars scrambles to his feet, but he's weaving like his body is moving a few seconds ahead of his brain. I'm torn between concern for Lars and concern for my furniture. A gun appears in Deirdre's hand. The cats disappear into the bedroom. Lars raises his large hands and makes a noise that sounds like *Eep*. I slide between the two of them.

"Deirdre!" I say, "You can't kill him."

"Oh, I can," Deirdre says, her cold eyes focused on Lars, "It won't be particularly hard. Now, if you could please step aside."

I hold my hand in front of me, as if it could stop a bullet. "You can't fire that thing in here. Everyone in the building will hear it. They'll call the cops. Believe me. It's happened before." And that's kind of a sad statement. But I'll contemplate it later.

Deirdre lowers the gun. She twirls it slightly before slipping it into the holster behind her back. "You're right, sweets." She slips her hand into her boot and comes up with a knife bigger than my head. "This will be so much quieter."

Lars jumps back over the coffee table, shouting "Whoa, momma!" as he goes. I'm fast enough to stay between the two of them, though I doubt Deirdre would have much difficulty getting me out of the way. I keep my hands up, but closer to my body in case Deirdre decides to go slashy-slashy.

"Look, Lars won't tell anybody anything," I say.

Lars pats my shoulder. "You're right. But just out of curiosity, what *is* going on?"

I speak out of the corner of my mouth. "You're safer if you don't know."

"No," Deirdre says, "He's not."

Since I'm caught between a rock and a hard place, I blurt out the short version of everything that's gone on the last twelve-or-so hours. To her credit, Deirdre lets me do it without objection. (Fuck, it's not like Lars can get into any *more* trouble with her.) Lars leans back in the corner as he takes in the story.

"Quite a funky conundrum," he says, "But I don't think killing me is going to solve it."

Deirdre responds with a casual flick of the knife. "I beg to differ."

Lars is calm. "You have to think this thing through." He slips past me before I can stop him. "If you kill me, you'll have to dispose of the body."

"Not a problem," she says.

"Not for you," Lars says, "*I* would be rather inconvenienced. But the point is, if I disappear, my friend Chuck will get worried and call the police."

I whisper to Lars behind his back. "I thought Chuck hated the police."

Lars half-turns his head. "He claims to. But when push comes to shove, Chuck has an incorrigible streak of cowardice in him." He turns to Deirdre again. "If Chuck calls the police, they'll come around, asking questions. That's going to make it harder for Joe to investigate. And harder for you to hide. Really, you're far better off keeping me alive."

Son of a bitch. From out of the mouths of not-particularly-bright babes. Lars—*Lars*, mind you—has actually made a decent point. Deirdre lowers the knife a little.

"How do I know you won't tell anyone about me being here?" Deirdre asks.

Lars gives her a slight bow. "Because unlike my unfortunate friend Chuck, my disdain for the *federales* is all too real. I'd rather let you stab me right here than waste my valuable time squealing to them."

Lars's argument carries the day. He's too good-natured to sound genuinely disdainful of the police, but something in his words gets through to Deirdre. She slips the knife back into her boot.

"Just don't change your mind about saying anything," Deirdre says, "Or I'll have to kill you. Over a four- or five-day period."

As with everything, Deirdre says it with the same tone of voice I use when saying I have to run some errands. It gives me the willies, but Lars simply strokes his scraggly beard.

"That sounds proper," he says, "I'm glad we could come to an agreement."

Deirdre goes into the kitchen. I grab Lars's arm and yank him over to the arch windows. He has no choice but to follow, arms and legs flying about, looking like a bag of disconnected body parts. We lower our voices.

"May I ask what in the hell you're doing here?" I say, my teeth gritted.

Lars's head snaps back. "Now is that any way to greet a friend? I thought we were operating on a *mi casa, su casa* basis. Why the sudden hostil—"

"Lars!"

He holds up his hands. "Fine. I was hoping we could talk about the fundraiser."

"What about it?" I ask.

"Carol said it would be a good idea to include you. I think so, too. It might mean a larger-than-average turnout on the part of the socially awkward, but we need all the help we can get."

I can agree with the last part. "Like I told Carol, I'll think about it. I've got a lot on my plate at the moment."

"I get it. Just think about it. That's all I ask." He drops his hands into the pockets of his robe. "I certainly understand where you're coming from. I've got a lot on my plate with Iris."

"When we were leaving Fong's last night, I noticed she was, um, expressing herself to you. In no uncertain terms."

"She was unhappy with the menu. Iris is more a gluten-free, nondairy, vegan sort of a girl. I'm afraid I won't be going to Fong's while I'm with her."

Well, if that isn't a slap in the face. Abandoning a beloved local restaurant because it threatens your supply of nookie? This will not stand. This aggression will not stand, man.

"You sure this woman is right for you?" I ask, "No offense, but she sounds kind of…demanding."

"She is," Lars says, propping a hand on the wall in a sort of jaunty pose, "But into each life, a little rain must fall. Besides, I think you're missing the bigger picture."

"Which is?"

"The sex is absolutely spectacular."

Now if Carol were here, I'm sure she'd say something like, "Lars, you're really going to let yourself get bossed around just because the sex is spectacular?" But I know better, guys in general and Lars in particular.

"That good, huh?" I ask.

"It's amazing," Lars says, "Wild, uninhibited, perverted. The Holy Trinity. And loud. I'm amazed you didn't hear us last night, brother. My bedroom's right below yours."

I don't need him to remind me, since I constantly work to erase that thought from my head. But something he said jogs the memory banks.

"I think I did hear you two last night," I say, "I thought it was a dog howling. I nearly called Animal Control."

"Oh, there was an animal involved," Lars says, "But you can't control her. And I don't know if I want to."

I'm not getting anywhere with Lars. Besides, he's a big boy. He can make his own choices (and hopefully survive them). Meantime, I've got troubles of my own.

"Just be careful," I say, dropping my voice to a whisper, "And make sure you don't say anything about my houseguest in there."

"Lips are sealed, my friend," he says, throwing a look toward the kitchen, "But I've got to tell you: you're taking a hell of a chance here. How long before someone else walks in and sees her? Or walks by and sees her? Or—"

I hold up a hand. "I get the picture. But I don't have any options."

I pick up the blanket and pillow and carefully organize them. Deirdre is at the breakfast bar, munching toast and getting crumbs all over the place. She's spilled some coffee and is making no effort to clean it up. Son of a...

Lars snaps his fingers. "I might be able to help you out," he says, "Both of you."

Deirdre sets her toast on the breakfast bar (with no sign of a plate or a napkin). "How do you mean?" she asks.

Lars glides toward the front door, enjoying his moment of triumph. "It just so happens that the apartment across the hall from me is vacant. If I'm not mistaken, that would make a better hiding place for you than Joe's apartment. Very little traffic and I don't believe there are any showings in the foreseeable future. Since you're traveling light, I wouldn't have to do much more than give you the keys."

Deirdre picks up the toast and chews as she thinks about it. "You might be on to something."

"I have an old mattress down in my storage unit," Lars says, "The rest of the accommodations would be a bit spartan, but I imagine you're used to that."

"I can make do," Deirdre says.

I glance into the kitchen. The bag of bread is still open. There's a trail of crumbs leading out of the kitchen. I grab the paper towels and wipe down the breakfast bar. Then I grab the broom and dustpan out of the closet and go to work on the crumbs.

"You can take the extra towels and blankets with you," I say, as I work, "I can help get you outfitted with clothes and food and stuff. Whatever you need."

Deirdre squares me with a look. Apparently, the enthusiasm in my voice makes *Whatever you need* sound like *Whatever I need to do to get you out of here.* (And I'm not going to say that's incorrect.) Nonetheless, Deirdre nods her approval.

"That sounds like a good idea." There's a moment where her mouth quivers, as if she's struggling with the words. "Thank you."

I can't imagine it's easy to thank someone you were willing to kill just three minutes ago. (Having never been in that position myself.) However, Lars, as he has a tendency to do, takes the compliment with extreme grace. He gives Deirdre a little bow.

"It is my pleasure, madam," he says, "I'll fetch the keys and be back momentarily."

As Lars opens the door, letting in the cold air, I ask: "What about Iris? What are you going to tell her?"

"Nothing," Lars says, "I'll just run in, spout some gibberish, grab the keys and run out again. She won't know what hit her."

Sort of like *my* every interaction with Lars. I guess you've got to play to your strengths.

***

Two hours later, I'm sitting at the counter at Glacier's, my local coffee shop. It's on Selby Avenue, just a few blocks from my place and a stone's throw from the St. Paul Cathedral. The place is a converted café with checkerboard tile floors, straight-back chairs, brass rails and picture windows. The shades are up, but it doesn't do much for the view. Snow and ice cover everything and make for a pretty bleak landscape. I know Minnesota's supposed to be a winter wonderland and all that. But if you live here, that shit gets old right around the time you put the Christmas decorations away. That, and the temperature, is probably why I chose a seat at the bar rather than a table at the window. There are only a few people in the place, but like them, I'm huddled over my drink. I'll be honest, being here without my laptop makes me feel a little naked. And the thought of being naked in this kind of weather makes me shiver.

The bell rings over the door and a heavyset Latino guy walks in, possibly from the forties. He's wearing a gray fedora and a matching wool overcoat. (Even that can't be warm in this weather.) He unbuttons the coat, revealing a natty striped suit that (partially) disguises his bulk. He slips off his glasses, allowing them to clear up after the heat mists them over. Somehow, he's able to spot me at the bar. He ambles over and stops at the stool next to me. He takes off his black leather gloves and the fedora, tosses the gloves into the hat and sets it on the bar. That done, he slips off the overcoat and carefully drapes it on the stool next to his before finally taking a seat. Hannah, the barista, just out of college but greatly experienced in social awkwardness, comes over to take his order. I speak for the guy.

"Large Americano to go, room for cream."

Hannah seems slightly confused. The guy gives his consent. She slides down the bar to get the drink ready. I set the creamer in front of him in a *checkmate* fashion. He points at the beverage in front of me.

"Turtle mocha," he says, "and you let it sit until the whipped cream had melted into the coffee."

"Well done," I say, "Your instinct for the truth remains untrammeled."

The guy on the next stool is Alberto Castillo. He and I have known each other since I first came to the Twin Cities. He had just started working for the *Pioneer-Press* and I was working for a little suburban newspaper and doing odd jobs on the side. We were both roughly (very roughly) in the same line of work and both liked to frequent Glacier's. We also, strangely, had a love of competitive cycling (watching, not participating) and struck up a conversation around it one day. The bonding experience only lasted a handful of months. Castillo was hired at *The Star-Tribune* and moved across the river. We've stayed in touch here and there. It would be a stretch to call us friends, but we're certainly friendly acquaintances. This is the first time I've ever hit him up for information, though. We'll have to see how this goes.

"How have you been?" Castillo asks, carefully straightening his red tie.

"Hanging in there," I say, propping an arm on the bar, "Rallying my army of geeks."

"Good to hear."

There's a bit of disapproval in his tone. Castillo is among those who feel my potential is wasted on writing a column that's largely for laughs. Most of that crowd, though, is Carol and certain ex-girlfriends, so Castillo is unique in that regard. Unlike the others, he's allowed to get on his high horse. The man has been a crusader for social justice, frequently writing about corruption in city hall and in the police department. If he tends to look down on my in-depth analysis of *The Ghost and Mr. Chicken* and why Don Knotts should have been nominated for an Oscar, he's earned the right. We chitchat, getting caught up until Castillo's

Americano arrives. He slowly adds some sugar from the shaker and carefully stirs it with a spoon, making sure not to spill a drop.

"Something on your mind?" he asks, carefully setting the spoon on the counter, "I got the feeling this wasn't a social call."

I'll hand it to him. He's perceptive. And he's probably hoping I didn't drag him all the way over from Minneapolis just to rap about the Tour de France, still five months off. I set my mocha aside and try to make sure Hannah doesn't overhear us. Not a worry. She's reading a play script. (*Sweeney Todd*. Ick.)

"What do you know about Alex Hollins's murder?" I ask, lowering my voice, "Everything I've read online is pretty sketchy."

Castillo sips his coffee. "Why are you interested in that?"

Excellent question. I can't tell Castillo, "Oh, I've got the woman who was hired to kill him hiding out in my place." Castillo has a reasonably good bullshit detector (comes with the territory he's covered), so I proceed carefully. And vaguely.

"What if I said I couldn't tell you that?" I ask.

"I'd think you had a story to tell, and you weren't telling it to me."

Yep. Perceptive. "I'm going to be as honest with you as I can. Yes, I've got something going on and it has to do with Alex Hollins's murder. I can't give you details right now. But when I can, I'll give you the whole story. All I need is some information."

Castillo's mouth is open slightly, confused. "You're going to give me a story? You aren't going to write it yourself?"

"You know what I write. If it doesn't involve pissing on a Kardashian—figuratively or literally—it's not in my purview."

"That's not exactly true, my friend," Castillo says, giving me a knowing look, "I read _The Daily Bugle_ from time to time. Near as I can tell, you've taken down a corporate conspiracy, a drug ring, and a suburban police department. You've also solved two murders and kept your own ass out of jail. You're not exactly restricted to writing about _Star Trek_ and Marvel movies."

Shit, he's right. What happened to the good old days, when I spent all my time chasing women and writing dick jokes? I'll have to take that up with my staff. Meantime, there's the matter of prying info out of Alberto Castillo.

"You're just going to have to trust me," I say, "I'm working on something and if it pans out, I'll give everything to you. It'll be your story. All I need is information."

Castillo contemplates this over another sip of his Americano. I might be flattering myself, but if it were anybody but me coming to him with this, he'd tell them to take a flying leap. Even now, he's weighing the cost of giving me information, sight unseen. Finally, he gives me a sidelong glance.

"You still think Indurain doped his way to five Tour titles?" Castillo asks.

"Oh jeez, yes. He had to. You've seen the power-wattage output study they did. No human being could put up those numbers unless he was doped to the gills."

"All right, that's the first thing you've said that didn't sound completely ridiculous. Now I know you haven't gone totally insane." He takes a breath. "All right, I'll do it. But I'm going to hold you to your promise."

"You're welcomed to all of it. Last thing I need is a reputation as an actual reporter."

Castillo chuckles. "What do you want to know?"

"Who's investigating the murder? I'm assuming the Excelsior mall cops aren't dealing with it."

"You assume correctly. BCA is taking over. A guy named Jim Street is in charge. Heard of him?"

I have. Oy. Apparently, everything that's old is new again. I ran into Jim Street about a year ago, the same night I met Deirdre. His detail was working with an informant to take down a drug ring. Said informant was killed and I was dragged into it for reasons I won't go into here. He's with the Bureau of Criminal Apprehension; sort of Minnesota's version of the FBI. Street also helped save my life. Not that it will do me a lot of good here.

"The name sounds familiar," I say.

"Street's good," Castillo says, "Bit of a maverick, but that doesn't bother me."

"Me neither," I say, "You heard anything about the investigation itself? Suspects or anything?"

"Heard they saw someone leaving the scene."

And I know who that someone was, so that doesn't do me a lot of good. I scratch my chin. There's some stubble there. I've been debating growing a winter beard. Not sure it's quite my style, though.

"I did research on Alex Hollins," I say, "I saw a blonde on his arm in some of the photos. His wife, I assume?"

"You are correct. Chelsea's her name."

"Trophy wife?"

"Not exactly. She handles a lot of their community outreach. Helping out with fundraisers. Getting them good publicity. They've needed it lately."

Hmm. The wife is usually a suspect in these cases, but Chelsea gets a pass thanks to Deirdre's involvement. She'd be a natural to talk to first. She works with community outreach. I have an *in* there.

"They need good publicity, huh?" I say, "For reasons other than their CEO being brutally murdered?"

"Yeah," Castillo says, "They got an issue with the Green River Project."

"And what is the Green River Project?"

That tickles Castillo's funny bone. "You don't know? Green River is up near your hometown. You should have heard of it."

Son of a bitch. He's right. Why didn't I put two-and-two together? Porter's Bay, my hometown, is in the northeast part of the state. I've heard of Green River. It's a little stream that winds its way through a couple forests and empties into Lake Hadley. Nothing to write home about, but certainly nice.

"I've heard of it," I say, "What's going on?"

Castillo rolls his eyes, exasperated by my ignorance. "Apparently, there's a decent vein of copper near there. Hankerson-William formed a subsidiary called Green River Mining. They're looking to tap into it. Right now, they're haggling with the state."

"About what?" I ask.

"Environmental concerns. A goodly number of state reps and senators aren't thrilled with the idea of strip mining a stretch of forest land. Mostly DFL."

For those not aware, *DFL* is what we call the Democratic Party in Minnesota. It was formed in the Nineteen-Forties when the Democrats merged with the Farmer-Laborer party to form a powerful party of the left with an unwieldly title. They're generally the party who's going to stand up for environmental concerns in this state.

"I'm not surprised," I say.

"There are also concerns about how mining will affect the drinking water up there," Castillo says, "Both the river and Lake Hadley provide a goodly amount of that. Hankerson-William insists there's absolutely no risk. That opinion is backed up by legislators who have received generous campaign donations from Hankerson-William."

"Make America great again."

We bump our coffee cups in a sarcastic toast. Castillo starts to take a drink of his coffee, then stops and rubs his jowls.

"There *was* something unusual," he says, "Somebody working on the project, a guy named Dustin Felt, died a few months ago. Right after he tried to set up a meeting with me."

My eyebrows go up. "He was murdered?"

"No, no, no. Are you kidding me? If I thought that, I would have been all over Hankerson-William. At any rate, this Dustin Felt guy didn't show up for our meeting. Next thing I heard, he died in a car accident, over in Wisconsin. A little town called Durham. His car went off the road and into a river. I talked to the sheriff there, a guy named Scott Mitchell, just to follow up. He said everything checked out. No reason to suspect foul play. I made a few other calls, just to doublecheck. They all backed up the sheriff. End of story."

Now, that's interesting. But probably fruitless. Castillo's right. If he had even an inkling of something suspicious, he would have attached himself to Hankerson-William like a tick. Still, it's an interesting coincidence. Meanwhile, Castillo swirls his coffee.

"You're really not going to tell me what's going on?" he says.

"Not yet. But I will."

Castillo gives me an appraising look. "I'm wondering if I should believe you."

"Al, please. We're not dating. Just take my word."

He holds up his hands. "All right, we'll play it your way. But remember: if you jerk me around on this, I will smite you with the power of my pen."

"Smiting noted."

With that, Castillo stands, slides into his coat, retrieves his gloves from his fedora and pops said topper on his head. He pushes his chair in and reclaims his coffee. "Good seeing you again, Joe. Good luck with whatever it is you're working on. I hope this is worth your while. And mine."

I feel the same way. Both that it will be worth Castillo's while and that I'll live to tell him about it.

***

Here's a thing you need to know about me: my obsession with keeping my apartment clean isn't due to any compulsion or neurosis on my part. (My mother will testify to the disaster area that was my room when I was a little boy.) It's simply what I need to do to create. As I've said, *Orderly space, orderly mind.* I discovered this in high school when I had my first column for the school newspaper and found I could bang out the work a lot faster when my room was in order. This continued into college, when I wrote for the school newspaper there, and on into adulthood. Since writing is now my job, I try to keep the apartment spotless as often as I'm able. It gets complicated, though, when I have friends over. Particularly those friends who belong to the slobby set.

"You ought to see this guy Ron," Mike says, propping his feet on my coffee table (even though I've told him a hundred times not to do that) and opening a grape soda (with

59

a nary a coaster in sight), "He's a complete disaster. And not just as a delivery guy. He doesn't know anything. He can't cook for himself, he doesn't know how public transit works, he doesn't know shit about politics or what's going on in the world. He's gonna be thirty this year and you'd think he's never left his parents' basement. But he's got a college degree and he was in the military. So much for that shit preparing you for life."

I could remind Mike that he is not an apostle of learning or doing things for himself. If he's not living in his parents' basement, it's only because they live on the West Coast. (Although if they follow through on their constant threats to move back to Minnesota…) And I'm an expert in the subject. Mike and I met about five minutes after we got to college, and we've been best friends ever since. Mike grew up the only child in a rather strict (read: smothering) military family. Once he got to college and escaped his family's supervision, he became a one-man Animal House. He's never entirely recovered. So really, Mike's only a step ahead of Ron in being skilled at their largely unskilled labor. But Mike's feeling good about himself (for the first time in a while) and I don't want to spoil that. Besides, I've got bigger things on my mind.

"It's amazing," I say, dusting off the desk and trying to ignore both Mike and the cold seeping in from the nearby window. (Lenny, stretched out on the top of the radiator, watches me, partially fascinated. Mostly he's intrigued by the movement.)

Mike finally gets his freakin' feet off the coffee table and turns to face me. "I decided to help Ron out," he says, "Show him a few of my tricks."

"You have tricks?"

"Of course, I do," he says, vaguely offended, "How do you think I've gotten to be the top delivery man? You learn how to cut corners. Run the occasional stoplight. Park in the handicap spots. Double-park if you have to. Mount the occasional curb. Know the unlocked entrances to all the apartment buildings. That sort of thing."

"That's nice of you to teach Ron your evil ways."

"It was Biyu's idea. She mentioned it while we were making out in the alley last night."

I drop into the desk chair. Hoo-boy. "You were what in the where? With whom?"

Mike props an arm on the couch, shit-eating grin firmly in place. "I was making out in the alley with Biyu. Quite the kisser she is. Benefit of having a father who constantly watches over you. Lots of repression and shit."

"In the alley? It was below zero last night."

"We take any opportunity we get," he says, adjusting his *Fong's* cap, "Biyu lives with Fong. He watches her like a damn hawk. I won't be going over to her place, and she won't be coming over to mine."

Oh boy. You'd think Mike would have learned his lesson about making out with the boss's daughter, but a cornerstone of Mike's personality is that he will never learn any lesson from any experience. I go back to my dusting.

"Good luck with that one, slugger," I say.

Mike jerks a thumb toward the door. "How is your…*friend* downstairs?"

Yes, I decided to tell Mike about Deirdre. He was there last year when she made multiple attempts to kill us, so he's familiar with her. Plus, Mike drops by my place so often (frequently unannounced—make that *exclusively* unannounced) he would have found out about Deirdre sooner or later. Best to dispense with the suspense.

"She could come up here at any time," I say, "You prepared for that?"

Mike gets a faraway look in his eyes. "Oh, I think I am."

Jeez. Messing around with the boss's daughter and he still has time to renew a year-old crush on our resident contract killer. I snap my fingers, trying to bring him out of it.

"Just be careful, okay?" I say, "Deirdre spared me because she needs my help. I don't think that kind of charity extends to you."

He flips a hand at that. "We'll be fine. Deep down, I think she really likes me."

"Do me a favor and don't bet your life on that."

The front door opens and Lars bursts into the room. His red smoking jacket billows out, revealing a white A-frame t-shirt and polka dot pajama bottoms. He makes his way to the liquor shelf. I watch his progress.

"Something I can help you with?" I ask.

Lars studies the shelf. "I'm wondering if you have any Asbach Uralt?"

"I'm going to say no. Since I have no idea what in the blue fuck that is."

He closes his eyes, as if reciting from memory. "It's a German liqueur. Technically a brandy, but similar to cognac." He opens his eyes and looks at me like I'm supposed to give him a gold star.

"Well, that *does* clear it up," I say, "But it doesn't help you, since I don't have any."

He throws a hand in the air in frustration. "Iris is down at my place. She wanted to have a little pre-dinner cocktail. Asbach is her drink of choice. She's a little…miffed that I don't have any on hand."

I get the feeling Lars uses *miffed* as a euphemism in the same way Mike uses *incident*. But I'm not going to pry. "Sorry I can't help," I say.

Lars is understanding, though maybe a tad defeated. "Don't worry about it, brother. I'll think of something." Then he mutters, "I hope."

Mike hops off the futon and into Lars's path. "Hey, I talked to Fong. He's willing to cater the fundraiser. He just needs details from you."

Lars claps his hands together. "Thank you, brother. I knew I could count on you."

Mike gives him a faux-modest bow. (He's getting good at that). The word *fundraiser* jogs my memory. I set the dust can and the rag aside.

"I want to talk to Chelsea Hollins about the fundraiser," I say, "You have any problem with that?"

Lars extends a flipper-like hand. "I'd be delighted, brother. You're finally on board, huh? Ready to fight the good fight?"

I take the hand, hesitantly. "Um, I've got kind of an ulterior motive. I need to question her about the thing with our, uh…friend. This would give me a decent excuse."

"Whatever it takes," Lars says, pumping my hand, "Let's forget that you're late to the party and only showed up because you're out of beer and just be glad you came at all."

"Sure," I say, wrenching the hand free, "Assuming I'm able to get an appointment with her, can you get me some information on the fundraiser?"

"Sure thing. Be glad to."

"Good," I say, sinking into the desk chair, "And ulterior motive or no, it might be a big help to the fundraiser. Hankerson-William could add some big-time money and exposure."

Lars scratches his beard. "I'm not normally one for suckling at the corporate teat. But this is for a good cause, so what the hell?"

He spins toward the door, then pauses, perhaps thinking about the task ahead downstairs. He takes a deep breath and closes his red smoking jacket. His body sags as he leaves. Mike sets his empty soda bottle on the breakfast bar (even though the recycling bin is just four feet away).

"I should get going, too," he says, swaggering toward the front door, "I've got work in a few hours. I should get a nap in."

"Is that all you do during the day? Take naps?"

"No. I masturbate as well."

I turn to the computer and mutter, "Jesus."

"Hey, if you didn't want the answer, you shouldn't have asked the question."

Mike wraps his scarf around his neck, zips up his leather jacket and heads for the front door. He's almost there when the door opens and Deirdre walks in. Everyone freezes (save for the cats, who make a beeline for the bedroom). Deirdre squints, taking a moment to remember Mike.

"You're a friend of Joe's, right?" Deirdre asks.

Mike is out of breath (and this time, not from the smoking). "Yeah, that's me." He offers a hand. "My name's Mike."

"That's right," Deirdre says. She ignores the hand and asks me, "Can we trust him?"

I rotate in the desk chair. "In this situation, we can. Anything else is fair game, though."

"Understood," Deirdre says.

Mike scampers out of the apartment. Deirdre's body language loosens, almost imperceptibly. She lounges on the arm of the futon and fixes me with a look. I become aware of her nearness and the smell of the berry bodywash I keep around in case I have female guests (something that amused Deirdre to no end). I wander toward the liquor shelf. Deirdre flips the honey-colored hair off her face.

"Have you got anything so far?" she asks.

"Not a lot. I talked with my friend Alberto Castillo. He's a reporter. He told me a few things going on at Hankerson-William. I'm going to chat with Chelsea Hollins, Alex's wife. Assuming she'll talk to me."

"Why *would* she talk to you?"

"About a fundraiser. Apparently, she helps out with that for Hankerson-William. Gives me an excuse."

Deirdre doesn't look convinced. "She just lost her husband. You think she's going to talk business with you?"

"I won't know until I ask. My friend Lars is going to help set something up."

"You think he can pull it off?"

"I've learned never to underestimate Lars," I say, "Or to overestimate him. Truthfully, he's beyond estimation."

There's a flicker of amusement on Deirdre's face. She gets up from the futon and slips her hands into her back pockets. "This friend of yours. The reporter. Did he say anything else? About what the police are doing? Anything like that?"

I return to my desk chair, very aware, once again, of Deirdre's proximity. "He said the Bureau of Criminal Apprehension is taking over the case. The BCA is—"

"I know what the BCA is. Who's got the case?"

"A guy named Jim Street. He—"

"I know him." Deirdre takes a few steps away from the desk. Her back is to me, but her head hangs slightly, telling me she's thinking. "He's on this, is he?"

"That's what I'm told."

"He's been after me for a while. He hasn't gotten anywhere." Deirdre props a fist on the back of the futon.

"But if he thinks he's got a physical description of me, he might put that out to the news people. If he does that, I am, as they say, completely fucked."

I pat my hands on my lap, looking for some way to calm her. (An agitated Deirdre is more likely to do something I'll regret.) "Let me ask you something: were you going to stab Alex Hollins?"

Deirdre gives me a sharp look. (I get the feeling this is a *Never ask me about my business, Kate* kind of moment.) "No. Not for this kind of hit. It's not efficient. A gun, especially when the house is shielded like the Hollins's, works faster. Two shots, placed correctly, and the target is done. No chance of them fighting back or something going wrong."

"Get you in, get you out, get you on your way."

"If that's how you want to put it." Deirdre tilts her head to one side. "Is there a point to this?"

"Just that using a knife to kill Alex Hollins isn't your M.O. And James Street is likely to come to the same conclusion."

Deirdre considers this. "You may be right."

"From the little I understand about it, a knife means something personal. Meaning the murderer would be someone close to Alex."

"Or the knife was the handiest weapon available."

"Either way, it doesn't feel premeditated," I say, "Not to knock your profession, but it's nothing if not premeditated. This feels more like a crime of passion. Or something like it."

Deirdre runs a finger along her jaw as she considers this. "Can you prove that?"

"Not yet."

"Then you'll pardon me if that doesn't seem particularly comforting."

"Sorry. It's all I've got. For now."

Deirdre slinks into the kitchen and returns with a highball glass. She makes her way over to the liquor shelf and pours two fingers of whiskey. I prop my elbows on the arms of the desk chair and steeple my fingers. Deirdre sits in the nearby comfy chair.

"Seems like a lot of trouble," I say.

Deirdre sips her drink. "Taking me in?"

"No, no. I mean hiring a contract killer and then doing the job yourself. A lot of expense when you could have framed—I don't know—a maid or somebody."

"The butler did it?" Deirdre says, raising one corner of her mouth.

"Exactly. It all comes down to what the motive is: personal or professional. Either way, why go through all the trouble?"

Deirdre is quiet while she considers this. Finally, she gulps down the rest of her drink and sets the glass on the coffee table (rather than in the sink). She sashays to the front door.

"I hope you find something," Deirdre says, "I don't like to wait."

That makes two of us. Watching Deirdre head out the front door, thinking about the possibility of the neighbors seeing her, I'm aware this situation is just waiting to blow up in my face.

And these situations don't like to wait, either.

CHAPTER FOUR

One of the many complicated issues in dealing with relationships is that the etiquette battle never really ends. Even when the relationship has.

One particularly thorny issue involves the timing of you or your former significant other moving on to another significant other. When do you move on, and should this be an issue for the former significant other? It shouldn't be. But it frequently is.

When I was in college, a girl broke up with me on Friday night and slept with a guy from work before the weekend was out. The breakup was bad enough, but knowing I meant so little to her that she was canoodling with another guy within hours of kicking me to the curb was a particular twist of the knife. In the interest of full discretion, I once broke up with a girl and slept with her roommate just forty-five minutes later. (The fact I was sleeping with the roommate for three weeks prior to the breakup may have figured into the timing.)

Regardless, it's difficult to know how to thread that needle. Yes, you can rush it. At the same time, you can't expect someone to pine away for years and years, wearing black and swearing off relationships of any kind.

Unless it's my high school girlfriend. I'm hoping she's remained celibate. (What are the odds? Good, right? Right? Yeah, I didn't think so.)

Obviously, the death of a significant other is a different ballgame. I'm not certain how Chelsea Hollins is dealing with her husband's death—if she's moved on or not. But she's still willing to meet with me. Maybe she's not that broken up. Maybe she needs to focus on work. Whatever the case, I've scored (or rather Lars has scored) the meeting.

Chelsea agrees to meet me in the Hankerson-William Headquarters. It's a tall building, about thirty stories, dwarfing the four-story bank building next door. Not the tallest building in downtown Minneapolis, but impressive. It's solid glass and tinted blue. It seems perfect for this time of year.

Our meeting is on the third floor. A perfectly coiffed blonde receptionist greets me and directs me to the large, glass-enclosed conference room behind her. She's kind enough to take my (borrowed) tweed overcoat and scarf. I tug at my dark suit. I had hoped never to wear this damn thing again, save for my funeral (which could be nigh). In the conference room, picture windows portray the frozen vista of downtown Minneapolis. There's a large screen on one end and a small table for coffee and rolls at the other. The place is spotless. I assume any dust particles would have to report to H.R. Chelsea waits at one end of the large conference table that dominates the room.

She's younger than I expected, maybe about my age. (I turned thirty-five a few weeks ago.) She's tall and the white sweater and dark blazer don't hide her curves. (Statuesque, one might say). Her blonde hair is clipped behind her head. Her features are porcelain perfect. Almost too perfect, leading me to wonder if she's had some work done. (Awfully young for that, but…) Her eyes are clear and blue but have a dull look to them. Maybe that's grief, maybe that's her normal look. Chelsea stands to greet me, offering a hand as I come around the table.

"Joe Davis," she says, her tone dulcet but businesslike, "It's a pleasure to meet you."

"You as well," I say, taking her hand (the handshake is dry and brief), "Thanks for meeting me. It must be a long drive in from Excelsior."

"I have an apartment in the city."

"Got it." I clear my throat. "I'm sorry for your loss."

A corner of Chelsea's mouth twitches. It might be grief. It might be amusement. She slides gracefully back into her chair.

"Please have a seat," she says, "and tell me about this fundraiser."

I drop into the (nicely padded) chair and launch into the sales pitch. Thankfully, Lars has filled me in on everything I need to know about the Kellen Community Center and the fundraising efforts. I give Chelsea the entire spiel about the need for the center and what the planned event entails. We go into the need for corporate sponsorship and how Hankerson-William can help. Chelsea listens placidly, her hands folded on the table in front of her. When I'm done, she sits back in her chair and balances a pen in her fingertips.

"It certainly sounds like a worthy cause," Chelsea says, "We've been trying to reach out to more communities, particularly in St. Paul. The Kellen neighborhood might be a good fit."

"That would be great," I say, shifting in the chair, trying to find a comfortable position, "My friend Lars is organizing it, but I can act as a contact for you."

"Interesting that a celebrity like you would be doing the grunt work here."

I give her the faux-modest look I use whenever I'm recognized. "You read my column?"

"Frequently," she says, "You're very amusing."

Huh. It's a compliment, but her tone and word choice feel a little forced. Plus, the dull eyes are still focused on me, not blinking. It leaves me feeling a little uneasy. I cover it with a shrug.

"Lars is a friend," I say, "I like to help him out. He needs it. And let's face it, being involved with this is good PR for me, too. Win-win deal all the way around."

"Then we understand each other," Chelsea says, "That's a good start to a working relationship."

"I hope so." We stand. I fumble with my pad of paper and pen. "Thank you for meeting with me," I say, "I know it can't be easy…under the circumstances."

She takes a breath in through her nose. "Thank you."

"Have you heard anything from the police?" I ask.

Okay, it isn't the most tactful thing to say. But Chelsea doesn't know me from Adam, beyond what she's read in my column. For all she knows, I'm a classless tool. Might as well lean into that portrayal. Especially if it gets me some answers.

"No, I haven't," Chelsea says, "They have a suspect, I hear, but they haven't caught her. I don't even think they know who she is."

Chelsea doesn't seem too particularly broken up about it. We might be making small talk about the headlines, for all anyone would know. Still, I'm not going to let that stop me from blundering in.

"Were you home when it happened?" I ask.

"No. I was out with a friend. We went to a movie. I came home and found the police and the ambulance crew there."

"Who was the friend you went out with?" I ask.

Chelsea's eyes narrow. "Her name is Linda Dotter. We're friends from the tennis club."

"You went to an early movie?" I say, toying with my pad of paper, "What did you see?"

"*The Crossing.* The five o'clock show over at St. Anthony Main."

Hmm. If I've read my movie reviews correctly, *The Crossing* is about two and a half hours long. Five o'clock show means Chelsea's out by seven-thirty. The murder occurs around nine. Plenty of time to get home. That puts a little hole in Chelsea's alibi.

"Sounds like fun," I say, "You do anything afterwards?"

"No. I just went home."

I'm pushing it. The line between casual (if clueless) inquiry and interrogation will be crossed if I'm not careful. I nod my head, as if sharing part of Chelsea's mourning.

"Must have been a real shock," I say.

"It was," Chelsea says, but again she doesn't sound broken up about it.

"How are you coping?"

She shuffles through some papers on the table. "I'm supposed to be sad, aren't I? The fact is, though, that Alex and I weren't that close."

That explains why she would be back at work so soon. "I suppose the people here are a comfort."

Again, the hard-to-read look in Chelsea's face. She says, "They have been."

One big happy family. Although, now missing its daddy. And mommy isn't all that bothered by it. I can only tap dance here so long. I may have to rattle her cage a little.

"You know anything about the Green River Project?" I ask.

Chelsea's face freezes (and it wasn't exactly animated before). "What are you talking about?"

"Oh, it's just something I saw on the internet," I say, "I didn't even read the article. I just saw the headline." I add an uncomfortable laugh (doesn't exactly require a Tony-winning performance). "It's the last time I saw Hankerson-William in the news."

Chelsea collects her paperwork. "I don't know much about it. Alex didn't talk about his business with me. And my focus here is the charity work."

"I guess he didn't talk about Dustin Felt, either?"

Chelsea nearly drops her papers. After a second, she regains her composure. She draws a strand of hair away from her face. "How do you know Dustin Felt?"

"I don't," I say, "That's another thing I saw in the news. He, uh, he died, didn't he?"

"I guess so," Chelsea says, "It was just a couple months ago. I remember people talking about it. But I never met Dustin."

I'm not sure I believe that. The reaction was too sharp. Chelsea makes a decent attempt at being casual, but she also avoids eye contact. Still, I can't call her out on it without the conversation getting unfriendly.

"Did Alex ever mention it?" I say, "It must have been a real shock."

Chelsea stuffs the paperwork into her briefcase. "He might have mentioned it in passing. I really don't remember."

I look for a way to bring the temperature in the room down. I'm not sure if Chelsea will appreciate a compliment about her appearance, but I'm going to give it a shot.

"I like your necklace," I say, gesturing toward it.

Chelsea's hand instinctively goes to the necklace hugging the nape of her neck. It's white gold, with hearts on either side leading to an emerald shamrock. While my dad's side of the family is Welsh (along with several hundred other ancestral stains), my mom's side is (largely) Irish, meaning

Mom keeps a lot of Celtic bric-a-brac around the house. It's the sort of thing that catches my eye.

"Thank you," Chelsea says, protectively fingering the necklace, "It was a present."

"From Alex?"

"No. From a…from a friend."

I'm not sure how to approach that without seeming more a buttinski than I already am. Maybe it's best that we're interrupted by someone approaching the conference room. It's a thin, middle-aged guy with graying black hair and green eyes. He wears a dark suit with a red power tie. He's not tall, but he carries himself with a quiet confidence. The beady eyes and the cruel mouth give you the impression he knows more than you, no matter the subject. Chelsea's face brightens when she sees him. He opens the conference door and pokes his head in.

"Chelsea," he says, as if I'm not in the room, "I heard you were down here. I'm…surprised." *Then* he notices me. "Am I interrupting anything?"

"No," Chelsea says, "We're just wrapping up."

The guy steps into the room and gives Chelsea one of those not-quite-kisses on the cheek. "It's good to see you."

She waves a hand toward me. "This is Joe Davis. We were just talking about a fundraiser for a community center in

St. Paul. Joe, this is Payton Hicks. He's the CFO for Hankerson-William."

Payton Hicks offers his hand. "Pleasure to meet you," he says, not sounding at all like he means it, "If you're doing a fundraiser, you're in good hands."

"I'm sure I am," I say.

Chelsea and Payton exchange little looks but say nothing. I get the feeling they're waiting for me to leave so they can talk. Then I'm hit with a moment of inspiration. I tuck my folder under my arm.

"I wonder if it would be possible to get a meeting with you, Mr. Hicks," I say, "Maybe you could make an appearance at the fundraiser. It would really help."

Hicks's face freezes, like I just asked permission to urinate on the floor. He looks toward Chelsea, who gives him nothing in return. He slips his hands in his pockets.

"You have to understand I'm very busy," he says, "I'm not only doing my own work, I'm filling in as best I can for Alex."

"It wouldn't be a long meeting," I say, "And the fundraiser is for a really good cause."

Hicks looks toward Chelsea again. She simply raises her eyebrows. Hicks face falls, slightly (though he looks more constipated than anything). He reaches into his coat, pulls out a business card and offers it me, held between two fingers.

"My number is on here," he says, "My assistant can set something up."

I snatch the card. "I appreciate that. Thank you." Having overstayed my welcome, I move to the door of the conference room. "It was nice meeting you. Both of you."

Chelsea and Hicks barely acknowledge me. I slip out of the conference room and head for the elevators, smiling at the receptionist as I go. She plasters on a return smile and goes back to her work (whatever that is). I hit the *down* button and wait for the elevator. I slip a look toward the conference room.

Chelsea and Hicks stand close together and their heads incline toward each other as they talk. Hicks reaches for Chelsea's hand. She pulls back, slightly. He lays his hand on her forearm. This time, she makes no move to pull away. They remain like that. The elevator dings. I'd like to go on spying on Chelsea and Hicks, but the receptionist is looking at me. Best to beat feet. I step into the elevator.

Quite the lonely life we voyeurs lead…

***

When I was in high school, I had no opportunity to skip school. My mom stayed home with the kids, so there was never a time when I could call in sick and go wander around Chicago with my best friends, ala Ferris Bueller. Even Senior Skip Day was a mild affair. I just hung out at Rudi's Pizza for a little longer than normal at lunch. I feel like I was robbed of a crucial high school experience. I've been considering legal action against my mother ever since.

Then again, watching Carol jump headlong into the whole skipping thing, maybe fate was on my side in that case.

"I'm in trouble," Carol says, slamming my front door behind her.

Her cheeks are flushed and I'm not sure it has anything to do with the cold. I should have known something was up as soon as Carol rang the door buzzer. It's one o'clock in the afternoon. She would normally be at work or at a meeting. And a cloudy, three-below-zero afternoon isn't the kind that inspires you to play hooky. I spin around from the desk, leaving my latest column behind, and pick up my *I'm Working on My Novel* coffee mug.

"In trouble, huh? I say, "Well, you were warned to stay away from those boys who hang out down by the railroad tracks. They only have one thing on their minds."

"It's not that kind of *in trouble*, you idiot," Carol says.

She whips off her tam, black trench coat and leather gloves and tosses them indiscriminately on my sofa. (Thanks, Carol.) The cats, curled up together in a furry ball, lift their heads, then go back to sleep. Carol casts a longing look toward the liquor shelf but decides it's too early in the day. She goes into the kitchen, probably to get some coffee. (All

my friends seem to know the layout of my place. I may have
to rearrange, just to keep them on their toes.)

I walk to the breakfast bar. "What kind of trouble are
we talking about?"

Carol rummages through the cupboards, looking for
sweets (making me cringe at the disorganization she's
wreaking). "My boss, Mr. Pratt, is pissed at me. He knows I
wasn't in the office on Friday."

"How did he stumble across this information?" I ask.

"There's a project we've been working on. I thought
it was all settled. The client was happy. We were good to go.
Then apparently, the client called Friday afternoon and
wanted some changes made. Mr. Pratt was looking for me,
but I wasn't there, obviously. Nobody knew where I was."

"Did he try calling you?" I ask.

"He did. But I have a personal cell phone and a work
cell phone. I sort of…ignored the work cell phone. For the
weekend." She stops, one of the cupboard doors half-open.
"The whole thing was time sensitive. Mr. Pratt had to do the
job himself. But he's pissed. He said he wanted to talk to me
after lunch."

I look at the clock. "Isn't right about now *after lunch*?"

"Yeah. I had to get out of there. I sent him an IM,
told him I had a dentist appointment. Then ran out of there
before he could reply."

"You think that's going to make the situation any better?"

"I don't know!" Carol says, "I just know I didn't have an excuse and I had to think." She throws her arms out. "So, here I am."

We sit on opposite sides of the breakfast bar. I feel for Carol, I really do. I don't condone her skipping out of work, but an argument can be made that *my* entire adult life has been an act of skipping out of work. Besides, I know Carol loves her job. Getting fired for the kind of negligence she displayed might prevent her from getting a similar job. It's a problem, no doubt.

After a prolonged silence (interrupted only by the hissing of that damn radiator), I ask, "What are you going to do?"

"I'm not sure," Carol says, drawing out the words as if she's contemplating it right now, "I might have to make something up. Find an acceptable reason to have left the office early on Friday."

"And the truth need not be a part of it?"

Carol winces. "I don't know if I feel right about lying. Mr. Pratt has always been really nice to me. I don't want to betray his trust."

"As opposed to betraying his trust by skipping out of work?"

"Yes, Joe," Carol says, giving me a look that's colder than the temps outside, "As opposed to that."

It feels unusual to consult Carol in a situation like this. Normally, she's the diligent and mature one in the group. Now, without warning, she's descended to our level. Yet another child growing older. And we had such high hopes for her.

"Any plans for the possible lie?" I ask, "If you go that direction?"

Carol massages her temples. "Not really. It's got to be good, though. Mr. Pratt will see right through any *dog ate my homework* stuff."

"How about saying you had a family emergency? That's tried and true."

"It won't work. Mr. Pratt knows I don't have family around here. He's actually a fan of my dad's. He'd insist on calling him and checking in."

Carol's dad, Walter, is a semi-famous mystery writer. He specializes in the hard-boiled genre. I'm not surprised Carol's boss would be a fan. I'm a fan myself (even after meeting Carol's dad). On top of that, Carol has worked for Mr. Pratt for several years. They're friends on top of everything else. This will take more than your garden-variety tall tale.

"If you need a convincing lie," I say, "you may want to consult an expert in the field."

Carol, munching on a bag of chocolate chips from the pantry, instantly knows who I'm talking about. "Mike?" she says, her mouth half-full, "No. No way. What I've done is bad enough. I can't lower myself to *that*."

"Then what are you going to do?"

She doesn't have an immediate answer. After downing more chocolate chips, Carol comes to a conclusion. "I'm going to tell Mr. Pratt the truth. I've got a good reputation there. Mr. Pratt and I have a good relationship. He won't be pleased, but I'm sure he won't come down on me too hard. I just have to face the music."

Except I'm not sure Carol's going to like the tune. Once you've dented an employer's trust, it's hard to get it back. I should know. Last spring, I was caught in a situation where I was dating a married woman (in my defense, I didn't know she was married when we started dating) and it got more publicity than either my employer or myself would have preferred. (Her husband turning up dead on my deck might have had something to do with said publicity.) I kept my job, but my relationship with my editor, Lance, has been fairly distant ever since. (The fact I don't care much for Lance and am sort of thrilled with this change in our relationship should in no way to detract from my larger point.)

"You may still want to consult Mike," I say, "This *is* his territory. Besides, I've got enough on my plate."

I look toward the door, half expecting Deirdre to come through it. Carol follows my look. She knows exactly what I'm thinking. I had to let her in on my helping Deirdre. She makes no attempt to hide her disapproval.

"Deirdre is in the building right now?" she says.

"Yep. She's downstairs. Living across from Lars."

"And you haven't thought about calling the police?"

"Thought about it?" I say, "Sure. But Deirdre's gotten away from the cops once. If she gets away again, she'll come for me. And she won't be as friendly next time. Besides, there's the fact that…she is innocent."

"Of *this* murder," Carol says, brushing some hair out of her eyes, "How many others is she guilty of?"

"Probably for the best if I don't think too much about that." Carol gets up from the breakfast bar. I spin around on my stool. "Look, I know you don't agree. I respect that. But I've made my decision. The best way out of this is to help Deirdre."

"And if you get killed in the process?"

"That's a risk, no doubt," I say, "But think what happens if I pull it off. Deirdre leaves me alone. Justice is done. I might—well, Al Castillo might—get a decent story out of it. A win all around.."

Carol isn't convinced. "If you can live with it."

"I can."

"Good for you."

There's tension here, of course. It's not as if we haven't, either of us, skirted societal rules at one time or another. But what I'm doing is a different animal. Different species, almost. I turn back to the breakfast bar. Carol sits across from me.

"What's your next step?" Carol asks.

"I've got an appointment with Payton Hicks," I say, "He's the CFO for Hankerson-William. He was a friend of Alex Hollins. And a particularly good friend of Chelsea Hollins's, if I'm reading everything correctly."

I tell Carol about my conversation with Chelsea, my brief chat with Payton Hicks and what I saw in the conference room when I was about to leave. Carol twists her mouth to one side as she thinks.

"So, he's *very* good friends with the Hollins'?" she asks.

"At least he tries," I say, "I'm not sure what was going on with him and Chelsea. And I'm not sure how to ask."

Carol grabs more chocolate chips. "Just don't screw up the fundraiser. If this guy and his company are willing to help—and we need all the help we can get—we can't afford to piss him off."

"I will be the soul of discretion."

Carol doesn't seem thrilled, but she lets it go. The door buzzes. It's just past lunch. Maybe Mike is stopping by between shifts. I answer the buzzer.

It's not Mike's voice that comes through the intercom. "This is Jim Street. I'm with the Bureau of Criminal Apprehension. You have a minute to talk?"

Okay, Carol is not the only one who needs to come up with a story. Fast.

CHAPTER FIVE

When I was in high school, I was in the spring play. The cast and crew decided to have a party by the lake one night after a performance. We stopped at Terzich's Grocery, a little convenience store on the main drag, to grab some soda. We sent my friend Ken inside to do the honors. When Ken emerged, he had a case of soda…and a case of beer. Apparently, he looked old enough for Joe Terzich to sell him an adult beverage. (In his defense, Joe was older, and his eyesight wasn't all that good. Although Ken's letter jacket should have been a giveaway.)

We went to the lake and the party was rockin'. (Mainly from youthful exuberance, since twelve beers were only going to go so far among twenty-five people.) We were having a great time…until the cops showed up. As the squad car rolled into the parking lot, everyone dropped their beers and endeavored to kick the cans under the cars. We thought we were slick until the cop led with, "All right, first thing I want you to do is pick up all these beer cans!" So much for being slick.

See, things like that told me I was never meant to go into a life of crime. Nor are most of us. This isn't as pro-cop as it sounds. It's just that cops are built to find criminals and most of us aren't built to be criminals. Sure, we think we are. I'm convinced that most of us have plotted at least one crime we think is perfect. On the bright side, most of us don't bother to try it. It would only be in trying that we'd find all the holes. And sitting in the pokey is the not the time you want to look back and think, "Oh, I see where I went wrong."

A lot of it comes back to one thing: it's difficult to lie to the cops. They're lied to on a professional basis, so they likely know when you are lying. They're also trained to see things we think we can cover up. And if they don't see it, they'll probably plant it.

All these things roll through my head as I buzz the front door and let Jim Street into my building. First, of course, I'm wondering why he's here. Yes, he was on the case a year ago when Carol was accused of murder and Deirdre was there, meaning his visit is not likely to be a coincidence. Does he even remember me from that? The odds are he's not going to open with, "Just happened to be in the neighborhood. Thought you'd be up for a game of pinochle."

I peek out the front door to see if Deirdre's on the landing or if her apartment door is open. She's in the clear. Then I scan my apartment to see if there's any evidence of Deirdre's presence. None I can see, but I'm not certain what I'm looking for. Carol stands, frozen, at the breakfast bar.

"What are you going to do?" she asks.

"Simple. Answer any question I can and lie my ass off where indicated."

"You think you can pull that off?"

"Probably not. Enjoy the floor show."

There's a rap at the front door. I take a breath and answer it. Jim Street is on the landing, his sandy hair perfectly in place (save for a few strategically misplaced strands). He wears a black cashmere coat and a white silk scarf. (How the hell does a cop afford that? BCA must pay awfully well.) Next to him is a short, balding, dumpy Latino guy with bug eyes and a stained, tan overcoat resting over a rumpled gray suit. Ric, if I remember correctly, part of Street's crew.

"Joe Davis," Street says, his voice slightly gravelly, "Mind if I come in?"

Why is it that unwelcomed visitors always address me by my full name? It's a trend I could do without. I wave a hand into the room. Street and Ric step past me. Street's eyes casually scan the room. The cats perk up. Something in Street's manner tells them they dare not get any cat hair on his person, so they flee the room, just to be on the safe side. Street catches sight of Carol, who is keeping her distance at the breakfast bar.

"Sorry, Slick" he says, "Didn't realize you had guests." He studies Carol. "I remember you. You were the one they thought murdered your boyfriend."

Carol's mouth tightens. "Not my boyfriend. Not my murder."

Street grins. He undoes a button in his coat, and it falls open, revealing a burgundy suit and a yellow tie. (It should look ridiculous, but he makes it work.) This is maybe the third time I've met the guy and I still marvel at how he maintains a tan in the middle of winter (in Minnesota of all places). On top of that, he appears impervious to the cold. The slight drawl in his voice tells me he isn't native to this part of the world and yet he handles the chill better than me, a guy who's lived in this state all his life. (I myself am deeply jealous.)

"Funny thing is, Slick," he says, "I'd like to talk to you about that murder. Or something related to it."

Yep. It's about Deirdre. As I suspected. I try to be nonchalant (despite my heart going at hummingbird pace) and step toward the kitchen.

"Can I get you guys anything?" I ask, "Coffee? Hot chocolate?" Nice warm cup of Get The Hell Out?

"No, we're fine," Street says, "Just had a few questions."

I affect puzzlement. "What's going on?"

Street slips his hands in the pockets of his overcoat. "You remember a woman named Deirdre? She was hired to kill…" He glances at Carol. "Your friend."

"Carol," she says, not liking being referred to in the abstract.

Street gives her a little bow. "Carol. Sorry."

Nonetheless, Carol's nostrils flare slightly at the sight of Jim Street. This can't be good. I walk toward the breakfast bar, careful to keep it between me and the nice gendarmes.

"I remember Deirdre," I say, "She was the one with the rocket launcher. Kidnapped me and nearly killed me." Obviously, I'm not going to play dumb about those things. They tend to stick in your mind, you understand.

"That's the one," Street says, "Seems like she's back in town. You heard about Alex Hollins?"

Here I play dumb. I channel the Joe of a few days ago, the one who really didn't know who Alex Hollins was. Street and Ric are nice enough to fill me in on the murder and the suspect who fled the scene. I act surprised and maybe a little dismayed. (The surprise is faked. The dismay is genuine.) When Street is finished, I consider the information.

"That's nuts," I say, "You really think this Deirdre is the killer?"

Ric pauses in chewing his gum. "It would be a hell of a coincidence if she wasn't," he says, his voice avuncular, even when he's trying to be harsh. (The born *good cop* of this operation.)

Street, though, holds up a cautioning hand. "We don't *know* it's her. But the Excelsior cops got a brief look at the suspect. I think it's her. And if it is her, Slick, I thought she might come here."

My head snaps back, as I've seen Lars's do many times. *Heaven forfend. Who could dream of such a thing?* "Why would she come here?"

Ric crosses his hands in front of him. "Because she needs someone to run to. And you're pretty much the only one she knows in town."

I lean against the breakfast bar. "Should I be concerned?"

"I would be," Ric says.

"We don't *know* she's coming here," Street says, "We don't even know for sure that she killed Alex Hollins. But you might want to be careful."

I pick up my coffee cup. "I haven't heard much about Alex Hollins's murder. They haven't said much on the news."

"Not much to tell," Street says, "He was stabbed to death in his study. Nobody else home at the time. We found tracks in the snow leading away from the house and back to the woods. One of the windows had been forced. Very subtle. The Excelsior cops missed it."

"Who called the police?" I ask.

"It was an anonymous call," Street says, "Phone number wasn't traceable."

"A burner phone?" Carol asks.

"You know about those?" Street says.

"Everyone *knows* about them," Carol says, "It doesn't mean I deal in them."

He considers this then lets it go. Carol flashes him a big smile, then seems to wonder why she did. I play dumb. (*Certainly*, the fugitive accused of the murder is not living just down the stairs.)

"I'm surprised there wasn't a security system," I say, then quickly add: "Or was there?"

Street's cold eyes narrow. This is that Cop Sixth Sense I'm so afraid of; that thing that tells him *This son of a bitch is lying*. If he suspects such a thing, he doesn't say. Ric jumps in.

"It was turned off," Ric says, "According to the wife, they only turned it on at bedtime."

"And I assume the wife was out?" I ask.

"Went to a movie with a friend," Ric says, "Then she says she drove around for a few hours before going home and finding the police there."

"That seems kind of convenient," I say, "She doesn't have an alibi for the time of the murder."

"That doesn't always mean anything. In fact, it usually doesn't mean anything. Murderers are more careful about covering their tracks, making sure time is accounted for."

He's right there. I can't really share any information about Chelsea and how she seemed chummy with Payton Hicks. I might give Street the impression I've been looking into this thing. Which in turn would bring a host of uncomfortable questions.

"I take it there was no sign of the murder weapon?" I say.

Street tilts his head, ever-so-slightly. "The murderer took it when they ran."

Something in Street's manner catches my attention. He's unsure about something. He didn't refer to Deirdre by name. He simply said *the murderer*. And his countenance is normally so filled with self-confidence, any interruption stands out like a neon sign.

"Something about it bothers you," I say.

"Something, yeah," Street says. He looks to Ric, maybe for consultation, maybe for permission. Ric gives him only a brief raise of the eyebrows. "The stabbing," Street says, "Not Deirdre's style. It was too…"

"Personal?" Carol asks.

Street slips her a look. "Something like that. Maybe Alex Hollins resisted, and it had to get ugly. But that doesn't feel right."

"Sounds like an amateur," I say.

"Maybe," Street says, "Someone went through the study. A few drawers had been opened, a few papers out of place. Not Deirdre's style, either." He taps his fingers on the futon. "Someone had to hire Deirdre. She doesn't do this stuff on her own. I've questioned a few people. Hollins's wife. And the new CEO over there."

"Payton Hicks," Carol says.

Street's eyebrows go up. "You've heard of him?"

"We're working with them on a fundraiser for the Kellen Community Center."

I'll hand it to Carol. Maybe she *doesn't* need Mike covering for her. She can be pretty fast on her feet when she needs to be. Street looks toward Ric, who must be in charge of filling in certain details.

"We talked to Payton Hicks for a minute," he says, "He was Alex Hollins's best friend. And, uh, he used to date Chelsea Hollins."

I nearly slip off my stool. "I didn't know that."

"Neither of them made it sound like a big deal."

Shazbot. I'd love to ask for more details, but there's no way I can do that without Street and Ric getting suspicious (or more suspicious than they already are). Best to ask my own questions when I meet with Payton Hicks. Assuming I can do that without *him* getting suspicious.

"How much do you know about Deirdre?" I ask.

"I've got a file on her, going back a few years," Street says, "I've got a string of unsolved murders across five states—three of which I've worked in—and I had a few witnesses who thought they recognized her."

Carol beats me to it. "*Had* a few witnesses?"

Ric clears his throat. "The witnesses have a tendency to…disappear."

"Dead?" Carol asks.

"No," Ric says, "Just extremely…gone."

Carol and I exchange a look. As if I needed a reminder of the danger I'm in. *I* can identify Deirdre. Even if I clear her of Alex Hollins's murder, what's to stop her from doing away with me once I've outlived my usefulness? I could spill the whole thing right here and let Street take his chances on arresting her. But something tells me that would be a mistake. Incarceration would not stop Deirdre from getting revenge on me.

"What do you need me to do?" I ask, "I haven't seen her."

Street gives me the same cop stare I tend to get from Sergeant Frank Pike, a St. Paul homicide cop I've dealt with way too many times. It feels like my moral compass is getting X-rayed.

"If you see her," Street says, "if she contacts you in any way, you get ahold of me." He takes a card out of his pocket and sets it on my desk. "I need you to remember that this woman is dangerous. Every place she goes, the coroner's working overtime. I don't want you to be next, Slick. Understand?"

My eyes get glassy, as if the danger is only just occurring to me. It's not entirely an act. Yes, I've always known that Deirdre is dangerous. But I didn't know the full extent of what she's done. I don't know it now. But I suspect the more details I have, the worse I'm going to feel. I try to ignore that thought.

"I understand," I say.

Street waits a moment, to see if I'm going to add anything to that. Carol doesn't say anything, either, but she strokes her neck, as if the room is getting warm. (Good Lord.) Street looks toward Ric, then buttons his coat in one swift motion.

"Just hold on to the card, Slick," he says, "Get in touch if you have to."

"Will do," I say.

Street leads the way out the front door. He pauses before leaving. "Stay safe," he says.

With that, Street and Ric are out. My body sags, as if I have a slow leak. For several seconds, Carol and I don't move or say anything. I'm not certain either of us are breathing. I finally regain the use of my legs. I move toward the arch windows and peek out above the collected frost. Street and Ric are getting into a black SUV. It pulls away from the curb and disappears down Summit Avenue. I turn toward Carol.

"That was close," I say.

Carol arches an eyebrow. "Really? You think you're *out* of danger now?"

Good point. Lousy of her to say it, but a good point.

***

The trouble with all the intrigue going on (aside from my possible death and/or incarceration) is how it has interrupted my homelife. I like my apartment. It's small, but it's cozy. The same thing can be said about the building. I've always placed a high priority on feeling comfortable at home. This is particularly true in the winter when I have to spend so much time here. I don't much like skulking around the place.

I peek out of the front door and down the stairway, trying (and I'm sure utterly failing) not to look suspicious. The coast is clear. I hope my neighbor across the hall doesn't step out. She already thinks I'm kind of strange. The sight of me skulking around, carrying a casserole dish and a paper bag while wearing oven mitts isn't likely to change that. I slip down the stairs and stop outside the door to Deirdre's apartment. I peek around the corner and down the adjoining staircase. Again, no sign of anyone. In addition to the aforementioned casserole dish and oven mitts, the sight of me knocking on the door to a supposedly unoccupied apartment is bound to raise suspicion. I rap on said door, trying to be quiet at the same time. After several seconds, the peephole darkens and then the door opens a crack. There's just enough room for me to slip inside.

"I come bearing gifts," I say, hefting the casserole dish.

Deirdre closes the door behind me. She's wearing a blue robe that I recognize as Lars's. She fills it out a hell of a lot better than he does. I find myself staring at it. Deirdre runs a hand along the neckline.

"I'm washing my only clothes," she says, "Your friend loaned me a robe."

I take another second to get a hold of myself. Deirdre pulls the robe tightly closed. I avert my eyes and look around the apartment. It's a mirror image of mine but owing to its being on the other side of the staircase, everything is reversed. It's like Bizarro Joe's apartment. A straight back chair sits in the middle of the living room. A few books (borrowed from me) sit in one corner. Back in the bedroom is the old mattress Lars loaned Deirdre. The trashcan in the kitchen (also borrowed from Lars) is filled with to-go food containers. There are bits of dust and dirt spread about. I shiver slightly.

"It's cold in here," I say.

"I don't mind," Deirdre says, "Besides, if I turn up the heat, the person upstairs might get suspicious."

I can see the sense in it, but I'm wishing I had worn my peacoat down here. I set the casserole dish on the breakfast bar. A corner of Deirdre's mouth goes up.

"You brought me dinner?" Then she laughs and says under her breath, "Of course, you brought me dinner." She points to the bag. "What's in there? Wait, let me guess: a couple plates, silverware, and some napkins."

Now I feel self-conscious. "They're plastic plates and cutlery and paper napkins. I hope that's okay."

"I think I can make do." She peels back the tinfoil and takes a look. "What is it?"

"It's a Chicken Dorito hotdish. Recipe of my mom's."

"What's in it?"

"Chicken and celery and beyond that, absolutely nothing healthy."

Deirdre chuckles. "Comfort food. Just what I'm in the mood for." She gives me a slight smile. "Thank you. I appreciate this."

I fumble to get the plates, napkins and cutlery out of the bag. That done, I make sure everything is set just so. I use a plastic serving spoon to scoop two servings on to the paper plates. We sit at her breakfast bar and dig in. Deirdre eats heartily. (I wonder how many homecooked meals she gets in her line of work?) I wave a hand at her robe.

"I could help you out of that," I say, then quickly correct myself, "Help you out *with* that."

"You have a large collection of women's clothes?"

"No. But I've got a female friend who could do some shopping for you."

"What are you going to tell her?"

I scratch my ear. "I, uh, don't have to tell her anything. She…already knows."

Deirdre doesn't react strongly, but the tilt of her head conveys her displeasure. "Who is this person?"

"My friend Carol," I say, trying not to mumble, "You might remember her, actually."

"She's the one I was hired to eliminate. If I remember right, she got in a lucky kick on me as well." A kick that knocked Deirdre out, but she doesn't need me to fill in those particular details. She's displeased enough as it is. "You're not exactly busting your ass to keep this a secret," she says.

I hold my hands out, palms down, trying to be Mr. Reasonable. "I understand your concern. But Mike, Carol and

Lars are my closest friends. They're constantly around. They would have stumbled across this sooner or later. Besides, there's no one I trust more than them. Everything will be fine."

Deirdre arches an eyebrow. "They're not going to tell anyone?"

"No. They wouldn't put me at risk."

She strokes her neck as she thinks. "You're willing to stake your life on that?"

"Yes. Absolutely."

"Good. Because you are."

Deirdre goes back to her meal. I find myself sliding back on the stool, as if I need to get ready to run at any moment. If she wasn't happy about Carol, she's not going to be happy about my next bit of information.

"I did get a visit from someone we *should* worry about," I say, "Jim Street came a-callin'."

"I'm not surprised," Deirdre says, looking toward the windows, "What did he say?"

I run down the list of evidence Street gave me: the brief glimpse the police got, the sign of forced entry (Deirdre seems chagrined by this, an affront to her professional pride), and the questioning of Hollins's associates. I try to make it sound like Street's way off, putting in as light a touch as possible. Deirdre doesn't seem convinced.

"I'm his only suspect," she says.

"I wouldn't go that far. He knows you weren't acting on your own. You must have been hired to kill Alex Hollins. And there's something about the whole thing he doesn't like."

"What is that?"

I give her Street's observations about the use of the knife. They mirror my own, so it's not new information to Deirdre. But it's more intriguing that a guy like Street is thinking it. She contemplates this while she eats. I set my plastic fork aside.

"It gives Street the same vibe it gives me," I say, "The whole thing feels personal. Not the kind of thing a contract killer would do."

Deirdre weighs this info. "Doesn't mean he won't come after me."

I incline my head in agreement. "Then we still need to find out what's going on."

"Or I could eliminate him." I give her a sharp look. Deirdre smirks. "I'm kidding."

Okay, this is a breach of our partnership. *I'm* the one who's supposed to crack jokes and Deirdre is the one who kills people. If she's going to crack jokes…well, I should probably stop there. I pick at the hotdish.

"The sign of forced entry," I say, "I assume that was you?"

"A downstairs window. I had to jimmy it a little. I'm surprised Street spotted it. He's got a good eye."

That's disconcerting. I wonder what Street might have spotted (and not let me in on) when he was in my apartment. Best to shake it off. I tap my plastic fork on the plate.

"There's another thing that's bothering me. There are traces of you, but not the actual murderer. Meaning the murderer was able to get into the house without breaking in and get out without having to tramp through the snow like you did. All of which points to someone who had a pretty decent familiarity with the house."

"An inside job, so to speak."

"Exactly. It could only be someone who was close to Alex Hollins."

"Like his wife," Deirdre says.

"Like his wife. Assuming, of course, it wasn't his wife who hired you."

Deirdre pulls her ponytail free. Honey-colored hair spills around her shoulders. She puts it back into a tighter ponytail. "Did Street say anything else? About me, I mean?"

I debate telling her. There *is* one more thing, but I'm not sure I should bring it up. It might take us into a territory we'd best not go. I look down.

"No, nothing," I say.

"Are you sure?"

I hesitate. "Yes."

Deirdre doesn't seem to buy it, but she says, "All right."

We eat in silence. Every now and again, there's a creak or a buzz, the usual noises in an apartment building. Deirdre's head flicks slightly at every noise, as if something is about to happen. It's not paranoia so much as readiness. Her robe has fallen open a bit, giving me a slightly less-than-demure peek. Deirdre makes no effort to close it. I look down, avoiding the view. I can't help wondering who I'm having dinner with. I set my fork down.

"Can I ask you something?" I say.

"You can try."

"How does someone get into your line of work? I can't imagine you graduate from college with a degree in Cut A Bitch."

"No. You go to tech school." Deirdre looks down. I can't help laughing. Dear God, another joke. She's on a roll. Deirdre concentrates on her food. "It's a long story," she says. She tilts her head slightly. "Why do you want to know?"

"Just curious," I say.

Deirdre takes another bite. "Someone got me involved. It's a long story. But he…was a very interesting person." She pauses in her chewing. "I was a different person then. He rescued me."

"Rescued you?"

She stares at the plate. "Like I said, darling. It's a long story. Not worth getting into."

When someone like Deirdre tells you they won't tell you a story, that's the end of the discussion. Again, I'll probably stay healthier not knowing some of these things. But I can't help being curious.

"This guy you mentioned," I ask, "Does he have a name?"

"I'll keep that to myself, darling." She goes back to her food. "Anyway, that's how I got into this life."

A bite is halfway to my mouth. I set it down again. "How do you do it?" I ask.

"You want me to train you?"

"No, no. I just…when you do a, a job…and then you're home, living what I assume is a normal life…"

"You're wondering how I live with myself."

I nod, half-grateful that she cut to the chase for me. But it's an impertinent question. Asking someone about their background is one thing. Making moral judgements is another. The look Deirdre gives me is a tad forbidding. She sets her fork down.

"You learn to compartmentalize," she says, "The person I am at home doesn't touch the person who does the work. The person I am now doesn't touch the person I was back in the day. You keep these things separate." She looks off to one side. "It's like there's a little box in my mind. I put the job there. And I only open it when there's another job. Does that make sense?"

"Yes. But if you'll pardon my saying, it sounds a lot like a split-personality disorder."

Far from being offended, Deirdre gives it some thought. "I suppose it's similar in some ways. Except the disorder is the result of trauma. Mine is the result of training."

I tap my plate with my fork. "If I'm hearing you right, Deirdre is the part of you that does…the job. And you're somebody else when you're back home?"

"Yes."

"Does that somebody have a name?"

"She does."

"But you're not going to tell it to me."

"I am not."

Fair enough. There was only so much I was going to get out of this conversation, anyway. I couldn't exactly tell her a guy who has chased her through five states was asking about her and then hope she'll give me her entire biography.

Deirdre gets up from the breakfast bar and steps to the window. She gently peers through the blinds.

"Speaking of James Street, you might want to be a little cautious," Deirdre says, "He has men watching you."

A stab of panic shoots through my chest. "How do you know that?"

"There's a little green Corolla that's been sitting at the end of the block for the last several hours. It doesn't belong to anyone in the neighborhood."

"You're kidding me."

"I'm not. I've been keeping an eye on things around here. I know all the cars, casual or otherwise, that come through." She turns away from the window. "I can't sit here and play sudoku all day."

I push away my plate. (So much for my membership in the Clean Plate Club. Sorry, Mom.) Street's having me followed. Jiffy swell. At the same time, I haven't gone anywhere too suspicious. Yes, I've talked to Chelsea Hollins and I'm going to talk to Payton Hicks, but the fundraiser gives me cover there. As long as Deirdre stays in this apartment, we're fine.

The dryer buzzes, indicating its cycle is complete. I jump slightly, but Deirdre doesn't bat an eyelash. She walks from the window to the dryer and peeks in. "What's our next move?" she asks.

"I'm going to talk to Payton Hicks. He's the CFO of Hankerson-William. And a friend of the family. He might have something to tell me."

"A confession?"

"He's probably not going to make it that easy."

Deirdre pulls an armload of her clothes from the dryer. "I need to get dressed. You probably want to leave."

It's not as commanding as it might be. The slight smile returns to Deirdre's face. Weird. I didn't really want to come down here, and now I'm kind of disappointed I have to go. I toss my plate in the garbage, put the foil back over the casserole dish and put the dish in the fridge.

"It reheats really well," I say, "You just have to put the oven on two-fifty and give it about fifteen minutes."

Deirdre temporarily puts her face behind the armload of clothes. "Yes, mother." And I can swear I hear her laughing.

I head for the front door. "I'll let you know what I find out."

"Do that," Deirdre says, "And if you want to stop down again, feel free."

I pause at the door. Deirdre has one hand on the sash of the robe. It hangs loosely, not revealing anything, but only just. I scamper out, chuckling like an idiot as I go.

I'll admit: I've done better jobs playing cool. (Not many, but…)

CHAPTER SIX

I've always hated waiting in a reception area. Nothing good is ever on the horizon when you're parked on a couch, waiting.

It probably goes back to when I was a kid, and my mom would take me to the clinic for my shots. Sitting on a sofa, staring at a copy of Time *magazine that I couldn't comprehend, knowing any minute a nurse was going to step out and announce I was next is the closest thing I'll (hopefully) ever get to walking the last mile.*

It's never gotten better. Principal's offices, job interviews, legal offices; they all involve a certain amount of waiting and worrying. You never hear someone come out of a room and say, "The naked chicks and beer are ready for you now."

At least it hasn't happened yet. The search continues…

"Mr. Hicks will be with you in just a moment," the receptionist says.

As waiting areas go, I can't complain about the one outside Payton Hicks's office. A panoramic view of downtown Minneapolis is visible through the picture windows. It's probably nicer when the panorama doesn't consist of snow-capped buildings and steam rising from the street. But I can't put that one on Hicks.

"You sure you don't want me to go in there with you?" Lars asks, leaning toward me and invading my personal space, "After all, I'm organizing the fundraiser. And I have quite a way with people. Particularly people in power."

"I'll be okay," I say, leaning away, tugging again at this damn suit.

Lars goes back to his copy of *Better Homes and Gardens*. He insisted on coming along. I don't need his help, but I'm glad he's catching up on his reading. "Actually," he says, looking toward the receptionist. "I may do just fine out here."

Oy vey. Lars waggles his eyebrows on the off-chance I didn't know what he was talking about. The receptionist has the usual Stepford pleasantness, covering a general lack of interest. She has wavy brown hair, tightly clipped behind her head. Her gray blouse hangs loosely, giving me no idea what her figure looks like. A pair of reading glasses are perched on the end of her nose. She bears a disquieting similarity to Mrs. Grothe, my second-grade teacher. Lars gives her a little flutter of the fingers. The receptionist looks down and blushes. Her phone rings and Payton Hicks lets her know he's ready for me. Nice of Hicks not to keep me waiting.

Still, I'd rather have the naked chicks and the beer.

The receptionist leads me to the door of Hicks's office. I fumble with the folder of information Lars has provided. Lars himself glides toward the receptionist's desk. Great. If Hicks doesn't throw me out on his own, security will probably toss Lars out on a sexual harassment complaint. Surely, the Kellen Community Center deserves better than the likes of us.

Hicks's office is palatial and affords an even better view of downtown Minneapolis. Diplomas and framed awards line the walls. No photos with local celebrities, though. Hicks stands next to his desk, looking dyspeptic as ever. He wears a dark suit and a navy-blue tie. I wish the dude would wear a carnation in his lapel or something. *Anything* to add some festivity. He greets me with a mildly slack handshake. He indicates a chair and takes a seat behind a desk roughly the size of an aircraft carrier. It's bare of any decoration, save for a coffee mug with a few hearts on it. (There's a lighter touch, anyway.) He slouches slightly in the chair.

"How can I help you, Mr. Davis?" he says, as if this interview has already gone too long.

I run through the spiel about the Kellen community and how the much the center would mean and how the fundraiser will help. Hicks listens closely, if impassively. I rush to the finish.

"As you can see, it's a good cause," I say.

"It is," Hicks says, "What is it you need from me?"

I struggle to find a comfortable position in this chair. "As I said, Hankerson-William's participation is terrific. But I'd like to know more about what you do. That would help with the publicity for the event. And it means more coming for the CFO and, I'm guessing, interim CEO."

"De facto CEO would be more accurate," Hicks says, "Just until the board decides on a replacement."

"And will that replacement be you?"

Hicks lightly flips his hands open. "That will be up to the board."

I'm hunting for some confession of ambition. A motive for arranging Alex Hollins's murder. But Hicks is not going to give me that. If the guy has emotions (and I'm making a big leap here), he's not likely to wear them on his sleeve. He looks around his desk. He doesn't seem nervous. He just has better things to do. I shift, slightly, in my chair.

"Must have been a real shock," I say, "Alex Hollins's death."

"It was."

"Where were you when you found out?"

"I was here at the office," he says, "I was doing work."

I'm getting nowhere with the small talk. Hicks is a pro at deflecting anything that sounds like a personal question. I make a show of shuffling through my notes.

"How is Chelsea doing?" I ask.

"As well as could be expected."

"You're good friends with her?"

He looks away, dismissive. "She's a nice girl. After what happened to Alex, she needs someone to look out for her."

"I understand." I keep my eyes on the paperwork. "How long did you know Alex?"

"I met him when he first came to Hankerson-William," Hicks says, "He was just out of college. Bright. Eager to learn. Ambitious. You could see he was headed to the top. I was ahead of him on the corporate ladder, but I knew it was only a matter of time before he passed me."

"You were okay with that?"

"Of course," Hicks says, "That's a thing people don't understand. A person might have ambitions to lead, but if someone else is better suited for it, you've got to step aside. That way, we all win. That's all I've ever wanted in my career. It worked out well for both of us."

"Until last week."

Hicks winces. "Until last week."

I let him stew in his faux pas. I'm not getting a lot of bitterness toward Alex Hollins. Maybe Hicks is covering. Maybe he's as pragmatic as he says. I look up from my notes, trying to seem casual.

"I understand you and Chelsea used to date," I say.

Hicks looks stricken. "Where did you hear that?"

"I think she mentioned it."

She didn't, of course, but I'll let Hicks and Chelsea work that out. Hicks fumbles with some paperwork. "It wasn't anything serious. I met her at a cocktail party. She was working in…middle management. We went out a few times. Then she met Alex. They hit it off. Simple as that."

Translation: Chelsea was working in the secretarial pool, she agreed to go out with Hicks (whether she was a social climber or felt pressured to go out with an executive is a question I'll leave for others), then she met Alex, who worked a crowbar and eventually married her. But I keep my interpretations to myself, lest I antagonize Mr. Hicks.

"And you stayed friends with Chelsea?" I ask.

"Of course. There was no bitterness there. She and Alex were a good match."

"Huh. Chelsea made it sound like they weren't happy."

Hicks looks down for a second, maybe debating an answer. "They were happy," he says, "For a while." He shrugs. "I've never been married. I can't tell you what happens in a marriage other than sometimes people just…drift apart. I believe that happened to Alex and Chelsea."

"Did either of them talk to you about it?" I ask.

"Not really." Then he spreads his hands and says, "Is this relevant to anything?"

I nearly drop my notes. "Sorry. I didn't…I have a habit of asking questions and chatting with people and sometimes I just run off at the mouth. I'm, I'm sorry."

That gets a small bob of the head from Hicks. We talk about the fundraiser and the list of projects Hankerson-William has on tap. Nothing all that interesting, at least to a layman like me. For something that started as an office supply company, they've moved into a lot of diverse areas: mining, transportation, research and development. Next thing you know they'll be involved in the space program. I pretend to write it down, knowing full well I won't need the information and if I do, I'll just look it up online. I set the notes aside.

"This is all very interesting," I say, "What can you tell me about Dustin Felt?"

Hicks looks up, suddenly. "Where did you hear about him?"

"It was in the news. I remember reading something about it. He died shortly after he was fired. Something like that."

"He was." Hicks's eyes drop to the desk. "Dustin was emotional. Maybe a bit unstable. He had difficulty getting along with others. I don't have a lot of details. Most of this was handled on a level below me. After Dustin died and the story was in the media, I asked to be filled in."

"Dustin was working on the Green River Project, right?" I ask.

There's a hint of suspicion in Hicks's beady eyes, but I try to give him my most open face. I'm just making conversation, right? Clueless conversation, but here I am. There is a momentary debate, then Hicks decides to answer the question.

"Yes, he was," Hicks says, "He was doing research. One of many people working on it. I never met him, personally. As I said, most of what I know about him I got from reports."

I slip my notes into a folder and cross my legs. "I've read a little about the Green River Project. There's some controversy about it if I'm not mistaken."

Hicks's mouth tightens, like he's sucking a lemon. "There are some minor, completely unfounded concerns from activists who are long on passion and short on facts.

Unfortunately, they've got the ear of a few politicians looking to score points."

"That, that's *one* version of what I've heard."

"The Green River Project is going to create jobs. It's going to help the economy in a part of the state that badly needs it. Anything else is a diversion. And a damaging one at that."

"Then it's completely safe?" I ask.

Hicks strokes his power tie. "We're doing studies. Teams are researching it. We're completely confident the project is safe, and the research will bear that out."

I tuck the folder under my arm and stand to shake Hicks's hand. "Thanks for your time. It's really going to help the fundraiser. It would be great if you could be there."

"I will be," Hicks says, sounding like he's talking about an upcoming colonoscopy, "Chelsea felt the company should have a representative there and that I'm the best person for the job."

"That's great," I say,

Hicks says nothing in response. Probably best for me to get the hell out of here. (We'll call this a win-win.) I thank Hicks again and head for the door. He makes no effort to walk me out. Instead, he swivels his chair toward the window.

When I get to the reception area, Lars is deep in a flirty conversation with the receptionist. They're leaning close and giggling. Gross. When she sees me, the receptionist turns away from Lars and tries to regain a bit of professionalism. Lars merely turns toward me.

"How did it go, brother?" he asks.

"Jiffy swell," I say, "You ready to take off?"

"If we must."

He winks at the receptionist as he steps away from the desk. She looks down, smiling. The hook up is visible from fifty yards. I wait until we're out of earshot to address the situation.

"Let me guess," I say, "You got her number."

"I did indeed."

"Don't you already have a girlfriend?"

"I'm a man of the world, Joe. I'm allowed to make friends, meet people."

"Uh-huh," I say.

"Besides, what Iris doesn't know won't hurt me," he says, "Because if she knew…she'd almost certainly hurt me."

There he is, folks. My buddy Lars. The Minnesota Love Machine.

We're just about at the door to the elevator bank when someone barrels past us. She's about my age. Her curly hair is pulled back into a severe ponytail and her small mouth is puckered. The brown eyes look slightly wild and give me a quizzical look. It lingers for a second. I say hello, but she ignores me and makes a beeline into Hicks's office.

Welcome to Hankerson-William: now offering you the fuck you can go give yourself.

***

"I should have known this was going to blow up in my face," Carol says, staring into her Cosmo, "I just didn't know *how* it was going to blow up."

Oh, what a tangled web. But I keep the thought to myself. Carol is having enough trouble as it is. And this should be a pleasant occasion. We're hanging out at The Tav, the watering hole of preference in my neighborhood. The place is on Selby Avenue, down the street from the Cathedral. It's a combination restaurant, sports bar, and pub. Picture windows face Selby, all of them frosted over. (That's okay, there's nothing to see on Selby anyway.) Big screen TVs hang from various corners. A Wild game is on, but the bar is half empty and sleepy. No one is paying any attention to the game except Freddie, the three-hundred-pound Samoan gentlemen who acts as a bouncer and whose screams at the TV can be registered on the Richter Scale. There's a pool table at the back and a few dart boards. The atmosphere is cozy, the staff knows us and there's a collection of quality craft beers and other booze. Always a good time, even on a night as cold as this. Except Carol isn't having a good time.

124

I swirl the Grand Brewing Winter Ale in my glass, savoring the coal black richness. I can't help wondering if the cops are watching me. (Although the beer helps take the edge off.) I tug at my sweatshirt and scratch the legs of my jeans. (They irritate my dry skin, but they're still my clothes of choice. Summer will come sooner or later, right? Right?) Carol is resplendent in her black sweater and jeans (about as casual as she gets). Maybe focusing on her problems will help me with my own. (That's a nice thought.)

"All right, fill me in," I say, "What happened?"

Carol brushes a strand of hair away from her face. "Okay, I knew I'd have to tell Mr. Pratt something about skipping out on Friday. I was willing to tell him the truth and throw myself on the mercy of the court. As soon as I got into his office and saw the look on his face, I knew I couldn't do it."

"He wasn't happy, huh?"

"I imagine it's the look some people get before they give the order to the firing squad. Only less pleasant."

"Ouch," I say.

"Ouch is right. Anyway, I was stuck. I had to come up with something and I had passed up my chance to ask Mike what to do. I had to improvise."

I can't help wincing. Carol is too much like me. She's a creative person, hence her job as an ad writer, but improvisation is not her specialty. Then again, we've both been shockingly successful in that area lately. Maybe Carol's foray wasn't a complete disaster.

"What did you come up with?" I ask.

Carol blows out a sigh. "I told him I had a friend who needed my help. It wasn't complete bullshit. I *did* have a friend who needed help. It's just that the help involved cutting out of work and going day drinking."

I try to channel my Inner Mike. "That's a good start. You take an actual event, twist it to the left, and go from there."

"I didn't hang around Mike this long for nothing." She sips her Cosmo. "Mr. Pratt asked me for details—I knew he would—and I said my friend Evie was going to rehab. She had been on the wagon, but she fell off. She needed someone supportive to give her a ride to treatment."

Whoa. When Carol comes up with BS excuses, she doesn't ass around. The look on her face is half-chagrined, half-impressed. It probably mirrors the look on my face.

"Did he buy it?" I ask.

"Oh, he bought it. His attitude changed on a dime. He asked me all sorts of questions about my friend and if there was anything he could do to help. He was really interested. It worked like a charm. If not for the fact I felt like a complete shit."

"Ah see, you let your conscience get to you. Mike would never do that."

"I know. My bad." Carol tears at a napkin. "But I was free and clear. Or so I thought."

"You thought? Uh-oh. We have trouble? Right here in River City?"

"With a capital *T* that rhymes with all the rest of that shit." She pushes her Cosmo aside. "Mr. Pratt called me into his office today. He wanted to let me know how much he appreciated what I had done for my friend, asked me how she was doing. I made up some stuff. Said she was in a rehab center and things were going well. She was really making some progress. I was proud of her. All that shit. Then Mr. Pratt said his son is in the same boat. The kid's an alcoholic."

"That's too bad."

"It gets worse. Mr. Pratt wants to get him into treatment. And he wants to put his son into the same rehab center as my friend Evie. He wanted to know the name of the place."

Oh, dear God. When they say the devil is in the details, they might just be talking about lying. A good general lie will get you through. But when you have to start providing details, you get into trouble. Not only is there a chance you'll screw those details up, there's a chance you won't be able to repeat them the next time through. That is how you generally get caught in a lie.

"What did you tell him?" I ask.

"I just made up a name. Right off the top of my head. I said she was in the Amber Heard Center. But that it was very exclusive."

I try to hide my giggle behind my pint of beer and ignore the dirty look Carol is giving me. "Amber Heard?" I say, "As in Johnny Depp's crazy ex?"

"It just came out," Carol says, "Isn't that what they teach you when you're improvising? Just work off the top of your head?"

"If that's what you've got, maybe you ought to work off the top of somebody else's head."

She gives me the finger. "There wasn't time to do that. I just went with what I could think of. I must have seen her name on the internet recently. I don't know. It didn't matter, anyway. Mr. Pratt bought it. He said he'd look into it."

"Given that the place doesn't exist," I say, "I would think that matters a lot."

"I know," Carol says, "I volunteered to do it for him."

"Good thinking."

"It bought me some time, anyway. Now, I just have to figure out how to handle things with the kid."

I finish off my Winter Ale, trying not to smack my lips as I do. I'll admit it feels a little decadent to be enjoying this while we're talking about someone going to rehab. I set the pint glass down and signal Nick, the bartender, for another.

"What's your next move?" I ask.

"I don't know," Carol says, "Mr. Pratt isn't going to let this go, obviously. And he shouldn't. His son is in trouble. But there's no such thing as the Amber Heard Center."

"I suppose you could always build one."

"You're not funny."

"On the contrary, I think I'm hilarious."

"You can't exactly lecture somebody about lying," she says, "Not at the moment."

This is true. Stashing a contract killer from the police does make one's high horse rather lame. I exchange my empty pint glass for the full one brought by April, our server. I wait for April to walk away before continuing.

"I will drop the subject, if you wish," I say.

"I wish," Carol says, "At least as far as the thing with Mr. Pratt is concerned. How's it going with Little Miss Lucrecia Borgia?"

"Fine," I say, "But I don't think she'd appreciate you calling her that. Assuming, of course, she understood the reference."

Carol balances her Cosmo just below her lips. "You making any progress on getting her out of trouble?"

"I've talked to a few people. I don't know if I can say I'm making progress."

I update Carol about my chats with Chelsea Hollins and Payton Hicks, specifically the Hollins's not having a happy marriage and Payton Hicks dating Chelsea before Alex. I give her the few bits about the Green River Project and Dustin Felt's death and how those seem to be more unhappy coincidences than anything. Carol winces as I get to the end.

"Doesn't sound like you have much of anything," she says.

"I know," I say, "The motivation is what's bedeviling me."

"Bedeviling?"

"Thought I'd try it out." I rest my arms on the table. "Why would you hire Deirdre and then set her up?"

"To throw suspicion off yourself."

"But what's that going to get you? Unless you've found other ways to cover your tracks, the cops are going to figure out Deirdre is a contract killer. She's not going to act on her own. Someone would have to hire her. Why take the chance on having it boomerang back on you? Better to just let Deirdre take out Alex Hollins and disappear into the ether."

Carol twists her mouth to one side as she thinks. "You'd be taking a hell of a chance."

"Exactly. Street's already seen things he doesn't like. If you're going to go through all this trouble, why stake your life on the idea that cops are idiots?"

"Don't most DIY crooks work on that assumption?" Carol asks.

"True."

We lapse into a momentary silence, having come to a dead end in this thinking. Fortunately, we're distracted by something else. Lars whips open the front door and holds it for Iris. Carol turns their direction.

"What does Lars see in her?" Carol says.

Watching Iris slip out of her leather jacket and viewing the wine-colored sweater that clings to her chest, I say, "I can think of a couple of things."

"Come on," Carol says, "is he really *that* shallow?"

"You remember this is Lars, right?"

That settles that; temporarily at least. Lars gets Iris settled at a table on the other side of the bar and makes his way over to us. He's smiling, as usual, but it looks a bit plastered on.

"Good to see you all," he says, "Quite a surprise."

"Indeed," I say, "Given that we're here several times a week."

"Yeah, it happens," Lars says, distracted. He seems concerned about what's going on at his table. Iris sits with her arms folded across her ample chest; her hair pulled back into its usual severe ponytail. Her cold eyes search the room and don't appear to like what they're seeing. Lars taps the table in front of Carol. "We have to come up with something for the silent auction. I've been consulting Chuck about some ideas."

Carol gives him an extended blink. Lars's friend Chuck is the intellectual driving force behind all of Lars's ventures. Please note that I am using *intellectual* in the broadest sense of the word. Nothing Chuck suggests will result in something usable. Still, we have to give Lars room to express these ideas. (Although again, we must use *ideas* in a very broad…well, you get where I'm going with this.)

"What kind of ideas?" I ask, my voice hollow.

"Okay, Chuck has a friend who's a dairy farmer," Lars says, "He would be willing to donate some stock."

"Free milk?" I ask.

"No, the actual cow," Lars says, "Some of them simply outlive their usefulness. If someone can make the cow productive again, think of the possibilities."

Carol pinches the bridge of her nose. "You're proposing we put dried up old livestock in the silent auction?"

Lars sniffs. "If that's how you want to put it. Personally, I think you're only seeing the glass half-empty."

Before Carol can answer (and slap Lars), I jump in. "What else have you got?"

Lars starts ticking the points off on his fingers. "Going three rounds with the Hobo Boxing Champion—and I mean *the* Hobo Boxing Champion, not that pretender from the East Side—an evening with a Judi Densch impersonator, a manicure from Kim's Korean Barbeque and Salon, a complimentary entry to the Jugg's Mud Wrestling Invitational, and a gasoline-powered dog hair trimmer."

"Excellent," Carol says, "So, we're not going to use any of those and I'm going to order you not to consult Chuck again until the fundraiser's over. Unless, of course, you want me to kick you in the balls. Repeatedly."

Lars strokes his beard as he considers this. "It's a fair cop."

Before we can further discuss the fundraiser, there's a commotion on the other side of the bar. Not surprisingly, it involves Iris. She's confronting April, our server. Iris gets up from the table and shakes the drinks menu in April's face.

"Chopin Family Reserve!" Iris shouts, her face distorting, "It's the best vodka in the world! How can you not have it?"

There's panic in April's doe eyes. "It's…we just…don't!"

"This is ridiculous! How can you even stay open?"

Before April can offer a response (assuming she has one), Iris uses the drink menu to slap the tray out of April's hands. Thankfully, there are no beverages on it, and it clatters harmlessly to the floor. The whole bar has gone quiet, watching the scene unfold. This includes Freddie, who slides his bulk off the barstool to get a better look. Nick, the bartender, slips out from behind the bar and approaches the scene, waving his hands in an amiable manner.

"Hey now, we can't have that," Nick says, his voice jovial as usual.

Iris responds by grabbing two handfuls of Nick's beard and shaking his head. "Yeah? What are you going to do about it, you little toad?"

Carol and I hop out of our chairs, but neither of us is sure what to do. All I can say is: "Lars."

"I'm on it," he says, looking as if he's been asked to throw himself on a grenade (and in a sense…)

Lars approaches the scene. Unfortunately, Freddie is approaching it as well. And his solution is likely to be a lot less diplomatic than Lars's. That spurs Carol to action. Freddie has always had an unspoken crush on Carol. Hopefully, she can use that to de-escalate the situation.

Freddie opens the conversation with, "You need to get your fucking hands off my bartender."

Iris barely gives him a glance. "Who the fuck are you?"

"I'm the one gonna be throwing you outta here, you don't get your hands off my bartender."

"I'd like to see you fucking try."

Obviously, Freddie isn't going to pass up that invitation. He makes a move toward Iris. She responds by kicking him in the leg. Although, she could have thrown that kick at the wall for all the good it does her. Freddie keeps coming. Lars slides between them and Freddie ejects him from the scene. Lars winds up under a table, a tangle of arms, legs and quasi-pompadour. Carol steps in front of Freddie, stopping him just before he gets to Iris.

"Freddie, it's okay," Carol says, "This is a friend of ours. Well, actually..."

"She ain't no friend of mine," Freddie says.

"Just...calm down," Carol says, "We'll get this thing handled." She turns toward Lars and shouts, "Lars, handle this fucking thing!"

Lars frees his arm from the slats of a chair and gets out from under the table. He carefully approaches Iris and begins whispering to her, trying to calm her down. I can't hear what's being said, but Iris at least forgoes any further aggression. Carol, meanwhile, keeps a hand on Freddie's massive chest, preventing him from continuing his advance. The whole bar holds its collective breath.

Lars finally convinces Iris to let go of Nick's beard. She transfers her grip to Lars's beard, causing him to momentarily go weak in the knees. He gently drapes Iris's coat around her shoulders and guides her toward the door. Her hands are in Lars's beard and her eyes are still locked on Freddie, giving him the hateful look to end all hateful looks. April and Nick are huddled against the wall, afraid to do anything. When Lars and Iris get to the front door, Iris shouts over Lars's shoulder.

"I'm never coming into this shithole again!"

Lars looks back, giving the place a weak smile. "You all have a good night."

There are a few seconds of silence once Lars leaves, then the bar slowly regains its conversational mojo. Carol says a few words to Freddie, and he ambles back toward his stool. Nick makes sure April is okay, then returns to his place behind the bar. April picks up the tray, takes a deep breath, and goes back to work. Carol returns to our table.

"Nice work," I say.

"Lars did most of it," she says, before gulping the rest of her Cosmo, "By the way, I don't want to hear one crack about Lars being a *Bitch Whisperer.*"

"Of course not," I say, although I wish I had thought up the term myself.

Carol frowns. "I guess we're not going to see Iris in here again."

"We will not. I'm pretty sure management will see to that."

"I wonder what Lars and Iris will do?"

"Probably go back to his place and have spectacular hate sex." It then occurs to me that I'll be treated to the sounds of the aforementioned hate sex.

Maybe I need to hire Deirdre to take care of that matter. As long as she's out of work...

***

While The Tav is only five blocks from my apartment, I actually drove there. This whole *rugged northern Minnesotan* thing only gets you so far. My Saturn Ion (a vehicular Freeze Baby) isn't happy about it, but I'm the one making the car payments, so...

I park in the lot behind the building and sprint up the erector set of decks and stairs, trying to avoid the ice patches before my extremities freeze. This reminds me of when I was in high school and would have to park a few blocks away from the school (this was after my girlfriend Lisa wrote an article exposing the parking lot attendant as the beautifully corrupt asshole he was) and I would be nearly frozen by the time I got to the door of the school. I always imagined if I slipped on the ice and broke an arm or a leg, my only instructions to potential rescuers would have been, "Get me the fuck inside!"

As I pass Lars's deck, I notice all the lights are off. I'm sure he and Iris are home. I can practically hear the animal-like sounds. (I might be imagining it but why the hell would I imagine *that?*) I'm going to have to turn on the radio tonight and crank it up. I don't like where things are going with Lars and this woman. First Fong's, now The Tav. He's rapidly becoming persona non grata all around the neighborhood.

I dart up the stairs and make the final assault on the summit of Mount Apartment. The cold seeps under my coat and my legs are getting heavy. I step around the wall separating my deck from my neighbor's. And find a guy holding a gun on me.

Apparently, Lars isn't the only one who's persona non grata.

CHAPTER SEVEN

On the one hand, I benefit from an overactive imagination. God knows I've made a living off it. But the drawback is that I've never been allowed to enjoy horror stories.

You see, horror, like most genres, isn't hard to understand on the surface. It plays to our deepest unconscious fears. Freud knew that. And he threw a bunch of sex in there as well. (Really, he could have written any of the Friday, The Thirteenth *movies.) I certainly understand someone enjoying the momentary vicarious thrill of exploring these fears. A catharsis, if you will.*

My problem is that I can't leave it behind. Vicarious horror stays with me for days or maybe weeks at a time. I'm afraid of the dark. I'm afraid to be alone. I'm afraid someone is sneaking up behind me. I'm afraid someone will pop up out of nowhere and freak me out. It's best to keep my imagination and the horror stories in separate corners.

Horror stories aside, *this* is not going to help my fear of the unknown, either.

The light is thin, but I can clearly see the guy. He's a little shorter than me and dressed all in black, including a leather biker jacket and black jeans. He's got piggy eyes, a needle nose and a thin mouth. His round face is red, and he shivers slightly, underdressed for the weather. Not a particularly intimidating fellow, but the gun makes up for that.

"Joe Davis," he says. It's not a question.

"And you are…?" I say.

He raises the gun to about face level. (My face level, sadly.) "Looking for Deirdre. Where is she?"

Safe to say I'm conflicted. I'd like to live through this experience, but I don't want to give up Deirdre. Because if I do give her up and *she* lives through the experience, there's a good chance I'll still end up dead. A lot of thoughts going through the old noggin.

"Deirdre…" I say, as if jogging the memory banks (when I'm actually stalling for time).

The guy's not having it. "Don't fuck around! I'm sure she's been in touch with you. I want to know where she is. You got five seconds. One…"

"Look, I just met Deirdre the one time. A year ago."

"Two…"

"Why would she contact me?"

"Three…"

"You've got to calm down and listen to me."

"Four…"

I shake my hands. "All right! You win! You want to know where she is? I'll tell you."

"Good thinking," the guy says, "Where is she?"

"Right behind you."

The guy scoffs. "How fucking stupid do you think I am?"

Deirdre's voice floats in from the doorway. "From the look of it? Really fucking stupid."

The guy starts to spin around, but he's not halfway there before Deirdre grabs his arm and brings it down over her knee. The guy's gun drops to the deck with a soft *whump* in the snow. Still holding the guy's arm, Deirdre steps into him, ready hit him with an elbow.

However, she finds a patch of ice and goes down on one knee, swearing upon impact. The guy's arm comes free. He makes a break for it, coming right at me. I've got the angle to stop him.

And he plows right through me.

Next thing I know, I've hit the deck and slid into the rail. Snow seeps into my collar. Pain runs up my side. I went down right on my hip and elbow. (My high school nightmare come true.) The guy runs toward the stairs. I grab the rail and pull myself up, slipping a bit in the snow. I go after him, hoping my grasp of the erector set of stairs is better than his.

Deirdre runs to the opposite set of stairs. Our footsteps send *rat-a-tat-tat* sounds echoing into the still air.

The guy gets off the stairs and starts down the second-floor walkway, toward the other set of stairs. He doesn't get far before he realizes Deirdre is waiting for him on the other side. He turns just as I reach the second floor. The guy is trapped. He dances on the balls of his feet, trying to decide where, if anyplace, he has to go.

Then Lars stalks out on to his deck.

He's wearing a red silk bathrobe, his flap-eared cap and a pair of snow boots. He stops a few feet from the fleeing guy and surveys the scene.

"May I ask what in the hell is going on here?" Lars says, "Can a man not make sweet, sweet love to his woman without some kind of interruption?"

I keep my focus on the fleeing guy. "Lars, go back inside."

"I will not. I am the superintendent of this building. I need an explanation, Joe. So does Iris. Her particularly."

Sadly, that explanation will not be forthcoming. The fleeing guy spins around and shoves Lars out of the way. Lars winds up in the snow, flat on his bare ass. The guy disappears into Lars's apartment. I run toward Lars's deck and swing toward his apartment. Lars slips and slides, trying to get to his feet. High-pitched screams come from inside the apartment.

"You son of a bitch! Get out! Get out! Nobody sees me naked without my approval! Or fifty bucks!"

Despite my better judgment, I plunge through the backdoor and into the apartment. The fleeing guy is barely visible up ahead. Iris stands in the doorway of Lars's bedroom, a bedsheet draped over her otherwise naked frame. I'm momentarily distracted, but she throws a framed picture at me, getting me back on track. (Can't say she never did anything for me.) The guy gets through the front door and runs down the front stairs. I follow, with Iris hurling profanity (and perhaps some breakables) at me as I go.

The guy beats me to the front door. He hesitates, then turns back, heading for the backdoor on the ground floor. I run down the front stairs, maybe touching them twice. The guy is nearly to the building's backdoor by the time I get him in sight. He plunges back into the cold. I try to close distance. I have no idea where Deirdre is. The chase into the building may have dissuaded her (assuming Deirdre can be dissuaded).

I come through the backdoor and look around the parking lot for the fleeing guy. I spot him, rounding the carriage house on the far side of my parking lot, and heading for the alley behind it.

I cut a diagonal path across the parking lot. The frigid air slices into my lungs. I struggle to keep my balance as I get around the carriage house. (I must look a bit like Charlie Chaplin.) There's no sign of the guy. I run into the alley.

And get hit by a car.

Sadly, when it comes to being hit by a car, this ain't my first rodeo. I catch sight of the thing right before we get on intimate terms. I'm going too fast, and the footing is too unsure for me to stop in time. I leap into the air, instinctively. I hit the hood, hip-first, and roll. For a second, the world goes into a blender. Colors fly past in streaks. My body is twisting in space and I'm not sure which direction is down. I spot the ground about a second before I hit it. Just in time to get my hands up and break my fall.

For a second, I can only lay in the snow and try to catch my breath. Slowly, I push myself to all fours and run a diagnostic. No huge pain. Everything functional. No dizziness or nausea. All systems normal. Mr. Scott, prepare for warp speed.

I get to my feet, my body not responding quite as fast as I'd like. The car is further down the alley. It's stopped. One of the taillights is out. They're probably going to check on me, make sure I'm not dead. The fleeing guy reappears, running toward the car. He's going to take a hostage. I have to stop him.

Except the guy doesn't take a hostage. He falls into the car and the car takes off. It rounds the corner out of the alley and disappears, probably heading for downtown St. Paul and anonymity. I stop and stand in the middle of the alley, breathing hard, hands on hips.

Shit. I couldn't catch the guy. I couldn't even catch his name. And I got hit by his getaway car. Other than that, I really kicked ass.

***

Getting hit by a car in sub-zero weather is one of those things you think about later and wonder, "Did that really happen?" But there's plenty of physical evidence to tell me, yes, it did happen. My hands are slightly skinned up (one patch of exposed pavement and I manage to find the damn thing), I'm bruised up one side, particularly on my hip, and I'm limping slightly from the pain in my right knee. On the bright side, my apartment is warm and my distance running experience has taught me there are very few aches and pains that can't be remedied by a beer or seven. I limp into the kitchen and despite my freezing self, stand in front of the open fridge, ready to grab a beer.

A familiar voice emerges from the shadows. "Are you okay, darling?"

I spin around, bumping hard into the refrigerator door. (Fortunately, I wasn't holding a beer, or I would have dropped it. The night has been difficult enough, thank you very much.) I fetch a beer and close the refrigerator door behind me. Deirdre stands in the shadows at the entrance to my kitchen.

"How do you do that?" I ask, "Are you Batwoman or something?"

"I was always more of a Catwoman fan." She scrutinizes me. "Back to the original question: are you okay?"

"I'm fine," I say, "I try to get hit by a car at least once a winter. Makes spring seem all that much sweeter, y'know?"

Deirdre meets that with her usual smirk. I grab a seat at the breakfast bar and Dierdre joins me. She doesn't take off her coat or pour a drink of her own. I feel guilty slugging a beer in front of her, but on the other hand…beer. Deirdre looks me over.

"You did good work," she says, "You kept your cool."

"Really?" I say, "I didn't notice. I was hyperventilating through a lot of it." I knock back a good bit of the beer. "You have any idea who that guy was?"

"None. But apparently, he knows who I am."

I shift around on the stool, trying (and failing) to find a comfortable position. "Where did you disappear to?"

"The roof. I thought if I could get a clear shot at him, I could slow him down for you. But he got to the alley before I could do that."

"It was a nice thought. But the guy had help. I don't suppose you have any idea who *that* was, either."

"I'm afraid I can't help you there."

Shazbot. A mystery attacker. Just what we needed. As if all this shit wasn't confusing enough to begin with. I put the cold beer bottle against my forehead. It at least soothes the headache that's developing.

"Thanks for the assist," I tell her, "You're doing sterling work keeping me alive."

Deirdre drops her eyes to the counter. "It seems like the right thing to do."

"Because you need my help."

"Because it's the right thing to do," she says, sharply, "You didn't do anything to deserve that guy coming to your door. You didn't deserve to get hurt. So, I helped you."

I lower the beer, not sure what to say. "Thank you."

Deirdre's eyes return to the countertop. "I'm returning a favor."

"To me?"

"No. Not entirely. Someone else."

I wait for her to expound on that, then realize she's probably not going to. A thought hits me. "The guy you talked about," I say, "The one who got you into this life. Right?"

"Right." Deirdre's voice gets quiet. "He kept me safe when…well, he kept me safe. He protected me. I owe him."

"I get that," I say, "But where do I come in?"

A slight hesitation. "You remind me of him."

Wow. I have a hard time picturing the aspects of my personality that would fit with a contract killer. I conjure up the image of a dude emptying a clip into some poor bastard while humming the theme to *The Flintstones*. It's disturbing even to me. But there's a slight pain in Deirdre's eyes, even though she's not looking at me. I'll respect that.

"I take it this guy isn't with you anymore?" I ask.

"No," Deirdre says, "he's long gone."

There's a story there, obviously. But if there's pain involved, I'll let Deirdre decide when—or if—she wants to tell it to me. But I can't help being curious.

"What was his name?" I ask.

Deirdre pauses before answering. "Warren."

"Not his real name, I'm guessing?"

"No, he insisted it was. I never saw his birth certificate, but I took his word on it."

We stay silent for several seconds. I wonder if Deirdre's going to tell me the story of Warren, but it's not forthcoming. I finally take a sip of my beer.

"I'll take it as a compliment," I say.

"It is," Deirdre says. Then her voice drops to barely above a whisper. "It is."

The silence returns, lingering for what seems like a long time. I'm hoping Deirdre will grab a drink, loosen up, something. Hell, I'd even be willing to watch *Phineas and Ferb* with her if it would lighten the mood. Finally, she gets up from the breakfast bar and heads for the door. I call after her, with the only words I can think of.

"Thank you," I say.

Deirdre pauses at the door. "It's okay. Keep yourself safe. Understand?"

"Understood."

She's still for another moment, her hand on the doorknob. Then she flips open the door and steps out. I wait at the breakfast bar. I'm certain I'd hear something if one of my neighbors began shouting for help or something. All remains quiet on the western front. Deirdre must be safe in her temporary apartment. I down the rest of my beer.

Never a dull moment around here. Although, I'll be honest: I'd be fine with some dull moments.

***

One of the most misunderstood phrases (in our large litany of misunderstood phrases) is the one stating *Charity begins at home*. The saying actually means that the charitable spirit must begin in the home; a spirit embraced by parents,

149

passed on to children, and then to the entire community. Over time, of course, Americans have interpreted this to mean, *Fuck everybody who isn't me.* Because Americans are, to put it politely, a bunch of complete bastards.

It hasn't always been this way. Back in the Eighteen-Hundreds and early Nineteen-Hundreds, the well-to-do were expected to contribute a certain amount of charity work. It was the price of obtaining great wealth. After time spent making money by standing on the neck of his workers, a wealthy magnate was expected to give to the underprivileged. Underprivileged generally defined as *The Poor Suckers Who Work for Me.* Nowadays, you can't even get the wealthy to do that much. After all, why should a billionaire CEO donate to charity when he can spend that money on a solid gold commode, thus allowing to literally do what he metaphorically does to his employees every day.

But the spirit of charity is still alive in *some* people I know. Even if they tend to be misguided and idiotic in their everyday lives.

Lars huddles into his ratty green parka and circles around the lobby of the Kellen Community Center. "The city closed the place years ago due to budget cuts. No one's really attended to it since. As you can see, it needs a bit of work. But it has nothing but upside."

I look around the dilapidated place. "It would have to."

Carol tucks her chin into her scarf and pulls her tam down a little tighter. "It's for a good cause."

"I get that," I say, "Does this good cause involve heating?"

Lars glides up, taking a shorter stride than normal. (When faced with freezing cold, it's best to not let the extremities get too far from the groin.) "It will," he says, "We've got enough funding to get the heating system repaired by the date of the fundraiser. In the meantime, the collection of space heaters will keep the pipes from freezing. I hope."

Carol briefly closes her eyes. It's not hard to picture what's going through her mind. *It's for a good cause. Keep telling yourself that. Even if you're working with Bozo the Clown.* I struggle to see the same possibilities Carol and Lars see. There's a large gymnasium at one end of the building and a lecture hall on the other. The lobby rests in the middle and is currently housing the three of us. The lobby isn't large and, like the place in general, seems more utilitarian than anything. The sad remains of a front desk rest opposite the front door, and a few offices (one of them without a door) are located behind the desk. According to Lars, there are some small storage rooms tucked behind the lecture hall. These could be used as dressing rooms if some unsuspecting theatre company decided to produce shows there. Even when the heat is working again, I can't help wondering how they're going to handle the detritus of years of disuse in a crappy neighborhood: stained walls, accumulated trash, graffiti, broken windows and a subtle but very present bad smell floating through the air (best not to consider the source of said smell). It's definitely a fixer-upper. Or we could just go outside, give the building a good push, and let it collapse on its own.

"You're really going to be able to clean this whole place up?" I ask, flexing my gloved fingers, hoping frostbite isn't setting in.

Lars tightens his flap-eared cap. "We don't exactly have the manpower for that. It's a rather…extensive job. But we thought a sufficient number of decorations and a lower level to the lighting might mitigate those factors."

"So, your plan is to paper over the bullshit, turn down the lights, and hope no one notices," I say.

"Fuckin' A, Bubba," Lars says, relieved I'm on his wavelength.

Carol puts a leather gloved hand over her face. Judging by her body language, she's ready to run, screaming, from the building. But she remains. Carol is nothing if not a trooper. I tuck my hands into my peacoat and wonder if I should start wearing a stocking cap. (I'm fundamentally opposed to them but given the number of times I've frozen my ears…)

"It's good that we're all pulling in the same direction," I say. Yep. Right on over a cliff.

Lars gives me a thumbs up and spins toward the door to the lecture hall. "If you'll excuse me, I wanted to check out the storage areas. I've heard rumors the local homeless population may have left some…items back there."

Carol gives him a panicked look. "Are you going to clean it up?"

"Oh dear God, no," Lars says, "I just want to know if we should close those rooms off from the public. Or perhaps burn them down. Pardon me."

With that, Lars disappears into the auditorium. I turn to Carol and raise my eyebrows. She holds up a hand, acknowledging my concerns.

"I know, I know," she says, "It's like working with someone who has brain damage—"

"Are we sure he doesn't?"

"But the kids in this neighborhood are really going to benefit from it. As long as I can steer him in the right direction—"

"And assuming the brakes work."

"We should be fine."

I tilt my head in a gesture of dismissal. This is Carol's and Lars's show. Yes, I'm involved tangentially, but that's just so I can snoop around a major corporation. Beyond that, I don't really have a dog in this fight. (Okay, there's the health and safety of my city, which in turn affects the health and safety of my community and my own personal health and safety. But beyond *that*…)

Carol lowers her voice. "Everything okay after…last night?"

Her blue eyes are laser-focused on me. I had to tell Carol about last night's adventures—she would have dragged it out of me eventually—and I've just been waiting for her to bring up the subject. I slide my eyes away, even though I can sense (if not see) Carol's glare.

"So far, so good," I say, "No further assailants, anyway."

Carol hugs herself and shivers. "I thought Jim Street and his men were watching your building. How did they not see all that?"

"They were watching the front of the building. This guy must have come up the back."

Carol and I are close together. I'm not sure if it's for secrecy or because we're trying to huddle for warmth. Either way, it looks as if we're plotting the death of Trotsky. Carol pulls her black trench coat tighter around her.

"I hope all this is worth it," she says.

I'm hoping the same thing. But the jury's out on that. I decide to deflect from my shortcomings to Carol's.

"When is your boss getting here?" I ask.

"Mr. Pratt should be here soon," Carol says, "I hope this will show him I'm a decent person. Willing to help out my community. That sort of thing."

"You *are* a decent person," I tell her, "You don't need to prove it."

"I'm not exactly feeling like one at the moment. Mr. Pratt isn't just meeting me here to see the community center. He's coming to meet his son's sponsor."

My eyebrows go up. "His son has a sponsor?"

Carol looks toward the front door, probably checking to see if her boss is coming. "I worked out an alternative to checking the kid into rehab, but it isn't exactly..."

"Honest?" I say.

"No."

"No, as in it's not an honest solution, or no, as in honest isn't the right word to describe it?"

She looks up. "Both. I think." Then Carol waves a hand, like she's erasing a blackboard. "Can I just tell you what the fuck is going on?"

"That would be lovely."

"I convinced Mr. Pratt that the detox center might not be necessary," Carol says, "We might be able to get the kid to quit cold turkey. If my friend Evie could act as his sponsor, it might help *her* recovery as well. It took a little doing, but I got him to come around. He's bringing the kid here to meet Evie."

The cracks in Carol's rather cracked plan make their appearance. "Your friend Evie is on board with this?" I ask.

"Of course," Carol says, "She's always willing to help."

"Even though she's not actually in recovery?"

"She's not in recovery *now*. But she's been there a few times. She knows the lingo."

I could probably explain to Carol the perils of putting someone who's failed at recovery in charge of someone who's attempting to recover. But I don't think it would gain any traction. Not with Carol's job on the line. I switch from moral difficulties to practical ones.

"You think Evie can pull it off?" I ask, "It sounds like a tall order."

"It'll be fine," Carol says, "Evie's used to this kind of ruse. She's like a female Mike."

I consider this. "You think we should get them together?"

"Oh God, no," Carol says, "The combined evil would bring an end to life as we know it."

Yeah, if Mike is to hook up with someone, it must be a decent person who can drag him (likely kicking and screaming) toward the light. Then again, that seems like a waste of a perfectly good decent person. Oh well. Sometimes, you have to take one for the team. Sacrifice a metaphorical (or in this case perhaps literal) virgin.

"Good luck to you," I say, "If Evie's in Mike's league, you'll be fine."

"I hope so. I already feel like I've let Mr. Pratt down enough. I like him."

"Good boss, is he?"

"Huh? Oh yeah. He's that. Definitely."

There was something in Carol's answer that seemed a little rushed. She looks away from me. I cup my chin with my gloved hand (more for effect than anything).

"Do you like Mr. Pratt or do you *like* like him?"

"He is a good boss and I respect him and let's leave it at that."

"Of course. We'll just ignore that nice round ass of his."

Carol snaps me a look. "How did you know—" Then she catches herself and looks away. "Fuck."

"Well, let's not even get into *that*."

Before Carol can punch me out, the front door opens, and two people walk in. One is a middle-aged guy with wary brown eyes, a tan overcoat and a flat gray cap. His face is round, and he has a scraggly goatee (sort of like Mike if Mike were African American). Mr. Pratt's companion is younger and taller. Beyond the ears that stick out a bit, the family resemblance is clear. The kid's face is emaciated, and he wears a dirty gray hoodie and saggy jeans. Carol straightens her scarf and tam and steps over to the older guy. Ah. This must be Mr. Pratt.

"This is the place, huh?" Mr. Pratt says, in a tone more conversational than I would have expected. (For some reason, I imagined an uptight businessman whenever Mr. Pratt was mentioned. Maybe because Carol is generally so uptight.)

"It is," Carol says, forcing some pleasantness, "We've got high hopes for it."

Right after she says it, Carol has to fight a look of chagrin. Perhaps she realizes, just as I do, how much she sounds like Lars when saying things like that. Mr. Pratt looks around, his face impassive.

"It's got…" He searches for the right word. "Potential." He looks toward the kid in the hoodie. "This is Shawn."

Shawn looks at the floor and doesn't see Carol offer her hand. He mumbles, "'S up?"

Mr. Pratt lightly whacks Shawn on the arm. Shawn takes Carol's hand, briefly. (Bet he gave her a dead fish handshake.) Carol slips her hand into her pocket.

"Evie should be here any minute," she says.

Mr. Pratt crosses his hands in front of him. Shawn says and does nothing. I sit back and enjoy the floorshow. As if things couldn't get more awkward, Lars makes a reappearance. He charges into the room and comes to a sudden halt when he sees Mr. Pratt and Shawn. He straightens his jacket and strolls over to them, hand outstretched.

"This must be one of our benefactors," he says, "My name is Lars. I'm in charge of this shindig."

Mr. Pratt looks to Carol, perhaps wondering if Lars is a homeless guy who's strolled in. (He's not entirely off the beam.) Carol studies the wall. Mr. Pratt takes Lars's hand, hesitantly.

"My name is James Pratt," he says, "I work with Carol. I'm afraid I'm not a benefactor. We're just here…for a meeting."

Lars takes the news smoothly. "You've come to the right place. Soon enough, there will be a lot of meetings here. We'll be a prime location for them."

Mr. Pratt indulges Lars by giving him more attention than he deserves. Carol laughs for no reason. She probably thinks it will lighten the mood. Shawn continues to do nothing. This little circle jerk is broken up by the arrival of Carol's friend, Evie.

"Carol!" she says, her voice ringing across the lobby, "Great to see you! Why did you want to meet in this dump?"

I bury my face in my gloved hands. Lars's head snaps back. Evie approaches the group. Her face is angular and interesting, if not quite pretty. Her eyes are green and there's something wild in them. They flit about without focusing on anything for too long. Her straw-colored hair is swept back and hangs down past her shoulders. She's huddled into a white winter coat that's a little soiled at the edges. I've met Evie before, so I know she's built like a brick shithouse. But this is Minnesota in the winter. Until the coats come off, everyone's built like a polar bear. (We're sort of Victorian in that sense. Horny, freezing Victorians.) Carol greets Evie with more uncomfortable laughter. She holds a hand toward Mr. Pratt.

"Evie, this is Mr. Pratt," she says, "My *boss*." This is accompanied by a little *Get your shit together* look. "And this is his son, Shawn."

Shawn doesn't react. Mr. Pratt nudges him, none too gently, with his shoulder. Shawn slips the hood off and lets out an audible, "Whoa." Mr. Pratt whacks him on the arm. Evie, meanwhile, assesses Shawn with a low "Ooo," prompting Carol to whack *her* on the arm. I snicker, causing Lars, for some reason, to whack *me* on the arm. Great. The Three Stooges, everyone.

Mr. Pratt removes his cap, revealing a brush of graying black hair. "Shawn is trying to get things straightened out. I'm hoping you can help him."

Evie gives Shawn an appreciative look. "Oh, I can do that." Then she catches the look from Carol and straightens up. "I think this would be a good time for me and Shawn to talk. Is there someplace we can go?"

Nobody says anything right away. I pipe up. "There's a coffee shop down the street."

That gets me dirty looks from Mr. Pratt and Carol. Apparently, neither want to let Shawn and Evie out of their sight. But Evie jumps on the idea.

"Sounds good to me," she says, "I'm parked in the lot. Shall we?"

Shawn gives that a half-smile, flips his hood back up and turns toward the door. Evie falls in behind, placing a hand on the center of his back to guide him. She looks back toward Carol and waggles her eyebrows. Carol stifles a response, not wanting to make Mr. Pratt aware of anything untoward.

"I think they're off to a great start," she says.

Mr. Pratt doesn't seem convinced. "I hope so. I've had enough of Shawn's antics. It's time he got his life straightened out." He gives Carol a warm look (and it's about the only warm thing in this place). "I appreciate it. I hope your friend can help."

Carol keeps laughing, nervously, and flits a hand. "It will be fine. If anyone knows about alcoholism, it's Evie."

At that, Carol looks stricken, perhaps realizing what she's said. I put a hand to my face, covering my laughter. We're spared any further embarrassment by Lars commanding the scene. (And when have I ever been able to express *that* thought?) He takes a position in the center of the room and claps his gloved hands together.

"It's great that we're all together," he says, "Why don't we discuss more of what we can do with the center? We can go to one of the classrooms, start a fire."

Carol throws a look that direction. "There's a fireplace in one of the classrooms?"

"No," Lars says.

Mr. Pratt looks at Lars, as if he's looking at the membership of a carnival freakshow. (And he's not wrong.) Carol takes Mr. Pratt's arm and guides him toward the door.

"We should probably get back to work," she says, "Plenty to do. At work. Always."

Lars starts to floridly thank Mr. Pratt for his presence, but Carol is already speeding him toward the door. Lars goes back down one of the hallways. As Carol and Mr. Pratt reach the front door, Mr. Pratt can be heard, faintly, asking, *"These are your friends?"*

My cell phone rings. I don't recognize the number, and it doesn't appear to be spam. I debate answering but decide to do it. (I'm in the mood to tell off a telemarketer.) After I pick up, there's a pause and then a woman's voice comes on the line. "Joe Davis?"

"Who's calling?" I ask.

"I work with Payton Hicks. I need to talk to you."

Whoa. This is definitely not a telemarketer. "About what?" I ask.

"I don't want to go into it over the phone. I'd like to meet with you."

Of course, she does. I don't like this. Perfect stranger calls me up and wants to meet. It's got the ring of heebies with a side of jeebies. This is probably a setup. But I can't help being intrigued. (Hell, it's not like I do a lot of looking out for my own good.)

"When and where would you like to meet?" I ask.

"Do you know the Stone Mill in Minneapolis?"

"Very much so."

"I can meet you there. Ten o'clock tonight."

That makes me feel a little better. The Stone Mill is on the corner of Hennepin and Lake, in the heart of Minneapolis's Uptown district. It's generally crowded, no matter what night of the week. Not the kind of place one staffs an ambush.

"That sounds good," I say, "How will I know you?"

"I'll know you," she says before hanging up.

I slip the phone back into my pocket, wondering what fresh hell I've gotten myself into. I look around the dilapidated building and head for the exit. If this is hell, it's the frozen center of Dante's Inferno.

I'd make some crack about *Out of the frying pan and into the fire* but that actually sounds kind of good right now.

CHAPTER EIGHT

I have noticed, over time and bitter experience, the basic dichotomy of a first date. It's supposed to be an opportunity for two people to get to know each other. In truth, it's exactly the opposite.

See, the advice everyone gives you before a first date, if you're nervous at all, is, "Just be yourself." Anyone who's been on an actual first date knows this is terrible advice. You never want to lead with yourself. At least not yourself as you know you. "Me? Well, I work at Dunder-Mifflin. My co-workers all suspect I steal food out of the breakroom fridge, and they would be right. I throw all my fast-food bags and wrappers into the backseat of my car. I have no idea what's even back there anymore. I'm afraid to look. If I had to guess it's probably the garbage monster from Star Wars. *My bathroom generally looks like it houses the filthiest toilet in Scotland. I spent the whole afternoon cleaning it up on the off chance you and I will be back there tonight. Also, I like to pick my nose when I think no one's watching and I'd be lying if I said I never blew my nose on my shirt. And how about you? Tell me a little something about yourself."*

Being yourself is bad strategy, as you're probably the only one who can stand the company of your unvarnished self for ten consecutive minutes. You need to isolate only the best parts of yourself (or if need be, make some of those parts up) and stick the majority of who you are in the deepest recesses of your being. If the relationship has any legs, that part of you will eventually show itself, sort of like The Wizard of Oz telling someone to pay no attention to the man behind the curtain. Thus, all relationships, good or bad, begin with a lie.

Now, if you'll excuse me, I have to put some additional BS in my Tinder profile.

This meeting at The Stone Mill isn't a date, but it kind of feels like one. It gives me the same butterflies, if nothing else. The only difference is that a lack of chemistry here could mean somebody's going to emergency and somebody's going to jail rather than me going home to Pornhub and some Jurgen's Lotion. There's a lot on the line.

As stated previously, The Stone Mill is in the Uptown section of Minneapolis. The neighborhood is generally young and trendy, but that's in the summertime. Right now, everyone rushes from car to bar and back again. Hard to see and be seen in these circumstances. The Stone Mill itself is cozy, with its soft lighting and (faux) wood décor. There's a bar area and a restaurant area, separated by a large stone fireplace. The bar itself is horseshoe shaped. Tonight, it's only half-full and rather sleepy. But it's warm.

After I walk in, a woman at the bar stares at me. I've seen her before, just outside Peyton Hicks's office. Her wavy brown hair is pinned back, and her round face has just a hint of makeup. She wears a tight-fitting black sweater (which she fills, amply) and a brown suede skirt that stops just above the knee. A burgundy double-breasted maroon coat hangs from the back of her chair. A martini rests near her on the bar. The stools on either side of her empty. I walk to the bar, unbuttoning my peacoat as I go.

"Joe Davis," she says, her voice a little high, her tone a little clipped, "Let's get a table, shall we?"

"Sounds good," I say.

She picks up the martini and we walk to a booth in the corner. She hangs her coat on a hook and primly takes a seat. I slide into the seat opposite, keeping my peacoat on. (The turtleneck sweater is plenty warm, but the peacoat feels like added protection.) The table is dark wood and has a candle inside a red painted glass candleholder. A server wearing a white dress shirt and black slacks is right there as we sit. I order a beer. Once he leaves, we're quiet for a moment.

"You know who I am," I say.

"I've read your column. I recognized you from the profile picture." She sips her martini. "I'm a fan."

"Thank you," I say, "Speaking of names, what's yours?"

She waits a moment before saying, "Kendall. Kendall Lucas. I'm Mr. Hicks's executive assistant."

"I thought I met his receptionist."

Oops. Obviously, my understanding of the Hankerson-William power structure is deficient, at best. Kendall's entire body stiffens. She speaks slowly and in a tone that's colder than the weather outside.

"I am *not* Mr. Hicks's receptionist," Kendall says, "I am his executive assistant. I am upper management at Hankerson-William, not an entry level pencil pusher. I hope you understand the difference."

"I believe I'm getting the gist of it. Sorry."

On that pleasant note, there's a slight pause while my beer is delivered. Grand Brewing Winter Ale, as per usual. Just what I need. I toy with my beer, letting the tension pass.

"What is it I can do for you?"

Kendall sets her martini aside. "I'm concerned that Mr. Hicks is in danger."

"What kind of danger?"

"The same kind Mr. Hollins was in." She decides to lay things on the line. "I'm worried that the same person who killed Mr. Hollins is going to come after Mr. Hicks. This person is still at large, right?"

"As far as I know," I say, dancing around my personal elephant in the room, "What makes you say that? Apart from Mr. Hollins's untimely death?"

Kendall squares me with a piercing look, annoyed that I'm trying to be funny (when I'm actually just being an idiot). "It would stand to reason, wouldn't it? Mr. Hollins and Mr. Hicks were best friends. They had business dealings together. If someone would target one of them, they might target the other."

"I suppose. The bigger question is: why come to me? I'm glad you're a fan, but I don't know how I can help you."

"Because I think you know the killer."

Uh-oh. Danger, Will Robinson. My panicked look is fleeting, covered by my look of confusion. (A look that's not entirely disingenuous.)

"Why would you think that?" I ask.

Kendall folds her hands in front of her. "I did some research. You had a friend who was suspected of murder last winter. You proved she was innocent. I read your column about it."

Nuts. I've really got to stop writing columns about the scrapes I get into. Or I need to stop getting into scrapes. Either would be fine.

"That still doesn't explain why you want to talk to me," I say.

"You mentioned a woman in the article. A contract killer. You didn't give her name, but you gave a description. It matches the description of the killer. It's not hard to figure out."

Smoley hokes. I sit back, trying to maintain a casual air. (Not easy when your inner Don Knotts is trying to get out.) "Interesting," I say, "But I'm afraid I haven't heard from De…uh, de woman."

"De woman?"

"It's a running gag with me and my friends." Mental note: make that a running gag with me and my friends.

Kendall's eyes narrow. "Not at all?"

"I'm afraid not."

"Then why were you in Mr. Hicks's office?"

"Talking about a fundraiser my friends are organizing. I thought he would have told you that."

"He did. I thought he was covering."

"He wasn't. My friends are organizing a fundraiser for the Kellen Community Center in St. Paul. They need some help. They…need a lot of help. I went to talk with Mr. Hicks. Chelsea Hollins recommended it. We chitchatted. He was pleasant. If not exactly warm and cuddly."

Kendall gives that a knowing look, then her eyes slide away. I get the feeling Kendall's interested in something other than just Payton Hicks's safety. I swirl my beer.

"I'm sorry about Alex Hollins," I say.

Kendall keeps her eyes down. "Thank you. It was quite a shock."

"Did you know him well?"

"Of course. If you worked closely with Mr. Hicks, you worked with Mr. Hollins."

"What did you think of him?"

Kendall runs a finger around the rim of her glass. "He made Hankerson-William into what it is today. I admired him."

"What about Payton Hicks? What's your opinion of him?"

"He's a good executive. Detailed, even-tempered, professional."

"How did he compare to Alex?"

Kendall contemplates this. "A business needs more than one type of personality to make it work. Mr. Hollins was ambitious. He drove us forward. Mr. Hicks is calm. He steadies us. It was a perfect blend."

"And there was never any tension there?" I ask.

"Between Mr. Hollins and Mr. Hicks?" Kendall asks, her jaw dropping slightly, "Absolutely not. They were close friends. Everyone knew that. Again, it was what made them such a great team."

And much like the 1998 Chicago Bulls, the team has been broken up. Possibly too early for some. Kendall doesn't seem to suspect Payton Hicks of having a hand in Alex Hollins's murder. I wonder if she feels that way about everyone.

"Did you know Alex Hollins's wife, Chelsea?" I ask.

"I met her a few times." She gets a distasteful look. "We didn't talk much."

Not getting a real sisterhood vibe here. "Were she and Alex happy?"

"I don't know," Kendall says, coldly, "I've heard rumors they weren't. But it was none of *my* business."

Ah, Kendall. Rising above the joys of office scuttlebutt. She swirls the martini, as if that will make it disappear more quickly. I've been in her shoes. You invite someone out for drinks, get the information you need, and then you're stuck in conversation with them because your drinks are only half-finished. Well, she made this bed...

"Where were you when you found out about Alex Hollins?" I ask.

Kendall takes a less-than-dainty sip. "I got a call from Mr. Hicks. I was at home, working on a project"

"The Green River Project?" I ask.

"Yes," she says, struggling to avoid an eyeroll (one of those *Nobody asks about anything other than that* sort of looks),

"We have some meetings coming up with state legislators and Mr. Hicks wanted to be prepared."

"Have you had those meetings yet?"

"No. They've been delayed because of, well, the circumstances."

Now *I'm* swirling my drink, more out of nerves than anything. It's like we're involved in some sort of weird drinking game. I glance toward the window, trying to maintain a casual air.

"A guy named Dustin Felt worked on that, didn't he?" I ask.

Kendall stops swirling her drink. "Where did you hear about him?"

"It was in the news," I say, "Something about him being killed. I didn't get the details. I just know he worked for Hankerson-William. I guess that's what happens when you read the headlines and not the article."

Kendall looks away. "Dustin *did* work on the Green River Project. That's really all I know. I only met him once, briefly. I heard about his death, of course. But I didn't hear any details."

Nuts. That seems to be the company line regarding Dustin Felt. My phone buzzes in my pocket. There's a text message from Deirdre. It reads *Someone is watching you*. I look up. We're sitting next to a small window. I have no idea where Deirdre is or where the someone watching me might be. I don't see anything out the window. Then again, it's a lot like when I have car trouble and look under the hood. It takes only a second to realize I have no idea what the hell I'm looking at. I hold the phone below table level and punch in a reply.

Cops?

The answer comes back: *No. An amateur. Watch your back.*

Swell. Watch my back. What if the guy attacks my front? Experience has shown I'm not exactly the Immortal Iron Fist when it comes to hand-to-hand combat. Kendall, meanwhile, has figured out I'm on my phone. It gives her the perfect excuse to finish her martini and get the hell out of here. She takes her wallet out of her purse to leave a tip. (There's a heart stitched on the wallet. Cute.) She grabs her coat off the hook behind her.

"I need to go," she says, "Thank you for meeting with me."

I down the rest of my beer in one swallow. (Ah man, that seems like sacrilege.) "I'll walk out with you."

Kendall doesn't look particularly thrilled with this idea. Then again, what can she do? She leads the way to the door and out into the street, moving at a good clip. My head is on a swivel, trying to spot my potential attacker. I'll admit, my walking Kendall out is less about chivalry and more about using her as cover. Once we're on the street, the cold hits us like an uppercut. Kendall's car is just a few spots away from the entrance. Great. I'm parked down the block and around the corner. It's like I was setting myself up for a mugging. Kendall's car is a black Chevy Cruze. She hustles to it.

"Thanks again," she says, looking briefly over her shoulder. "It was nice meeting you. I enjoy reading your column."

She's in the car before I can thank her. A moment later, Kendall accelerates away from the curb. (Geez, she doesn't even warm the thing up? That's cruel.) A car across the street flips its lights on, does a rather dangerous U-turn (just pulling out of a parking space on Hennepin can be death-defying), and pursues Kendall's car. It's a green Lexus and a rather sporty one at that. Kendall stops at the light. I can't help noticing her car has a taillight out. It's only a brief look, as the Lexus slides in behind Kendall's car, blocking the view. No one gets out and approaches Kendall. The light changes and both cars proceed peacefully. My phone buzzes once again. Another message from Deirdre.

That was the guy.

I won't be able to pursue said guy. He'll be long gone by the time I get to my car. Maybe Deirdre will pursue them.

(Although I sincerely hope she doesn't.) Guess I'm just going to have to let this one go.

So much for chivalry.

***

Asking Deirdre to watch my back while I met Kendall was supposed to bring me peace of mind. It did until she told me someone was watching me. Now, it's got me so unsettled I've started drinking. (Ah, who am I kidding? I would have started drinking regardless.)

I fetch a beer out of the fridge and peek around the corner. Deirdre stalks my apartment like a caged panther. "You want something?" I ask.

"Whiskey would be great," Deirdre says, stopping in front of the futon, "I can get it myself. Just grab some ice."

I bring Deirdre a lowball glass with some ice and she pours herself a few fingers of whiskey. I plunk down in the comfy chair. We sip our drinks and unwind for a moment (assuming unwinding is a thing I can still do, and Deirdre is even capable of).

"I don't suppose you got a look at the guy in the car?" I say.

"Not from the angle I was at, no. He stayed in the car the whole time."

"How about the license plate?"

"No." She levels me with a look. "And even if I did, what would I do with it? Give it to the cops and have them run it through the system? It's not exactly how I work."

"Actually, I've got a contact with the police," I say, thinking of Sergeant Pike, "But he wouldn't do me any favors without asking a ton of questions."

"I'm sure." Deirdre sips her whisky. "Did you find out anything interesting?"

I sip my beer. "It's possible Kendall had something to do with the guy who came around here. Her car has a taillight out, just like the one that hit me in the alley." I bob my head. "But that's not a lot to go on. Thousands of cars in the naked city. It's entirely possible two of them have a taillight out."

Deirdre takes in a breath through her nose. "What do we do next?"

I lean my head back as I think. "We're still back to the original question. What's the motive? Personal or professional? I honestly don't know what the professional motive could be. I've dangled the Green River Project and Dustin Felt in front of a few people, and nobody seems nervous. There's some personal motive, at least with Chelsea and maybe with Payton Hicks. The murder itself, with the use of the knife, feels very personal. But it doesn't explain the double-cross."

"Doesn't sound like we've gotten very far."

I'd like to argue to the contrary, assure her that we've made some progress. But we'd both know that's a lie. Deirdre drains her whiskey and goes to the liquor shelf for another. She muses as she pours her drink. When she returns, she lounges across the futon.

"We should check out the Hollins's house," she says, "See what we can find in there."

I laugh at the absurdity of the idea, then stop after one look from Deirdre. "You're kidding," I say.

"I'm not." Deirdre arches an eyebrow. "You think it's a bad idea?"

I reposition myself in the chair, recognizing I have to put this delicately. "Okay, first off, there's a good chance Chelsea will be home. And she's not going to welcome us into the place. Second, it's still a crime scene. There might be cops hanging around."

"I'll take my chances," Deirdre says.

"Yes, but while I don't have a lot of experience in this area, I thought the whole idea of being a fugitive from justice was to *avoid* places you're likely to find the police."

Deirdre sets her drink on the coffee table. "I'm tired of sitting around. There might be something in that house that tells us what Alex Hollins was up to and why somebody would want him dead. If there is, I want to find it."

I try to sip my beer but can't quite get the job done. "There's nothing I can say to change your mind?"

"No. Now, let's finish our drinks. Then we can make some plans."

I'll admit: the thought of a break-in is harshing my buzz.

***

I grew up in a small town. One of the complaints I frequently hear about small towns is that outsiders don't feel welcomed. (Although my hometown, Porter's Bay, is a tourist destination, so the locals are a bit more friendly to strangers.) Personally, I feel the same way about the suburbs. The locals are just as wary of anyone they don't recognize or who doesn't seem like they're from around these parts.

Of course, in some cases, it depends on the suburb. First ring 'burbs like Robbinsdale, Crystal, Bloomington or St. Louis Park are largely blue-collar and largely welcoming. Places like Eagan, Edina, and Excelsior, though, are filled with money and a protective sense of entitlement. *Those* are the places you've got to keep an eye on.

So, you can imagine my discomfort hanging out in a car in Excelsior with a contract killer.

Alex Hollins's house isn't exactly secluded, but it's hardly in a neighborhood. It sits on a winding road, with a handful of other houses in the surrounding area. They're all spaced out so the owners can indulge the illusion they're the master of all they survey. Hollins's house is a multi-story number, screened from view by a collection of pine trees, firs and shrubbery. The outside light is visible through the foliage, but there are no lights on in the house (as far as we can see). Deirdre and I sit in my Saturn Ion, parked in a neighbor's driveway. (The neighbor's house is far enough from the bottom of the drive that we could take up residence here and not be caught until early spring.) My headlights are extinguished, but the car is still running. (Ain't no way I'm going without heat in this weather.) I wear a black turtleneck under my peacoat, and a pair of thick black boots and I *still* feel cold. Deirdre seems far more relaxed here than in my apartment, lounging in a corner between the door and the passenger seat. She notices the stank upon my visage.

"You don't look happy," she says.

"I wish we could have taken another car," I say, "We get spotted out here and the police run my plates, I'm in deep shit. Street will know I'm up to something and it sure as hell won't make my bosses at *The Bugle* happy. They still haven't gotten over what happened last spring."

"With the married woman?"

"Yeah. Wasn't good publicity for anyone."

Deirdre props an elbow on the ledge of the passenger window and puts a hand to her face, covering her laughter.

"All this and he cooks, too. You're an interesting person, Joe Davis. There's no doubt about it."

She huddles inside her trench coat and doesn't make any comment about the weather, which is great. The cold is hard enough to take without someone complaining (particularly someone I can't argue with). I look over the house.

"Where is Alex Hollins's study?" I ask.

"The ground floor, near the corner of the house. That's where I was told he would be. And he was. Just not in the condition I was told he would be in."

"You got in through the downstairs window?"

"I did," Deirdre says, her mouth tightening. She's still pissed about Street finding her out. "We'll try a different route. The basement apparently functions as its own apartment. It has a separate entrance."

"And you're sure nobody's home?" I ask.

"Yes. You said Chelsea's staying at an apartment in the city. The servants have gone home. No one's there."

"What about the security system?"

"I'll take care of it," Deirdre says, "Trust me."

Trust her. I don't have much of a choice on that front, do I? Deirdre slips a small pair of binoculars out of her trench coat and gives the countryside a once-over.

"There *are* cops hanging around," she says, "Just one unit, though. Further down the hill. They must be keeping an eye on the house."

I'm suddenly short of breath. I grip the wheel, fighting the desire to slam on the gas and get the hell back to St. Paul, where I belong. "If the cops are here, what are we going to do?"

"We'll be fine," Deirdre says, waving toward the far side of the house, "That path over there leads to the door. From that angle, they're not going to see us, even if they *are* paying attention. And that's not a given." She grabs the doorhandle. "Shall we?"

Before I can say anything, Deirdre plunges into the cold. I hasten to follow her. I can't believe I'm doing this. I'm going to get arrested or killed or worse. (I don't know what could be worse than those two options, but I get the sinking feeling I'll find out.) Deirdre sprints across the road. I'm a step behind her, trying to keep my balance on the ice-covered street, worried I'm going to fall and break a leg. (I told you about my fear of that in high school, didn't I? I'm pretty sure I did.) We disappear behind the foliage screening Alex Hollins's house.

The driveway takes an S curve past the front door and around to the back of the house. Deirdre and I tread the edge of the snowbanks, trying to stay out of sight. Our crunching footsteps echo in the still air. (Although, who the hell is close enough to hear them?) Behind the house is a parking area next to an A-frame garage. There's a small patio with a snow-covered firepit in the center. The backyard extends into the distance, dropping nearly out of sight toward the tree line. The smell of woodsmoke is in the air. It reminds me of when I was a kid and some houses in my neighborhood were heated by woodstoves. Nice that I can get sentimental when I'm this close to death and/or incarceration. A roof is visible near the tree line.

"Any idea what that is?" I ask.

Deirdre barely looks that direction. "No. A garden shed for all I know. It doesn't matter." She throws a hand out, stopping me. "Watch your step. The motion sensor."

I fall in behind Deirdre, who leads the way along the house. We slink down a small set of steps to the basement door. The stairs are completely clear of snow and ice. (I should find out who does the work. They do a much better job than Lars does at my building.) Deirdre makes short work of the backdoor and steps inside. She waits a few moments, then signals for me to follow. The warmth of the house is a vast relief. It's all I can do not to issue the patented Minnesota Groan of Relief once being spared from the cold.

"Did you short out the security system or something?" I ask.

"No need. It's been turned off. Maybe Chelsea figures there isn't anything here to protect."

We look around the long basement. There's a stairway on the far side, next to a small kitchen. Deirdre leads the way up the stairs and on to the main floor. We head down a long hallway that opens to a large living room. Beyond the living room is a glass-enclosed study. Plush carpeting covers the floor. A few bits of dust have collected, telling me no one's been here since the murder. Everything else is white and sparse. Austerity R Us. Deirdre takes careful, measured steps. She opens the study door and makes a beeline for the computer.

"What are we looking for?" I ask.

"Anything unusual."

More unusual than breaking into someone's house for the pleasure of being back at the scene of the crime? But I keep that thought to myself. Deirdre's fingers fly over the keyboard. I'm getting flashbacks of Scotty at work in *Star Trek IV*. She's looking for a password to get in. While she does that, I look around the desk. At one corner is a sticky note with the name *Donna Rousch* written on it. I pick it up.

"Does the name Donna Rousch mean anything to you?" I ask.

Deirdre keeps her focus on the computer. "It doesn't."

"Maybe it's a password."

That becomes academic a few seconds later when Deirdre's accessed the desktop. She pauses in her typing. I peek over her shoulder. There are a ton of files. We page through the various files and documents. There's nothing marked *Incriminating Evidence*, which is an annoyance. There's a file marked *Meeting Minutes* and it covers Hankerson-William board meetings, executive committee meetings and a few personal meetings, all in the last year. We page through them but don't find anything particularly interesting. Deirdre keeps flipping through the files. I decide to see if there's something in the desk (at least make myself useful).

At first glance, I have to give Alex Hollins credit. He kept his desk immaculate. All papers organized and clipped together. Notebooks and files arranged neatly and in order. From one neat freak to another, I salute you, sir. I go through the drawers, but don't find anything worth noting. I look through the paper files on the desk and come across one marked *Meeting Minutes 9/15*. Something about it strikes me as odd.

"Could you go back to the 'Meeting Minutes' file?" I ask.

"Why?"

"I want to check something."

Deirdre seems annoyed but goes back to the *Meeting Minutes* file. We browse through it. No meeting notes for 9/15 in the computer. The only record is the paper copy I'm holding. I tell Deirdre as much.

"What does it mean?" Deirdre asks.

"Potentially weird wild stuff."

I study the paper copy for 9/15. There was a presentation by Dustin Felt, regarding the Green River Project. There's a subheading marked *Impact File*. Four people present in the meeting: Alex Hollins, Payton Hicks, Dustin Felt, and Kendall Lucas (acting as the recorder). No details about the meeting. We go back to the computer files and open some of the other meeting notes. No further mention of Dustin Felt or the Impact File. I set the paper down. Deirdre looks it over.

"I'll ask it again," she says, "What does this mean?"

"Well, it *does* mean something, and it *doesn't* mean something."

Deirdre squares me with an unpleasant look. Before I can expound on my rather cryptic thought, the lights come on in the study. And Chelsea Hollins stands in the doorway.

CHAPTER NINE

I'll be honest, I'm not a big fan of horror movies. Never have been. Sure, I like the old atmospheric types: Frankenstein *and the* Universal monster flicks *or* Horror of Dracula *and the Hammer Films series. But modern-day slasher flicks? No thank you. And it's not just because I have a low tolerance for gore (although, don't rule that out). It's because I really don't care about the people getting killed.*

Before you label me a sociopath, please know this disdain is not derived from any personal animus toward the human race (although again, don't rule it out). It's that the characters getting stabbed, filleted and lopped are so ridiculously dumb, it's hard to feel any sympathy for them. Nobody calls the police. Nobody gets the hell out of the house. Nobody checks caller ID to find out where the damn call is coming from. Nobody avoids going into the darkened basement. Tommy and Becky don't stop to think that going off alone in the woods and getting naked might be a bad idea. (Although, there I have sympathy. Teenagers with raging hormones aren't going to let a little thing like consequences stop them.) In all these cases, Freddie or Jason or Jigsaw are less responsible than Natural Selection (which, come to think of it, sounds like a beer for stupid people).

Right now, I think breaking into a house where you only narrowly escaped the cops a few days ago would fall into that same category.

The second the lights go on, Deirdre spins toward Chelsea Hollins in the doorway. I dive under the desk. (Plenty of room under here. This is really a quality desk.)

"Who are you?" Chelsea says, "What are you doing here?"

Deirdre doesn't say anything. I venture a peek. Deirdre's body mostly obscures the view, but I get a sterling view of the gun in Chelsea's hand. She's wearing a long white winter coat. Our preoccupation with the computer must have distracted us from her coming in the house. Deirdre holds her hands out.

"You're going to want to put that away," Deirdre says.

There's a pause. "You're her," Chelsea says, "You're the one who…who killed Alex."

The last part is a little rushed, as if Chelsea was going somewhere else with the first part of the sentence. But that's on the backburner right now. A shooting and/or possible arrest are on the front. Deirdre takes a half-step forward.

"This is the last time I'm going to tell you," Deirdre says, "Put the gun down."

"You stay right there. I'm…I'm calling the police."

Chelsea reaches into her coat to get her cell phone. She tries to turn the trick of dialing, holding the gun, and keeping an eye on Deirdre at the same time. She doesn't quite pull it off. For a split-second, Chelsea's eyes drop to the phone. Deirdre throws a thrust kick at Chelsea's head. Chelsea screams and dives out of the doorway, her white overcoat flapping behind her. Deirdre's kick shatters one of the small windows in the door. She brings the foot back and draws a gun from her coat. I slide out from under the desk.

"Don't," I say.

Deirdre scowls in a rather horrible way. Then her eyes drop to the gun and the reality of the situation hits her. If she fires it, the cops will come running. Besides, if she shoots Chelsea, it won't matter if she's innocent of Alex's murder. Deirdre shoves the gun back inside her coat.

"Let's get the hell out of here," she says.

We charge out of the study. Chelsea can't be seen, but her voice is audible nearby. She's on the phone. As we run across the living room, Chelsea's words come into focus.

"In the house. Right now. I think it's the same person who…who murdered my husband."

Deirdre swings into the hallway. Chelsea is a few feet away, babbling into her cell phone. She spins toward us and drops the phone. Deirdre's fist cracks Chelsea's jaw. Chelsea manages to stay on her feet. Girl can take a punch, though it looks like she's out on her feet. Deirdre follows with a left hook and Chelsea goes down faster than the phone. Deirdre steps over Chelsea's carcass without breaking stride.

She leads the way to the foyer near the backdoor. Something gets her attention. She stops. Then she takes a few steps toward the hallway that bisects the house.

"The police are out there," she says.

"I don't see anything."

"I heard the car pull in. They don't have the lights going, but they're still clumsy." She turns her head, straining to listen. "Just the one unit. For now." She steps past me, again heading for the backdoor. "Step lively, darling."

We slip out the backdoor and make our way along the house. There's no sign of a cop, yet. We're careful to avoid the motion sensor light. My heart pounds in my ears. Deirdre might as well be doing the laundry, for all her face gives away. We have to get past the police, back to my car and get the hell out of here without anybody noticing. Yes, I'm in the company of Batwoman, but this is a tall order even for her. Deirdre carefully approaches the corner of the house.

And practically runs into one of the cops.

You know what they say about the bear being as frightened of you as you are of the bear? In this case, the cop is as startled to find Deirdre as she is to find the cop. He goes bug-eyed and fumbles for his gun. He holds it on us, swallowing hard.

"Just stay right there," he says, "Don't move." He reaches for the radio on his shoulder. "This is Officer Lynch. I've got eyes on the suspects. Repeat—"

Before he can repeat, Deirdre makes her move. Strangely, it's not against the cop. She grabs the shoulder of my peacoat and chucks me to one side. I hit the snow and slide. Two things happen. I get snow down the back of my pants. (Not since Dave Hill gave me a snow job in third grade have I liked snow less.) And the motion sensor light goes on, flooding the backyard. It catches the cop right in the eyes.

Officer Lynch puts up a hand, trying to block the light. He lowers the gun ever-so-slightly. Deirdre throws a thrust kick at the officer's head. This one connects. Officer Lynch goes down like a shot, winding up face-first in the snow. (I guess getting shoved isn't quite so bad.) Deirdre grabs me by the scruff of the neck and hauls me to my feet.

"Move quick," she says, "The other cop will be on to us."

This is great. The other cop won't hesitate to shoot. I don't think Deirdre fears the possibility. She hauls ass down the driveway. I'm a step behind her. The other cop is coming our direction. We've got just enough room to get to the street.

Then the cop starts shooting.

I'm not sure if there was a warning issued. If there was, I didn't hear it. (Then again, do suburban cops—any cops, really—need an excuse to start shooting?) On the upside, the cop is a terrible shot. Bullets ping off the yard light high above us and *whump* into the driveway well behind us. On the downside, he only has to be accurate once. Deirdre fires a warning shot that backs him off. It allows us to get into the street and head for the Saturn.

Halfway across the street, Deirdre stops. "You get to the car. I have something to do."

She runs back to the Hollins's driveway before I can ask what that something is. I head for the car. I'm almost there when I hear three gunshots behind me. I slide around the front fender and drop down. I venture a peek. Deirdre is running right for the car.

"What did you do?" I ask.

"Saved us a car chase," she says, "Get in and let's go."

I do as I'm told. I try to get the key into the ignition. But my hand is shaking so much, I can't turn the trick. (My first sexual experience was a lot like this, but I'll save that story for another time. Assuming I have another time.)

Deirdre grabs my hand and guides the key home. (Again, a lot like my…let's just leave that there.) The car roars to life and I punch the gas.

The Saturn does three-quarters of a complete spin as it swings on to the street. I turn *into* the skid (one of those weird things you learn to do in cold weather states) and the Saturn rights itself. We race down the hill. I'm vaguely aware that lights are coming on all over the neighborhood. (Gunplay will do that.) I glance into the rearview mirror. No sign of the cops.

"What did you do?" I ask, barely able to find breath.

"Shot out two tires on the squad car," Deirdre says, casual as you please.

"Are the cops still alive?"

"They are. Hopefully, they're smart enough not to come after us."

The road winds down the hill. It will eventually spill on to a cross street that feeds Excelsior Boulevard and then winds back through the suburbs to the Cities. Deirdre grips the dash, her face taut. Something occurs to her.

"Take a left," she says.

"What?"

"Take a left! Right here."

Said left reveals an even smaller street that drops out of view. Everything around here seems to be built on a hillside. The Saturn cruises along peacefully. After another few seconds, Deirdre puts her hands on the dash.

"Stop here," she says. There's no shoulder to the road, so I pull over as far as I dare. Deirdre looks back. "Kill the lights." I douse the lights. I hope she doesn't ask me to turn the car off. I've grown so fond of the heat. After several seconds, Deirdre says, "I think we're clear."

"Of what?"

"The police." Deirdre waves a hand toward the street where the Hollins' live. "If the cops are coming to the house, they're going to come up that way." She looks toward me. "Take out your phone. Look up this street. It's…"

"Bedford Avenue. I saw the street sign when we passed."

Deirdre gives that a half-smile, pleased that her partner in this particular crime isn't a complete idiot. I look up our location on my GPS. I nearly do a fist pump when I see the results.

"There's an outlet for this street," I say, "If we follow it far enough, it will lead us through downtown Excelsior."

"And we can get home from there?"

"Yes. Assuming the police don't have the make and model of the car and we're pulled over, arrested and possibly shot. In that order."

"We'll be fine. We got out of there fast enough. I doubt anyone got a look at the car." Deirdre pats me on the leg. "Home, Jeeves."

I throw the car into gear. "As you wish."

I ease down the street. There's just enough light so I can wait until I'm at the bottom of the hill before I throw the lights on. No one is coming after us. We're safe for now.

For now.

***

I think we all have our niche in life, that little something which, in our minds at least, makes us special. The thing we can point to and say, "This is what I'm known for." It doesn't matter what that thing is. You can be the person who provides snacks for the office on Friday or the neighbor who puts out the most elaborate Christmas display or the manager of the best damn Denny's on this stretch of Highway 35. Whatever it is, it gives you that little sense of self-importance. Even if, in reality, you are, as my father liked to put it, "King of the hill on a pile of bullshit."

Yes, I have my column, but I also like being known as a decent cook, particularly in the area of soup. Normally in the winter, chili is the best option (and I make a kickass chili) but man cannot live (or be lived with) on chili alone. Therefore, it's good that I've mastered that Minnesota staple: chicken wild rice soup.

My preferred way of making it is to cook the chicken in the crockpot and then shred it with two forks. I'm in the process of doing that now, working at a cutting board on the breakfast bar. The wild rice is cooking in chicken broth in the oven and with one thing and another, the apartment is filled with a rich, delicious smell. I am in my happy place. (And after last night's harrowing escape, I really need a happy place.)

So, I probably should have expected Mike to come along and screw it up.

"I've got a problem," he says, stepping through my front door, pulling his Vikings stocking cap off his head and tossing it on the couch (even though there's a place for it on the coat tree, two feet away).

"You've been able to narrow it down to one?" I say, setting aside the forks and moving to the refrigerator, anticipating Mike will need a grape soda. Or something stronger.

"I'm serious!" Mike says, striding to the breakfast bar, "It's a real problem."

I set a can of grape soda in front of him. "What is it? Late deliveries? Car problems? Sexual advances from a Yeti?"

"No!" He runs a hand through his disheveled hair. "This kid Ron is challenging me."

This ought to be good. I go back to shredding the chicken. "Challenging you how? A knife fight? Fifty-yard dash? Macrame guns at ten paces?"

Mike stops the grape soda short of his lips. "You got anything to offer but snark?"

"We both know the answer to that question."

He turns away from the breakfast bar and tosses his gloves on my futon. (Goddammit, Mike.) The cats, huddled together on said futon, each open an eye, then go back to sleep.

"Okay, you remember Ron from Fong's?" he asks.

"Captain Incompetent? You were helping him out, as I recall."

"It's backfiring on me." He rubs his forehead. "I know all the shortcuts around the neighborhood. I told him where to cut corners, literally, which lights he could run without worrying about the cops, where the side entrances are to apartment buildings, where, when and how to park illegally. Sure enough, he started getting better. The problem is he's turning in delivery times nearly as good as mine."

I finish with the chicken and bring it over to the stockpot on the stove. "Mission accomplished, then."

"No! Mission not accomplished! *I'm* top dog at Fong's. I can't have this guy challenging me. Worse, Biyu's started talking to him. She never gave him the time of day before."

Mike takes off his coat and tosses it over the back of the futon. (Sigh.) He chews his goatee as he paces. I take the wild rice out of the oven and add it to the stockpot.

"On the bright side, you helped him out," I say.

"Fuck the bright side! I didn't help him out of the goodness of my heart. I was trying to get laid. Now I'm getting screwed."

Mike should have been born a hundred-and-twenty-five years earlier. He would have made a great robber-baron. If, of course, brains, follow through, and social graces didn't enter into the equation. I get some chicken stock out of the pantry and pour it into the pot.

"What are you going to do?" I ask.

He vigorously runs his hands through his hair, freeing a large amount of dandruff. "I need to get better. Maybe you can help me out. We can brainstorm something."

"I don't think that would work. You know this gig better than I do."

"Maybe you can do a ride along with me. Come up with some ideas."

Oh boy. I can see my answer is going to be a problem for Mike. But I have to be honest with him. I move to the counter where the rest of ingredients—chopped carrots, chopped onions, almond slivers, spices, etc.—are sitting in little bowls, like you see in the cooking videos.

"I don't think that's doable," I say, "First, Fong probably wouldn't go for it."

"Why does he have to know?"

"Second, lying to your boss isn't really a way to get *out* of trouble. Third, I've got enough on my plate right now."

It's this last argument that hits home with Mike. Moral obligations be damned. When you're working for a contract killer, you can't really take your eye off the ball. Mike holds up his hands, surrendering the point.

"I'll figure something out," he says, "This job is too important. I'm not about to let the Dipshit Kid get the better of me."

I dump in the carrots then hold up the empty bowl in a toast. "That's the fighting spirit you're known for," I say, knowing full well that is *not* what Mike is known for.

Mike chews a corner of his goatee. "I'll figure out some new routes. Find a way to double time here and back. Push myself like I've never pushed before. And if all that doesn't work…" He smacks the counter, lightly. "I'll cheat."

Okay, that last part? *That* is what Mike is known for. We're quiet while I dump in the rest of the ingredients, then give the soup a gentle stir. I pour myself a cup of coffee and join Mike at the breakfast bar. He looks up from his grape soda.

"What's going on?" he asks, "Something with your, uh…friend?"

Why does everyone call Deirdre that? They know her name as well as I do. "Yeah," I say, "We broke into the Hollins's place last night. Didn't go entirely well."

I fill in Mike on the aborted break-in and near escape from the local police. Mike listens impassively, an expert in the field. When I'm done, he sets his grape soda aside.

"Why the hell didn't you call me?" he asks.

I should explain. In addition to his abundant skills as a delivery and/or con man, Mike was a cat burglar in college. He wasn't exactly a one-man crime spree. It was only when he needed money and couldn't hit up his parents. He'd grab small ticket items and bring them to the local pawn shop. Mike hasn't used those skills since then, except for a few occasions recently when I've needed them. (Although when he's used those skills, he, uh, hasn't exactly looked rusty.)

"It was Deirdre's idea," I say, "There wasn't really time to call in reinforcements."

Mike gives that a *hrumph*, his professional pride wounded. "You find anything interesting?"

"Yes and no," I say, "We went through Alex's files and found mention of something called *The Impact File*. But we were interrupted before we could look for it."

"You don't know what was in this Impact File?" Mike says.

"No. But it must have something to do with the Green River Project. The file was discussed at a meeting about the Project. But I won't know for sure unless I see it. There was something I *did* find."

"And what was that?"

"Dustin Felt was at that meeting."

Mike's eyebrows go up. "The guy that died?"

"Yeah. It was a meeting with three people, two of whom claimed they barely knew Dustin Felt. Payton Hicks was one of them, and he specifically said they'd never met."

"You caught him in a lie."

"Exactly," I say, "And I found a sticky note with the name Donna Rousch on it."

"Who's that?"

"Excellent question." I look toward the computer. "I did some looking on the internet. Didn't find anything. Nothing related to Hankerson-William, anyway."

"It's a big company."

"But you'd figure everybody working there at least has a LinkedIn profile or something. And it's not like Rousch is a common name. But I'm not finding *anything*." I take in a breath through my nose. The rich smell of the soup, warm and comforting, fills the apartment. So, I've got that going for me. Which is nice. "I may have to give Al Castillo a call."

"The reporter?" Mike says, "Does he know about Deirdre?"

"Not really. He knows a woman with Deirdre's description is a suspect in Alex Hollins's murder. But he doesn't know any of the details. Might not take him long to figure out, but I think he's on my side. I promised him a big scoop when this is all over."

"You think you'll be able to deliver on that?"

"Or die trying. I mean that literally."

Mike looks toward the front door. "Is Deirdre still downstairs?"

"Yeah. We have to be careful. The cops are watching the building."

His eyebrows go up. "Seriously?"

"That's what Deirdre tells me. And she's good at spotting cops."

Mike walks over to the arch windows and separates a few of the blinds. "It's hard to believe they're going to spend the kind of man hours required to watch...oh, look at that. There they are."

I throw up my hands. "Does everybody know how to spot cops except me?"

"Comes in handy if you need it." He stiffens up. "Speaking of which, it looks like they're headed this way."

"Seriously?"

"Yep. Tall guy with kind of blondish hair, looks like he'd be at home wearing a zoot suit." He lets go of the blinds. "Wasn't he part of the silliness with Deirdre last year?"

"Yeah," I say, "James Street. Is there a dumpy Latino guy with him?"

"No. Should there be?"

"His partner, Ric, is usually with him. I wonder what the hell Street wants with me?"

"Excellent question. Be sure to tell me later."

Mike gathers his coat, gloves and Vikings cap from the places he's strewn them. I step around the breakfast bar.

"You're going to abandon me?" I say.

"Cops are involved," he says, heading for the backdoor and leaving his grape soda on the counter. (The sink and the recycling are just a few feet away, man.) "Cops give me hives," he says, "I can't be here for this. You know my policy. Have a good one."

Mike disappears out the backdoor. I hope his escape is smooth and orderly and doesn't involve him falling down my stairs and suffering compound fractures to both legs. He's just cleared out when the front door buzzer sounds.

"It's Jim Street," the voice on the intercom tells me, "You got a minute?"

"Uh, sure."

I do the honors (if that's the word I'm looking for) and buzz him in. A few moments later, there's a knock on the front door. I open it and let Jim Street into the apartment. He's wearing the same black coat and white scarf as usual. This time, he has a blue suit with a yellow shirt and no tie. His eyes are slightly red and there are a few hairs out of place. The cats flee into the bedroom. (Thanks, guys.) Street sniffs the air. The soup is becoming fragrant, rich chicken with just a hint of curry. (Yes, curry. I know it isn't particularly Minnesotan, but it's nature's perfect spice. I owe the public nothing.)

"Something smells good," Street says.

"Chicken wild rice soup," I say, "I'd offer you a bowl, but it just started cooking."

"No worries."

"Can I get you a cup of coffee?" I ask.

"I'm fine," Street says, helping himself to a seat at my breakfast bar, "Could have sworn I heard someone going out the back."

This guy is good. Better keep my Spidey-Sense active. "That was my friend Mike. He had to…go." I sit opposite Street at the breakfast bar. "What brings you by?"

He affects puzzlement. "Strangest thing. I got a call from the Excelsior police. Seems someone broke into the Hollins's place last night. Chelsea Hollins found them. They knocked her out and made a break for it. Guess they got away. But she was able to give us a description of the intruders."

I affect interest. (Truth is, my heart is hammering at several hundred beats per minute.) "Oh?"

"One of them is a tall woman with blondish hair. Apparently hits like a piledriver. Chelsea didn't get a good look at the guy, but she gave us a general description. He's about six-one. Thin build. Brown hair. Sound like anyone you know?"

"Yes," I say, "Half the male population of the Twin Cities."

Street gives that his usual cocky grin. "The woman, at least, sounds a lot like our suspect in Alex Hollins's murder. Might be a mutual friend of ours."

I incline my head. "Makes sense."

"As for the guy, that *does* sound like someone a little closer to home, right?"

"It does. But she left out devastatingly handsome. It couldn't have been me."

The grin fades ever so slightly. The hard cop look comes into Street's eyes. "It's interesting, though. Alex Hollins gets murdered. Someone matching the description of a contract killer named Deirdre is spotted fleeing the scene. Then someone matching her description and *your* description—you, a guy who's familiar with Deirdre—breaks into Alex Hollins's place and knocks his wife senseless. It might be a coincidence. But a lot of coincidences add up to a pattern. And that's what I'm seeing here."

I take a breath, as if I'm trying to maintain patience (when, in reality, I'm trying to maintain bowel control). "And sometimes coincidences are just that."

Street debates this, looking not at all happy with the results. "You're telling me you haven't seen Deirdre at all?"

"I have not seen Deirdre at all," I say.

We're quiet, each waiting for the other to blink. I put everything I've got into it. I just have to believe I'm innocent and refuse to back down. I'm not going to let Jim Street intimidate me. Finally, Street gets up from the breakfast bar and wanders toward the arch windows.

"I've got an obsession with Deirdre," he says, "I'll admit that much, Slick. Been like chasing a white whale.

Started back when I was in California. Bay Area. You ever hear of Ricky Pinzollo?"

"No."

"No reason you should. He was this little scumbag who owned a trucking company. Had his hands in fifty different rackets, including high-end loan sharking. He bled a lot of people dry, made himself a decent chunk of change. He must have pissed off the wrong guy somewhere along the line. Turned up dead in his nice little penthouse apartment. Bullet through his right eye." He gazes at the floor, maybe picturing the scene. "Thing is, Pinzollo was careful. He had security all over the place: men and cameras. Forensics figured he had been shot with a high-powered rifle from at least a mile away. An impossible shot. But there it was." He looks up at me. "Before the week was out, his lawyer, his top enforcer and his righthand man were all in the ground. A complete housecleaning. No trace of the murderer. The only thing we caught was a woman in black on a security camera. Picture wasn't clear enough to identify her. Nothing we could use. But it was a hint."

"And thus, an obsession was born," I say.

Street inclines his head, acknowledging the idea. "I started checking databases, making contacts with other parts of the country. Every now and again, I'd hear a mention of a woman in black, right around the time of some unsolved murder of some bigwig. When I was working Kansas City, I even got a name. Deirdre. That was a big one, Slick. I'm ninety-nine percent certain it's fake, but it was something anyway."

"A fake name to put to the face you can't quite make out."

"Now you know how hard it is to track her, Slick." He gives me the cold cop look. "But I know this much: she's dangerous. Far as I know, you and your friends are the only ones who got that close to her and lived to tell the tale."

This time, I can't disguise the shudder. I think back to a brief phone conversation I had with Deirdre, right after the craziness last winter. She seemed to be contemplating whether she could let me live. And she decided she would. For now. I wondered then like I wonder now: how long is *for now* going to last?

I shake it off. Street's manipulating me. He suspects I know something about Deirdre and he's trying to scare me into giving up what I know. I push my coffee aside.

"Let me ask you something," I say, "If you really think it's Deirdre, you could blast her name to the TV news and the internet and to the six people who still read newspapers. But you haven't done it. Why?"

"Maybe I still will."

"I think it's because you know she didn't kill Alex Hollins. You just said Deirdre's been like a phantom this whole time. You think she'd be clumsy enough to let the cops—the Excelsior cops of all people—nearly catch her?"

Street's jaw momentarily tightens, but he covers it with his patented grin. "Maybe not. But if she's in the Cities, she was here to kill Alex Hollins. Either way, I want to find her."

I gesture toward the arch windows. "Is that why you're having me watched?"

Street doesn't even flinch. "Don't know what you're talking about there, Slick. You got anything you want to tell me?"

Ah, finally, the direct question. "I'm sorry, I don't."

It takes a second, but Street finally accepts that as my final answer. He buttons his overcoat, pushes a few stray hairs back into place, and heads for the front door.

"You want to talk, Slick," he says, "you got my number."

"I'll give you a buzz. We can chat about the Wild."

"Not much of a hockey fan. If I'm going to be honest? Not much of a fan of this whole state. Not this time of year." The door slams shut behind him.

Yeah, there's a lot of that going around right now.

***

Once upon a time, evading the cops must have been a simpler task. Everyone paid in cash. Cameras were only found on movie sets. DNA was strictly a theory. All you had to do was dye your hair, make up a name and/or move out of the house you lived in. You could cruise for years on that.

It's a different ballgame these days. You can't go anywhere. You can't spend money. You can't even cruise the internet. And if the cops have the infrared stuff going, you can't even hide out. Even felons have lost their privacy.

The bright side here is that the Bureau of Criminal Apprehension is not likely to spend the money necessary for infrared technology. As far as I know. As long as we keep the shades drawn, we're okay. At least that's what I keep telling myself.

I slip down the stairs and stop in front of Deirdre's door. Across the hall, a one-sided argument is raging. Iris is screaming and Lars is babbling. Something about cheating. I'm going to stay *far* away from that. I switch the paper bag I'm carrying to my left hand and use the special knock Deirdre and I have developed. It's two quick knocks, followed by four slower knocks. (Essentially, the opening guitar lick to *Last Train to Clarksville*, but Deirdre doesn't know that.) I look around, hoping no one comes out of their apartments. The peephole darkens. A second later, I scurry inside. Deirdre gently closes the door behind me.

"What have you got in the bag?" she says.

"Brought you dinner again," I say, "Chicken wild rice soup."

Deirdre might at least look grateful. She might, but she doesn't. She just stalks into the kitchen and pulls a bottle of vodka out of the freezer. I set the bag on her breakfast bar and take out the small Tupperware bowl and the plastic spoon. I push them toward her.

"It's still warm," I say, "No need to heat it up."

Deirdre hesitates, then peels the cover off. The soup is still steaming in the plasticware. She sits down and picks up the spoon.

"Another recipe of your mother's?" she asks.

"Well, this exact recipe is my mom's," I say, "but pretty much everyone in Minnesota makes it. I think you're required to know the recipe before they license you to be a restaurant or a housewife."

Deirdre smiles, ever-so-slightly. "You aren't eating?"

"No, I'll have the leftovers. I'm meeting someone for dinner."

"Who?"

"Alberto Castillo. He's, uh, he's a reporter. He's looking into something for me." Responding to the look from Deirdre, I add, "Just researching some of the stuff we found at the Hollins'. He doesn't know about you."

"He's a reporter. You think he's not going to guess?"

"We have an arrangement. He isn't going to write anything without my approval. And when he *does* write the story, he'll keep your name out of it."

"I'd love to believe that, darling, but…"

"You've trusted me this far, right?"

Deirdre debates that. She picks at the soup with her spoon. "What is wild rice? I've never heard of it."

"I'm not entirely certain. I just know Minnesota has a shit ton of it, and this is the only form in which it's acceptable."

She tries a small spoonful, considers it, then digs in. (It's the curry. Bet you anything.) I'm jealous. I really wanted the soup but the easiest way to get Al Castillo to do you a favor is to buy him dinner. He jumped on the offer of Fong's with the kind of alacrity one doesn't normally associate with a man of his girth. I'm stuck being a spectator to my own soup. Deirdre looks at me between spoonfuls.

"I get the feeling I'm never getting out of here," she says.

"You'll be fine. We'll figure this out. Then you can go back…doing what you do."

She doesn't seem convinced. She rapidly finishes the soup, then rinses out the bowl in the sink. I look around the apartment. The place is spotless. Deirdre has developed into a decent caretaker. (Although I suspect the motivation is a combination of covering her tracks and being bored out of her mind.) A TV, a DVD player and a stack of DVDs have been added to the apartment. I step over to the DVDs.

"Where did you get these?" I ask.

"Your friend across the hall," Deirdre says, "It was a nice thought, but all the DVDs are old black-and-white French movies."

I pick up a copy of *The 400 Blows*. "Yeah, for a moron, Lars has excellent taste in film." Deirdre paces the room, holding the bottle of vodka, looking again like a caged panther. I set down the movie. "I, uh, I had a visitor today."

Deirdre stops. "Jim Street wanted to talk about the break-in. What did you tell him?"

She's good. But I knew that. "I was spectacularly obtuse. Seriously, I could be a press secretary or a diplomat, the kind of work I do."

Deirdre sits on the shelf above the radiator. "He still suspects you, though, doesn't he?"

"He suspects everything. He just can't prove anything. And for what it's worth, I think he has his doubts about you killing Alex Hollins."

She slugs the vodka and contemplates that. "He's not going to let it go at that, though. Everything's too high profile. Sooner or later, he's going to feel the pressure and he'll do whatever he can to bring me in. Including leaning on you. More than he is now."

Well, there's a pleasant thought. If Street having me followed and dropping into my apartment anytime he likes in order to ask me a lot of insinuating questions isn't leaning on me, I look forward to when he *really* gets nasty. I assume it will involve rubber hoses and bamboo shoots. I join Deirdre on the shelf above the radiator.

"He *did* tell me a little story," I say, "About a guy named Ricky Pinzollo."

Deirdre's face lights up and her eyes glaze a little. It's the same look I get when saying, "Oh, I remember that song. That was awesome."

"That was a good one," she says, "Tall order. He had decent security and was a little paranoid. Problem was, he wasn't paranoid enough. Left me an opening."

"Street called it an impossible shot."

"Wasn't impossible if I actually did it, darling."

I get a chill, even though I'm sitting on a radiator. "Street also said a lot of Pinzollo's people turned up dead right after that."

"Price of doing business," Deirdre says, sipping her vodka.

I tilt my head. "You really do lock that stuff away, don't you?"

"Part of the game." Deirdre looks at me, her face placid. "Am I really some kind of monster to you?"

"I didn't say that."

"But you're thinking it."

"I am not." I clear my throat. "Was Pinzollo the, uh, the first?"

"No. But it was the first one worth talking about."

"Warren," I say, "was he part of it?"

Deirdre looks down. "Not by then, no. He was…gone."

We're quiet. Deirdre's face is placid, but the eyes give me a look behind the mask. There is something soft and inexpressibly sad in them. As if she's looking for something that was lost a long time ago. I turn a little toward her.

"Does it ever get lonely?" I ask.

Deirdre doesn't look up. "The life?"

"Yeah. As far as I know, you've got this Emily person and I get the impression she might just be an employee. I can't imagine you can make any real friends or…others when you have to go out of town on a moment's notice. Unless, of course, you *do* live like Batwoman and you can do this while the world thinks you're a rich, ne'er-do-well socialite."

Deirdre's head tilts back slightly. "I get by. If you work at it, you find you don't need people. It just takes some discipline."

"Doesn't make it sound any less lonely."

"I'm alone, darling. I'm not lonely. I don't get lonely. That's the discipline."

"Warren taught you that?"

"He did. He was a good teacher."

"I get the feeling he was more than that," I say.

Don't ask me why I said that. It isn't a good idea to pry into the personal life of a woman who doesn't just value her privacy, she bases her entire life and security on it. I'm not the least surprised by the sharp look she throws me. I stand my ground, hoping she remembers the whole *I need him to get me out of this mess* thing. Deirdre takes a pull off the vodka bottle.

"We were lovers," she says, flatly.

Lovers. That word has always sounded funny to me. Boyfriend-girlfriend, husband-wife, even significant other, all those sound just fine. But would you really introduce someone as your *lover*? Sort of implies you'd be willing to get on the floor and do it for everybody if requested. (Not that I'm against that sort of thing.) At any rate, Deirdre takes it seriously, so I keep my goofy thoughts to myself.

"You can tell me about him if you want," I say.

Deirdre shakes her head. "I don't want to go into it. Let's just say he meant a lot to me. He was my teacher and my mentor. And more. That's all you need to know."

Per Deirdre's command, I let it go. Whatever hurt is lingering there, I'll accept it's none of my business. Not that I'm ready to let things go that easily.

"Can I ask you something?" I say.

She slips me a look. "Oh, please do. I was just thinking you hadn't asked me quite enough personal questions."

I push through the snark. (It's more fun when I'm on the other end of it.) "Do you have an exit plan? From the life, I mean. I know you don't want to end it now, but is there something else you'd like to be doing one day?"

Deirdre's face gives nothing away. I half-wonder if she's going to shoot me and call it a day. Finally, she sets the vodka bottle down. "I have an island picked out. I'll keep the location to myself. But I go there once a year. Walk on the beach, go snorkeling, read. That's where I want to go when…it's time to have a 'rest of my life.' I even have a place picked out."

"What if it's not available when you retire?"

"I'll kill the rightful owner." Responding to my look, Deirdre holds up a hand. "I'm kidding. It'll be available. I have an understanding with someone. When the time comes, I'll be there. And I won't have to be Deirdre anymore."

"You'll be the real you. The one whose name you won't tell me."

"Exactly."

I drum my fingers on my leg. "What if you don't get there? Even if I get you out of this, you're not in the world's safest line of work. You really want to wait?"

Her eyes slide away. "I've made my choice. It is what it is."

It is what it is. The great throw-up-your-hands-and-end-the-conversation catchall. But it's the only answer I'm going to get out of Deirdre. I set my hands on the radiator shelf, ready to push myself up. Deirdre does the same. Our hands touch. We both react as if shocked, pulling away immediately. I'm ready to apologize to Deirdre. She lays a hand on my forearm. We look at each other for a few seconds. Then, she lets go and turns away.

"Thank you for the soup," she says, "It was good. Surprisingly."

I head for the front door, unsure about leaving. But equally sure I should. I flip open the door and begin to back out of the room.

"I'll talk to you soon," I say, "Keep you updated."

"Sounds good. You know where to find me." A pause. "Any time."

There's something warm in her voice. Not the usual half-amused mockery. I look back and find Deirdre staring at me. I get the feeling she wouldn't object if I closed the door and announced I was staying. But that's not certain and this is one circumstance where I wouldn't want my instincts to fail me.

"I'll see you," I say.

I close the door behind me and stand on the landing, trying to figure out what's bothering me. Then again, maybe I shouldn't contemplate it. Nothing good comes of thinking too much.

And if I had a mission statement in life…

CHAPTER TEN

I occasionally get questions from people who can't fathom doing what I do for a living. "How can you just write all the time? Aren't you worried about job security? Isn't it a hand-to-mouth existence? How are you going to retire on that kind of money?" (To be fair, most of these people are my parents.)

This speaks to a deeper concept that society, or at least American society, has difficulty grasping: that some people could no more work a nine-to-five job than they could fly. Yes, some people are fine going to work in the morning, working a mundane job until quitting time and going home to wife, kids, cat, dog, empty apartment with a big stack of porn, what have you. They're fine with the routine and the security. They're okay with snatching bits of freedom in the evening, on the weekend and on the occasional vacation and holiday; always knowing the great reward, retirement, waits for them, beyond the years in which they could actually enjoy it. Boredom is simply the price they pay.

People like me, though, are cut from a different sort of cloth. Routine is the enemy. Life needs constant change. A new column or book to write, a new film to make, a new play to do, a new town to live in, a new season, what have you. That spice of life—variety—is the thing that keeps us going.

If retirement is a little less enjoyable when you're dying in a puddle of your own piss in a welfare hospital, well, you can't make an omelet and all that…

I wonder where Alberto Castillo fits into that little scenario. He's a damn good reporter (don't tell him I said that) but he's in an industry that's still undergoing a seismic shift. Newspapers as my parents knew them barely exist anymore. Websites offer news but are moving increasingly toward clickbait. (*The Daily Bugle* was never exactly a neutral source—*liberal rag* was the term most often applied—but even now it's devolving into headlines like *I Bet You Didn't Know…*and *X Number of Things You Won't Believe About Blank…*and *Click on This, Chucklehead.* That's to say nothing of an increasingly large set of internet "news" sources consisting of "facts" derived from rumors overheard in the waiting room at "Jiffy Lube." The reporting of actual news gets pushed aside for entertaining hot takes designed to draw viewers, readers, sponsors, troglodytes, what have you. How does a reporter, even a good one like Castillo, navigate that minefield?

I'd ask him, but he'd just tell me to mind my own business.

That's not his attitude regarding this case, though. Maybe it's intrigue that's driving him. Maybe it's the quest for truth. Maybe it's the promise of free grub.

I'm sitting at a small table, one aisle over from the picture window with *Fong's* stenciled in red. If this were summer, I'd sit at the window, but the frost lining the edges of it discourages me. It's getting late and the restaurant is half-full. I peruse the menu and sip my ginseng tea. (Hey, don't look at me like that. On a cold night, it's really lovely.) I'm still distracted by thoughts of Deirdre, remembering the moment when our hands touched. Should I have done something there? Or would I have gotten my arm broken? Or worse? Before I can think about that too much, someone plops into the seat across from me. But it's not Castillo. It's Mike. Far from the bundle of insecurities he was a few hours ago, he now wears an insufferable expression.

"I think I've gotten the Ron situation taken care of," he says.

"So soon?" I say, setting the menu aside, "Did you leave his head on the city gates as a warning to the others?"

"Metaphorically, maybe. Is 'metaphorically' the word I want to use?"

"It is."

"There you go," Mike says, "He just left on a delivery. He should be stumbling back in here any second."

I ask, for perhaps the ten-thousandth time in our friendship, "What did you do?"

Mike holds up his hands, Mr. Innocent. "Nothing at all. If his tires are flat, that must be some act of God."

"Uh-huh. Think quite a lot of yourself, do you?"

Before Mike can respond, Fong calls out: "Mike! Delivery up!" Mike speaks to me as he slides out of the chair.

"This should settle, once and for all, who is the top delivery man. And who Biyu should be interested in."

"But given that her father would chop your head off—the larger head if you're lucky—if he finds out about you and Biyu, maybe that's not a good thing."

"No. No way. Ron is finished. This…" He taps the table. "Is *my* domain."

"Really?" I say, jerking a thumb toward the stenciled name on the front window, "You mean all this time Fong has been fronting for you?"

"Shut it."

"Besides, 'your domain?' What are you? Tarzan of the Apes?"

Mike ignores me, though I doubt he normally extends his middle finger quite that far when scratching his chin. He heads to the front, grabs the to-go order off the counter, and maintains the same insufferable countenance as he dashes out the door. I pick up the menu and wonder how badly Ron will suffer Mike's handiwork.

I get one more chance to peruse the menu before Castillo comes through the door. He wears a large tweed overcoat with a fedora and a plaid scarf. The Latino Frank Sinatra, ladies and gentlemen. He slips off the coat, scarf and hat and hangs them on the coatrack by the door. (Mental note, invite Castillo over sometime. The man knows where outerwear belongs.) He undoes the button on his gray suitcoat before easing his bulk into the seat opposite me. He picks up a menu without looking at me.

"Food better be good," he says.

"You better eat light," I say.

He looks over the menu. A few minutes later, the server comes by. I order the Slayer Stir Fry with an eggroll to start. Castillo orders the Drunken Noodles with cream cheese wontons. He has a soda to drink. (Philistine.)

"I did your research," Castillo says, "Can't say it's real promising."

Nuts. "Did you find *anything?*"

He takes a folded piece of paper from his coat and peruses it. "Donna Rousch. Born in Durham, Wisconsin. Has lived there her entire life there. Graduated from Durham High School. Lives with her elderly mother. Donna is her primary caregiver."

"Any connection to Alex Hollins?"

"None that I could find. I even called Sheriff Mitchell again and asked a few questions."

"He get suspicious?" I ask.

"A little. Two calls from a Twin Cities reporter in the space of six months? Probably two more than he's gotten his whole life. I told him it was background on something. I'm not sure he bought it."

"You losing sleep over it?"

Castillo snorts. "Yes, how could I live under the scrutiny of Officer Barney Fife?"

Our appetizers arrive. We split them, family style. (Fong's eggrolls are gigantic. They could double as cricket bats.) Castillo carefully arranges the cloth napkin on his lap. He eats with his usual gusto. (Sure, the man could stand to lose a few pounds, but he certainly enjoys his food.) I look toward the window as I eat.

"Dustin Felt dies in Durham, Wisconsin," I say, "Alex Hollins has a sticky note with the name of a woman from Durham. Now Alex Hollins is dead. No way all that is a coincidence."

"I'm thinking that, too," Castillo says, "I pushed Sheriff Mitchell a little about Alex Hollins. If he had ever been to Durham, if there was any connection between him and Donna Rousch. Mitchell said he had no clue. First time he'd heard of Alex Hollins was after Dustin Felt died and that was only because Hankerson-William released a statement of condolence with Alex's name on it."

"The sheriff didn't say anything more about Dustin?"

"Nope. I asked, but it was a nonstarter." Castillo dips his cream cheese wonton in the sweet-and-sour sauce. "You got anything to tell *me*? Or am I just your research guy?"

"What do you want to know?"

"Where you're hiding the woman who might have killed Alex Hollins."

On the bright side, I wasn't chewing anything when he said that. Otherwise, I might be choking on it as we speak. Still, the way I dropped my eggroll wasn't exactly smooth. Castillo's head is placid, giving his eyes a much more penetrating effect. I dab my lips with the napkin.

"What makes you say that?" I ask.

"A year ago, you wrote about how you ran around after your friend Carol was accused of murder. You mentioned a woman who was a contract killer. Now, there's a woman—probably a contract killer—who is accused of murdering Alex Hollins. And you just happen to be looking into Alex Hollins's murder for reasons you refuse to state." He picks up a cream cheese wonton and carefully dips it in the sauce. "You think journalism degrees are something they give away at the State Fair? I can put two-and-two together.

In fact, I'm pretty good at it. Where is she and what is her name?"

Castillo takes a bite of his wonton. I pick up the eggroll, but just tap it against the plate as I think. I've got to give Castillo an answer. But I can't give him the whole truth.

"I can't tell you those things," I say, "But I meant what I said. When all this is over, I'll give you the whole story. And there will be plenty to it. But when I *do* give you everything, I'm going to ask you to keep her name out of it."

"Why would I do that?"

"Because we both might live longer if you do that."

"I don't like being threatened," Castillo says, coldly.

"It's not a threat. I'm giving you a reasoned prediction based on the facts at hand. I'm sure you and your journalism degree can appreciate that."

That *does* get through to Castillo. I don't know about his religious beliefs—we've never gotten that deep into conversation—but he's enough of a sensualist to shudder at the thought of eating his last cream cheese wonton.

"Okay, do you have anything I *can* use at the moment?" he asks.

I go back to my food. "I think Dustin Felt had something on Hankerson-William."

Castillo stops chewing (but only for a moment). "Do tell."

"There was a meeting last fall. It involved Dustin Felt, Alex Hollins, Payton Hicks and Hicks's assistant, Kendall Lucas. Assistant, not receptionist, you should probably be clear on that. Anyway, at the meeting Dustin presented something called *The Impact File*. Thing is, save for a single piece of paper, there's no record of that meeting. And I don't know what the Impact File is or where I can find it. Meantime, Payton Hicks said he'd never met Dustin Felt. Kendall said she barely knew who he was. One is lying and the other is at least stretching the truth."

Castillo props an elbow on the table. "Interesting. Maybe it's time I had a chat with Payton Hicks."

I set aside my eggroll (through a hideous force of will, I can tell you). "I'd rather you didn't."

"Why?" Castillo asks.

"Because it would help us both. Right now, I'm able to ask these people questions because they think I'm just some idiot humor blogger—"

"You *are* just some idiot humor blogger."

"So, they have no reason to take me seriously. Maybe I can get answers they aren't prepared to give. But if you start badgering them, they're going to circle the wagons, and nobody is going to get through to them."

The entrees arrive, temporarily breaking up the conversation. We thank the server and sit quietly. Fong's voice booms across the restaurant, ordering the kitchen staff around as they begin closing preparations. Castillo is poised over his food but is not eating. That alone tells me how preoccupied he is. Finally, he sets his fork aside.

"I don't suppose you're going to tell me *how* you got this information about the Impact File?" Castillo asks.

Oy. That would mean confessing to a crime. Actually, given that it involves breaking-and-entering, trespassing, harboring a fugitive and assaulting a police officer, it's more like confessing to a crime spree. Castillo already suspects these things but if I don't confess, he doesn't have to be in on the conspiracy and compromise his journalistic ethics. Not when I can give him the gift of plausible deniability.

"That's going to have to remain on the downlow as well," I say, "Just for now."

Castillo's face creases, annoyed. (Honestly, I didn't expect any other reaction). "The rate you're going, there better be a Pulitzer in this for me when all is said and done."

"Can't guarantee that," I say, "But it should be worth your while."

"That's going to be in the eye of the beholder." He lowers his fork. "Listen, I like talking cycling with you and I don't find many people to do that with. I'd hate for all this to end with me raking you over the coals."

"*Obscure Local Reporter Drags Beloved Humor Columnist.*"

"Geeks Take to the Streets. Dozens Annoyed." His face turns serious. "These are pretty high-level people you're fucking with. I don't want to say you're out of your league, but…"

"You're out of your league."

"Yeah." He pauses. "You sure there's nothing else you want to tell me?"

"There is," I say, "I think they should go back to national teams in the Tour de France."

Before we can get into a discussion of cycling or anything else, a delivery guy comes through the front door. It's Ron, Mike's sudden rival. He gets a little applause from the kitchen. Nothing huge, but certainly appreciative. Fong looks at his watch.

"You back already?" Fong asks.

"It wasn't easy," Ron says, in that Bullwinkle Moose voice of his, "Good thing I know how to patch tires."

Ron grabs a seat at one of the tables. Biyu passes by and gives him a little nod. A moment later, Mike speeds through the same door, as if he's running the Mental Hospital's Fifty Yard Dash. He nearly crashes into our table as he passes. He spots Ron and comes to a complete halt. He gives Ron a hateful look and mouths, "What the fuck?" He steps out the door again and can be faintly heard screaming,

"Fuck!" to the heavens. Castillo uses his fork to gesture toward the front door.

"What the hell is that?" he asks.

"Now, there is a story I *can* tell you."

***

Anyone who has ever played with a Chinese finger puzzle or gotten stuck in quicksand or tried to get bubble gum off their fingers and wound up with stickiness over seventy percent of their body will know that sometimes our best efforts to extricate ourselves from a situation only lead us deeper into it. As proof, sadly, I must offer my friend Carol as an example.

"I thought I had taken care of the situation," Carol says, wandering around my living room, "but I just made things worse."

I'm at the breakfast bar, eating some leftover chicken wild rice soup and wondering if giving Carol a cup of coffee was a good idea. Caffeine appears to be the last thing she needs. Squiggy puts his front paws on the stool and reaches up to tap my leg, as if to say, "Sir? Sir? Do you require my assistance?" I don't, but I pick him up and set him on my lap.

"What's up now?" I ask Carol.

Carol stops. "Evie's fallen off the wagon."

"Fallen *off* the wagon. I wasn't aware she was *on* said wagon."

"It's part of the ruse, you idiot!" Carol holds up a hand, apologizing for her outburst, and steps to the breakfast bar. "Evie was supposed to be helping Mr. Pratt's son. Well, she's helping him all right. She's helping him get shitfaced every night."

"Uh-oh."

"Exactly. All Evie had to do was keep an eye on Shawn and try to help him. Y'know, fake a bunch of Twelve Step bullshit and hope he got his act together."

"I'm starting to see the flaw in your plan."

"I know! I know!" Carol says, resuming her pacing, "But I was desperate. And Evie was the only one who could help me. She's the best liar I know." Carol holds out a hand, knowing what I'm going to say next. "Except for Mike." She sits on the arm of the futon. "At first, she was willing to go sober for a while, just to make the part look convincing. Then she had her first session with Shawn. If the goal was to create a bond between Evie and the kid, it was a spectacular success. If the goal was to keep Shawn away from drugs and alcohol, it was…not."

"What happened?"

"It started just fine. They went to the coffee shop, like we suggested. And they really hit it off. Evie said they were talking like old friends in no time. I guess Shawn reminds Evie of an old boyfriend of hers."

"I assume the guy's currently doing time."

"It wouldn't surprise me. At any rate, Shawn started talking about why he's into drugs and alcohol. The kind of kick he gets out of them. Evie just listened. She was doing her job. But the more Shawn talked about the fun he had, the more Evie thought it sounded like fun, too."

"Oh dear."

"Yeah. Pretty soon they were both at The Tav, doing shots. They got kicked out when they refused to stop doing a thing where Shawn was drinking Tequila Shooters out of Evie's cleavage. They hit a few more places and then Shawn remembered he had a friend nearby who'd sell him a dime bag. Everything went downhill from there. Evie doesn't remember a lot. Only that they pantsed a guy and stole his wallet."

"In the middle of winter?"

"Actually, in the middle of a strip joint," Carol says, "Evie doesn't remember how they got there, but she remembers running from the cops. It must have been a hell of a night. Considering it was two days ago and Evie called me an hour ago to tell me it had just ended."

Ouch. I'm not really one to talk vis-à-vis running from the cops. But I like to think I did it in a (somewhat) good cause. "What are you going to tell your boss?" I ask.

"I don't know," Carol says, walking into the kitchen and setting her coffee cup in the sink, "No one at the office knows, thank God. I'm not sure I can keep this whole thing a secret."

"Well, long about the time they go on a *Badlands* style killing spree across the upper Midwest, it might be a little difficult to keep things on the downlow."

Carol frowns. She's not bothered by my sarcasm so much as she's bothered by the possible truth that lays behind it. She grabs her coat off the coat tree and steps to the front door.

"How are things going with your, uh, friend?" she asks.

Eyeroll. "Not sure." I update Carol on my chat with Castillo and what he found (or more accurately did not find) out about Donna Rousch. "It's frustrating," I say, "Donna Rousch is from Durham. Dustin Felt died in Durham. Alex Hollins—and maybe some others at Hankerson-William— were trying to cover up something called the Impact File. It all fits together somehow. I'm sure of it."

"Just a matter of how."

"Exactly."

Carol thinks about it, as if she can come up with something to assist me. Finally, she opens the door. "Good luck," she says, "I'd hope you find something before you get in real trouble, but it looks like you're already in real trouble."

"Thanks," I say, "Give my regards to the Betty Faux Center." Carol stops. Her head pops back around the door. "Yes, I've been working on that one," I tell her.

Carol's face grows serious. "Be careful. Okay?"

"Got it," I say, quietly.

She slips out the door. The apartment is quiet, disquietingly so. I finish my soup and set the bowl in the sink. Squiggy stands nearby, his butler instincts quietly approving my keeping up appearances. (In reality, he's probably angling to be fed.)

Alex Hollins. Dustin Felt. Donna Rousch, Durham, Wisconsin. How do they all tie together? The Impact File. That was something Dustin Felt was working on. There had to be something in it. Something Hollins didn't want to get out. He fires Dustin Felt and tries to cover up the existence of the file. I can divine that much from the evidence. Everything else requires some speculation.

There's some connection between Hollins and Donna Rousch. Maybe a love match. He arranges for her to take out Dustin Felt. But how does Dustin Felt get to Durham? Of all the gin joints in all the towns in all the world, why would he go to that one? And it still doesn't explain who killed Alex Hollins. Or why. So near and yet so far. Fuck.

Lars comes through the front door. I can't even disguise my impatient groan (not that Lars will pick up on it). I love the guy, but sometimes his timing stinks. This visit, though, is a little more subdued. He carefully closes the door behind him and slinks over to the breakfast bar. He looks around to make sure we're alone. (Like I've got Reilly, Ace of Spies hiding in the bedroom.) He keeps his voice down.

"Got a little news for you," Lars says.

"You know who was on the grassy knoll in Dallas?" I say, "Was it Phil Silvers, just like I've always said?"

Lars's head snaps back. "No. What the hell are you talking about?"

"I'm wondering why we have to keep our voices down. Have you discovered the location of the Ark of the Covenant or what?"

Lars waves a bony hand at that, nearly whapping me in the face. "I've got some news, but I don't want Iris to overhear me. She's downstairs."

"The walls aren't *that* thin. As long as we're not screaming, you should be fine."

"I don't want to take any chances. What Iris doesn't know doesn't hurt me. You get what I'm saying?"

Now I'm intrigued. And apprehensive. What does Lars have that he doesn't want Iris to overhear? And do I even want to know? I give him the benefit of the doubt (despite my misgivings).

"Go ahead," I say, "Temba, his arms wide."

Lars cocks his head to one side. "Temba? I don't get it. Is that a reference to something?"

"It's *Star Trek: The Next Generation*. The 'Darmok' episode. You, you don't…you know what? Fuck it. What do you have to tell me?"

"Okay, you know I'm seeing the receptionist from Hankerson-William? Megan is her name, by the way."

"I knew you got her number," I say, "I didn't know you were seeing her."

"Just once. She's a delightful woman. Intelligent. Well read. Open-hearted. And her blowjob technique is simply sublime."

"And the point to all of this is…?" (I'm taking a giant leap in believing there *is* a point.)

"Alright, so Megan and I were pillow-talking. If relaxing in the backseat of a Cadillac after spectacular sex can be considered pillow-talking…"

"Lars!"

"Fine, fine. Keep it down." A look around. "Megan was talking about rumors at the office. I didn't think much of it, but I humored her. Not making conversation after a BJ is simply gauche."

"I've heard."

"And she started talking about sexual rumors. Who's doing who and such. And Chelsea Hollins's name came up. Apparently, she was having an affair. With someone at Hankerson-William."

Finally, he's got my undivided attention. "Who?"

"A guy named Dustin Felt. Have you heard of him?"

Holy shit. Chelsea and Dustin Felt? "I've heard of the guy," I say, "What else did this Megan say?"

"Not much. Just that there were rumors of an affair. I thought you might be interested."

"I *am* interested. Thank you." I'm stunned to be saying this, but: "Good work."

He drops his head, modestly. "Think nothing of it, brother. All in a day's work. And I mean *work*. Megan, I'll tell you, she's insatiable. You wouldn't know it by meeting her, but…"

"I'll take your word on it."

"Just don't tell Iris. She's getting suspicious."

"Of the receptionist?"

"No," Lars says, "Of…our friend next door."

Danger, Will Robinson. There's a little wrinkle I didn't anticipate. Lars has a girlfriend *and* he's harboring a fugitive. Those worlds were going to collide eventually. I've got no suggestions regarding security, so I focus my wrath on Iris's existence.

"Lars, I've got to ask: why are you with this woman? I don't mean to offend, but from everything you've told me, she's temperamental, abusive and violent."

"You left out narcissistic," he says, "She has quite the substrata of narcissism."

"What's the appeal? Beyond the fact she's gorgeous?"

"Well, she's gorgeous," Lars says, "And it's the most incredible hate sex I've ever had. Well worth the pain."

"Hate sex?" I ask.

"I've come to the conclusion that hate sex is the only sex Iris has. But I can handle it."

I wonder if that's the case. Mike once broke up with a girl who, in the throes of passion, told him she had a knife under the bed and asked if he wanted her to plunge it into his back. He let the question go unanswered, but as soon as he finished (come on, you *knew* he was going to finish), Mike got dressed and fled the house. Not necessarily in that order. The moral of the story (if *moral* even applies here) is that good sex only goes so far.

"Good luck to you," I say, "I hope Iris doesn't find out about the receptionist. That probably can't be made up with hate sex."

That gives Lars a shiver. (Welcome to the club, pal.) He slinks out the front door without saying another word. I slump against the breakfast bar and try not to beat my head against it. Iris might be on to Deirdre. All right, fuck it. One disaster at a time. Best to think about the investigation and where I'm going with that.

Wait, that's the *pleasant* thought? Fuck me.

CHAPTER ELEVEN

A common misconception about us neat freaks is that we have some kind of disorder. Neatness has become so associated with obsessive compulsive disorder that people assume if you are one, you have the other. Sort of like how being an introvert has become associated with being shy or socially awkward. There are plenty of introverts who have perfectly normal social interactions. There's just a limit to how much *social interaction your average introvert can handle. (And if you met my friends, you'd realize why* I *prefer limits.) The bottom line is that society has somehow deemed people like my slobby friend Mike—a guy who cleans only when the state department of health orders him to do so—to be normal.*

I'm not going to deny that there are *compulsives in the neatnik set. But we're not always driven by some form of illness. There are people like me, who prefer an orderly space in which to create. Or people like my mom, who just like a neat home. Mom always turned the trick of keeping our house neat without insisting that everyone keep it that way. Rather than make everyone walk on eggshells, afraid to spread dirt or*

spill a beverage, Mom just let everyone go on about their business,
figuring if something got messy, it would give her something to do later.
(Of course, since she had three boys who were relatively close in age, this
might have been a defense mechanism.)

I wonder what approach Chelsea Hollins takes. Then again, can you be much of a neat freak when someone cleans your place for you?

I pull the Saturn up to the front door of the Hollins estate, guiltily hoping none of the neighbors recognize the car from the break-in. (A black car driving around after dark. I'm probably in the clear.) I wear my peacoat over a black sweater and jeans, meaning I'm a whole lot more comfortable than the last time we met. A maid greets me at the front door and says she'll get Chelsea. I stand in the foyer and try to convince myself I haven't been here before (lest I adopt a guilty look that Chelsea will pick up on). Chelsea comes along and greets me with a dry handshake. She wears a simple white blouse and black pants. Her hair is pulled back and held in place by a black clip. A light dusting of makeup covers her face. The same shamrock necklace adorns her neck. She's trying to appear casual but doesn't quite get there.

"You have a lovely home," I say, waving a hand about. (That's right. It's a lovely place I've never been to before. Never. This is all new to me. I'm not hyperventilating. *You're* hyperventilating.)

"Let me give you the tour," Chelsea says, though I sense it's more out of obligation than pride.

The tour *does* afford me a look at portions of the house I didn't get a chance to break into. There are three floors, multiple bedrooms, many of them repurposed as sewing rooms or sunrooms or studios. Everything is neat and clean and polished. I tip my hat to the household staff. Chelsea's voice is rather perfunctory, as if she's proud of the house, but not enthusiastic. As we go down one of the staircases, I glance into the backyard.

"Looks like you have a little cottage back there," I say.

Chelsea flips a hand at that. "It came with the house. We never use it. In fact, it's falling apart, so I never let anyone back there."

That makes sense. My layabout uncle Gordie inherited a cabin from a former girlfriend (perhaps as revenge for their relationship) and discovered the thing was in such a state of disrepair the décor could only be improved by having a tornado hit it. Since my dad and my uncle Mel refused to help him remodel it and his friends' knowledge of tools extended only to those used for breaking-and-entering, Gordie had to let the cabin go. Last I heard, it's the ancestral estate for several generations of racoons.

The tour ends with Chelsea guiding me to a small room off the kitchen. More like a breakfast nook on steroids. It has a small table with a few chairs. There are windows on two sides, affording a view of the countryside. It's sunny, even if the sun is deceiving. (The temp is still below zero outside.) I'm directed into one of the chairs and offered coffee, which I gladly accept. Chelsea gives discreet orders to the maid, who returns a few minutes later with a tray containing two ornate coffee cups and a French press pot. I thank her, but the maid leaves the room without further interaction. I leave the coffee untouched while it steeps.

"Thank you for meeting me," I say.

"Thank you for coming to the house."

"I'm surprised you're here." And not for the first time. "I thought you were staying at an apartment in the city."

Chelsea hugs herself, maybe getting some of the chill from the window. "I came back a few nights ago, just to check on it. And there was a break-in. Two people, I think. I walked in on them. It was horrible. I'm surprised you didn't hear about it on the news."

Well, when you're *part* of the news… "Sorry. I spend too much time looking at the sports."

Chelsea doesn't seem overly concerned. I'm just another shallow sort. (Read my column, for crying out loud.)

"I'm going to stay here for the time being and keep an eye on things. I'll go back to the city eventually."

"Do you feel safe being here?"

"I do. The security system will be on *all* the time now. And we've got at least two police units patrolling the neighborhood. I'll be fine."

Huh. I guess there won't be any future break-ins at the Hollins estate. (Not that it was even on the table.) I silently wish the French press would hurry along. I could really use the java.

"Where is the apartment located?" I ask, trying to make conversation.

"Near Uptown. Over by Lake Bde Maka Ska." She's switches the subject. "How's the fundraiser coming?"

"As well as can be expected. Given who's involved."

Chelsea slowly lowers the plunger on the French press, compressing the grounds. "So, what's on your mind?"

"Dustin Felt," I say.

Sure, I could have been more tactful. Make small talk and eventually slide a mention of Mr. Felt into the conversation. But this approach has the benefit of getting an honest reaction. Chelsea's hand slips off the plunger. She snaps me a look, then her eyes drop to the table.

"What have you heard?" Chelsea asks.

At least she's not trying to bullshit me. "That Dustin worked for Hankerson-William. That he was fired. That he died last fall. And…a few other things."

"Things about he and I?"

"Things like that. Yeah." I take over with the plunger. (I could *really* use the coffee.) "Is it true?"

"It is." She turns her coffee cup up and I pour for each of us. "Why do you want to know?" Chelsea asks.

That puts *me* on the defensive. This really falls outside the purview of someone helping out with a fundraiser. Let's hope spending all that time around Mike hasn't gone to waste. I stir some sugar into my coffee. (I could use the extra comfort.)

"It involves the fundraiser," I say, "You know how these things go. You want people to donate to a good cause. You don't want any hint of scandal gumming up the works."

"Scandal? It doesn't need to be a scandal if everyone minds their own business."

I accept the jab. "I understand that. But with your husband passing away—"

"You mean being murdered."

"Um, yes. With that happening, the media might put Hankerson-William under more scrutiny. You never know what they're going to turn up. I mean, I found out about you and Dustin Felt and I'm barely a reporter."

"How *did* you find out?"

"Sorry. Can't reveal my sources. I'm that much of a reporter, at least."

Chelsea fingers the shamrock necklace. "Do you *know* there are reporters snooping around Hankerson-William?"

"I know of one. Alberto Castillo. You heard of him?"

"No, I don't think I have."

"He's good. He may look like a Latino version of the Pillsbury Doughboy, but don't let that fool you. The guy is a shark."

Chelsea stares at the tabletop. "I see."

"You'll understand why we're concerned. If Castillo is digging around, we'd like to head any bad publicity off at the pass. So to speak."

I try to give Chelsea that "still look" Castillo uses, hoping I can intimidate her into giving me some answers. I'm sure the look is failing miserably, witness the way Chelsea is eyeing me, warily. But it works nonetheless.

"What do you need to know?" she asks.

I set my coffee aside. "You *were* having an affair with Dustin Felt?"

"Yes, I was having an affair with Dustin."

"Did Alex know?"

"He did. But he didn't care." Chelsea stares into her coffee. "You need to realize what things were like with Alex.

He wasn't just distant. He was nonexistent. He gave me nothing but an income. In the end, that's all he was to me."

"And now he's not even that."

"In a strange way, he *is*," Chelsea says, "According to the will, I'm getting almost everything. Including the house."

She says it with the usual lack of enthusiasm. For some, I guess it's better to be bored and rich than poor and entertained. But I don't need to get into that.

"Tell me about Dustin," I say.

"In some ways, he's—he *was*—like Alex. Very committed to his work. But Alex was…cold. He had an air of command about him, but he was like a machine. At first, I was attracted to his drive. But then I realized there wasn't anything else to him. It was like he checked the box for *Wife* and now he was moving on." She fingers the necklace. "Dustin was a real person. He had fire. Passion. He believed in things." She holds up the necklace with her thumb. "He gave me this. He cared. It was more than you could have said of Alex."

"How did you meet Dustin?"

"He was helping with a charity drive I was working on. We talked about politics and literature and philosophy. All the things Alex didn't have any interest in."

"Dustin was working on the Green River Project, right?" I ask.

Chelsea stiffens. "I think so. Dustin didn't talk a lot about his work. I've heard of the Green River Project, of course. It's in the news and Alex and Payton both mentioned it. Dustin didn't give me any details."

I prop an elbow on the table. "Was the relationship with Dustin over when he died?"

"Yes." Chelsea picks up her coffee cup but doesn't drink. "Alex had found out. He might not have cared, but he wasn't going to let it go on. And I wasn't going to leave Alex. It was best to end things with Dustin."

"How did Alex find out?" I ask.

"I honestly don't know. Alex was well-connected. If he suspected—and just my being happy would have given him cause to be suspicious—he could find things out."

Eek. Just in case you were wondering what it was like to be married to The Godfather. A servant peeks in, then slips out without saying anything. Welcome to life in the fishbowl.

"When did you break things off with Dustin?" I ask.

"Shortly before he died."

Wow. There's some heavy-duty guilt. I don't feel particularly good about badgering Chelsea on this topic, but I need answers. I take in the faint smell of woodsmoke. (A little aroma therapy never hurts.)

"What do you know about Durham, Wisconsin?" I say.

There's a moment, just a moment, where Chelsea's fingernails claw the table. Something has gotten to her. "I don't know anything about Durham," she says, "Should I?"

"It's where Dustin died. I thought you'd know that."

"I know Dustin died someplace in Wisconsin. I didn't memorize the name of the town."

"Sorry," I say, "Do you have any idea why Dustin was there?"

"None," Chelsea says, "Maybe he knew somebody there. I don't remember him ever mentioning it."

Fair enough. Maybe Dustin was just passing through Durham and had some bad luck. Or maybe he has some connection there that nobody knows about. It's a long shot, though.

"Did Payton Hicks know about the affair?" I ask.

Far from shocking Chelsea, it simply amuses her. "No, Payton didn't know. If he had, he would have talked to me. Try to patch things up between me and Alex. He's that kind of guy."

I toy with my coffee cup. "And Alex was faithful to you?"

Chelsea freezes me with a look. "I think so. Why do you want to know?"

"Just wondering." I clear my throat. "Does the name Donna Rousch mean anything to you?"

"No," Chelsea says, drawing the word out, "Should it?"

"I'm not sure. It was just a name Alberto Castillo mentioned. Donna Rousch is from Durham. He says he didn't find any connection to Dustin. I'm wondering if there's a connection between her and Alex."

I'm on thin ice here (or whatever winter metaphor you'd like to throw in). Knowing the name Donna Rousch comes perilously close to admitting *how* I know that name. Chelsea, though, just looks amused and doesn't press me for details.

"I'm sorry," Chelsea says, "It doesn't mean anything to me."

Yeah, it was a reach. The notion of a wealthy CEO sleeping with a small-town woman who lives with her mother is absurd on the face of it. But there must be *some* connection there. Whatever it is, I'm not going to get it out of Chelsea. She and I have finished our coffees and she doesn't appear to be in a rush to order refills.

"Thanks for meeting me," I say, standing up from the table.

"I'd like to say it's been a pleasure, but…"

"I'm sorry. I know I'm prying, but the fundraiser is for a good cause and…"

"Everyone involved must be pure of heart. Is that it?"

I step out of the room. Chelsea walks me to the door (probably to make sure I completely leave the grounds). The maid fetches my peacoat, scarf and gloves. I stand in the doorway as I put them on. I look for something pithy to say, but I'm withering under Chelsea's cold look.

"Sorry," I say.

"You're protecting your friends," she says, "That's nice. Maybe I'm just jealous."

"Jealous?"

"I don't have anyone looking out for me."

Chelsea's eyes cut toward the door. I take the hint and move into the bitter cold, allayed only by the sweet smell of woodsmoke. Behind me is the faint sound of the alarm system being activated. I haven't made a friend in Chelsea or gotten a ton of information. All in the name of supposedly looking out for my friends.

If Chelsea only knew who I was *really* looking out for…

***

I worked briefly as a pizza delivery man after I moved to the Cities. I had a day job at a small suburban newspaper, but it didn't pay enough to cover the bills. I compensated by delivering pizza on Friday and Saturday nights. I liked the job. I wasn't stuck in the store the whole time, I could listen to the radio while I drove, and I could take home discounted pizzas anytime I liked. While the job assisted me in developing my Rules of Pizza (I'll have to tell you about those sometime), I also got tired of pizza by the time I quit. Maybe the Vulcans can find infinite variety in infinite combinations, but with pizza, you run out of that pretty quickly.

So, it's beneficial to have a *friend* who's a delivery person. You get the discounted eats but don't have to put up with the annoyance of the job. Though I doubt I'll ever get tired of the cuisine from Fong's. Even if their delivery man is threatening my digestion.

"I tried everything," Mike says, pacing the living room while I unpack the sesame chicken he's brought me, "I've taken every shortcut I know. I've broken the speed limit I-don't-know-how-many times. I run in and out of the place like I'm LeBron on a fast break." He blows out a breath. "I think I've peaked."

"It happens to all the great ones. You'll just have to be content with being a first ballot Hall-of-Famer."

Mike drops on to the stool across from me at the breakfast bar. "I can't believe the tire thing didn't work. The kid is three of the most helpless fuckers you'll ever run across. You'd think a thing like that would have been paralyzing. No luck. One of the few things the asshole knows how to do is patch a tire. Must have picked it up in the army."

"Does Ron suspect you?"

Mike scoffs. "The guy would have to have a fully functioning brain to pull that off. No, he still thinks we're besties. Keeps thanking me for the help. It's all I can do not to puke."

I take two square plates to the breakfast bar and spoon jasmine rice on to both. "I take it the playing field is still even?"

"More or less," Mike says, "Even worse, Biyu admired the way Ron handled the flat tire business. She's paying even *more* attention to him. And today, she gave me a 'That's nice' when I was in the middle of telling her something and went to talk to Ron. Bad scene, man." He takes a deep breath. "Something drastic has to be done."

I nearly drop the rice container before I get it to the fridge. "This drastic thing doesn't involve just doing your job and leaving the competitive stuff alone, does it?"

"Of course not. What are you? Insane?"

"Wasn't me I was thinking of."

Mike hops off the stool and paces the room. He looks like a mad scientist who lost the lab to creditors. "Fong might not be so in love with the guy if he realized what a safety hazard he is."

I come back from the fridge. "*Is* Ron a safety hazard?"

"Not really. There's the stuff he picked up from me, but I can't rat him out on that without getting myself into trouble. No, I'm thinking Ron's too intoxicated with his own power. It's made him arrogant."

"He's Anakin Skywalker?"

"Yes," Mike says, "But in a less crappy story."

"I beg to differ."

He ignores me, continuing to form his dastardly plan. "Ron thinks he's invincible. It's only a matter of time before something terrible happens and I'm Fong's undisputed number one delivery man again!"

If it wasn't the middle of winter and well below zero outside, I'd expect lightning and thunder to accompany Mike's pronouncement. I'm getting the willies over here. I need to pull Mike back from the brink of insanity. But if I haven't had any success for the first sixteen years of our acquaintance...

Before the situation gets any more ridiculous, Lars comes through the front door. (Seriously, this is where we're at? *Lars* is here to cut the silliness?) He carefully closes the door behind him and glides over to the breakfast bar. Once again, his usual bonhomie is missing, replaced by a skulking furtiveness. He draws us into a huddle around my breakfast bar.

"Gentleman, I may need some relationship advice," he says.

"Sorry, but you've come to the wrong place," I say, "The only woman I've seen lately is a contract killer who may be plotting my grisly death. And Chumley over there is plotting someone's grisly death as a path to nookie. Unless, of course, you're planning to kill Iris."

"No, no, not at all," Lars says, "But let's keep all options on the table." He keeps his voice low. "No, I'm talking about the best way to arrange a tryst."

"A tryst?" Mike says.

"A tryst, yes," Lars says, "I have found a woman with whom I wish to be trystin' the night away."

"Iris?" I say, "What's stopping you? You guys are always doing the tryst. Believe me, I can hear it."

If that causes Lars any chagrin, he disguises it well. But I'm almost certain it doesn't. He grabs the container of sesame chicken and a fork and starts in. (Guess I'm having plain jasmine rice for dinner.)

"It's not Iris," he says, "It's Megan. The receptionist at Hankerson-William. She's proposing a little get together. I'm not sure if I should follow through on it."

"Why not?" I ask, "It hasn't stopped you yet."

"This is different," Lars says, "She wants to get together formally."

"Like a date?" Mike asks.

"No, like a tryst," Lars says, "Michael, please try to follow along." He takes a bite of the sesame chicken and talks with his mouth full. "Megan feels we've passed the sex in frozen vehicles and shagging in single occupancy bathrooms phase of our relationship and wants a more formal setting."

"Like a bedroom," Mike says.

"Precisely," Lars says, "That, however, presents a problem. Megan has a roommate who is rather close-minded on the subject of gentleman callers. Neither of us can afford a decent hotel room. And clearly, we can't come over to my place."

"Have you told Megan about Iris?" I ask.

"Oh, certainly," Lars says, "I believe in complete transparency in a relationship. Unless said transparency would put me at risk of physical injury or death. Then I tend to be more…subversive." He picks up another forkful of sesame chicken but speaks without eating it. "Megan is completely okay with Iris. She even brought up the idea of a three-way."

Mike's eyes bulge. "Holy shit."

"It's a nonstarter, my friend," Lars says, a touch wistful, "Iris would never go for it. Oh, she might be into it if I wasn't there. But sharing me? No way."

I feel the sudden need to jump in. "Before you even bring the subject up: no, you can't use my apartment."

"You can use mine," Mike says.

"That's not the issue," Lars says, "Joe, I couldn't use your apartment because it's too close to mine. I need a demilitarized zone in which I'm safe from Iris finding things out. And Mike, I appreciate the offer, but Megan has a bit of an allergy to dust. And an aversion to the sort of aromas that accompany the single slovenly male. I hope you understand."

"I'm totally cool with it," Mike says.

"Megan *does* have a place she can use," Lars says, going back to his (by which I mean, my) food, "The problem isn't the location. It's the sense of commitment. Seeing Megan on the sly was one thing. But a whole—or maybe the better part of a—night together? I'm not sure I'm ready for that kind of thing."

I pick at my rice. "Particularly when you consider the homicidal possibilities."

"Exactly," Lars says, "I just don't know. Should I go for it?"

"Of course," Mike says, "Double your nookie, double your fun. Don't look back."

"Absolutely," I add, "and when Iris removes your johnson like a Lebowskian marmot, this sort of conundrum won't even be on your radar."

Mike shoots me a look. "Did you just come up with that?"

I pause in my eating. "Surprisingly, I did."

We lapse into silence, each contemplating our various situations. Lars on how he can continue getting skinny on the side without finding himself a paraplegic or a eunuch. Mike on how he can possibly murder a co-worker and make it look like an accident. Me on how I've arranged my adult life such that these chuckleheads are two of my three closest friends. I leave the rice behind and go to the fridge for a beer.

"If it's not a hotel room or her apartment," I say, "where is this place Megan wants to meet?"

"It's an apartment in Uptown," Lars says, still plowing through the sesame chicken, "It used to belong to Alex Hollins. I guess his widow has been using it. But it's unoccupied for now. And Megan has access to it."

Isn't that interesting? I stand at the refrigerator, door open (even though I know better), contemplating this bit of information. If there was something between Alex Hollins and this Donna Rousch woman, maybe this apartment was used for a rendezvous or several. Regardless, it was Alex's place. Maybe there's something there we can find. Yes, I vowed not to do another break-in, but I'm not getting anywhere otherwise. I slowly close the refrigerator door, the beer temporarily (but only temporarily) forgotten.

"You know where this place is?" I ask.

"I don't know the exact address," Lars says, "but I could get it from Megan."

"You think you could get access to it?" I say, "Without bringing Megan along? Or getting a lot of awkward questions?"

Lars contemplates this as he chews his food. "If I massaged it right—and her right—Megan might be open to that kind of thing. She's a very understanding girl."

"You think you could get it tonight?" I ask, "Like ASAP?"

"Possibly," Lars says, "I won't know until I ask. Is there, uh, a reason you need it so soon?" I get the feeling he wants to waggle his eyebrows but chooses to resist.

It's hard to ask a favor of somebody and not give them the full info. Oh sure, I can do it with someone like Al Castillo, but Lars is closer to me than that. (Even if he's significantly more annoying.) I approach the breakfast bar.

"I need to take a look around the place," I say, "See if I can find some information on Alex Hollins. Or anything related to this case."

Lars strokes his beard and considers the matter. "I can probably talk Megan into it. But I'll have to come along. She won't hand the keys over to anyone else. And it sounds like fun."

Oy. Only Lars could consider something that could result in his murder and/or incarceration to be fun. Well, only Lars unless you stop to consider…

"I want in on this, too," Mike says, "You left me out of the last break-in and you saw how that went. You're going to need expert help."

I tried to throw the brakes on the Idiot Express. "I'm not sure this is a good idea. The fewer of us, the less chance of getting caught."

"We'll be fine," Lars says, "We're a good team. The Three Musketeers."

"Or the Three Stooges," I say, "Or the Three Amigos. Or the Three Musketeers candy bar."

Mike sniffs at that. "I was always a Whatchamacallit kid."

"I didn't care for Whatchamacallits," Lars says, "I didn't know what made it crunch. I don't trust any candy bar in which I can't identify the source of the crunch."

"Come on, it was chocolate covered," Mike says, "You can't lose when there's chocolate all over it."

"I dated a girl who thought that same way," Lars says, "She was an adventure."

My head is getting closer and closer to the breakfast bar. I'm planning a break-in with these yahoos? I might as well go downstairs and ask Deirdre to shoot me through the head.

It would be the merciful thing to do.

***

The Hollins's apartment is in the heart of Uptown, but on the Lyndale Avenue side rather than the Hennepin Avenue side. The building is not exactly a high rise. It's about five stories and has been built recently. It's striving to achieve the kind of charm that older buildings achieve naturally. There's marble in the lobby and some pillars near the elevator. A few Art Deco touches here and there. A lot of mirrors. But it all seems so forced, and likely done on the cheap, that the effect is muted. ("Sincerity? I can fake that!")

The revolving door to the lobby is recessed a bit, as if trying to hide from the riffraff. The lobby itself is empty but there are security cameras posted in all corners. We try to follow Mike's mantra of always looking like you belong in a place, even when you don't. Our results are mixed. Mike is a born con man and Lars genuinely feels comfortable any place he goes. I'm the only one struggling to pull it off. Mike elbows me in the ribs every time I look furtive. Meaning I get elbowed a lot. The elevator bank is just around the corner from the lobby. We get there unmolested. Mike hits the *Up* button, and we wait. Lars passes the time by humming *The Girl from Ipanema.*

"What floor are we going to?" Mike asks.

"Five," Lars says, "The apartment in the corner. Rather secluded, I'm led to believe."

"Good," I say, "I wouldn't want our deaths to inconvenience any of the neighbors."

Neither Mike nor Lars seem particularly concerned. The elevator doors open, and a guy starts to step off. He's probably a heavy-set guy but given the size of the parka he's wearing, he might be a buck-sixty and skinny as a rail. He stops, effectively blocking the entrance to the elevator. Great. Let the molestation begin. (Maybe I should phrase that another way.)

"You guys just move in?" the gatekeeper asks, a little bass in his voice (though I suspect he's working to keep it there).

Mike sizes up the situation. "Building management sent us."

The gatekeeper flinches slightly, as if he can't believe what he's hearing. "Building management? About what?"

"I'm afraid that's between us and building management," Mike says.

The gatekeeper shows no sign of moving. "You're telling me building management sent you three guys here practically in the middle of the night? You're not carrying anything. You sure as hell don't *look* like workmen. Suppose you tell me what's really going on?"

If we were smart, we'd run as fast as possible for the exits, forgetting this building even exists. Of course, if we were smart, we wouldn't be here in the first place. Mike doesn't bat an eye. Instead, he gets right into the gatekeeper's face.

"You a fan of mold, big fella?" Mike asks.

"Mold?"

"Mold. Indeed."

The gatekeeper looks to me and Lars, probably to see if we're serious. I can only look down. Lars is incapable of looking serious under any circumstances. The gatekeeper focuses on Mike, who's still up in the gatekeeper's grill.

"No, I'm not a fan of mold," the gatekeeper says, "What's going on with mold?"

Mike scoffs. "You think I'm going to waste my time telling you? I've already wasted enough time as it is. *And* I've told you too much as it is. You think I want to create a panic?"

"A panic?"

"A mold panic, my friend," Mike says, "The worst kind there is."

The gatekeeper is now thoroughly rattled. "Wha…what about the mold?"

"It ain't good," Mike says, staring at the gatekeeper without blinking, "Suffice to say, if we don't get up there in time, every man, woman, and child…you have children?"

"Yeah, yeah. Lots of 'em."

"Gross. Still, every one of them is in grave danger—notice I used the word 'grave'—if we aren't allowed to do our work. You don't even want to know the disastrous health effects."

"Like what?" the gatekeeper asks. Apparently, he *does* want to know.

"That depends," Mike says, "How many orifices are you cool with bleeding from?"

"How many? No…none."

"Then, for the eight-hundred-and-fourth time in the last two minutes, get the fuck out of our way and let us deal with this."

Now the gatekeeper can't get out of our way fast enough. In fact, he nearly slips on the marble. (No worries, since I'm certain his parka could stop a bullet.) We get into the elevator, ignoring the gatekeeper. I contain my sigh of relief until the doors close.

"One of these days," I say, "That aggressive bullshitting of yours isn't going to work."

Mike is unfazed. "It ain't gonna be today. And it ain't gonna be because of that guy."

Great. Thank you, Ferris Bueller.

The doors open on the fifth floor. The hallway has hardwood floors and each of the doors is oak-wood paneled with gold number plates. Another attempt to look charming that just looks contrived. That's it. I'm reporting this place to *Architectural Digest*. Lars takes a set of keys from the pocket of his ratty winter coat and leads us to a corner door. He takes a peek over his shoulder, making sure we're clear of nosy tenants, and carefully unlocks the door.

For a crash pad in the city, this place is bigger than the house I grew up in. The ceiling is several miles above our heads. A stairway leads to a second level (probably a bedroom and a bathroom). Picture windows along two walls provide a view of Uptown and the neighborhoods directly south. Matisse prints are scattered along one wall. A Persian rug and a giant flat-screen TV dominate the living room. The kitchen is visible down a small corridor. There are airplane hangars that would envy this kind of space. Mike takes a step forward and turns to the rest of us, as if he's the host of this shindig (which he more or less is).

"All right, what are we looking for?" he asks.

I look over the place. "Anything about the Impact File, the Green River Project, or Dustin Felt. Or Donna Rousch. Or Durham, Wisconsin."

"So, just that," Mike says.

Lars claps a hand on each of our shoulders. "Not to worry. We're an unbeatable team. Let's get started. I'm going to make a sandwich."

He lets go of our shoulders and starts down the hallway to the kitchen before I can stop him. Son of a… I turn to Mike. "Why don't you take the upstairs?" I say, "I'll look around down here. Maybe Erbert and Gerbert in there will give us a hand when he gets a chance."

Mike climbs the winding staircase. I wander around the living room until I see a study. I step into it and look around. It's just a desk, a few chairs and a couch. I search the desk, but don't find anything. I feel around the walls. No secret passages or a safe or anything. It's looking like Alex Hollins didn't keep anything here. At least nothing worth finding. Maybe this was a waste of time.

All that proves to be irrelevant once we get jumped.

CHAPTER TWELVE

As a society, we tend to venerate those who are extremely focused. One drawback to that kind of focus is the inability to see the bigger picture. You get so focused on the me-wantee aspects of what drives you that you don't think about consequences. You don't take the chess game approach of thinking four or five moves ahead. You become Daffy Duck as Robin Hood, trying to remember the sequence and what part of it must have gone wrong.

I'm feeling very Daffy myself right at the moment. And I never could play chess to save my ass.

There is a tremendous crash from upstairs. I rush into the main room, worried that Mike has fallen over something or possibly killed somebody. (This *is* Mike we're talking about.)

A few seconds later, two bodies tumble into view, crashing through a door. In the thin light, I can't get a clear look at them. One is dressed in black and has a big bulldog head. That's obviously Mike. The other guy is, near as I can tell, buck ass nude. That makes identification rather more difficult. The two of them are locked together like two kids on a playground trading haymakers. (Or a reasonable facsimile.) Suddenly, they come tumbling down the stairs.

The whole thing sounds like a Warner Brothers cartoon. ("Oof! Ah! Gah! Oy! Kretch!") They sprawl at the bottom of the stairs. Amazingly, they're both still intact. Even more amazingly, they're both still trading punches. (Actually, they're closer to slaps. Really wussy slaps.) I circle around them, my back to the stairs, looking for a way to help Mike.

I don't get the opportunity. Someone hits me from behind. I wind up face down on the hardwood floor, with someone thrashing away on top of me. Fingernails rake one of my cheeks and slash across my ear. Then someone has two handfuls of my hair and is trying to slam my head into the floor. I try to get out from under this person, but they follow my every move. It's like one of those nightmares where something has got you pinned, and you can't get up. Except this shit hurts a hell of a lot more.

It stops all at once, accompanied by a high pitched, "Hey!" The pressure on my back is relieved. I roll over and find myself among a collection of tomatoes, bread and lettuce (all covered in oil). The front door is being wrenched open and what looks to be a female form is fleeing, silhouetted in the hall light. Lars stands over me, holding a half a loaf of French bread.

"You okay, brother?" he asks.

"Who was that?" I ask.

"Not sure. A woman, I think. She looked to be naked. Or maybe that was wishful thinking on my part. I saw her attacking you and I had to help."

I start to get up. "What did you do?"

"I hit her with my sandwich."

On the one hand, I should be pissed with Lars for taking the time to satiate his appetite in the middle of a sensitive operation. On the other hand, I can't help being touched that he sacrificed his sandwich for the greater good. We turn to Mike, who's still rolling around on the floor with The Nude Bandit.

The two of them roll toward the sofa. We wait for the naked guy to roll on top of Mike before we make our move. Lars gets the guy under one armpit, and I get him up the other. We manage to pull him off Mike. Mike springs up and helps us secure the guy. We wrestle him over to the sofa and toss him down. The fight finally leaves him, as he realizes he's outnumbered. Lars flips on a table lamp.

I find myself staring at Payton Hicks. Pretty much all of him.

Hicks crosses his legs. "You mind getting me something to…cover…myself."

Lars agrees to help, dashing up the stairs to the bedroom. Mike and I position ourselves on Hicks's right and left, giving him no escape route. Lars returns with a lush red velvet robe and a sizeable canary yellow bath towel. He tosses Hicks the bath towel and puts on the robe. Lars's fingers trace the large heart on one of the lapels. Hicks pulls the towel over his torso. I look to Lars and Mike.

"Check the hallway," I say, "See if the woman is still out there."

They step out while Hicks and I stare at each other, saying nothing. They return, both shaking their heads.

"No go, brother," Lars says, "All quiet on the western front."

If anybody is going to spot a naked or near-naked woman, it would be Lars and Mike. I'll take their word on it. Hicks, surprisingly, is able to make eye contact with me.

"Is there something I can do for you, Mr. Davis?" he asks, "Before I call the police?"

"I need to ask you some questions," I say.

"You can ask. I'm under no obligation to answer."

"I thought that's what you'd say."

I take out my cell phone and punch in a message. A few seconds later, the response comes. I sit next to Hicks on the couch, hefting the phone in my hand.

"Here's the deal," I say, "Right now, there is a high-powered rifle aimed at your heart. All I have to do is give the word to the person holding the rifle and you're going to be saying hi to Alex Hollins in the great hereafter. You get me?"

Hicks's jaw tightens. "You're bluffing."

"You probably think I am." I tap another message into the phone, then nod toward a vase on the side table. "That thing valuable?"

"No," Hicks says.

"That's a shame."

There's a *whump* somewhere near the window. Then the vase shatters. Hicks throws his hands over his head. Mike jumps back a few feet. Lars calmly chews what's left of his sandwich. I set the phone down.

"That was a little demonstration," I say, "The next bullet hits home. You feel like talking?"

Hicks pulls his hands away, looking over the vase's mangled corpse. "Yes. I'd…I'd love to chat with you. Here. In the nude."

I get up from the couch, putting some distance between me and Hicks. He might get shot and come on, the dude's naked. I grab a chair from the dining room table and drag it opposite the sofa. Hicks's eyes constantly move toward the window.

"Can I…ask what it is you're doing here?" he says.

"I might ask you the same thing," I say. (I know, Dad. It's impolite to answer a question with a question, but…) "Seeing as how this apartment belongs to Chelsea Hollins."

"Actually, it belonged to Alex."

"Who left most everything to Chelsea," I say, "So, what are you doing here?"

"Alex used to let me use the apartment when I had…need of it. Chelsea and I came to the same arrangement."

"Uh-huh. I assume you weren't working late."

Hicks carefully slicks his hair, rudely ruffled by the fight with Mike and I'm guessing, other activities. "I was…entertaining."

Mike snorts. I cut him off with a look. We *do* need Hicks's cooperation here. Lars returns to the kitchen, probably to make himself a replacement sandwich. He doesn't bother to clean up the detritus of the first sandwich. I turn to Hicks again.

"Who was it you were…entertaining?" I ask.

Hicks's eyes search the room. "I'm afraid I can't tell you that."

"Really? You're not going to be cooperative?"

"Not on that subject. No."

He's sweating. I could probably browbeat him on this subject, but I'm sure Deirdre is freezing out there. And the naked woman might be calling the police right now. I have to pick my battles.

"The Impact File," I say, "Tell me about that."

Hicks pauses in slicking back his hair. "Where did you hear about that?"

"Not important," I say, "What *is* important was a meeting between you, Alex, your assistant Kendall and Dustin Felt. A meeting in which you all apparently discussed the file. Which is interesting because you told me you'd never met Dustin. It's also interesting that the only record of the meeting is a paper copy of the notes Alex apparently kept."

Hicks mutters under his breath. "Son of a bitch…"

"Shortly after this meeting, Dustin Felt was fired from Hankerson-William. He contacted a reporter named Al Castillo but didn't make the meeting. Instead, he turned up dead in a little town in Wisconsin called Durham. It's a very interesting chain of events, don't you think?"

There is silence. Hicks's body is still but the look in his eyes gives me the unmistakable impression he'd like to bolt from the sofa and strangle me with his bare hands. Then his eyes cut toward the window. He tries licking his dry lips.

"Are you accusing me of something?" he says.

"Not at the moment," I say, "I just thought I'd get your take on it. Seeing as how you're rather closely involved with all of it."

He's breathing heavier now. He's either nervous or on the verge of a coronary. Perhaps both. He slaps a hand on his thigh, a little show of temperament.

"What is your interest in all this?" Hicks asks, "It can't just be about a fundraiser."

That brings me up short. I've unwittingly blown my cover. No one concerned about a fundraiser is breaking into apartments in Uptown in the middle of a frosty February night. The only story that makes sense is the truth. But I can't tell him that. Payton Hicks is the kind of guy who would go directly to Jim Street and tell him everything he knew. Mike senses my discomfort and steps into the breach.

"We represent an interested party in this case," Mike says, "We're doing some investigation for them."

Hicks doesn't seem impressed. "What interested party is this?"

"We could tell you that," Mike says, "but then our friend with the high-powered rifle would have to splatter you all over that nice sofa. Then nobody wins. Especially the sofa."

Hicks's face goes red. "I understand completely. Please ask me anything you like."

"The Impact File," I say, "It has something to do with the Green River Project, right?"

"We put Dustin Felt in charge of it," Hicks says, his voice getting quiet, "I'm being honest when I say I barely knew Dustin. He had apparently done some environmental work for us in the past. He was known as a bit of a fanatic on the subject. At least, according to his file. But Alex seemed convinced that would just mean Dustin was thorough. We were sure the project was completely safe."

"But the Impact File said otherwise," I say.

"Yes. It said that seepage into the groundwater would eventually make its way into the drinking water. There would be drastic long-term health effects for anyone who lived near the mine. And the radius for *near* was pretty large. The report went over it again and again and in great detail." He clenches an ineffectual fist. "Absolutely everything the DFLers had been trumpeting in the press was right there in the file. It was a disaster."

"So, you decided to bury it."

Hicks picks at the hem of the towel. "You have to understand, it's going to be years—decades, really—before any of those long-term effects are felt. By that time, the company will be able to build a credible wall between what we knew and what we didn't know. It's also possible that Hankerson-William will have sold the mine and be completely out of it by then. All we had to do was keep that report quiet. That's what I advocated, anyway."

"And Alex went along with this?" I ask.

"He did. At first. He agreed to suppress the report and remove any trace of its existence. We swore everyone in the meeting to secrecy. Only Dustin didn't agree."

"Because he had a conscience?"

Hicks gives me a sour look. "We assigned Dustin Felt to collate the information, run an analysis, and present a report. He did that. What we do with the information is our business."

"Save for the people who were going to be poisoned," I say, "But why let that get in the way of a good time?"

Hicks drops his eyes. "Dustin badgered us about what we were going to do with the file. When we didn't give him the answers he wanted, he threatened to go to the press. We had no choice but to let him go."

"But he tried to go to the press, anyway," I say.

"That was unfortunate," Hicks says, "It wouldn't have come to anything. Every part of the Impact File was property of Hankerson-William. It would have simply been Dustin's word against ours."

"But pretty crappy publicity."

"Those who hated the project already would have believed Dustin," Hicks says, "Those who backed the project would believe us. Very little would change."

He seems sincere in saying that. But there are always those timid souls who sit on the fence between two parties. What would their opinions be if Dustin shouted long enough, loud enough, demanding the release of the Impact File? But all that is speculation and Hicks isn't likely to engage in it.

"Alex held on to a paper copy of the meeting notes," I say, "Did he keep a copy of the Impact File?"

Hicks looks up and away. He pauses a second before saying, "I don't believe so."

Mike jumps toward me, waving a finger at Hicks. "He's lying. You see that? Looks up and away. Pauses before answering. Those are two tells. The son of a bitch is lying."

A vaguely offended look drifts across Hicks's face (offset by the panic in his eyes). "How would you know that? Are you a cop?"

"No, I, uh, I work the other side of the street," Mike says. Then he lowers his voice as he speaks to me. "You need to know what to avoid. This guy's lying. I'm completely sure of it."

I give Mike a reassuring nod, cueing him to back off. I pick up the cell phone and begin working on a message. "I agree with my friend. You're lying. I'm just going to send a message to my other friend—"

"No!"

"And then we'll wish you a good night," I say, "And good luck. Though you're not really going to have either."

I start to get up, finishing the message as I do. Lars and Mike are already on their way to the front door. Hicks holds a hand out, trying to stop me, half-getting up himself.

"Wait, wait, wait," he says, "I'll tell you." I pause. Hicks's eyes slip toward the window. "Yes. There was an actual copy of the Impact File. A paper copy. Alex had it."

"Where is it now?"

Hicks speaks slowly. "You have to absolutely believe me on this. Please." A breath. "I don't know where the file is. The last I knew Alex had it. He…he was going to release it to the press."

That sends a little charge though me. I completely forget about the phone, focusing all my attention on Payton Hicks. "*Alex Hollins* was going to release the Impact File?"

"I couldn't believe it, either. He was going to kill the project. After everything he'd done to spearhead it, with all the company stood to profit from it…he was going to kill it. He was completely in favor of everything we did until then. Things…changed."

I put two-and-two together. "Because of what happened to Dustin Felt?"

"Yes. He thought he was responsible."

"Why would he have thought that?" I ask.

"Because we fired Dustin. Because we were going to fight him in the press. And in the courts, if necessary. Dustin went into a spiral and...you know what happened. Alex felt responsible for all that. He was going to release the file. Make everything right."

I guess that's one of those cases where you have to forget someone came late to the party and just be glad they came at all. Except coming to the party got Alex killed. I give Hicks my hardest stare. (It isn't that hard, really, but it's all I've got.)

"What were you going to do about Alex releasing the file?" I ask.

Hicks seems thrown by the question. "I tried to talk him out of it. I owed him that much. As a friend and a co-worker. I couldn't let him throw away his whole career like that."

"And that was it?" I ask.

"Of course." Hicks suddenly sees where I'm going with this. His eyes get wide. "You think I killed him? Is that what you think?"

That's exactly what I think. But the vehemence of Hicks's reaction gives me pause. I slip a look to Mike. He nods in response. Hicks is on the up-and-up. Still, I'm having a hard time believing that.

"What do you know about Alex's death?" I ask.

"That some blonde woman stabbed him and that was that. I don't know anything else."

"Do you know who the blonde woman is?"

"No. No idea. I assume the police are looking into it."

"You aren't even curious?" I say, "Alex Hollins is killed by some unknown woman, for some unknown reason, and you're not even curious who she is?"

Hicks looks down and says, lamely, "I just thought the police would handle it. I wouldn't kill Alex. The idea is preposterous."

"Really?" I say, "You *never* considered the idea? Even for a minute?"

"No!" Then Hicks relents slightly. "All right, I'll admit the idea crossed my mind. When you're in extreme situations, extreme thoughts will come. But I never would have followed through on it."

I examine Hicks's face. Again, I read sincerity. (Nothing but sincerity as far as the eye can see and Jesus, why is *that* in my head right now?) Furthermore, if Hicks was bullshitting us, Mike would be quick to point it out. I prop my forearm on my knee.

"You're not going to tell me who just ran out of here?" I ask.

Hicks's voice becomes small. "I can't tell you. It's between her and I."

I look toward Mike, who briefly cuts his eyes toward the window. Ugh. I *could* threaten to have Deirdre shoot him, but it would be a bluff. And what if Hicks called me on it? I'm not going to have a guy killed because he won't share the identity of the woman sharing his bed. Not when there are more important things with which I can threaten him. I join Hicks on the sofa.

"Here's the deal," I say, "My friends and I are going to leave. You're going to forget we were ever here. If a cop, a thug, a candy striper—I don't care who it is—comes up to me and accuses me of something or tries to make a move on me, my friend out there is not going to be happy. You can probably imagine what will happen next."

Hicks's voice is hoarse. "I can. Yes."

"We'll keep this between ourselves," I say, "I would suggest passing that along to *your* friend. Wherever—and whoever—she is. Understand?"

"I do. Yes. Definitely." Hicks's skull looks like a bobblehead.

I get up from the sofa and walk to the door with Mike and Lars, who is apparently taking his sandwich to go. I hope he doesn't finish it too soon. If the woman who attacked me is lurking around out there, Lars may have to defend me with it. As we slip out the door, I send a message to Deirdre, telling her we're clear. She responds a moment later.

Did you get anything interesting?

I punch in my response: *Maybe a few leads.*

You sure you don't want me to kill him?

NO. I WILL FIGURE THIS OUT.

A moment later, Deirdre's response: **Make it soon. Before I come up with a new plan.**

A feeling of dread runs through me. Just what would that new plan entail? Killing everyone involved? Killing Jim Street? Killing me? I don't like any of those options.

Certainly not the last one.

***

"It's a matter of ingenuity," Lars says, moving a chair to a corner of the lobby, "If you have a goal in mind, you can't let anything stop you. Money, the media, government restrictions…"

"Common sense," I say.

Lars turns to Carol and waves a hand toward me. "Naysayers."

I hold up my hands. Aside from being outnumbered, I can't deny the facts looking me in the face. The Kellen Community Center is once again a heated facility. If the place doesn't exactly look appealing, it's at least clean. The rubbish has either been thrown out or moved out of sight. A few strategic curtains screen off the graffiti and the holes in the walls. The place looks exactly as it ought to: presentable but badly in need of funding to make it look pretty.

"I'm guessing the next step is to decorate for the party?" I say.

"Way ahead of you," Lars says. He rummages behind the front desk and comes up with a box of decorations, flourishing a stream of crepe paper. "We'll do this place up in no time."

"Make it look like the prom from *Carrie*, will you?" I say.

"Haven't seen it," Lars says, "But if it's a lovely and festive space, that's what I'm aiming for."

I clap a hand on his shoulder. "I'm sure you'll get there."

Lars gives me a little bow. Carol looks toward the front door and absentmindedly pulls at her ponytail. She's in her usual professional attire, highlighted by the black trench coat, but she looks haggard. I step over to her while Lars spreads the decorations out on the counter.

"Any sign of your friend Evie?" I ask.

"Not yet," Carol says, "I just hope they get here. Clothed and sober, preferably."

"But you'll take one or the other?" I ask.

"I'll be lucky if I get *one*," she says.

Carol and I walk down the hall to the dilapidated gymnasium, where the bulk of the fundraiser will be held. It's a decent-sized place. Sunlight filters through the cracked windows. However, the warped floor and the dirty backboards, at least one of which is missing a hoop, give it a forlorn feeling. Carol and I stand in the doorway.

"Lars has done good work," I say, "The fundraiser should be a success."

"Should be," Carol says, "I hope you live to see it. Are you getting any closer to getting your friend out of town?"

"Maybe. I talked to Payton Hicks at Hankerson-William. It was…interesting."

I fill in Carol on the visit to Chelsea's apartment in the city and what we found. Her eyes bug out, then she gets an annoyed look. I suspect she's miffed at being left out of the excursion. Then she probably realizes I didn't want Lars and Mike along in the first place. More would definitely not have made for merrier.

"Who do you think the woman in the apartment was?" she asks.

"I don't know. It was semi-dark, and Lars didn't get a good look at her. I didn't see her at all. Mike was a little preoccupied."

"Lars didn't see *anything*?"

"Nothing he could identify. It's a guy thing. When you see bare flesh, it tends to distract from other features."

Carol power-rolls her eyes. "Dear Lord…"

I lean against the doorframe. "If I had to take a guess, I'd say it was Chelsea Hollins."

"What makes you say that?"

"It's her apartment. Hicks would have needed Chelsea's approval to use it. He asked Chelsea out once upon a time. They've stayed good friends. When I saw them together, when they thought they were alone, they looked very…comfortable with each other."

"I suppose you've got a point."

"There's also the matter of the Impact File. Hicks knew Alex was going to release it." I turn toward Carol. "I've been wondering if this thing is personal or professional. If Hicks stands to lose a fortune in business *and* he's sleeping with Alex's wife, he's got *both* reasons to hire Deirdre."

Carol twists her mouth to one side. "But it doesn't explain the double cross. Why would he hire Deirdre to kill Alex and then pull the rug out from under her?"

"I don't know. It's like when I was in math class in high school or college. I'd work on a problem, know all the information was there, but I couldn't remember the damn formula to put it all together. And God forbid someone would ask me to show my work."

"They tend to do that in these situations."

This just gets better and better. A case where it feels like the more information I gather, the further I get from the answer. On the bright side, Carol's friend Evie arrives, her addict/boyfriend in tow, to distract me from my troubles. Carol practically sprints down to the lobby. Evie appears to be using Shawn to stay upright.

"Hey lady," Evie says, her voice a little smoky, her words a little slurred, "How's tricks?"

Shawn seems happy but can't muster any actual words. Say what you will about the morality of the situation, they *do* appear to be having a good time. And that's the only thing that looks good about their appearance. Evie wears a ratty parka over a soiled skirt and ripped leggings. Her eyes are glassy, and her face is flushed (though everyone in Minnesota has a flushed face this time of year). She has new makeup applied over the dried remains of her old makeup. Shawn wears a blue hoodie with no jacket or hat. I doubt he's wearing gloves, since his hands are jammed into the pockets of his jeans.

"What the hell are you two doing?" Carol says.

Evie focuses her bleary eyes on Carol. "We're having a good time. Just a little coffee. And whiskey. And blow."

I stroll up behind Carol. "All FDA approved," I say.

Carol tries to elbow me in the stomach but misses. Evie blearily recognizes me.

"Joe Davis!" she says, "Has anyone told you how funny you are?"

"This morning?" I say, "No."

Carol steps between us, turning her lecture on Shawn. "What happened to your coat?"

Shawn's voice is jovial. "No fucking clue."

Carol moves to one side of Evie, as if she can disguise the conversation from Shawn. (Judging by the state of him, she might pull that off.) "You are supposed to be keeping him on the straight and narrow," Carol says, "You think this is how it's done?"

"Carol," Evie says, "has anyone told you how much you resemble an albatross?"

I shouldn't laugh, but I do. Come on. How often do you hear someone called an albatross? And how often do they perfectly fit the description? Carol gives me a glare, clamming me up. She turns to Evie.

"This isn't what I asked you to do," Carol says.

Evie dismisses this with a cluck of her tongue. "You didn't say I had to keep Shawn from having a good time. I'm just supposed to *pretend* to keep him from having a good time. You're supposed to be helping me with that by lying to his dad." She points at Carol (or at least one of the three Carols she's seeing). "You're really dropping the ball here, babe."

Again, I have to laugh. Carol looks ready to strangle someone and just about any someone will do. Lars steps out from behind the desk and walks toward the front door, his eyes fixed on something.

"Carol, isn't that your boss?" he asks.

Instantly, everyone's head spins toward the front door (except for Shawn, who now seems incapable of movement). Sure enough, Mr. Pratt is stalking up the front walk of the community center. Carol's eyes widen. My heart is in my throat. Only Evie seems unconcerned.

"Fuck him," she says, waving a hand, "He needs to lighten up. Most of you guys do." Her head lolls toward Lars. "'Cept maybe you. You look cool."

Lars glides up to her. "Oh, I'm cool, sister. You want a look around the place? You and your, uh, friend over there?"

Evie shrugs, nearly dropping Shawn in the process. "Sounds like fun." She looks toward the back hallway. "You got anything back there?"

Lars guides Evie and Shawn across the lobby. "Oh, I'm sure we'll find something. If not, we'll just make our own."

Evie pats Lars on the shoulder as she stumbles. "I fuckin' knew you'd be a good time."

When the Katzenjammer Kids disappear into the distance, Carol bolts to the front door, arriving in time to meet Mr. Pratt. She whips open the door.

"Mr. Pratt!" she says, "So good to see you. What are you doing here?"

The boss seems impervious to Carol's friendly greeting. His eyes search the room. "I'm looking for my son."

"Here?" Carol says, "Why would you think he's here?"

Mr. Pratt removes his phone from his coat pocket and holds it up. "I can track him. Since I haven't heard much from him or his sponsor lately, I put an app on his phone that lets me track where he's at. According to the app, he's here."

I take a half-a-second to contemplate how close we're getting to *Star Trek* (two hundred years before *Star Trek*). I look around the lobby, not as casually as I'd hoped, and see that Lars and the kids have disappeared. Carol makes a show of being befuddled.

"I haven't seen him," Carol says.

"You mind if I take a look around?" he asks.

"Of course," Carol says through a forced smile, "A very brief look around."

Mr. Pratt pushes his way through the door and looks around the lobby. He doesn't seem to remember me. Or seem remotely interested in *trying* to remember me. He slips off his leather gloves and holds them in one hand, smacking them into the palm of the other.

"They've got to be here," he says.

"I don't know," Carol says, playing dumb, "Is there a problem with the app?"

Mr. Pratt starts to retort, then hesitates. He looks at the phone. "I *did* just get the damn thing."

"See?" Carol says, tamping down a laugh of relief, "Why don't I help you look around?"

Carol leads Mr. Pratt toward the staircase on the opposite side of the lobby, far from the Katzenjammer Kids in the gym. Mr. Pratt calms slightly in Carol's presence. She slips me a look that says *Get Evie and Shawn the hell out of here before we get back.* I run across the lobby, heading for the gym. If I recall correctly, there isn't much back where Carol and Mr. Pratt went. Just meeting rooms and storage. Time is of the essence.

Lars and the kids are in the gym. That part is good. Shawn is stretched out on the dusty gym floor. Evie's on her knees next to him, laughing to beat hell. That's not so good.

"You've got to get up," Evie says, "We can't sleep here."

Shawn snags her head, pulling it toward him. "Who said anything about sleep?"

A second later, the two of them are rolling around on the gym floor, making out furiously and kicking up clouds of dust. Lars half-heartedly reaches toward them.

"You, uh, you can't do that here," he says, uncomfortable as the voice of authority.

They ignore him, as could be expected. I take a few steps into the gymnasium and give them my best stage whisper (which carries more than I'd like, thanks to the acoustics).

"Your dad is here," I say, "He's looking for you."

That gets their attention. They freeze in position. Shawn looks at me upside down, an expression of abject panic on his face.

"What's he doing here?" the kid asks.

"He's tracking you with an app," I say.

Shawn slides out from under Evie and pulls out his cell phone. "The son of a bitch."

I don't know who he feels more betrayed by, his father or his phone. Frankly, I don't care. We've got to get Shawn and his "sponsor" the hell out of Dodge. They both bounce to their feet, then stagger. Lars guides them toward the hallway and then to the lobby. Carol and Mr. Pratt have not returned. There's a clear path to the front door. All of a sudden, the Hee-Haw gang comes to a halt in front of me. I crash into Lars.

"What the hell are you doing?" I ask.

His voice is filled with dread. "Iris."

I poke my head around Lars's shoulder and sure as shit, Iris is coming up the front walk. As usual, she looks gorgeous and not particularly happy. Evie and Shawn don't know who she is, but they sense the trouble. Iris whips open the front door and storms into the lobby, pulling the hood of her white parka away from her face. She freezes at the sight of Lars's hand around Evie's waist.

"What the fuck is going on?" Iris asks, her voice ringing through the lobby.

Lars gives her a weak smile. "Honey! What a…surprise."

Iris looks at Evie. "Who's this whore?"

Oh boy. Let the games begin. Lars slips his hand away from Evie and moves toward Iris. Evie, though, steps in front of Lars.

"Who's *this* whore?" Evie asks.

The question is barely out of Evie's mouth before Iris attacks. She opens by punching Evie in the forehead. Evie reels. Lars manages to sidestep her, and she crashes into Shawn. Shawn sprawls. Lars and I back away. No sense getting involved.

To her credit, Evie is not felled by the force of Iris's blow. She spins around, annoyed, her eyes holding a focus they haven't had heretofore. "Fuck you, bitch!" is how Evie greets her, before tackling Iris to the floor.

Normally, Lars and I and, I suspect, Shawn would be completely into a cat fight breaking out in front of us. (Though I'd probably be the only one to feel a little guilt over my enjoyment. But only a little.) This, however, is not an occasion to enjoy. Both Lars and Shawn make half-hearted attempts to pull the ladies apart. I keep an eye on the stairs.

And get a perfect view of Carol and Mr. Pratt approaching.

I start up the stairs. The melee is temporarily screened from view. The sounds, however, echo throughout the lobby. My approach brings Carol and Mr. Pratt to a halt.

"I'm sorry," I say, "We've got a situation down here."

Mr. Pratt looks confused. Carol asks, "What kind of situation?"

"Oh, just a little disturbance," I say. This is followed by Iris screaming, "Die, you fucking whore!" I stay focused on Carol and Mr. Pratt. "Okay, maybe a big disturbance."

Mr. Pratt comes down a few steps, trying to get a look at the proceedings. That forces me to come up a few steps and cut him off. Carol grabs Mr. Pratt's arm. He cranes his neck.

"What's going on over there?" he asks.

I block his view. "You know what happens in these neighborhoods. People come in when they aren't supposed to. Don't want to leave. It's nothing to worry about. We've got the situation under control." This is followed by Evie screaming, "I will piss in your dead skull!" I add, "More, uh, more or less."

"Maybe we should give them a chance to clear the room," Carol says.

"Good idea," I say, "This should only take a minute." This is followed by Iris screaming, "I will rip out your vag and shove it down your throat!" I add, "Maybe, maybe two minutes."

Mr. Pratt allows Carol to drag him up the stairs and out of sight. I drop back to the lobby and find things unchanged from thirty seconds ago. Iris and Evie are rolling on the floor, attempting to do each other grievous bodily harm. Lars and Shawn are hesitating to get involved.

"Would you break this fucking thing up?" I tell them, "We need to get them the hell out of here!"

I'm not sure what clinches it, my tone of voice or the urgency of the situation, but Lars and Shawn finally dive into the fray. After a few fraught seconds, they're able to pull the two women apart. Lars has Iris around the waist, hoisting her into the air and carrying her across the lobby. Her hair has been pulled out of its ponytail and her white parka has been torn. She kicks the air with her heavy boots. Lars, showing a strength I didn't know he had, carries her into a back office and kicks the door shut behind them. Shawn grabs Evie's arms and pulls her toward the front door. Evie looks unchanged, save for a black eye and a cut lip (which actually fits with her overall aesthetic). They get out the front door, treating the lobby to a blast of cold air. Both women spend a goodly chunk of the time screaming threats to each other. Finally, the various doors close, and I'm left alone in the lobby.

Well, that went swimmingly.

A few minutes later, Carol and Mr. Pratt come down the stairs. Neither of them sees me or seem remotely concerned about the scuffle. As soon as they reach the lobby, Mr. Pratt straightens his tie, tips his cap to me, and hustles out the front door. Carol carefully puts her ponytail back in place. She runs a hand over her blouse. I approach her.

"The kids got away," I say.

"Good, good," Carol says, throwing her scarf over her blouse and pulling her coat closed, "I'm glad to hear that."

"Nice job distracting Mr. Pratt."

"Good. That's…good."

"How did you do it?"

"Oh, I just took him to the back. And…started making out with him."

Ah. That would do the trick. I open my mouth to reply, but I've got nothing. I'm half-hoping Carol is kidding. But I know she's not.

"I guess…" I say, struggling for the words, "We should probably…" Carol puts a hand over her face. "It's not that bad," I say, "After all…"

I'm interrupted by noise coming from the office where Lars and Iris are stationed. (That's fine. I had no follow up to *after all*.) There's a lot of shouting and crashing. I'm worried Iris is tearing apart either Lars or the office apart. (Really, it's hard to wreck either of them. They're both kind of a shambles.) Then Iris's voice rings out.

"That's it!" she screams, "That's it, my man! Rip my tits off!"

I take Carol by the arm and lead her out of the lobby. She throws a few looks back before we're through the doors and into the cold.

"What the hell is wrong with them?" she asks.

"I don't know," I say, bracing against the cold, "But apparently, it's the same thing that's wrong with everyone lately."

***

On more than one occasion, I've compared my relationship with Mike to that of a parent and a child. That's accurate only in that I'm privy to whatever idiot thing Mike has done and I offer criticism and correction (which is roundly ignored). Where it's inaccurate is that he actually shares this information with me, which is more than he offers his actual parents. Frankly, I'm not sure who comes out ahead. Watching Mike pace the floor of my apartment, running his hand through his hair and fighting the urge to chain smoke (something strictly verboten at my place, though he smells as if he's been doing it off-site) I'm feeling like the loser.

"I'm in trouble," Mike says, "I think it's all fucked now."

"At Fong's?" I ask, turning away from the column I had been working on.

"No. At the Vikings' practice squad. Of course, at Fong's, you moron!"

One would suspect it has something to do with Mike's people skills. But I know it's something else. "What happened?" I ask.

Mike kneads the stocking cap in his hands. "Ron got a little shaken up."

Glaven. "And by 'shaken up,' you mean…?"

Mike trudges over to the breakfast bar and drops on to a stool. I fetch a grape soda out of the fridge, thinking it might induce him. I can't help speculating what we'd be doing if the weather was warmer. Probably hanging out on the deck, giving me the chance to enjoy the sunshine and Mike the chance to chain smoke. (Yep. Definitely getting cabin fever here.)

"Ron got into an accident," Mike says, "There's a…chance I might have had something to do with it."

"How?" I ask, drawing the word out.

"I don't know," Mike says, "I cut his brake line. That might have had something to do with it."

I drop on to a stool. "Mike!"

He throws his hands out. "I didn't mean for him to get hurt! Things just got out of hand."

If there's a better description of Mike's entire adult life, I haven't heard it. Squiggy, always wary of Mike, watches from the edge of the futon, ready to escort Mike out if necessary.

"Why don't you give me the whole story?" I say.

Mike takes a bracing sip of his grape soda. "Okay, Ron was hanging out at the restaurant during the afternoon. We get almost no deliveries then. The asshole was spending his time talking up Biyu. And she didn't stop him."

"So naturally, you…"

"Decided to cut his brake lines, yeah." He holds his hands up, asking me to hear him out. "It's a little thing I learned to do in auto shop in high school. You just drain the brake fluid out and then the brakes are useless."

"Good to know your education didn't go to waste."

"I didn't want Ron to get hurt. I thought he'd have to brake as he's leaving the parking lot, he wouldn't make it and he might just bump into the sign on the edge of the lot. Just enough to take his car out of commission and leave me to do most of the deliveries." Another sip of grape soda. "How the hell was I supposed to know Ron never hits the brakes going out of the parking lot? Or for the first few blocks of a delivery?"

"Where did he learn that trick?" I ask.

Mike chews a corner of his goatee. "I might have taught it to him. Anyway, Ron took a delivery and got as far as Ramsey Hill before he realized he didn't have brakes."

Dear God. Ramsey Hill is just down the street from my place. It connects the Cathedral Hill area with downtown St. Paul and has a gradient that best resembles a ski jump.

"Wait a minute," I say, "it's *blocks* from Fong's to Ramsey Hill. How the hell did Ron not realize his brakes were out before then?"

"He caught all the lights," Mike says, "and he ran a few stop signs. One of those tricks he must have picked up from someone." He's careful to avert his eyes.

"All right, what happened to Ron?"

"Well, the details are fuzzy," Mike says, "Between the speed of what happened and Ron shitting his pants—literally and figuratively—it was a little hard to piece together. Rollover. Street signs down. Jaws of life. Pins in Ron's ankle. I didn't catch all the details. Bottom line: I might be in trouble."

"*You* might be in trouble?"

"The good part is no one saw me working on Ron's car. But Biyu hasn't talked to me. She's all concerned about Ron. Even went down to the hospital to visit him." He sighs. "Some guys have all the luck."

I slip off the stool and step over to the coffee maker, pouring myself a refill. It was only a matter of time before Mike got homicidal, even unintentionally so. It's not that he's unconcerned about Ron (or so I keep telling myself), it's just that Mike's eternal self-involvement won't allow for it. And I'd be lying if I said I didn't welcome the distraction. (Sorry, Ron.)

I step past Mike and return to the desk. The blinds are closed and it's starting to irritate me. Even if the only view is a monochrome landscape, it was at least *something* to look at.

Or maybe it's not having the option to open the damn things. Maybe it's just feeling stuck in a situation and not seeing the path out.

My cell phone rings. It's Jim Street. How the hell did he get this number? And why the hell is he calling? My heart pushes up into my throat. I answer it, trying to sound calm.

"Joe Friday's Cop Shop," I say, "You mug 'em, we plug 'em. Hunter speaking. How can I help you?"

Street, though, doesn't have time for my bullshit. He opens the conversation with, "Chelsea Hollins is dead."

And just like that, *I* don't have time for my bullshit, either.

CHAPTER THIRTEEN

I don't know about you, but when someone dies suddenly, it overshadows everything else about them. It's like their entire life was lived specifically for this end. Kobe Bryant, Amy Winehouse, Kurt Cobain, Marilyn Monroe. I wasn't there for all those deaths, but for the ones in which I was, the end became the most significant thing about them. For a time, anyway.

I wonder sometimes if we ever get over that sudden end. Can you really talk about John F. Kennedy without talking about Dallas? Sometimes, the end is all *there is to discuss. William Henry Harrison, for example, was the first president to die in office and he triggered a Constitutional crisis. That's pretty much all history will remember Harrison for. Sure, he was a general and got himself elected President. But he's just another in a line of faceless white guys who pulled that off. And he isn't particularly distinctive as a general-cum-president. Less statesman-like than Washington. Less beloved than Eisenhower. Less psychotic than Jackson. Less spectacularly drunk than Grant. History will remember him for his death and his death alone.*

On the other hand, I know who William Henry Harrison was and he has no idea who I am. So, who am I to judge?

In the years to come (assuming I have years to come), I wonder how I'll remember Chelsea Hollins. First, though, I should get into *why* I have to remember her rather than see her.

"What happened?" is the first question I ask Street.

"That's what we're trying to figure out," Street says, "She was found at her apartment in Uptown. Stabbed in the chest and the abdomen."

"Just like Alex," I say.

"Exactly. You're going to tell me you still haven't heard from your friend?"

I struggle to keep my breathing under control. "I haven't."

I had to answer promptly. If I hesitated, even a second, Street would know I was lying. He lets a breath out through his nose.

"You're at your apartment now?" Street says, and it doesn't sound like a question.

"I am."

"I'll be there in a minute."

Street hangs up. I have no doubt that by *in a minute*, he means exactly that. I set the phone down on the desk and tell Mike that Street is on his way up. He slides off his stool and starts for the backdoor. I catch him by his coat collar.

"You're not going anywhere," I tell him.

"What? You're kidnapping me?"

"You walk out now, and Street will think it was Deirdre sneaking out."

"Where *would* he get that idea?"

"Just sit your ass down," I say.

Mike gives me a sidelong glance, then slowly returns to the breakfast bar, again adopting his grumbly teenager persona. Street buzzes and several seconds later, he and Ric are in my living room, staring at me with twin cop faces. Street wears a bright blue suit with a white shirt and no tie. Ric wears the same cheap gray suit. (Does the guy take *any* fashion advice from his boss?) The cats make no attempt to leave. (Sadly, they're getting used to cops in the place.) Mike keeps his back turned. I stand next to the breakfast bar, trying not to fidget. Good to have the band back together.

"What happened with Chelsea?" I ask.

"Stabbed," Ric says, taking off his stocking cap, sending stray thinning hairs flying in all directions, "Housekeeping service found her in the living room. Called us."

"Someone broke in?"

There's no trace of a grin on Street's face. "Doesn't look like a break-in. There was some stuff out of place in the study. Looked like someone rummaged around."

Despite his studied disinterest, Mike half-turns his head and asks, "Did the neighbors see anything?"

Ric throws him a look. "No, they didn't. Then again, it probably happened in the middle of the night."

"Did Chelsea put up a struggle?" I ask.

"A little bit," Street says, "There was a chair knocked over. A table looked like it was out of place. But it was over pretty quickly." Street's cop eyes bore into me. "It looked like it might have been a professional job, Slick."

"You'd know better than I would."

Street scrutinizes me. The lines in his face are clear, as if he hasn't been sleeping. I fight the urge to look toward the door. I keep wondering if Deirdre is going to walk in. Maybe there's a way to lock the door. Then again, Deirdre would probably just shoot her way in. Street drops his hands into the pockets of his overcoat.

"This one doesn't make sense," he says, "If Deirdre was hired to kill Alex Hollins and that got botched, she wouldn't be taking any other jobs. She's got no motive to kill Chelsea. Unless that *was* Deirdre who broke into the place in Excelsior and Chelsea saw her."

Mike peers over his shoulder. "Killed just for seeing her?"

Ric squares Mike with a look. "Scorched earth. It's how someone like Deirdre stays in business."

Mike and I exchange a look, trying not to be obvious about it. We've seen Deirdre. We've worked with her. Does that *scorched earth* business extend to us? I guess we'll find out, whether we like it or not.

"You don't have any leads on Deirdre?" I ask.

"I have you."

"I'm not a lead," I say, "I don't know anything."

"Or so you would have me believe. But I'm not buying it." Street closes in on me. "Let's quit playing grab-ass, shall we? If Deirdre's been out of sight this long, she's getting help. Who else would give her that?"

"She got to the Twin Cities and tried to carry off a job without my help. She's resourceful enough."

Street strolls around the room, addressing his audience. "You want to know what I think? I think Deirdre was hired to kill Alex Hollins and the whole thing blew up in her face. She needed a place to hide out and she came to you. Maybe you didn't want to help her. But I'm guessing Deirdre has a way of persuading you. You've been hiding her out here. Maybe even trying to help her. Whatever that's supposed to look like." He puts a hand on the breakfast bar, giving me the feeling I'm trapped, even though I've got the rest of the apartment free behind me. "You want out of this?" he asks, "I can get you out. You tell me where Deirdre is, and we'll take care of it from there. You'll be out of the whole thing. What do you say?"

Here's the deal: I'm not an ass-kicker of any kind. I can't beat anybody up (at least not in a fair fight). I don't browbeat people or try to bend them to my will. But I don't like being bullied. I might not fight back with my fists, but I have an unlimited supply of obstinance. I'm not giving up Deirdre when she's innocent.

"You want to know what I think?" I say, sliding away from Street, "I think you know Deirdre didn't do it. But you have no leads, no evidence, nothing but your own suspicion. You're taking a stab in the dark and hoping you can browbeat me into telling you something." I go face-to-face now. "But I can't help you. Because I don't know where Deirdre is. And all the browbeating in the world isn't going to change that."

For a second, Street looks like he's going to take a swing at me. Then a corner of his mouth goes up and the familiar grin returns. He tucks his scarf into his overcoat and smoothly buttons it up. He turns toward Ric.

"I guess the man has nothing to tell us," he says.

Ric slips the gum out of his mouth, stuffs it in a tissue and tosses it in the wastebasket under my desk. "Sounds like it."

Street walks to the door. "You know where to find me."

"And you know where to find me," I say, "You and all of your guys."

"Oh yes, we do," he says.

Street and Ric slip out the door, not even saying goodbye (not that I'm broken up about that). Mike finally turns around.

"That guy," he says, "is a bit of a dick."

"Agreed," I say, "But he's a dick who can put me in jail."

"Let's hope it doesn't come to that."

Again, I'm in agreement with Mike. The question, of course, is: will I figure out what's going on before Street figures out what I'm up to? And will I even live to see that moment?

***

When I was a kid, my parents attended church regularly (they still do), frequently (too frequently for our tastes) dragging my brothers and me along. Despite my best efforts to be bored, some of the sermons linger in my brain. A bit from one of Pastor Tony's sermons that has stayed with me is very simple. He just said, regarding charity work, "You can always do more." In short, don't do a little and then fritter away your time patting yourself on the back. Look for more opportunities. You can always do more.

Watching my friends plot a fundraiser, I'd like to go back and tell Pastor Tony: sometimes you need to do less.

"The band is all lined up," Lars tells Carol, going over an itinerary paper placed in the middle of the table, "Great group. They're exclusively Seventies and Eighties R&B. Something everyone loves."

"What are they called?" Carol asks, picking up her Cosmo.

"Funky Chicken," Lars says, "Trust me. Four of the greatest soul brothers you'll ever meet. Oh, we may need to provide them with a kazoo."

Carol frowns. "There's a kazoo in the band?"

"It's all kazoos," Lars says, as if this should be obvious.

I look down, trying to suppress a laugh that would only irritate Carol. And frankly, we've had enough drama at The Tav lately. The three of us are parked at a high-top by one of the picture windows. The window only affords us a view of the parking lot, but as per usual, it's not like there's anything to see out of *any* of the windows. Lars and Carol are making final plans for the fundraiser. I'm here as an excuse to get out of the house (and away from police surveillance).

Carol puts her head in her hand and then uses the hand to cover talking to me. "Do you still have the friend with a band?"

I speak from behind my pint of Winter Ale. "Keith Prusack? Yeah, we're still friends."

"You think his band would be available on short notice?"

"I can always ask."

"Do it," Carol says, her voice dropping to a hiss.

We sip our drinks. Lars hovers over the itinerary, oblivious to everything else. April, our server, stops by to check on us. She pointedly does not address Lars. Freddie hovers at the bar, staring holes into the back of Lars's head. Our friend may have been allowed to return, but he's practically persona non grata.

Not that his persona needs any grata. Lars is cheerfully oblivious to everything around him. "We've got our speakers lined up," he says, "City Councilwoman Carolyn Pool. Payton Hicks from Hankerson-William. And Brennan Wonka."

Carol's brow creases. "Who is Brennan Wonka?"

"He's a local drug dealer," Lars says, "Decent guy, save for dealing the smack and the crack. I thought it would be important to hear from the exact element we're trying to save the community from. After all, it can't be all ivory towers and charitable intentions."

To her credit, Carol manages to keep her temper. (She *does*, however, gouge the tabletop with her nails). She speaks slowly to Lars, as one might speak to a person coming out of a coma (or still in a coma).

"We are not going to have a drug dealer speaking at our fundraiser," Carol says, "If I see the guy there, I will have him thrown out."

Lars crosses out something on the paper. "Brennan will be very disappointed. He's cleared everything off his schedule. Made quite a few sacrifices. He doesn't appear in public much these days, what with the price on his head and all."

I lean toward Carol. "You *were* looking for entertainment."

Carol uses the back of her hand to gently push me away. "I will find a third speaker," she tells Lars, "Tell your friend Brennan he's out." She sips her Cosmo and mutters, "We'll have enough drug addicts there as it is."

I turn to Carol. "Your friend Evie and her new beau will be there?"

That elicits a cluck of disgust from Carol. "Evie insists on it. She thinks the community center is a good cause."

It's heart-warming when heavy substance abusers take an interest in their community. Judging by the stressed-out look on Carol's face, though, she doesn't see the humanitarian aspects of her friend's outlook. I swirl my beer.

"Evie and Shawn still walking on the wild side?" I ask.

"Oh, they're still wild," Carol says, "They crashed at my place the other night."

My beverage stops short of my lips. "Your place? Why would they do that?"

"Because Shawn is hiding his behavior from his parents. And Evie's roommate threw her out. And because Evie is doing me a favor in this little ruse, I was sort of over a barrel."

"How did that work out?" I ask.

"Oh, they drank three bottles of Stoli, including one of mine. I'm not certain what it was they were putting in the pipe, but it smelled like someone dung-bombed a wig factory. And they had incredibly loud sex until four."

"Four in the morning?" I say.

"No, four in the afternoon," Carol says, "They were at it all night and according to my neighbors, most of the day."

"Coke can give you a lot of energy," Lars says. Then he notices us staring at him. "So I hear," he adds.

Carol returns her focus to me. "Needless to say, I spent a few hours apologizing to my neighbors. And I tried to politely explain to Evie that they can't stay at my place anymore. She was okay with it. Apparently, they found a room at a local hotel."

"They can afford a hotel?" I say.

"No, they break in late at night and leave early in the morning."

Wow. I wonder if they take advantage of the breakfast buffet. I imagine one needs a good breakfast to stoke up for a long day of abusing your body. Lars pauses ever-so-slightly in his writing, telling me he's considering the merits of the idea. I'm sure a completely stupid, entirely unworkable get-rich-quick scheme will arise from this experience.

All this pleasantness is shattered by the arrival of Alberto Castillo. When I first see him, I do a doubletake. I didn't know Castillo hung out at The Tav. I've never seen him here before and I'm here often enough that the odds of us just missing each other constantly are pretty long. I assume he's tracked me down, something he confirms as soon as he arrives at the table, removing his fedora and tossing it down.

"Got some information for you," he says by way of greeting.

I introduce him to Carol and Lars. He shakes Carol's hand. She gives his trench coat an admiring look. He's polite, but it's obviously a strain. I pull out the fourth chair at the high-top.

"Join us, won't you?" I say.

Castillo hesitates, slipping looks to Carol and Lars. "Are you sure about that?"

"Whatever you have to tell me, you can tell them," I say.

He thinks about it a moment, then slips off his trench coat. He carefully drapes it over the back of the chair, undoes a single button on his suitcoat and hefts his bulk into the seat. Carol watches the scene, shocked at watching a guy who actually cares about his clothing. It annoys me a tad. That gives way to curiosity about Castillo's appearance.

"How did you find me?" I ask.

"You've mentioned this place. It didn't look like you were home. I thought I'd take a chance. I didn't want to get into this over the phone."

Nor, I assume, at a crowded local pub. Fortunately, the self-involvement scale at The Tav is rather high, so he's perfectly safe. April comes by and Castillo orders a strawberry margarita. Carol's eyebrows go up. She's impressed with Castillo's taste in girlie drinks. I take a swallow of my beer.

"You said you had info," I say.

"I found out something about Donna Rousch," he says.

I set my beer down. "A connection to Alex Hollins?"

"You might say that. It's more a connection to Chelsea Hollins."

Better and better. "What kind of connection?"

"The most intimate kind," Castillo says, straightening his tie, "Donna Rousch is—or should I say was—Chelsea Hollins."

CHAPTER FOURTEEN

I once had a relationship founder on the notion my girlfriend expected me to be the same person around her friends that I was around her. She couldn't understand why I would not unbend around her friends the way I would around her. "You're so sweet and funny when we're alone, but when you're with my friends, all you do is make smartass remarks." I never met her family—we didn't date that long—but I'm wagering she would have been even more disappointed because she wouldn't have even gotten the smartass remarks.

Now, it's not as if I'm Patrick Bateman from American Psycho, *but I'm not the same person around every group I meet. And I hardly think I'm alone in this area. Can you honestly say you're the same person around your parents that you are around your friends that you are around your co-workers that you are around your significant other that you are around the person you chat with on the bus? All of us have variations on the theme that is us and we apply those variations differently depending on the company. Frankly, I think it's abnormal to be the same person all the time in all settings. If that's the case, you're the human equivalent of humping the same note over and over again on the piano. And if that's the case, I don't want to know what you've got hidden in your basement.*

I'd be *really* curious to know what this old girlfriend would think of someone literally creating a new person for themselves.

For some reason, I'm not comfortable having this conversation with Castillo at the high-top. Too much traffic around. (Although the traffic isn't likely to eavesdrop or care.) There's a small table in the corner, over by the dartboards, that's somewhat secluded. The four of us grab our drinks and head over there, assuring April it has nothing to do with her and asking if she could make sure no other servers disturb us. She is, as always, agreeable, although she does give Lars the stinkeye. Once we're at the table, Castillo puts a file in the center.

"After Chelsea Hollins died, I started doing some research," he says, "According to her biography on the Hankerson-William website, she went to Brenfield Academy, a private school out east, and then attended Purdue University in Indiana. I checked with Purdue. They'd never even heard of her. Same thing with Brenfield Academy. No record of her parents, any family, *any*thing about her. I contacted HR at Hankerson-William to see if I could get a copy of her application and resume. Shockingly, they wouldn't play ball. In fact, the woman seemed anxious to get me off the phone."

"That can't be a new experience for you," I say.

Castillo ignores me. "The more I looked into it, the more I realized that prior to her employment at Hankerson-William, Chelsea Hollins simply didn't exist."

Lars strokes his beard. "A phantom woman."

"More or less," Castillo says.

I set my beer aside. "How did you make the leap to Donna Rousch?"

"Guesswork," Castillo says, "If Donna Rousch was connected to Alex Hollins, I thought I should do some deeper research. I started poking around things in Durham—carefully avoiding the sheriff—and found out a few things about Donna Rousch. She was married right out of high school, to a guy named Roy Rousch. I called Roy a few times before I got him on the line. He called me a prick and said he didn't want to talk about Donna. Then he hung up on me."

"Nice guy," Carol says.

"I can deal with it," Castillo says, giving her a shy smile before returning his focus to the file, "There's no record of a divorce between Roy and Donna. Her official residence is her mother's. The mother's name is Angela Barker. You want to guess what I found out about her?"

"She played the Wicked Witch in a porn version of *Wizard of Oz*," I say, "Had a brief but bitter affair with Ron Jeremy."

Again, Castillo is unfazed. "She's dead."

I stare at the file on the table. "So, I was way off."

Carol sets her drink down. "Was she…?"

"No, nothing like that," Castillo says, "Complications from lung cancer. She died in a hospice facility a few years ago."

"But according to the sheriff, Donna lives with her mother," I say, "She's the primary caretaker to a dead woman?"

"Amazingly, I'm starting to doubt most everything Sheriff Mitchell in Durham told me," Castillo says, "I went online and looked up Donna's graduating class at Durham High School. They have a website and a Facebook page. I found a picture of our Donna."

He slips a picture out of the file and places it in the center of the table. It's one of those senior photos taken on a sunny fall day somewhere in the country. A young woman is propped against a wooden fence, looking distractedly toward the camera. The photographer could have filtered out the sunlight a little better, but the subject of the photo is clear enough. The hair is a little darker and the face a little younger.

But there's no mistaking it: it's the person I knew as Chelsea Hollins.

I pick up the photo, study it for a second, then pass it to Carol, who's been looking at it over my shoulder. "She gets married out of high school," I say, "Leaves the guy. Creates a new persona for herself. Marries Alex Hollins."

"Bigamy, anyone?" Carol says.

"But this Roy Rousch never comes looking for her," I say, "And the sheriff in Durham covers for her. Why would he do that?"

Castillo reaches into the file. "I might have an answer for you there. Got this off the graduating class's website. It's from the Durham High yearbook."

It's the page for the class awards. There are several pictures on the page, but Castillo has been nice enough to circle the photo we're looking for. It's for Cutest Couple. Chelsea/Donna is one half of the couple. The other half is a guy named Scott Mitchell. It takes only a second to put it together.

"Scott Mitchell is the sheriff in Durham," I say.

"Correct," Castillo says, "I did some looking into him. He went into the army right out of high school. Did a two-year stretch. I'm not sure what happened with Donna and Roy, but it must have been pretty whirlwind. Graduation was in June. Mitchell left for the army in July. Donna and Roy were married by October."

Lars props his chin in one hand. "I love an October wedding."

Castillo throws Lars a look, but like the rest of us, is learning to ignore him. "Mitchell comes back from the army and becomes a sheriff's deputy. A few years later, he gets elected sheriff. Shortly after that, Donna Rousch's official residence becomes her mother's."

"And Chelsea Hollins appears in the Cities?" I say.

"That is the case," Castillo says, "It's just speculation but it looks like Mitchell's been using his job as sheriff to cover for Chelsea."

"Why would he do that?" Carol asks.

"If I had to guess," Castillo says, "maybe as a favor to an old friend. Maybe Donna wanted out of Durham and used her old relationship with Mitchell to get his help."

Carol waves a hand, as if trying to clear her thinking. "Wait a minute. I don't get something here. This Roy Rousch guy. Why would he just let Donna disappear? Not go after her or anything?"

Castillo pulls a piece of paper out of the file and sets it on the table. "This is guesswork again. But this is Roy Rousch's record. In addition to a large number of arrests for drunken driving, drunk and disorderly and urinating in public, he was popped a few times for possession with intent to sell. If you look at the dates…" He runs a finger down the paper. "You'll see that these arrests dry up right about the time Donna Rousch would have left Durham."

I sit back. "That was the bargain. You let Donna go and I keep you out of jail."

"Again, it's guesswork," Castillo says, "If I write the story—and I still might—I'll see if Sheriff Mitchell is willing to connect the dots. For now, we can definitely say he was covering for Chelsea. At least on the Durham end."

Carol sips her Cosmo. "What about on the Twin Cities end?"

Castillo props his chin on one hand. "That I couldn't tell you. Once Chelsea rose to a position of prominence, she would have needed someone pretty prominent to cover for her. Alex would seem an obvious choice."

"Or Payton Hicks," I say.

"Or Payton Hicks," Castillo says.

I pick up my beer, though I don't feel much like drinking it (yet). Chelsea Hollins is Donna Rousch. How does that tie into two murders? It has to, right? The coincidence would be too enormous. Alex had to know who Chelsea was. Otherwise, why would the sticky note with Donna Rousch's name be posted in his office? Was Chelsea nervous about having her dual identity exposed and so she killed Alex? But then who killed Chelsea? And why? And why the double-cross of Deirdre? Why hire her at all? Huge news and I have no idea what it means. *Now* I take a sip of my beer.

"What are you going to do with this?" I ask Castillo.

"Print it," he says, "Eventually. Unless you got something better to tell me."

"I don't," I say, "Not yet."

"But you keep telling me you will."

There's an undertone of impatience in Castillo's voice. I can't say I blame him. He knows something is up, he's got a journalist's impatience to break a big story and I keep teasing him with one. And then not delivering. If he knew the kind of pressure I'm under, he might be more understanding. But if he knew the cause of the pressure I'm under, I'd be reading about it in his newspaper. Assuming I lived long enough to do so.

"Go ahead and run it," I say.

Castillo's eyebrows go up. "Really?"

"I don't think it's going to make a difference," I say, "Whoever killed Chelsea is still out there. It's not like they're going to run to ground over this kind of information. You got a story, print it."

"And you can still deliver the bigger story?" he asks, slowly.

"I can. I will." I don't really have a choice, do I?

Castillo considers the matter. He stands up from the table, drapes his coat over one arm and pops the fedora on his head. Carol and Lars watch him, both appreciating the panache.

"Pleasure doing business with you," he says, "You let me know if anything else comes your way."

"Same here," I say, "Maybe we'll wrap this up before the northern classics."

"Or at least the Giro," he says.

Castillo tips his hat to Carol and Lars, slips his coat around him, and departs. Carol watches him go, then turns to me.

"What was that last part about?" she asks.

"Cycling," I say, "We're both into it."

"He's a cyclist?" Carol asks.

"No, he just likes competitive cycling," I say, "I don't know if Castillo's ever been on a bike."

Carol looks in the direction Castillo went and contemplates this. Lars returns to his notes, this flurry of criminal investigation having passed. I'm left to wonder what, if anything, I can do with this information. I get up from the table and go to the bar for another beer. I just need something to help clear my head. Maybe another beer won't help.

But it sure as hell won't hurt.

***

As stated previously, it's not easy getting around my building these days. When two tenants are hiding a fugitive from justice (and one of them is facing the suspicions of his insane girlfriend), things get a little hairy. Normally, I would use the interior stairs to reach Deirdre's temporary pad. Since I can't be sure Iris isn't spying through the peephole or listening at the door of Lars's place, I have to abandon this route. Instead, I go out the backdoor and use the erector set of stairs and decks to get to the second floor. I'll reach Deirdre's deck before Lars's, thus I can avoid prying eyes. The deck hasn't been shoveled (thanks, Lars) so my shoes are full of snow by the time I reach Deirdre's backdoor. I give it the *Last Train to Clarksville* knock and a second later, Deirdre lets me inside. We make our way to the main room. Since the blinds are down, I make a beeline to the front, slip off my shoes and put my wet feet next to the radiator. Deirdre stops by her breakfast bar.

"Going through all this trouble for little ol' me, eh?" she says.

"Figured it would be the best plan," I say, "Things are getting a little dangerous."

"Because of Street?"

"Well, him. And others. Lars's girlfriend thinks you and Lars are having an affair."

Deirdre cocks an eyebrow. "First off, your friend is very nice, but dear God, no. Second, why does his girlfriend know about me?"

I hold up a cautioning hand. "She doesn't. She just knows Lars is skulking around and thinks he's having an affair with someone in the building."

Deirdre throws a look at the door. "I heard them arguing a little while ago. There was a lot of crashing and banging."

"They might have been having sex. It's kind of hard to distinguish between fighting and fucking with them. I'm not sure Iris even tries."

"It's an interesting building. I'll give you that."

"Yeah. I'm thinking maybe it's time we found you a new hiding place, though."

Deirdre wanders into the kitchen and gets a bottle of vodka out of the freezer. "Worn out my welcome, have I?"

"It's not that," I say, "It's just getting a little dangerous around here. I'm not saying you have to be afraid of Iris, but she can certainly create trouble. And with Street's guys watching the place, it's the kind of trouble we really can't afford."

"You aren't getting any closer to getting me out of this mess?"

"I *did* come across some new information," I say.

I fill her in on the info about Chelsea Hollins. Deirdre takes a few pulls off the vodka bottle as she listens. Otherwise, she's completely impassive. (Then again, it's not like she's exactly a live wire at the best of times.) When I'm finished, she sets the vodka bottle on the breakfast bar.

"What does all that mean?" she asks.

"It means Chelsea had a secret to keep," I say, sitting on the shelf over the radiator, "If someone was using that against her, it provides a certain amount of motive."

"But she's dead now. What good does her motive do us?"

"I don't know. I was thinking maybe she killed Alex to keep her secret. But it doesn't explain who might have killed her."

"In short, this may or may not be anything worth talking about," Deirdre says.

A door slams somewhere in the building. It sounds close. Could be my neighbor upstairs or one of the people downstairs. It still gives me the willies. Maybe it's Iris skulking around the hallway, waiting for a chance to spring on Deirdre. We can't keep this up for much longer, can we? I turn to Deirdre.

"I'll figure it out," I say, "Trust me."

Deirdre shrugs, as if to say, "I don't really have a choice."

She takes another pull off the bottle of vodka. I'm impressed by how she can do that without showing any effects. Most people I know either get chatty or slurry when they start slugging hooch like that. My cell phone beeps. Text message coming in. I don't recognize the number. The message reads: *I'm going to call you. Suggest you answer.* A second later, the promised call arrives. I answer after the first ring.

"This is Joe Davis."

"I got your friend," a voice says, "And his girlfriend."

The voice sounds familiar. It's thin and reedy, trying to add some bass. This is the guy who was waiting for me on my deck. Nothing good can come of this.

Okay, maybe we *won't* have to worry about Iris…

CHAPTER FIFTEEN

One of the drawbacks to having friends is the trouble they can get you into. Here's an example.

Back in the day, me and some buddies (Mike, Stoner, Robbie, T.J.) went to an Adams College baseball game. (Go Rangers!) Stoner liked bellowing at the umpires in a loud, gravelly voice that best resembled Vince McMahon using a bullhorn hooked up to an amplifier. "Come on, BLUE!" "That was outside! Use your eyes, BLUE!" As the game progressed, we discovered one of the opposing players had a serious case of rabbit ears. Ergo, we had to heckle him. Since we'd had several beers and were in a loopy mood anyway, we somehow decided the guy must have smelly feet and began taunting him thusly. "What is that stench?" "He's got the stanky feet!" "What's wrong with his shoes?" "Aaaathleeeete's Fooooot!" "There's a fungus among us!" We let Rabbit Ears have it every time a fly ball came his way or when he was up to bat. The way his neck flushed, and he kept glaring at us, we knew we were getting to him.

The climax occurred when Rabbit Ears came up to bat in the seventh inning and we started in with another round of "Smelly feet,"

*"Those poor shoes," and the like. With an 0-2 count, Rabbit Ears finally slammed his bat against the plate, turned to us and shouted, "If you stupid motherf**kers don't knock it off, I'm coming up there and kicking all your asses!" The whole stadium (such as it was) was struck dumb by the outburst. Everyone remained silent while Rabbit Ears stepped back into the batter's box and the Adams pitcher went into his windup. Just as the pitch was about to be delivered, Stoner shouted, "Come on, SHOES!"*

Needless to say, none of us—me, my buddies and Rabbit Ears—saw the end of the game. For further details, I'll have to direct you to the police report.

While I'm pretty sure, Stoner, Robbie and T.J. are in the clear, I'm not sure which friend of mine has been taken hostage. Then I hear a familiar female voice shouting curses at the other end of the line. The guy has taken Lars and Iris. Frankly, I'm not sure who I feel sorry for.

"Where are you?" I ask.

"I'm gonna tell you," the guy says, "but I'm also gonna tell you this: I see one sign of a cop, or a gun, and they're dead. You got me?"

"I do."

"Good. Now, this is what's gonna happen: you're gonna come to an apartment in Uptown. You're gonna bring Deirdre. You're going to hand her over to me. She is not gonna be armed when you guys get there. I've got a gun that's eight inches from your friend's head and it's not going anywhere. Any—and I mean *any*—funny stuff and your friend is a dead man. Did I make all of that clear?"

"You did."

"That's good. Here's the address." He gives it to me. Sure as shit, it's Chelsea Hollins's apartment in the city. Who the fuck is this guy working for? I pretend to scribble down the address. The guy asks me: "You got it?"

"I do."

"Remember the instructions. I'm giving you a half hour."

He hangs up. I lower the cell phone and rest my hands in my lap. Deirdre leans on the breakfast bar.

"What's going on?" she asks. I give her a rundown of the call. We're already on the clock. I'll give the guy credit. The shorter timeframe gives us less chance to fuck around and think of something. "He doesn't want us to try anything?" Deirdre says.

"He does not."

"Sounds like an invitation for us to try something."

"I'm not sure about that," I say, "The guy's got a gun to Lars's head."

Deirdre walks around the breakfast bar. "I'm supposed to come unarmed and throw myself on the mercy of this idiot?"

"In less than half an hour."

She slips a small handgun out of an ankle holster. She fetches a knife from her boot and a slightly larger handgun from a holster behind her back. She lays them all on the breakfast bar.

"Then I guess we better get going," Deirdre says.

"You're going to give up?"

Deirdre smirks. "To this guy? Never. We're just going to think of another way."

Oh. Great.

***

The trip to Uptown doesn't take that long, given that I'm hauling ass down the highway. (There's been no snow recently, so the roads are clear.) I call the guy when I get to the lobby, and he buzzes us in. I'm curious as to how he got access to this particular apartment, but that's on the backburner for now. We have to rescue Lars and Iris. (Well, Lars). We're quiet on the elevator ride up. Deirdre's face is placid. I look as calm as Jim Carrey on a cocaine binge.

We get off the elevator and walk to the door of the apartment. Deirdre stands with her back to it, looking down the hall. I knock gently. A voice says, "It's open." Deirdre and I go inside.

Lars and Iris are on the couch. They've been bound with electrical cord. Both (hallelujah) are gagged. Their captor stands behind them. He looks the same as I remember, except he's dispensed with the leather jacket. His dark hair is slicked back, and his piggy eyes lock on to us. He holds a small handgun behind Lars's head.

"Good," he says, licking his lips, "The two of you get over there, on the other side of the coffee table. Keep your hands where I can see them. Deirdre, take off your coat and leave it on the floor."

Deirdre complies. The guy's eyes bulge upon seeing Deirdre's figure. He uses the gun to indicate our designated spot on the other side of the coffee table. Deirdre keeps her hands away from her body. I follow suit.

"We had a deal," I say.

"That's fine," the guy says, "You get over here and untie your friends. Remember, I got the gun right here."

I make my way over to the couch. The guy takes a step back, keeping the gun on Lars's head. From this position, he can keep an eye on Deirdre and still react in case I try something foolish. (It's not as if foolish activity is beyond me.) The electrical cords aren't easy to negotiate. They'd be a lot easier if I had a knife or scissors to cut them, but there's no way this guy is going to allow me *those*. For a guy who quit Cub Scouts after two years, I do a pretty good job of getting Lars free. He then unties Iris. She turns at Lars.

"You did *nothing* to protect me," she says.

Lars avoids eye contact. "We, uh, we should probably discuss this later."

"Oh, we'll discuss it," Iris says, "And you're going to beg me for mercy."

I'm not sure if that's a sexual thing, but I *am* sure I don't want to know. The guy with the gun wearies of our presence.

"Okay, you three," he says, "get the hell out."

I take a half step back from the couch and keep my eyes on the guy. "What are you going to do with Deirdre?"

"None of your business," he says, "Get out."

"You aren't concerned we're going to call the cops?" I ask.

"No."

I step aside to let Lars and Iris pass. Lars, ever the gentleman, allows Iris to go first. The guy has his eyes locked on Deirdre. As Lars passes me, I hope he can read the apology in my eyes.

I stick out a foot, tripping Lars. A little push in the back guides him right into Iris. They fall to the floor, nearly taking out the coffee table. The guy's eyes flick toward the crash site, just for a second. That's all Deirdre needs.

It feels like one of those moments when life does an edit. One second, the guy looks toward Lars and Iris. The next second, he's got the handle of a small knife sticking out the shoulder of his gun arm. The moment in which Deirdre extracted the knife from her sleeve and threw it at him has gone entirely unnoticed. The gun falls to the floor. He weaves slightly, staring at the handle of the knife.

"What the fuck?" is all he gets out.

Deirdre temporarily ends his confusion by vaulting the couch and delivering a thrust kick to the guy's jaw. He's probably out cold before he hits the floor. He lands next to his gun, which Lars scoops up. Deirdre looks down at the guy.

"Joe, gather up that electrical cord," Deirdre says, "Lars, go into the kitchen and wait for me. I'll have some instructions for you."

Little does Deirdre realize that going into the kitchen is Lars's specialty (or maybe she *has* doped that out). I rummage through the electrical cord on the couch. Iris stamps her foot.

"What am *I* supposed to do?" she says.

Deirdre gives Iris a brief look. "You, dear, are going to sit down and shut up." Iris starts to say something, but Deirdre simply says, more slowly, "Sit down. And shut up."

A hint of doubt comes into Iris's eyes (possibly for the first time ever). She stalks to a nearby chair and sits down. And shuts up.

Okay, there is *some* survival instinct floating around in there.

***

Despite what hours spent watching Keifer Sutherland in 24 might tell you, torture is not an effective method of interrogation. Yes, there's a certain visceral satisfaction in stringing up some recalcitrant asshole by their thumbs or shoving bamboo under their fingernails. But it's not going to get you reliable answers. Give somebody pain and they'll cop to anything in order to make it stop.

It's more effective to create a connection with the subject because they're more likely to give up reliable information. It takes time and patience, of course, and is not as fun as punching them until they puke blood. But it works better.

And if that doesn't work, just waterboard the son of a bitch.

Deirdre must come from the Torture school of thought.

I'm not going to argue since this is more her area than mine. Deirdre deposits the guy into a straight-back chair from the dining room table and uses the electrical cord to strap him in. She doesn't look pleased with her work, but given the materials, it's the best she can do. She carefully slips back into her trench coat. Lars stands near the entrance to the kitchen. Iris is in the nearby chair. I'm next to the sofa, watching the scene. The guy's slicked back hair is coming loose, and his head lolls to one side. A siren sounds somewhere in the distance. I can't help wondering if this activity has gotten the neighbors' attention.

A groan signals the guy is coming around. Judging by the wincing and grunting, he's got a nasty headache. He looks around the room, trying to get his bearings. He finally focuses his piggy little eyes on Deirdre. He swallows hard. Deirdre sits in a chair opposite him.

"Welcome back," she says, "I'm going to ask you a few questions. I suggest you answer them."

It takes a few seconds, but the guy finds his voice. This time, there's no attempt to put bass into it. "Wha…what are you going to do?"

"We'll get to that," Deirdre says, patting him on the knee, "Let's start with an easy one. What's your name?"

Sweat slides down the guy's forehead. "I'm, uh, my name is…they call me Skizzy."

As names go, it doesn't have the same sting as *They call me Mister Tibbs!* But in his defense, Skizzy doesn't look as if he expects to impress anyone with his handle. It certainly doesn't impress Deirdre. She lowers her head, and her shoulders shake as she tries to contain her laughter. She clears her throat and looks up.

"It's nice to meet you, Skizzy," she says, "Suppose you tell me why you're interested in me."

Skizzy tries to regain what passes for his mojo. "I can't tell you that."

"Are you sure about that?"

"Yeah. Yeah, I am."

Deirdre's voice is calm. "That's too bad." She gets up and circles behind Skizzy. She nods toward Lars, who disappears into the kitchen. Deirdre speaks into Skizzy's ear. "Guess we're going to have to try another way."

Iris's eyes are flashing. "What are you going to do?"

Deirdre ignores the question. She steps behind Skizzy, reaches into her boot and comes out with the knife she had previously put in his shoulder. I tense up, wondering what she's going to do. Before I can say anything, Deirdre grabs the back of Skizzy's shirt and plunges the knife in, ripping it from neck to asscrack. She slips the knife back into her boot.

"I'm sorry about this, sweets," Deirdre says, "It might get a little uncomfortable."

Deirdre throws out a hand and Lars puts a candlelighter in it. She brings the lighter around, holding it in front of his face. She flicks it on and the flame dances in front of Skizzy. His sweating is turned up to eleven.

"Wha…what are you going to do?" he asks, his voice a rasp.

"Just a little controlled burn," Deirdre says, "Pardon me a moment."

She brings the lighter away from Skizzy's face and holds it close to the bare patch on Skizzy's back. His upper body tenses as he feels the heat. He struggles against the bonds.

"Don't…don't do this," he says.

"It's not going to be as bad as you think," Deirdre says, "The pain is livable, if a little intense. The tough part is not throwing up from the smell of your own flesh burning. Just put yourself in your happy place. Try to imagine it's happening to someone else."

I step forward, ready to stop this. A single look from Deirdre backs me up. Her other hand comes up, unseen by Skizzy. Lars puts an unwrapped popsicle in it. What the hell? Snacks during torture? That seems a bit gauche. She brings the lighter closer to Skizzy's back. His eyes bulge.

"Wait! Wait! No!" Skizzy screams.

"Don't worry," Deirdre says, "It will all be over soon. Here we go."

The lighter lingers near Skizzy's back. At the last second, Deirdre substitutes the popsicle. The sudden cold feels exactly the same as the burning sensation Skizzy has prepared himself for. He screams out in pain.

"Stop it! Stop it!" he shouts, "I'll tell you anything you want to know!"

Deirdre pulls the popsicle back. She flicks off the lighter. Iris watches the scene and, dear God, she's actually smiling. I didn't know she was capable. Deirdre hands the implements of torture to Lars, circles to the front of Skizzy and returns to her seat.

"Start talking," Deirdre says.

Skizzy gulps. "Can I, can I get something for my neck?"

"In due time," she says, "Just let it burn for now. And tell me what you want with me."

"I, uh, I was supposed to…" Skizzy swallows as he searches for the words.

"Eliminate me?" Deirdre asks.

Skizzy hangs his head. "Yeah."

Deirdre doesn't seem remotely concerned. "And whose idea was this?"

Skizzy debates answering, long enough for Deirdre to lose patience. She gets up from the chair, takes the lighter back from Lars and re-ignites it. Skizzy thrashes around.

"Don't!" he yells, "I'll talk! It just…takes a little explaining."

"Great," Deirdre says, "Explain."

Skizzy collects himself. "I'm, uh, I'm the guy who hired you."

A charge runs through the room. The heat kicks on with a bang, causing everyone except Deirdre to jump. She returns to the chair, still holding the lighter.

"You communicated with Emily," Deirdre says.

"Yeah. I worked through her."

"You're an operator," Deirdre says. Skizzy nods. Deirdre speaks slowly. "Who hired you?"

Skizzy runs his tongue over his dry lips. "Kendall," he says, his voice barely audible.

I move closer, standing over Deirdre's shoulder. "As in Kendall Lucas? From Hankerson-William?"

"Yeah. She's my cousin." Skizzy looks to the floor. "It was all her idea."

If he was expecting sympathy from Deirdre, Skizzy was sadly mistaken. "The setting me up and then double-crossing me?" Deirdre says, her voice colder than the wind chill outside, "You're telling me that was her idea?"

"No, not that," Skizzy says, "That wasn't the plan. I don't know what happened there." Deirdre plays with the lighter. Skizzy picks up the pace. "It all started last fall. Kendall called me up, got together with me. I haven't seen her in forever. We're…we're not all that close."

"A shame," Deirdre says, still flicking the lighter, "Are you going to get to the point?"

"Kendall wanted me to…to eliminate someone."

My first thought is Alex Hollins. But that doesn't gibe with the timeline. It hits me a second later.

"Dustin Felt," I say.

"Yeah, that was the guy," Skizzy says, "I thought the whole thing was a fucking joke, but she said she would wire five grand into my bank account. Sure as shit, there was five large in there the next day. Then she said there'd be five more when I got the job done."

"You killed Dustin Felt," I say.

"No! No, I did not," Skizzy says, "I mean, I tried. It just…didn't exactly work out. Tried getting him in a parking garage. But I've never been a great shot. He got away. You ever had a Volvo drive over your foot?"

"Once," Lars says, "I haven't taken an Uber since."

"Anyway, that really chapped Kendall's ass," Skizzy says, "But I guess the guy wound up dead anyway. I don't know who she hired to do that. But I was pretty surprised when she called me a few weeks ago, said she wanted this Alex Hollins guy taken out. This time, she said she wanted a professional to do it. Said I should just do the arranging. Kind of hurt my pride, but she was willing to pay me another ten grand. So, I got over it pretty quick." He turns his head toward Deirdre. "I'd heard about you and how to get ahold of you. I got in touch with this Emily and there we were."

"And later Kendall hired you to kill me?" Deirdre asks.

"She did," Skizzy says, "Said everything had gone to shit and she wanted to clean house."

I stand over Skizzy. "How did you know where to find Deirdre?"

"Took a little research," Skizzy says, "I heard Deirdre was in town last year. That whole thing with the liquor store. I found out you wrote an article on it. Then I looked up your address and figured I'd give it a shot. If Deirdre was going to run to anyone, she'd run to you."

Son of a bitch. Even this douchebag figured out Deirdre would come to me. I'm kicking myself for ever writing that article. In my defense, I had hoped I'd never see Deirdre again. Only now do I realize the depth of my wishful thinking.

"The night you tried to attack me," I say, "That was Kendall in the car, right? She got you out of there."

"It was her," Skizzy says, "She wasn't happy. Threatened to take back all the money if I didn't get shit straightened out."

I put things together in my head. Kendall was in the meeting about the Impact File. She's loyal to the company. Loyal to her boss. She wanted Dustin Felt killed when he tried to go to the press. Hicks probably told her about Alex's plan to release the Impact File. She arranged for Deirdre to eliminate Alex Hollins. Although that makes me wonder…

"You say you didn't double-cross Deirdre," I say, "Did Kendall?"

"No," Skizzy says, "She was right there with me the night Hollins got killed. She knew right away the cops were after Deirdre. That everything got fucked up. She was pissed about it."

Deirdre takes command again. "Why should I believe you?" she says.

Skizzy's mouth hangs open, slightly. "It's…it's the truth."

"I've got bad news, sweets," she says, "I'm not sure I believe you."

Deirdre gets up and circles behind Skizzy. She again flicks on the lighter and holds it toward Skizzy's neck. He thrashes around. "It's the truth!" he says, desperately, "You have to believe me!"

"Do I?" Deirdre says. Again, she holds the lighter close. Again, she substitutes the popsicle and again, Skizzy cries out as if he's being burned. Deirdre pulls the popsicle back. "Last chance."

Skizzy's on the verge of tears. "That's exactly how it happened. I don't know what else I'm supposed to tell you."

Deirdre pauses, then steps around to the front of Skizzy. "I'll take it under consideration. Wait here." She stuffs the popsicle into Skizzy's mouth.

She walks to a far corner of the room and signals for me to follow. We huddle near a window looking out over Lyndale.

"What do you think?" Deirdre asks.

"I believe him. He doesn't look bright enough to come up with a lie. And I don't think abject panic helps that situation."

"I think you're right. Now, we just have to get rid of him."

An uneasy feeling gnaws at my guts. "You mean let him go?"

"In a sense. From this apartment and the cares of life."

Deirdre starts to step past me. Without thinking, I grab her arm to stop her. She looks at me and I let go.

"You can't do that," I say.

"Of course I can, darling. I've done it many times."

"The guy's told us everything. He's too damn scared to make a move on you now. You don't need to do this."

Deirdre glares at me. "I don't like loose ends. He'll disappear and no one will miss him."

"Kendall will."

"I'll deal with Kendall when the time comes."

I'm losing control the situation. Again, Deirdre makes a move toward Skizzy and again I move to block her.

"Think about it," I say, "Skizzy just got done saying—swearing, actually—that he and Kendall didn't set you up. That means the actual killer is still out there. Eliminating the two of them won't solve anything."

Deirdre turns her glare on Skizzy. "They still wanted to eliminate me." I start to reply, but Deirdre stops me. "What are we supposed to do? Leave him tied up and call the police? They've got him on what? Breaking and entering? He could probably manufacture a story about why he's here. He clearly had the key. He would be out on the streets before morning. In the meantime, he could also spill everything he knows to the police, tactfully leaving out his role in hiring me." She slips the gun out of her holster. "That is precisely why I don't like loose ends."

Deirdre pushes past me. I try to think up a way of dissuading her. Maybe find something to knock her out. Lars, sensing trouble, drifts back toward the kitchen. (Either he's going to hide or make himself another sandwich. It's an even bet.) Iris gets up from her chair.

"Are you finally going to kill this motherfucker?" she asks.

Deirdre ignores the question and looks toward Lars. "I need you to find some towels. Kitchen, bathroom, doesn't matter."

Lars doesn't move, though he does turn an interesting shade of green. Skizzy's eyes bulge. Iris, though, stands her ground with Deirdre.

"I'm getting a little sick of you ordering Lars around," Iris says, "He's not your boyfriend. He's mine."

Deirdre doesn't look Iris's direction. "That's your problem, dearie."

A thought occurs to Iris. "You've been hiding out in Lars's building, haven't you? You're the one he's been catting around with, right? In that empty apartment. You think I wouldn't figure it out?"

Deirdre can only laugh. "Listen—"

Iris turns her voice up to *Screech*. "You think this is funny? I'll show you how funny this is! You and that lousy bastard Lars!"

Iris rears back and throws a punch at Deirdre. It doesn't come close to landing. Deirdre catches the fist, then throws one of her own into Iris's face. The crunch of Iris's nose echoes throughout the apartment. Iris drops to the floor, landing on her butt. Blood streams from her nose. She reaches up and touches it, looking more shocked than anything else.

"Sit there and let it bleed, sweetie," Deirdre tells her.

Then all hell breaks loose.

Unnoticed during our debate, Skizzy has managed to free himself from his electrical cord prison. He spits out the popsicle and dives off the couch. Lars, who's been distracted by his possible role in a murder and dismemberment, doesn't notice until the last second. Skizzy snatches the gun from him. He takes aim at Deirdre.

I dive toward Deirdre and tackle her. The shot explodes in the confined space of the apartment. There's a small yip from Deirdre, then we both hit the floor. Her gun clatters on the floor.

Deirdre's down just long enough to slip a small knife out of her boot. She pops back to her feet. Skizzy, not liking his chances, lowers his gun and runs to the front door. Deirdre jumps past Iris's carcass. Skizzy whips open the front door and charges into the hallway. Neighbors peek out their doors, alerted by the sound of gunfire. Skizzy ignores them, moving down the hall with a frenzied and not particularly athletic run. He shoves open the door to the stairs and disappears into the stairway. Deirdre has gotten as far as the door. She steps back at the first sight of the neighbors. Lars bounds over and flips the door shut.

"We need to get out of here," he says. Our Lars: he has a gift for stating the obvious.

Deirdre glances at her right arm. There's a small hole in her coat and blood is dripping from it. She ignores it. "The three of you go down the hall and get out of here. Don't talk to the neighbors. Just go."

I turn toward her. "What about your arm? Are you okay?"

"It's fine. I'll meet you at the car."

"How are you—?"

"Trust me. I will meet you at the car."

I head for the door. Lars collects Iris and follows me. Her nose is swelling, and her eyes are starting to blacken. Lars keeps her at arm's length. Once we're in the hallway, I look back into the apartment. Already, there's no sign of Deirdre. I put my head down and lead Lars and Iris past the neighbors. She glares at him through her watering eyes.

"Youb did nubbing to hep me," Iris mumbles.

"Sorry, darling," Lars says, avoiding looking at her.

"Youb'll pay ben we geb home," she says.

"Yes, I was thinking," Lars says, "with everything that's happened to us tonight, maybe we should go straight to sleep. In fact, I'll take the couch. Just so I won't disturb you."

Iris says nothing but doesn't seem happy. (Thank God, because I could barely understand what she was saying in the first place.) We go down the stairs, our steps echoing in the empty stairwell. I have to hope we get to our separate cars before the police arrive. I've got a contract killer waiting on me. Lars is going home with Iris.

For once, I feel like I'm in the better position.

***

The Ambassador Suites is located on the east edge of downtown St. Paul. It's about eight stories high. All floors are grouped around a sunken garden and a café in the middle. There's a lot of brass and tile floors and deep-colored wood. It has a nice little pub off the lobby. The place is generally out of my price range. But I recently solved a murder involving one of the guests and, when publishing my account in *The Bugle*, was discreet enough not to mention the Ambassador. That's enough to get me a discounted room for a few nights. The place also has several side doors allowing for discreet entry.

Just what I need to sneak Deirdre up to her room.

I lead her up a side staircase to the seventh floor. The suite I've been given is tucked into the corner. No one is in the hall or hanging around the railings on the other levels. Deirdre leads the way to the room. I keep an eye out while she works the key card and slips into the room. I follow her inside.

"As landing pads go," Deirdre says, looking around, "It's not bad."

The suite has a nice-sized outer room with a sofa, tables and chairs. A sliding glass door leads to a patio that will probably go unused. A short hallway leads past a decent-sized bathroom to an adjoining bedroom. A mini-bar rests next to the table and chairs. Everything is clean and comfortable. Deirdre steps over to the sliding door.

"Nice view," she says, "If you could see anything."

"St. Paul after dark," I say, "Nothing *to* see." I look at her arm. "We should probably take care of that."

She steps away from the window and pulls up a chair. "Grab the med kit your friend Lars gave me."

I rifle through the black duffel bag in which we threw a few of Deirdre's temporary possessions. The med kit is a small black pouch, not much different in appearance than the shaving kit I take on road trips. Deirdre slips off her long black coat.

"I'm surprised your friend had a med kit," she says.

"Lars has everything," I say, "It's just a matter of finding it."

Deirdre examines the wound through the hole in her sweater. "You're going to have to help me with this."

I nearly drop the med kit. "Me?"

"I only have two hands, darling."

"Of course," I say, my stomach rolling. Deirdre traces her fingers around the wound. I search the med kit for a pair of scissors. "I assume we cut the shirt sleeve open," I say.

"Oh, to hell with that."

Deirdre carefully, painfully, removes her black sweater. I stare at her in her black bra and pants. I should offer to help, but I'm not certain how Deirdre would respond. She sees me watching her.

"Come over here," she says, turning her attention back to her injury.

The wound is a jagged red mouth running across the outside of Deirdre's right bicep. There isn't a lot of blood because the sweater has soaked up a good bit of it. Deirdre doesn't seem impressed.

"Not bad," she murmurs, "Still going to need stitches." Deirdre looks up at me, a faint trace of amusement crossing her face. "I suppose you know how to sew?"

Ah damn. My brothers love to make fun of my domestic skills and I've always been rather defensive about it. Now *I'm* kicking myself in the ass for learning all that stuff. "I know how to sew on a button," I say, "but that's it."

"Works for me," Deirdre says, taking a needle and some thread out of the med kit, "Suit up, cowboy."

Deirdre walks me through the process. The wound has largely stopped bleeding, so we've got that going for us, which is nice. I use some vodka from the mini-bar and a hand towel from the bathroom to clean the wound. Deirdre takes the little bottle of vodka from me and downs in one shot. She tries not to acknowledge the pain, but winces slightly every now and again.

"Okay, good," she says, "Now close it up."

A little panic goes through me, like when I was in elementary school and Mr. Schlander asked me to turn in homework I hadn't finished. I prep the needle and thread. With Deirdre's help, I push the wound closed as best I can, then start sewing it shut. I'm trying very hard to ignore what I'm actually doing, letting my mind float off to an imaginary happy place—like when I'm on a really boring date or that one time I had an STD test—but I can't help noticing the tactile quality of human tissue is very different from fabric. Deirdre studies me and occasionally murmurs, "Good." I hope she feels the same way if I puke.

"What do I do after this?" I ask.

"We'll wrap it in a dressing," Deirdre says, "It will be easy. Easier than this, anyway."

I hope so. I can't help noticing that my urge to vomit eases as I get closer to stitching the wound shut. Dear Lord, am I getting used to this nonsense? I'll have to take that up with Him another time. I finish the stitching and cut loose the thread. Deirdre examines my work.

"Good job," she says, "Now grab the bandage."

At Deirdre's instructions, I carefully wrap the bandage around the wound. This is the easier part. I'm trying not to be distracted by the sight of Deirdre's black bra. She's warm and the scent of berry body wash is on her skin. Deirdre watches my work.

"You'd make a decent medic," she says.

"I'm better at mending garments," I say, "You need a decent seamstress in your organization? Wait. Seamstress or seamster? Is there such a thing as a seamster? I imagine there would have to be, but…"

There's a laugh. One of Deirdre's genuine laughs rather than her usual cool chuckle. I finish with the dressing. Deirdre fetches two more small bottles of vodka from the minifridge. She offers one to me. Now that I don't have to worry about keeping my hands steady, I gladly accept. We sit in the two chairs, close to each other. Deirdre brushes the hair out of her face.

"You did good back there," she says, "You saved me."

"Actually, I think I saved Skizzy," I say, "Shooting you only makes you mad."

Deirdre smirks, but it fades quickly. "Thank you," she says, her voice surprisingly soft.

We stay close, staring at each other. My face feels warm. Deirdre suddenly kisses me hard on the mouth. The hand of her good arm comes up to my face, gently stroking my cheek. I pull her into me, carefully avoiding her left side. After several seconds, we come up for air, our faces close together.

"Are you…?" I say, slightly breathless, "I mean, I'm not sure this…"

Deirdre stops me with a kiss. "You should probably stop talking." Her good arm reaches behind her back and unclasps her bra. She lets it slide off her and fall to the floor.

"You know what?" I say, "I should probably stop talking."

***

It isn't easy, of course, working around Deirdre's injured arm. But we give it the old college try. Deirdre tries to keep the arm elevated as we go. We have some success up against the wall and on the credenza. Less so on the sofa. The bed, as it generally does, works best, particularly when Deirdre straddles me and puts a hand on the wall. It bends my neck slightly, but what am I going to do? Complain? Eventually, we fall asleep in the queen-sized bed. Somewhere in the night, I wake up. The room is quiet and dark. Deirdre's face is next to mine. I'm not sure she's awake until she speaks.

"Christina," she says, sleepily.

"Hm?" I ask.

"Christina. My real name is Christina."

I look at her. "Is that a fact?"

"That's a fact. But if you tell anyone, I may have to kill you."

"You might do that anyway."

"Yeah," Deirdre says, her voice fading, "I just might."

She drapes an arm across me. I fall asleep staring at the ceiling.

CHAPTER SIXTEEN

The fallacy of using the word intimacy *to describe sex is that the act is rarely kept between just the participants. After all, what is the fun of keeping such a thing to yourself, particularly if it's new or unexpected? There's the cliché of a guy talking to all his buddies about it (a cliché because it's largely true) but women are not immune to it either. The only difference between men and women is the efficiency of the communications network.*

This isn't as salacious as it sounds. After all, if this new thing in your life is particularly exciting, are you expected to keep it from the people closest to you? Of course not. You're going to tell your best friend, your favorite co-worker, your siblings, Monty the barista at the coffee shop, the cashier at the grocery store, that Uber driver with the kind back of his head.

The key is to keep the circle small. After all, you have to be discreet.

Mike stares at me from his place at the breakfast bar. "You slept with a contract killer?" He contemplates this over his grape soda. "Your memoirs just got a fuckload more interesting, I'll give you that."

I regret sharing this news with Mike and Carol. I'm on the edge of my kitchen, where the washer/dryer is kept. The damn thing clangs away as it finishes the last of my laundry. Carol, sitting at the breakfast bar with Mike, looks as if a car accident is happening in my kitchen.

"Joe, are you out of your mind?" she asks, "This woman could kill you."

"I know," I say, staring at the dryer, "Strangely, that's part of the appeal."

Carol sets her coffee down. "You're hopeless."

"I agree," Mike says.

"You *agree*?" Carol says to her unlikely ally.

"Absolutely," Mike says, turning to me, "You need to have your life threatened to get turned on? Suddenly, tits aren't good enough for you?"

Carol drops her head into her hands. I sympathize with her. It can't be easy being close friends with a couple children growing older. She runs her hands down the side of her face as she tries to get a handle on things.

"So, you're dating this woman now?" Carol asks.

"I am not," I say, "It was just…one of those things that happens. Spur of the moment kind of deal, I guess.

Nothing about the situation has changed. The goal is the same. Clear Deirdre of the murder and get her out of town."

Carol gets up from the breakfast bar to refill her coffee. The cats crowd around her, thinking there might be food in the deal. They come up short on that, but they do get scratches on the ears. (Good enough for Squiggy. Not so much for Lenny, who is an eternal glutton.) Carol rejoins Mike at the breakfast bar but doesn't sit.

"Since you survived your…incident with this Skizzy character," Carol says (and it hurts when that euphemism is applied to *me*), "what's your next move?"

The annoyingly loud buzzer on the dryer goes off. That doesn't bother me, though. The kitchen is cold, and the laundry is warm. (Sometimes in a Minnesota deep freeze, it's the little things that get you through.) I start emptying the contents of the dryer into a laundry basket.

"Kendall hired Skizzy to kill Dustin Felt," I say, "That didn't work but Felt wound up dead anyway. Then she used Skizzy to hire Deirdre. She wanted Alex Hollins dead. Probably because he was going to release the Impact File and kill the Green River Project. But Skizzy insists they didn't double-cross Deirdre."

Mike rolls his eyes. "You think you can believe anything that guy says? Especially when Deirdre was sitting right in front of him?"

"I don't know," I say, folding a shirt, "Seems like you could frame someone who comes cheaper. And less dangerous."

"This Skizzy guy didn't exactly seem like a brain trust," Mike says.

"No, but Kendall's smarter," I say, "Then again, she did hire Skizzy."

Mike bobs his head. Carol smooths her black skirt and checks her ponytail in the hallway mirror as she considers the matter. She picks up her coffee, careful not to spill on her white blouse or black suitcoat.

"This Kendall is behind everything," she says, "Have you talked to her yet?"

"I've tried," I say, dropping the last of the laundry into the basket, "I called her cell phone. Shockingly, it appears I've been blocked. I tried calling the office, only to be told she's out. No word on how long. That's all I could get out of the receptionist."

Mike taps his foot on the stool (even though that drives me up a wall). "This the same receptionist Lars is doinking?"

"Megan, yeah," I say, bringing the laundry basket into my bedroom, "I believe they are engaged in the doink. You might want to keep your voice down, though, just in case Iris is down at Lars's place. Or listening at my door."

Without missing a beat, both Mike and Carol turn to the door and say, "Hi, Iris," in twin sing-song voices. (See? They can do things together from time to time.) I set the laundry basket on the bed, return to the kitchen, and fetch some coffee. Mike pushes his Fong's cap back on his head.

"Sounds like you may have to use Lars to get some answers out of Megan," he says.

I join Mike and Carol at the breakfast bar. "I might have to deploy the Lars Option."

Carol clucks her tongue. "Maybe not before tonight, though. We've got the fundraiser."

Mike does jazz hands and says, "Showtime!"

That gets a less-than-thrilled look from Carol (whose apprehension is generally in the right place). I'm wondering if Carol and Mike can smell Deirdre's body wash on me. (I *have* showered, but I can still smell it, faintly.) Neither of them shows an indication, though. Carol sets her coffee aside.

"You think Kendall will be at the fundraiser?" she asks.

"I don't know," I say, "Payton Hicks is supposed to be there. I'm not sure if Kendall is going to join him. She might be trying to protect him."

"Protect him how?" Carol asks.

"Think about it," I say, "Does Kendall have nearly the vested interest in the Green River Project that Payton

Hicks has? Why would she do all this stuff unless she's doing it on his orders? Something this big, going on at this level of the company, and Hicks has *no* idea? Not bloody likely."

Carol bobs her head as she considers this. "If that's the case, Hicks would have motivation to cover for Kendall."

That, of course, presents a major problem. How do you solve a problem like a powerful businessman? Sure, I can go after Payton Hicks, but is Hicks even touchable? Particularly, if I have no proof? He certainly has the means to avoid me like the plague. I can confront him at the fundraiser tonight (assuming he shows), but will that get me anything? Other than Carol's eternal hatred for screwing up that little gathering?

I need to get off this subject, even temporarily. Carol finishes up her coffee and brings her cup to the sink. I rotate on the stool to follow her movement.

"Are Evie and Shawn coming to the fundraiser tonight?" I ask.

"I hope not," Carol says, "But there's going to be free booze there, so what are the odds? Meantime, I have to keep lying to Mr. Pratt, telling him his son is turning a corner."

"He's turning a corner all right," I say, "Right into Desolation Row."

"Thank you, Joseph," Carol says, "That is so very helpful. When I'm unemployed and begging my parents for money, I hope your snark will remain untrammeled."

"It hasn't been trammeled yet," I say.

"Completely trammel-free, I'd say," Mike adds.

Mike and I raise our beverages in a toast. Carol gives us both a nasty look, then stalks out the apartment, closing the door a tad harder than necessary. (It causes Mike and I to flinch. Squiggy, his butler sensibilities disturbed, simply flees the room.) I set my cup down.

"You going to be at the fundraiser tonight?" I ask.

"That's the plan," he says, setting aside his grape soda without making any effort to put the can in the recycling, "Assuming I'm still working for Fong's by nightfall."

I collect the can and bring it into the kitchen. "Things still tense over there?"

"Pretty much," Mike says, kneading his Fong's cap in his hands, "Ron came by this morning, just as we were getting ready for lunch rush. He's moving around okay, what with the crutches and all. Everyone was fawning over him. Including Biyu. Even Fong was nice to him. I had to go in the next room to keep from puking."

"Yeah, you don't want to create a bigger mess than you already have."

Mike ignores me. "Everyone kept asking him about the accident. He says he doesn't remember much. Just that his brakes weren't working. He doesn't understand what happened."

"And he doesn't have any suspicions?"

"None that he said. He said the police wanted to look into it, but he told them it was just an accident. He also thought about having his mechanic look at the car, but he didn't want to pay the expense. The thing was totaled, so he'd just let it go at that."

"Sounds like you're home free," I say.

"You'd think that," Mike says, "but everyone keeps giving me these looks. Like *they* suspect something, even if Ron doesn't."

"Where *would* they have gotten that idea?"

Mike gives me a stinkface. I'm sure, somewhere in that mass of bad impulses he calls a brain, there's a recognition that he committed a potentially criminal act. But as usual, it's buried beneath his eternal self-interest. He gets up from the breakfast bar and heads to the front door. His hand rests on the doorknob.

"Is Deirdre still at the hotel?" he asks.

"For now."

"How did you two, uh, leave it this morning?"

"We didn't chat much. Just had coffee, breakfast and a shower together." Mike has no response to that, which is unusual for him. "Something bothering you?" I ask.

"It ever occur to you that we've gotten *way* too close to her?" he says, "All of us. And now especially you. Even if you figure out who double-crossed her, can she really afford to let us run around? You remember what she said about loose ends."

Mike's right. Thanks to Jim Street, it's always been in the back of my head that Deirdre might go completely scorched earth when this thing is over. I wave it off, trying to give Mike some assurance.

"We'll be fine," I say, "I trust Deirdre."

Mike looks unsure, maybe even a little uneasy. He opens the door. "Let's just hope those aren't famous last words."

With that, Mike's off, heading down the stairs. I let the door close under its own steam. Mike's right. I haven't conducted myself with an abundance of caution. But I need to have faith in Deirdre. Believe that she won't kill the guy who has helped clear her of murder.

Then again, where has faith generally gotten me?

***

I get into the Ambassador Suites completely unscathed. Even the front desk staff doesn't give me the usual suspicious looks. (Of course, wearing my dark suit and my peacoat for the fundraiser probably helps.) There's no sign of police activity or a riot, so I assume Deirdre made it through the day okay. I take the elevator to the eighth floor, keeping an eye out for anyone suspicious (well, more suspicious than me) and make it to Deirdre's room. I give the door a special knock. A moment later, Deirdre answers and I slip inside.

"On your way to something?" she asks, flatly.

"The fundraiser is tonight."

Deirdre closes the door. I'm unsure how to greet her. When last we left, there was a simple hug, and I was on my way. This time, Deirdre breezes past me and walks toward the sofa. She stands next to it without sitting.

"Have you heard from our friend Skizzy?" Deirdre asks.

"Not at all. If he's smart—and that's not a given—he's on his way out of town. To Guam, probably."

Deirdre doesn't react. She steps in front of the closed bedroom door, keeping her arms folded. "I'm not worried about Skizzy. He can be dealt with later. I'm curious what you're going to do with the information he gave us."

I keep my hands in my pockets. My whole body feels stiff (and not the parts that I enjoy feeling stiff). "I think we have to consider the possibility he's telling us the truth."

"Meaning?"

"Meaning there was no double-cross," I say, "That Kendall—through Skizzy—hired you to kill Alex Hollins and was perfectly content to let you carry out the killing and be on your merry way. But someone got to Alex before you. It threw her plan *and* yours into complete disarray. She thought the easiest way to cover everything was to have you eliminated."

"Bad choice."

"I'm guessing Kendall's new at this," I say.

"Too bad. The mistakes you make in this game aren't the kind you learn from." Deirdre moves toward the sliding door, far away from me. "If it wasn't a double-cross, then who killed Alex Hollins?"

I sit stiffly on the arm of the sofa. "If he wasn't killed for professional reasons, I'm going to return to the personal reasons. In which case, Chelsea Hollins is still the number one candidate. Alex was probably going to expose her actual identity. She hated him and wanted to make a move against him. If she wasn't interested in Alex's business, she didn't know about the hit. Wires got crossed."

Deirdre considers this. "Then who killed Chelsea?"

"That I don't know." I say, "Maybe it was Kendall. Maybe it was part of the same scorched earth thing she was trying with you. But that would mean Kendall found out that

Chelsea killed Alex. If the police haven't proven it and we haven't proven it, what are the odds she's proven it? And if she did, why kill Chelsea instead of just letting her take the fall for Alex's killing? If Chelsea didn't know about the intended hit, there's no harm, no foul for Kendall, particularly if she's able to get you eliminated."

"Easier than it sounds," Deirdre says.

"I guess so. This whole thing is like playing Whack-A-Mole. You think you've got everything covered, then something else pops up."

"Whack-A-Mole," Deirdre says, the slight smile returning, "I should have known that was the metaphor you'd go with."

"Actually, it was a simile."

So much for the smile. "Did you just 'actually' me?"

"Let's pretend I didn't."

"Good choice." Dierdre leans against the wall, her body language still stiff. "What are you going to do next?"

"Next? I'm going to the fundraiser. There's a chance I'll run into Payton Hicks or Kendall. If I do, I'll figure it out from there."

A moment passes. "Then you should probably go," Deirdre says.

"Oh," I say. I shouldn't be surprised. I've felt like an intruder since I walked in. I try to think of something to say, but all I come up with is a really pithy: "Okay."

The last part has a plaintive, junior high quality to it. Deirdre gives me an indulgent look and keeps her voice low.

"Last night was very nice, sweets," she says, "*Was.*"

"The tense didn't escape me," I say, trying not to sound petulant.

"This isn't going to affect the work, I trust?"

"Not at all," I say, "But I *am* wondering why it happened."

Deirdre's voice gets quiet. "Because I wanted it to."

"And that's that."

She looks out the window. "I have a life I'm trying to get back to and I'm pretty sure you don't want any part of it. I wanted you and it was very nice. But it had to end sooner or later. I prefer sooner."

I let a breath out through my nose. Whatever choler was there is now fading. For no other reason than Deirdre is right. I certainly wasn't kidding myself about any kind of future with her. I walk to the door.

"I'm going to get you out of this mess," I say, "And back to your life."

"Good."

"But I think you're better than that."

Deirdre keeps her eyes focused on the window and whatever lays beyond that. "Have fun at the fundraiser." Then she adds, with no small touch of sarcasm, "Say hi to the gang for me."

"They're my friends."

"I know that."

"Do you have any of your own?"

Deirdre looks at me, sharply. Then her eyes drift back to the window. I leave without saying anything. The door slams shut behind me.

***

Yes, I complain when I'm forced to wear my suit, but *I* have been told I clean up nice. The same can be said of my friends and, apparently, community centers they're looking to refurbish.

I slip through the main doors and look around the place. I can't help being impressed by the job they've done on the Kellen Community Center. It's scrupulously clean. Lamps have replaced the harsh fluorescent lighting. The offices at the back have been mercifully screened from view. Streamers and banners festoon the place, along with pictures of kids from the community and artists' renderings of plans for the center. They've made the place look nice but still needy. Not an easy trick.

It takes a moment to shake off the cold and orient myself. The lobby is pretty full, but the general flow of traffic is toward the gym. The door to the auditorium is open and a few people are mingling in there. A table has been set up to check everyone in. Lars floats around the table, glad-handing everyone he can find. He wears a red tuxedo with a plaid bowtie and his quasi-pompadour has been slicked down. He looks like the maître'd at the worst morgue in Glasgow. I unbutton my coat and start toward the table, trying to keep the mope out of my walk. Carol appears, wearing a blue gown. Her hair is up and her make up is exquisite. She hooks her arm into mine, slowing me down.

"Is your friend around here?" she asks.

"Probably not," I say, "But I never can tell."

Carol takes a prim sip of the martini she's holding. Long acquaintance with Carol tells me she's making a heroic effort not to guzzle it. I lower my voice.

"Your boss here yet?" I ask.

"No," Carol says, shivering slightly, "But he will be."

"What about Evie and Shawn?"

"Same thing." She sighs. "But they'll get here. In what condition, I can't say."

Carol and I step to the table, and I check in. I'm handed a name tag, which I promptly put in my pocket.

(We'll have to talk about my pathological hatred of nametags sometime.) Lars slaps a hand on my shoulder.

"Good to see you, brother," he says, "I'm sure your presence here will be a real boon. I can picture the geeks making their way in right now."

"Thanks," I say, not meaning it, of course, "Is Iris here?"

Lars lowers his head, slightly. "Not yet. I don't know if she'll show. The, uh, occurrence the other night startled her. She wasn't happy with…our friend."

I shoot Lars a look. "Is she going to tell anyone?"

"Ship already sailed on that, brother," he says, "She tried calling the police and reporting Deirdre. But between her broken nose and her towering rage, the police couldn't really understand what she was saying. They hung up on her."

"And she took it out on you?" Carol asks.

"Actually, no," Lars says, "I've, uh, decided it might be better if I gave Iris some space."

Our man Lars. Faithful and true until your face has been horribly marred by a contract killer. (I'll bet that's how he was described in his high school yearbook.) I look toward the gym, following the general flow of traffic.

"The VIPs are in the gym, right?" I ask.

"Indeed," Lars says, "We have a special corner set up. You'll see the velvet ropes as soon as you walk in."

"Is Payton Hicks here?"

"He is," Lars says, "He gave me a bit of a cold shoulder when he walked in. Said he'd sue me if I didn't get the hell away from him."

"What about Kendall? Any sign of her?"

"None," Lars says, "I'll have Chuck keep an eye out for her."

"Chuck?" I say, "I thought he was barred from the fundraiser."

"He was barred from the *planning*," Lars says, giving Carol the closest thing he's got to a dirty look, "But he's been allowed to work security. If he spots Kendall, he could always affect a citizen's arrest."

"That's not—"

"No, he'd do it. It would be his pleasure."

I'm sure it would be. I'll have to put out that particular dumpster fire when it occurs. I separate from Carol and start toward the gym. She spins around in time to see Mr. Pratt walking in. I'll let her deal with that issue. The gym is down a short hall. Crepe paper streamers arch over the entrance. I'm almost there when I bump into Mike coming out. He sports a hangdog expression I know all too well.

"How's the catering going?" I ask.

"Fine, I guess," he says, sounding not unlike a sulky teenager.

"Fong's in there?" I say.

"Yeah. He's running the whole show. Biyu is there, too. For all the good that does me."

That explains the expression and the tone of voice. "She's not welcoming, I take it?"

"Not in the least. She says she doesn't want to see me anymore. She suspects me in what happened with Ron."

"Ouch. Anything you can do?"

He chews his goatee. "Not much. I have to hope she doesn't say anything to Fong. Or if she does, that he won't believe her. I can try talking to him. Get him on my side. Tell him how Ron had a habit of driving recklessly and probably got what he deserved. Poison the water hole."

"So, lie?"

"Like a motherfucker, yes."

I clap Mike on the shoulder, wish him luck, and go into the gym. The place is filling up. Fong has set up the buffet on one wall. The VIP area is on the adjoining wall. A disco ball hangs from the ceiling. (It works well, assuming it doesn't bring down the whole ceiling.) Payton Hicks is dressed to the nines and working the crowd in the VIP area. Glad to see he's over his grief for Chelsea. I slip off my peacoat and hand it to an attendant. Then I get three steps away and realize that might not be an attendant. It could just be some guy currently showing his friends, "Hey look, free peacoat! Some dink just handed it to me." Guess I'm going to have to hope for the best. Like most of this night.

I approach the VIP area, currently guarded by Lars's friend Chuck. His straw-like hair has been combed as best it can be and he's wearing a dark suit. With his block head and bulbous frame, he looks like someone shaved an ape and stuck him in some formalwear. Chuck moves the velvet rope as I approach but otherwise ignores me. There is a bar in the VIP area. I make a beeline for it. Daddy needs some hooch. I fortify myself with a simple martini and drop a few bucks in the tip jar. (Two dollars for a martini. I stand by my assessment that the two most beautiful words in the English language are *open bar*.)

Small high-top tables, big enough for two people, are scattered throughout the area. I find one and take a lean (no seats available). I've just had my first beautiful bracing sip of my martini when I spot Al Castillo entering the gym. He wears a black suit with a red boutonniere. He dispenses with his black trench coat and fedora, handing them to the same attendant (who may be building a mini-collection if he's not employed by Carol and Lars). There's a manilla envelope in Castillo's hand. He powerwalks my direction. He moves fast for a bigger guy, but there's a trail of sweating leading away from his perfectly jelled hair. This ought to be good. I move to one of the ropes to intercept him.

"Alberto," I say, "I didn't know the kids were getting media coverage for this."

"They aren't," he says, "At least not from me." He holds up the manilla envelope. "I wanted to talk to you about this."

"What is it?" I ask, "The nuclear launch codes? Transcripts of the Nixon tapes? Nude photos of Nancy Reagan?"

Castillo doesn't bat an eye. "It's the Impact File."

I'll give him credit: he *did* make it good.

CHAPTER SEVENTEEN

Before I get too far into this, I have to be fair and say there are people on this planet who are completely sincere when they say, I'll help any way I can. *They will genuinely be at your beck and call if you need them. Run errands? Put a new roof on the house? Plow the back forty? They'll be there for you. Foot massage? There better be a medical reason involved, but if there is, they would do it for you. (Though if they have a brain in their head, they'll ask to see that doctor's order.)*

The rest of us view it from a What's in it for me? *perspective. After all, if we're going to give up a day off to help this worthless slug, there should be some kind of quid pro quo, mo-fo. There's a reason people ask for help moving by saying,* I'll buy beer and pizza *rather than saying* I'll be eternally grateful and think highly of you always. *Asking someone to give from the goodness of their heart only leads to disappointment and you hauling a couch up three flights of stairs by yourself.*

I'm not sure who's doing Alberto Castillo a favor, but I have to thank them for the effort. If Castillo had shown up sporting a second head, it wouldn't be more unexpected than this. I look at the file like it's the Holy Grail (and viewed from a certain angle…)

"How did you get that?" I ask.

"It was on my desk, waiting for me," Castillo says.

"Who sent it?"

"I'd love to know," Castillo says, "No return address." He rests the envelope against his chin. "The postmark is from Excelsior, though."

"Excelsior? Isn't that interesting?"

"I thought so," Castillo says, "But it was sent yesterday."

"After Chelsea Hollins died."

"Exactly. I'm guessing she was in no condition to send mail."

"Not unless George Romero got ahold of her," I say.

Castillo gives me a blank look. "I know that's a reference to something, but…"

"Disregard."

We become aware we're standing in the middle of a crowded fundraiser, holding what might be incriminating evidence against a major corporation. We decide to find some cover. I lead the way to an office, just off the gym. The place is cramped and filled with rickety furniture. The walls and floor are stained (with what, I don't even want to contemplate). I take the envelope from Castillo.

"Have you gotten a look at it?" I ask.

"Of course. You think someone's going to drop a thing like this on my desk and I'm not going to look at it?" He lets out a breath through his nose. "It says everything the DFL said it would. The Green River Mine would cause seepage into the river. Drinking water would be poisoned slowly. Long term health effects to the residents would be disastrous."

"Behold, the smoking gun." I put a fist on the desk. "Have you written the story?"

"Joe, if something like this shows up on my desk, sent from an anonymous source, I don't bang out the story and ask my editor to sign off on it. I check to make sure it's legit. What better place to do that than a fundraiser where the interim CEO of the company is hobnobbing?"

"Oh, he's nobbing his hob."

"We should go talk to him," Carol says.

I look toward the door. "You and the file stay here. I'll fetch him."

I slip out of the office and walk back to the gym. The place is officially packed assholes-to-elbows. If nothing else, there's going to be a hell of a community center in this neighborhood. Payton Hicks is in a corner of the VIP area. I drain the rest of my martini and approach. Hicks gives me his usual dyspeptic face. (I guess the open bar hasn't contributed to his bonhomie.)

"Mr. Davis," he says, stiffly.

"I need to talk to you," I say.

"About what?"

"The Impact File."

Hicks looks like he swallowed a pool ball. "What about it?"

"Alberto Castillo has it," I say.

Now Hicks is looking a little green. He's probably hoping I'm going to say, "Ah, I'm just yanking ya! Buy you some hooch?" When that isn't forthcoming, he takes a gulp of his red wine and steadies himself.

"He's...he's here, is he?" Hicks asks, trying to sound casual.

"He is."

"How, uh, how did he get the file?"

"He's trying to figure that out," I say.

"Then it could be a fake?" He sounds awfully hopeful about that.

"We were hoping you could give us an idea about its authenticity," I say.

If I had asked for an immediate stool sample, Hicks could not look more hesitant. I indicate he should follow me to the little office. We slip through the crowd and into the office. Castillo is still there, holding the manilla envelope. There's an awkward moment. I feel like I should introduce Hicks and Castillo, but judging by the way they're eyeing each other, they've already met. Hicks finally breaks the ice.

"Mr. Castillo," he says, trying to regain some air of authority, "I take it you have the Impact File there."

"That's what I'm guessing," he says, "It would be nice if you could confirm it."

Hicks nods, barely. Castillo opens the envelope. He carefully sets the pages on the desk, spreading them out. Hicks looks them over. He's making a show of being nonchalant, but his Adam's Apple is bobbing up and down like a rubber ball. He reaches for a page, but Castillo grabs it first. Hicks looks offended.

"You don't trust me?" Hicks asks.

"Only so far," Castillo says, "If you need a closer look at something, I'll show it to you."

Hicks points at a page and Castillo holds it up. They continue this ritual for a few minutes. Finally, Hicks looks toward the floor and takes a moment to think. He looks up.

"It's the Impact File," Hicks says, "The genuine article. How did you get it?"

Castillo puts the pages back together. "It showed up on my desk. No return address. No name. But now I know it's the real thing."

"And, uh, what are you going to do with it?" Hicks asks.

The file is returned to the envelope. "I'm a newspaper reporter," Castillo says, "What do you think I'm going to do?"

Hicks has no answer to that. He knows he can't bribe or threaten Castillo. He's up a creek. Hicks slumps against the wall, and that may be the only thing holding him up. I step over to him.

"Where's Kendall?" I ask.

Hicks seems slightly dazed. "She's not here."

"I realize that. Where is she?"

A voice comes from behind me. "I'm right here."

I spin around and see Kendall standing in the doorway to the office. Her hair has been weaved into some kind of updo and the neckline of her gown plunges more than what could be considered safe in a frigid February. Fortunately, the frown she gives me does not smear her lipstick. Before I can say anything, she reaches into her purse and pulls out a small handgun.

"You're going to give me the file," Kendall says, "Now."

Well, I wanted to know where Kendall was. Ask a silly question…

CHAPTER EIGHTEEN

My father never pushed me to be an athlete. He was a decent athlete in college and my two brothers were multi-sport lettermen who went to college on athletic scholarships. Thus, family honor had been more than upheld in that area. Dad could afford not to push me.

I do wonder sometimes when exactly he gave up on me as an athlete. Dad is too much a gentleman to tell me when or to give me the idea it even mattered. If I had to guess, it might have been the time we were playing catch in the backyard when I was eight. I had my Twins cap and my glove and was feeling like the next best thing to Kirby Puckett. Dad had the ball in his hand and was giving me instructions. "Okay, put your glove up." Up went my glove. "Now, you need to keep your eye on the ball. Remember, eye on the ball. Whatever you do, keep your eye on the ball. Got it?" I got it. Dad chucked the ball my direction and I kept my eyes glued to the ball, following every nuance of its path through the air. So much so, that I forgot to put my glove on it and the damn thing hit me right in the face. Dad was great about wiping away my tears and putting ice on my black eye. He would play catch with me again. He even encouraged me to try Little League. But his instructions were much less fervent after that. He knew when to cut bait.

If this situation with Kendall is any example, I *still* haven't learned my lesson about keeping my eye on the ball. If this thing goes down the way I think it will, an icepack isn't going to do me a hell of a lot of good.

Castillo and I put our hands up. One of Castillo's still holds the Impact File. Kendall steps into the room and closes the door behind her. There's barely enough space for the four of us. Kendall stands between us and the only exit out of the room. But I get the feeling Castillo isn't going to give up the file easily. Not that it will stop Kendall from trying.

She holds out her hand. "Give me the file."

Castillo doesn't move. "I'm not going to do that."

"It doesn't belong to you," Kendall says, teeth gritted, "Now give it to me."

"Actually, it was addressed to Al Castillo," I say, "That kind of makes it his. Possession being nine-tenths of the law and all."

"Shut up!" Even if the gun and the ferociousness in her voice didn't stop me, the way her face twists into a mask of hate certainly would. Kendall turns her attention to Castillo. "I will kill you right here in this office," she says, "Now give me the damn file."

Castillo looks at the file in his hand. He's giving it some serious thought. I'm not entirely thrilled by having my fate tied to his. Hicks looks toward Kendall, blankly.

"What are you doing, Kendall?" he asks.

Kendall doesn't answer right away, so I step in. "She hired someone to kill Alex Hollins," I say, "Because he was going to release the Impact File."

That just gets a disgusted look from Kendall. "You talked to Skizzy, right?"

"I did."

"I should have known. I haven't heard from the stupid son of a bitch. Probably for a good reason."

Hicks's head swivels from Kendall to us and back again. A few strands of hair fall out of place. (Heaven forfend!) "You…you arranged…"

I keep my eyes on Kendall. "You're still going to claim you didn't double-cross the contract killer?"

"I didn't," Kendall says, "I don't know who killed Alex Hollins. We did everything we could do to make sure the killing would go off without a hitch. Then the whole thing went tits up."

"Because someone got to Alex first," I say, "and you have no idea who that someone is?"

"No, I don't. I just want the Impact File back and for all of this to go away."

There isn't much chance that will happen. But Kendall is still eyeballing the file. Castillo's face is hard. He shows no signs of being willing to give up. This is going to get ugly. I turn toward Kendall, hoping I can stall for time (and get information).

"Did you kill Chelsea?" I ask, "Or did Skizzy?"

"No," Kendall says, "I didn't kill Chelsea. I needed her."

It takes a second for me to put that together. "She was helping you."

"Yes."

And another second to realize why. "Because you knew she was really Donna Rousch. You told Alex that."

"Yes," Kendall says, "And I would have told everyone else, too, if I had to. That's what I told her."

"So you could get her help," I say, "She was the one who turned off the security system."

"Exactly," Kendall says, "And she was supposed to find the file. But she couldn't even get that right. I'm not sorry she's gone. But I didn't do it. And Skizzy wouldn't do something like that without my say-so."

Kendall raises the gun. The heart locket hangs from her bracelet. The heart locket. Son of a bitch. Why didn't I put that together sooner? The heart mug on Hicks's desk. The heart on his bathrobe. It was all right in front of me.

"Hicks ordered you to do it," I say.

Hicks swings his head toward me. His jaw drops. Before he can answer, Kendall says: "Of course not! He's a good man. He wouldn't dream of doing something like this!"

"That's why you have to do it," I say.

"Yes. I have to protect him."

"Because you're sleeping with him."

"Yes." Then Kendall's voice gets quiet. "It's what you do when you love someone."

I hold up a finger. "That was you," I say, "The night in the apartment." My finger moves back and forth between Kendall and Hicks. "You two were…together."

Hicks turns red. Kendall sticks out her chin, defiant.

"Yes," she says, "and you and your idiot friends had no business being there. Or humiliating Mr. Hicks. He's a good man. I'm going to make sure no one destroys his work." She levels the gun at Castillo's face. "Now, give me the fucking file."

I'll admit: I'm in two places. Yes, I've always had this penchant for being physically in one place and mentally in another. I should probably put my focus on the crazy lady with the gun. But something she said struck me. About the things you do for the people you love. I've got an idea. Assuming I live to pursue it.

Sweat runs down Hicks's face. "Maybe…maybe you should give her the file."

Castillo curls the file into his chest. "I'm not going to do that."

"Then you're going to die," Kendall says.

Before her finger can close around the trigger, I step in front of Castillo, holding out a hand, hoping to be Mr. Reasonable. "Think about it," I say, "What good is that going to do? Castillo still knows about the file. So do I. So does whoever sent Castillo the file."

"It doesn't matter," Kendall says, "Without the file, there's no proof. You can say whatever you want."

"She's right," Castillo says, "That's why I'm not going to give her the file."

Kendall steps to one side of me, again taking aim at Castillo. I jump into her path, again putting myself in harm's way. (Seriously, do I even like Castillo this much?)

"You can't do that," I say, "Not here."

Castillo slips me a look. "Not *here?*"

"You fire that thing in here," I say, "and everyone in this place is going to hear."

Kendall falters slightly. "There's noise from the party."

"Not enough," I say, "You'll shoot Castillo, but people will come rushing in here and see what's happened.

Then you'll get arrested, and someone will grab the file before you can destroy it. The damn thing will be released anyway. Where does that get you?"

There's a moment where I think I've gotten through to her. Kendall lowers the gun. Her eyes search the room. She knows there is sense in what I'm saying, but it's swimming against a river of desperation and crazy. I hope good sense wins.

Kendall raises the gun directly at Castillo's face. "Fuck it. I can find my way out of here. Now, give me the fucking file!"

It was a nice thought. My fault, really, for believing that common sense will win under any circumstances. Castillo hugs the file, letting us know he won't be giving it up willingly. A crusading journalist to the bitter fucking end. (A thing I could admire if it wasn't likely to get us both killed.) I've got one Hail Mary play left. I spin toward the door.

"Oh my God, look out!" I shout.

It's a ridiculous plan. Who the hell falls for the *Oh no, look out behind you* ruse? But Kendall falls for my nonsense. Her head turns toward the door and the gun moves slightly off Castillo. I throw myself at Kendall, hitting her with a body check. Kendall bounces off the wall and the gun clatters on the floor.

Hicks drops behind a desk and covers his head. I dive toward the gun. Kendall elbows her way past me. She gets to the gun first. Castillo ducks out of the office, the file still clutched in his hand. I push away from Kendall and follow him, pulling the door shut as I go. Hopefully, it buys us a few seconds. (Castillo needs it more than I do.) Kendall screams incoherently in the office.

We run back into the gym. Everyone is sedately sipping their drinks. Castillo and I shoulder our way through the crowd. I'm wrestling with conflicting emotions. On the one hand, we need the crowd for coverage. On the other hand, I hate being the one to destroy this fundraiser my friends have worked so hard to put together.

So, Biyu attacking Mike turns out to be a good thing.

Our path takes us close to the catering table where Biyu is taking Mike to the proverbial woodshed. The dressing down takes verbal form but is threatening to go another direction. Mike cowers in the face of it.

"You did it!" she screams, "You cut Ron's brakes!"

"I didn't mean to," Mike pleads, "It was an accident."

"Accident? How was it an accident?"

Mike doesn't have an answer for that. Ron stands nearby, propped up on crutches. Fong has been supervising the catering but is obviously distracted by his daughter screaming at Mike. He moves around the table and toward them just as Biyu kicks Mike in the balls.

I look back. Kendall is in the gym, coming after us. We look for a way around the conflict. Mike is down on his knees. Biyu whacks him about the head and shoulders. Fong grabs her and pulls her off Mike. She shouts something at Fong, pointing to Ron as she does. Fong's head swivels between Ron and Mike. Then Fong attacks Mike.

We try to sidestep the scene. Mike slips away from Fong and hops to his feet. He makes a run for it. And crashes into me. The collision is like two pool balls crashing into one another. I go one way; Mike goes the other. I hit the gym floor. Mike crashes into Ron, knocking him to the floor. Ron clutches his side.

"Oh God, my arm!" he screams.

Fong and Biyu gather around Ron. Mike disappears into the crowd. Castillo follows. Kendall shoulders her way toward us. I pop to my feet and run after Castillo. Fong goes after Mike. Kendall goes after us.

We get out of the gym and into the lobby, fighting our way through the crowd. Kendall follows, struggling not only with the crowd but the limitations of her formalwear. We're halfway across the lobby when Kendall shoots Castillo.

You have to give her credit. It's a hell of a shot. Right through a crowd, hitting nothing but the intended target.

Then again, she shot my friend, so it dampens my enthusiasm. Castillo lets out a loud grunt and goes down, clutching his arm. He fingers the bullet hole. There's a distinct possibility he's more upset about his clothes being pierced than his person. The effect on the party is instantaneous. There's a round of screaming. Everyone drops to the floor, except me and Kendall. It gives her a clear shot. (Thanks, assholes.) Castillo shoves the file into my hand.

"Take it!" he says, "Go!"

Kendall aims at me. (Thanks, asshole.) I run with the file tucked under my arm. A shot rings out. A bullet slams into the wall near me. I cut toward the auditorium.

The auditorium isn't much to talk about. There's a lecture area shaped like a half-moon and rows of seats rising away from it. A few people mingle near the back. I stop in the middle of the lecture area, looking for an escape route. There's a small door at the back, leading God knows where. I take a chance on it.

I discover a simple hallway, moving in an L shape. I run around the corner of the L. The hallway beyond is long and white. There are three doors, two on the right and one on the left. There's no backdoor. I'm trapped. I've got to find a hiding place. I go to the first door and discover it's unlocked. I shove it open.

And find two people having sex on a metal desk.

The light pops on automatically when the door opens, so there's no way I can go unnoticed. The couple is not completely naked. The guy wears a dress shirt and socks. The woman is wearing a white blouse. Various clothing items are scattered on the floor. A near-empty bottle of whiskey sits on the desk. The aroma of pot lingers in the air. The woman pops her head over the guy's shoulder. She's got a round face and big eyes. Her blonde hair is tousled. Weirdly enough, I recognize her.

"Evie?" I say.

She holds up the whiskey bottle. "Hi Joe. What are you doing here?"

"I'm kind of in the middle of something," I say, "Sorry to interrupt."

Shawn speaks over his shoulder. "No worries. Hang loose, man."

"Yeah, you hang…yeah."

I slip out of the room and move to the next door. Again, it's unlocked. I shove the door open and see Carol making out with her boss.

They part as soon as the light comes on, then freeze in place like a couple of prairie dogs. A couple of disheveled prairie dogs, one of whom is sporting an obvious boner. Mr. Pratt tries to straighten his tie and pull his coat in front of him to obscure the aforementioned protuberance. Carol tries to simultaneously button up her blouse and tuck it back into her skirt.

"This, uh, this isn't what…what it looks…" Carol can't finish, probably because she knows it's *exactly* what it looks like. Then it hits her. "What the hell are you doing here?"

"Don't really have time for that," I say.

I step out of the room, letting the door clang shut. I have one door left, on the opposite side of the hallway. Before I can try it, though, Kendall starts shooting at me.

Something crashes into the door. I go down to one knee, ducking the wayward bullet. I lose my balance and fall back into the hallway. Kendall takes aim at me. I've got no place to go.

And several things happen in short order.

Evie and Shawn stumble out of their room, still half-dressed. Shawn is toting the near-empty bottle of whiskey.

Carol and Mr. Pratt step out of their room, still getting themselves together.

The two couples spot each other. Mr. Pratt greets this by saying, "What the blue hell is going on?"

Mr. Pratt screams at Evie, putting a finger in her face. Evie grabs the finger and tries to bite it. Carol struggles to separate them.

Kendall dances at the end of the hall, trying to get a clear shot at me. The skirmish is spoiling her aim.

Shawn grabs his father and throws him away from Evie.

Mr. Pratt crashes into Kendall. They bounce off the wall. Kendall hits the floor. The gun clatters away from her. Nobody but me seems to notice.

Mr. Pratt throws a punch at his son. He misses. The son swings the now empty bottle at his father's head. Mr. Pratt ducks.

Kendall grabs the gun and starts to get up. The bottle goes past Mr. Pratt's head and grazes Kendall's chin, knocking her back to the floor.

Mr. Pratt and Shawn grab each other's shirts, jostling and shouting. Evie goes after the father. Carol goes after the son.

Carol and Evie start shouting at each other. Then they start fighting.

Kendall gets to her feet and fires the gun into the air. Everyone freezes. A ceiling tile breathes its last.

"Everybody knock it the fuck off!" Kendall screams, "And get the hell out of my way!"

Despite everyone being nearly deaf from the gunshot, they divine what Kendall is saying and don't have to be told twice. Mr. Pratt, Evie and Shawn scurry into a room, trying not to be last and therefore in the line of fire. Only Carol stays in the hallway.

"You can't do this," Carol says.

Everyone keeps saying that. It's a nice thought. But I've seen Kendall in action. She's *very* well aware she can do this. And she's more than willing. Kendall takes aim at me.

"Last time," she says, "Give me the file."

I could say something pithy, like *You'll have to pry it out of my cold, dead hand* but I think that's her Plan B. I clutch the file to my chest. Kendall gets the message.

"Have it your way," she says.

But Carol moves first. She leaps forward, drops down and throws a foot out, trying to sweep Kendall's foot. Kendall, though, jumps back and avoids the move. She fires haphazardly, and puts a bullet in the wall, not far from Carol's head. Carol crabwalks back toward me. Kendall follows her with the gun, ready to fire.

"That was stupid," Kendall says, "You are both very, very stupid!"

A familiar voice emerges from the hallway behind Kendall. "They don't have an exclusive license on stupid, my dear."

Kendall turns in time to see Deirdre emerge from the hallway. She swings the gun Deirdre's direction. Deirdre's left hand comes up, grabs Kendall's gun hand and moves the weapon away. The right hand fires a straight jab to Kendall's mouth. (I guess the wound isn't bothering her too much.) Deirdre has possession of Kendall's gun once the rest of Kendall drops to the floor, out cold.

"Got everything under control, darling?" Deirdre says, disassembling the gun.

I'm vaguely aware of breath returning to my body. Carol gives me a dazed look, then notices Deirdre.

"It's you," Carol says.

"Yes, it is," Deirdre says, "You're the one who got the cheap shot on me as I recall."

"It wasn't…" With a look from me, Carol thinks better of that statement. "Yes, I am."

Deirdre regards her for a moment. "Nice work."

"Thank you," Carol says, stiffly. Then she adds: "What do we do now?"

"Call the police," Deirdre says, "Or just hang around. I get the feeling they'll be here sooner or later." She looks down at Kendall. "Is this the guilty one?"

"No," I say, "She tried to have you killed. But she didn't double-cross you."

"Then who did?"

"I have a theory. I need to test it out." Deirdre arches an eyebrow in response. I hold out my hands. "Trust me."

She contemplates that then says, "We'll be in touch."

Deirdre disappears around the corner and, for all I know, into thin air. I take out my cell phone and punch in a number, hoping I don't regret this. It takes a few rings, but Jim Street finally answers.

"I have a quick question for you," I say.

Street's tone makes it easy to picture the grin on his face. "You have a question for me? That's different. What's the question?"

"When Chelsea Hollins was found," I ask, "was she wearing a white gold necklace? One with shamrocks on it?"

There's a brief pause, as if Street is thrown by the question. "Hang on a second." He can be heard digging around for something. After several seconds, he comes back on the line. "No, she wasn't found wearing a necklace. There *were* scratches on her neck. Why do you—?"

I thank Street and ring off. I put the phone back into my coat and hand the Impact File to Carol.

"Give this back to Castillo," I say, "Check on him while you're at it. I need you to cover for me. Tell the cops I got freaked out and left. I don't have time to talk to them. I need to check up on a theory."

I start to move, but Carol grabs my arm. "What are you going to do?"

"I'll be fine. Trust me. Just taking a little field trip."

I slip free of Carol's grasp and walk away. I feel a little guilty. Carol not only has to handle cleanup from this nonsense, she probably has to deal with Mr. Pratt and his family crisis. But I've got a hunch to try out. And hope I'm right.

***

One of the charming (and infuriating) things about living in Minnesota is that no matter how long you live here, you are still, on some level, capable of being surprised by the weather. For example, when we go through a cold snap like this, where the temperature is generally a single digit or has a minus sign in front of it for days and days, we start to think it's always going to be this way. Sure, we know, intellectually, that spring will come. (Whether it's in March or June is a matter of debate.) But emotionally, we just can't picture it happening. We're always going to be in a deep freeze.

I'm vaguely aware of that feeling as I walk up the driveway of Chelsea and Alex Hollins's house. The cold is held at bay by my gloves and the scarf tucked into my peacoat. The air is still and the snow crunches lightly under my feet. In an odd way, I feel like I'm the last person on Earth. (Even though I'm not and nobody's making a crappy TV series about me.)

I follow the driveway to the back of the house and stop at the path leading to the cottage. Another few feet and I'd set off the motion sensor. I stand there, not moving despite the freezing cold. Again, the smell of woodsmoke. I take in a breath, watching it turn to fog as I let it out. As I walk down the path, I start to shiver. The cottage comes into view, resting at the bottom of the path. There are no lights on. My pace slows, despite the desire to get inside. I head for the door to the cottage.

The little wooden deck outside the front door creaks slightly as I go up the steps. I wait for a reaction. Nothing. No lights come on. No one calls out. All is calm, all is bright and all the rest of that shit. There's a small window built into the front door. A curtain falls across it. I try the doorknob. The place is unlocked. The door creaks as I open it (because of the weather and life's need to give me the finger at all times.)

The cottage consists of three rooms. The main room houses both the kitchen and the living room. There are two doors off to the right. A bedroom and a bathroom, probably. Rugs are tossed on the wooden floor. Wildlife paintings line the walls. Rustic, if a bit drafty.

The person I'm looking for sits in an easy chair in the living room, right in front of the stone fireplace. I close the door behind me.

The man in question is thin and gangly. He's curled into the easy chair as if he can sink into it and disappear. A plaid blanket is wrapped around him. Even in the thin light I can see something unstable in his brown eyes. His straw-like hair falls over his face and sticks out in all directions. For a few moments, we stare at each other. Finally, he speaks, his voice a little high.

"Are you the police?" he asks.

"No, I'm…a friend. I thought we should talk."

"Who are you?"

"My name is Joe Davis. And if I'm not mistaken, you are…" I pause before saying it. "Dustin Felt."

CHAPTER NINETEEN

Dustin Felt's head lolls forward, ever so slightly; a nod that confirms his identity. The blanket falls away, revealing a ratty sweater and an old pair of slacks. No shoes. I can't help wondering if he's got a weapon on him. He doesn't seem threatened by me. (Probably for the best. *Threatening* is not exactly the vibe I give off.) Still, I keep my distance.

"I'm a friend of Alberto Castillo's," I say.

Dustin's eyes widen. He struggles to speak, battling a stammer. "Did…did he…get the file?"

"He did," I say, "Did you get the file from Chelsea?"

Dustin gazes out the window. "I got it from that…apartment. Chelsea was…was in my way. She…she lie…lied to me."

"And you killed her?"

He closes his eyes. "They were going to poison thousands of people. So they could line their own pockets. They have to be stopped."

Dustin opens his eyes, looking at me as if to make sure he got it right. I keep my distance.

"Let me back up a bit," I say, "After you were let go, you called Al Castillo. Then somebody tried to kill you."

"Ye…yes." Dustin closes them again. "I realized I had to get away."

"And Chelsea helped you," I say, "Because you were having an affair with her."

"I thought she loved me. That's what she said. I believed her." He takes a breath through his nose. "Chelsea said she had a place I could run to."

"Durham," I say.

"She's from there. She had a friend who would help her."

"The sheriff," I say.

"That's right. He was supposed to protect me. Then Chelsea came to visit. She said they weren't going to give up looking for me. That we had to do something. We came up with a…plan."

"To fake your death," I say.

"Yes. Chelsea said Scott, the sheriff, would cover for me. We would fake my death and she would hide me."

And here he is. It's an odd sensation, talking to a dead man. I pull out one of the chairs from the kitchen table and take a seat.

"She hid you here," I say.

Dustin opens his eyes. "She di…did. Ho…how did you know?"

I wave toward the fireplace. "I could smell the woodsmoke. It was faint, but it was there. It told me, eventually, that the cottage was being used. Even though Chelsea wouldn't let anyone back here. Then Castillo discovered who Chelsea really was. That Sheriff Mitchell covered for her. That you died in Durham. It all made sense. Eventually." I lean forward. "What happened with Alex?"

Again, Dustin closes his eyes. "I kept asking Chelsea about the file. She said I needed to lay low, and she'd figure something out. She…she was trying to keep me away from the file. I didn't know it at the time," Dustin's eyes open only a slit then clamp shut again. "Chelsea went out. I wanted to see if the file was in the house. If I could get it to Castillo, Chelsea wouldn't have to hide me anymore. The information would be out there. I could accept the consequences, whatever they were."

"Did you know Alex was home?"

"No. I thought he'd be at work. He usually was. Every time Chelsea came down to see me, she said Alex was at work. That he always worked long hours."

"But he *was* home."

He runs his hands through his hair, scattering it further. "I knew where Alex's study was. I walked right in on him." He waves a hand toward the little kitchen. "I had a butcher knife. In case I needed protection. It took Alex a moment to even notice me. He was startled. Then he said, 'I thought you were dead.' I told him that I wanted the file. He said it belonged to the company. I told him it needed to be released. He agreed. He said he was going to do it himself."

"But you still killed him."

"Why should I have believed him? After everything he had done. He had lied to me. Fired me. Tried to have me killed. Why should I believe him? Sitting here right now, I don't believe him. I don't think he would have released the file."

Apparently, Dustin doesn't know who was actually behind the attempt to kill him. Not that it matters much now. He had more than enough reason to doubt Alex Hollins's sincerity in wanting to release the file.

"Then what happened?" I ask.

"I snapped. After everything…everything he had done. I…I just ran at him. I don't even remember all of it. I remember him not saying anything. Not even screaming. And there was blood. Everywhere. Then I looked for the file." He opens his eyes. "It…it wasn't there."

"Who called the police?"

"Chelsea," he says, "She came home and found Alex. She handled everything."

She certainly did. Chelsea calls the police and leaves, letting them find Deirdre when *she* eventually shows up. But there it is. The answer to the question that's been picking at me this whole time. Turns out I had it wrong. It wasn't a case of someone killing Alex and double-crossing Deirdre. It was one person killing Alex and *another* double-crossing Deirdre.

"You killed Chelsea?" I say.

Dustin closes his eyes. "I did."

"Why?"

"She lied to me." He slams his fists on the arms of the chair. "I was so stupid. It was hidden in her apartment. I followed her. I found her with it. She said she was going to give it to someone from Hankerson-William. She said she was protecting herself." He puts his face in his hands. "She *did* scream. I can still hear it. I'll *always* hear it." He's quiet for several seconds. Finally, he speaks to the floor, eyes still closed. "I took the file. I sent it to Castillo." Dustin opens his eyes. "Is…is he going…going to publish it?"

"I think so. Yes."

He collapses back into the chair. "I…didn't…know where to go. I just ca…came here."

"Why?" I ask.

"To…to die." He throws open his hands. "I have…nothing left. The file is…out there. Chelsea is…gone." His head lolls forward. "There's nothing left."

"You're not going to…"

He shakes his head. "I…can't. I've tho…thought about it. I…I'm…a…coward. I guess."

We're quiet for a long time. Dustin is suffering and not in his right mind. I have only one thing left to ask him.

"Where's the knife now?" I ask.

Dustin reaches under the chair and produces the still-bloodstained knife. "Here."

I try to disguise the shiver. My insides feel like Jell-O. "I need to take that with me."

He grips the handle. "I…can't let you do…that."

"Why not?"

"I…" He closes his eyes. "I won't let the police take me. I won't rot in a cell. I don't want to live, but…I'll decide how I die. And when."

"But…"

"I…can't let you…leave here."

Oh boy. This is what comes of getting chummy with a double murderer. I stay frozen in the chair. Any sudden moves and Dustin will come after me. I mentally calculate how long it will take to cover the distance between us. The answer comes back *Not long*.

"I'm going to stand up," I say, "I want us to talk about this."

"I'm…I'm sorry."

I start to stand. "Listen, you don't—"

That's as far as I get before Dustin charges at me. The knife is over his head. It comes down at me with frightening speed. But I'm fast. I sidestep the knife. The point drives into the chair and sticks there. It only takes Dustin a second to pull it out, but that gives me the opening to sprint for the door. I get there but realize I won't have time to open it before Dustin catches me. I take an instinctive step to the right and Dustin's overhead swipe barely misses me. He crashes into the door. I back away, toward the fireplace and the big chair. I don't really have an escape route here. There's a window, but if I couldn't get the door open, what hope do I have with the window? I could try to disarm Dustin, but if I haven't had success disarming anyone in my life, do I really have a chance now? As the band Squeeze might say, I'm up the junction. (Really, Joe? Brink of death and you're thinking about Squeeze?)

Dustin closes in, slowly. This time, he's careful, making sure he doesn't lunge at me willy-nilly. I'm running flat out of options. Dustin holds the knife in front of him. The blade comes closer and closer.

Suddenly, Dustin's body spins. His arm is thrown to the one side and the knife clatters against the wall. He drops to the floor, clutching his arm.

It takes a second to get my bearings. I step over Dustin and nudge the knife away from him. I'm almost back to the kitchen when the door bursts open and Jim Street charges in, Ric right behind him. They survey the scene. I slump against the wall.

"What took you so long?" I say.

Street turns to Ric. "Told you we should have gone right in after him, Enrique. But no, you said, 'Let's keep our distance, see if he comes out with anything.'"

"Always seems to work on TV," Ric says.

I try to get my breath back before an infarction sets in. "Got your murder weapon on the floor," I say, "Right next to your murderer."

Ric makes his way over, keeping Dustin covered with his gun. "Who do we have here?"

Street beats me to it. "Dustin Felt," he says, "Must be an interesting story there."

"It is," I say, "Speaking of interesting stories, how the hell did you two find me?"

"You call me, asking about the crime scene, then hang up without telling me why you're asking," Street says, "That's the sort of thing we're going to follow up on, Slick."

"You followed me," I say.

"We've had plenty of practice," he says, "Probably lucky for you."

"Probably."

Mr. Beret and Elvis crash into the room. They slip past Street and take possession of Dustin. He remains curled into himself, holding his arm. Mr. Beret turns toward Street.

"We're going to need EMTs, Jimmy" Mr. Beret says, "Gunshot wound. Bicep."

Ric steps out of the cottage to make the call. Street scans the room, silently putting something together. He walks along one wall, stopping when he comes to the window. He slips his hands in the pockets of his cashmere coat and bends to get a closer look.

"How about that?" he says, "A little bullet hole." He turns to me. "Lucky break. You have someone watching your back, Slick?"

I look toward the window. For once, my look of befuddlement is genuine. I *didn't* have anyone backing me up. But apparently, someone was keeping an eye out for me.

"Don't know what happened there," I say, "You got your man, though, right?"

Street lets out a breath as Elvis and Mr. Beret drop Dustin into a chair and stand guard over him. He looks out over the landscape and then to me.

"Don't really see anything out there," he says, "A damn near impossible shot. But you're not going to tell me about that, are you, Slick?"

"Nothing to tell," I say, "Nothing at all."

Street steps over to me. "Play dumb all you want. Just know that this could come back to bite you in the ass."

"You threatening me?" I ask.

"It won't be me," he says.

With that, Street takes charge of the scene, readying for the EMTs and the scores of police who will probably make their way inside. I look toward the window and strain to see my savior. No sign of her.

Probably for the best.

EPILOGUE

Those who know me will tell you I'm a creature of habit. But I wonder sometimes how long I can keep some of these habits going. And if I should want to keep them going.

I have no shortage of habits: coffee at Glacier's, drinks at The Tav, working out at Selby Fitness, running in the summer, touch football in the fall, broomball in the winter. I've driven the same car and lived in the same apartment for five years. Nothing changes and I like it that way.

But how long can this go on? Things do change, right? I'll give up running when the beating on my body becomes too much. I'll get too old for touch football and broomball. The car will break down. The apartment will get too cramped. Maybe I'll move to a different neighborhood and find new places to drink and eat and buy coffee.

Because that's the way of things. Life was meant to be fluid rather than static. It's why we grow old, finish school, find jobs, change jobs, get married, get divorced. Even if we try to keep things the same, the world around us will change. Nothing in life stays the same, no matter how much we like the same.

For now, though, I'll be happily stuck in my rut. When you've got a good thing going…

I think about these things as I walk to Fong's. Yes, *walk* to Fong's. The deep freeze has finally broken, and the temps have climbed into the upper thirties. If you don't live in a cold weather state, the thirties don't sound like much of an improvement. But after a couple weeks of temps starting with a minus sign, the thirties feel like a tropical heatwave. Thus, I'm merrily traipsing through the slush for the walk to Fong's.

I've been putting this off for a week, not knowing what kind of reception I'm going to get. This is why I had misgivings about Mike getting a job at Fong's in the first place. If something went wrong (and when Mike is involved, something going wrong is a matter of *when*, not *if*), it might screw up things with Fong. But I might as well face the Great Eggroll of Destiny. (I should mention: warm weather after a deep freeze makes me rather goofy.)

It's just after seven and the dinner rush is in full swing. I'm glad I ordered online. They didn't call me back to cancel my order and ban me from the building, so I take that as a good sign. Fong is at the cash register, ringing up checks and handling to-go orders. He looks as cool and efficient as ever. His face is tight as I approach the counter.

"Joe Davis!" he says, "You here to pick up?"

"I am. Order's under my name."

"We got it back here."

Fong rummages through the bags on the back counter and returns with my order. Three entrees and a ton of appetizers. He sets the bags on the counter but keeps his hands on them. He looks at me without blinking. My father used to do stuff like this when he wanted to get a lecture in before handing me money for a date.

"This not just for you?" he asks.

"No," I say, "It's for me and some friends."

Fong squints as he checks the bill for the list of items ordered. "Nothing here that Mike like. That good. Okay, you can pay."

I try not to let my relief show. Losing Fong's would have been a blow. Fong runs my credit card, and we wait for the receipt to print. I clear my throat.

"So, I guess Mike isn't welcomed in here?" I ask.

"Mike?" Fong says, his voice booming, "He a bag of shit. We hate him."

There is a chorus of agreement from the kitchen. As it dies down, a faint "Fuck, Mike" can be heard. Fong tears the receipt off the machine but holds on to it rather than handing it over. (Apparently, he's still in Dad Mode.)

"You wanna come in here," he says, "I don't want to see Mike."

It's a tough call. On the one hand, we're talking about a long and valued friendship. On the other hand, we're talking about the best Orange Peel Beef known to man. Actually, it's a rather easy call.

"You won't see Mike again," I say.

Fong hands me my receipt. I give him a smile and pick up my bags. I know what you're thinking, and I'll ask you to knock it off. If he were in my position, Mike would make the exact same call. I'd expect him to do it.

I catch sight of Ron sitting at a table. His arm is in a sling and his leg is in a cast. Biyu is feeding him sesame chicken with a pair of chopsticks. Ron is smiling. Fong beams at the sight. Maybe it's a good thing Mike isn't allowed in here.

The walk back is brisk, mainly because I don't want the food to get cold. I dodge the puddles on the wet sidewalk, enjoy the warm air on my face. I don't know how Deirdre would feel about this, but life feels a little more free without her around.

Deirdre is no longer a suspect in the murders of Alex and Chelsea Hollins. Her description has been completely forgotten and Jim Street doesn't even mention her when a reporter sticks a mic in his face. The focus has been on Dustin Felt and his motivation for the murders. And that's caused a hell of a lot of trouble for Hankerson-William.

One can't go into Dustin Felt's role in the murders without first mentioning the motive and the reason he was believed to be dead. This in turn has led to charges against Kendall (on top of the attempted murders of me and Alberto Castillo). Skizzy is still at large but it will only be a matter of time before he's behind bars (or so Jim Street keeps telling the press). Al Castillo has made hay out of the Impact File, breaking the story and making the rounds on the local news. Payton Hicks, though he claims no knowledge of Kendall's actions, has resigned from Hankerson-William for his role in suppressing the Impact File. The company has been in scramble mode ever since. Needless to say, the Green River Project will not be going forward.

I get to my parking lot and run up the erector set of stairs and decks behind the building. Yes, it creaks like it's about to step away from the building and look for shelter. But there's nobody hiding in the shadows, waiting to spring. Thank heaven for small favors, I guess.

I slip through the backdoor. Lenny and Squiggy are not waiting for me in the hallway, which is normally the case when I have guests. I drop the food on the breakfast bar and slip into the kitchen to grab the square plates. Carol gets up from the futon and makes her way over to the breakfast bar. Lars pops in through the front door, alive to the possibility of free grub. Mike remains huddled in the comfy chair, holding his glass of Winter Ale. He cranes his neck as Carol gets the food out of the bags.

"Anything for me?" he asks.

"No dice," I tell him, "Fong made that clear. You are banned from any and all delicacies from his place."

Mike gets a sour look. "C'mon, you can give me part of an eggroll or something. It's not like Fong is going to know."

"Forget it," I say, "If the last few weeks have taught me anything, it's never assume you have privacy."

Mike flips a hand at that. Carol spoons some Chicken Fried Rice on to her plate. Lars eats potstickers directly out of the container. I slide the Orange Peel Beef my direction. Mike watches the proceedings.

"You're just going to let me sit here and be hungry?" he says, in a pouty voice.

"I've got some leftover blackened chicken mac 'n' cheese in the fridge," I say.

Mike bobs his head, considering. For him, it's not as good as dinner from Fong's, but the mac 'n' cheese is homemade and not a bad consolation prize. He stalks into the kitchen, looking not unlike a sulking teen. He gets the Tupperware out of the fridge and puts it in the microwave.

"Not even fucking fair," he says, "I was a hell of a delivery man. Now they've cut me off. I tried sneaking in the other day to talk to Biyu. She wanted nothing to do with me. Then Fong found us and went after me with a broom handle."

Mike gets the mac 'n' cheese from the microwave and joins us at the breakfast bar. Carol uses her chopsticks to grab a potsticker out of the container, narrowly beating Lars to the punch.

"Speaking of taking chances," she asks him, "How are things with the girlfriend?"

Lars nearly drops his chopsticks. "Iris and I realized things were…not working out. We thought it was best to move on."

Mike pauses with his mac 'n' cheese. "You gave up having sex with a beautiful woman?"

"There were…other things to consider."

Carol grabs another potsticker. "Like her horrible personality?"

"That," Lars says, "and the broken nose Deirdre gave her. Really messed up Iris's looks."

Mike, living vicariously through Lars, is not willing to give up on this relationship. "Maybe you should just wait it out. Let the nose heal."

"I don't think that's going to work," Lars says, "The damage is pretty bad. Iris is thinking about plastic surgery. I gently suggested she consider therapy as well. She broke a lamp and threw a chair at me." He digs into his Slayer Stir Fry. "Seemed like the right time to move on. Besides, I'm much happier with Megan."

"The receptionist at Hankerson-William?" I ask.

"Absolutely," Lars says, "No more of this weird unpredictable behavior. Just a regular, normal girl who's into whips and chains."

We let that one pass without comment. As long as Lars gets out of the relationship with Iris, we'll turn a blind eye to everything else. Lars, eating with his usual gusto, turns to Carol.

"How did things turn out with your boss?" he asks.

"And the kid?" Mike adds.

Carol finds her fried rice very interesting. "Shawn is living at his parents' house. They've banned him from seeing Evie."

"You think it's working?" I ask.

"I don't know," Carol says, "I seriously doubt it. Evie is nothing if not determined. Shawn is pretty much the same way. I don't know how that one is going to end. Poorly, if I had my guess."

I toy with my Orange Peel Beef (which is practically a sin). "How about you and Mr. Pratt?"

"It's on a *Let's never speak of this again* kind of basis," Carol says, "Especially after I turned down his marriage proposal."

"Wait, isn't he already married?" I ask.

"That didn't seem to be a problem for him," Carol says, "So, I didn't answer any of his calls or emails. Didn't answer the door when he showed up at my place. Threatened to tell HR on him if he didn't knock it off." She dips an eggroll in some sweet-and-sour sauce. "I think we'll keep things professional from here on out."

We dig further into the food. It feels a little like a family dinner. Some relaxation in the midst of crazy times. Sure, Lars is dealing with a breakup and Mike has lost another job and Carol almost lost *her* job and I was almost killed or arrested about fifteen times over the last few weeks. But we're here together and we've got some decent grub. Things can't be too bad, right?

Carol sneaks a look at me. "Have you heard from Deirdre?"

"Not since the night I found Dustin Felt. She's disappeared back into the shadows."

I've just taken a bite of a cream cheese wonton when there's a knock at the backdoor. Everyone tenses. I slowly walk down the hallway. Most of the people who would knock at my backdoor are currently gathered at my breakfast bar. I have no idea who this could be. The peephole reveals Jim Street on my deck. For once, I'm relieved to see him. I flip open the backdoor.

"Mr. Street," I say, "I'm afraid you've caught us at dinner."

Street's face remains impassive. "You got a minute?"

I'm a little thrown by Street's demeanor. I wave a hand into the room. "Come on in."

He looks toward my friends at the breakfast bar and narrows his eyes. "Actually, I'd prefer if you step out here."

Okay, now I'm *really* thrown. I flip on the deck light and step out, closing the door behind me. With the halfway decent weather, my sweater and jeans will keep me warm for a few minutes. Street and I position ourselves on either side of the door.

"What's going on?" I ask.

He takes a second, then says, "I need to know I can trust you. So, this first part is entirely off the record. Understand?"

"That's a little vague, but let's say I do."

"When was the last time you saw Deirdre? The *actual* last time you saw her."

I debate the matter, then decide there's no harm in telling him the truth. "The night Dustin Felt was found."

Street's cop glare in full effect. "You haven't talked to her since? Phone, e-mail, anything?"

"No. She disappeared into the ether."

"You have no idea where she is?"

Now I'm getting irritated, despite the vague knowledge that Street has every right to question my integrity. "I just told you I don't. The whole thing was settled. She has no reason to contact me." I square him with a look. "Why do you want to know?"

"Because Kendall Lucas is dead."

A shock runs through me, stiffening every part of my body. Thankfully, I don't have to disguise the shock from Street. Blood rushes to my head and I totter a little. Street takes his hands out of his coat pockets, ready to catch me if I pass out. I put a hand against the wall, steadying myself.

"What happened?" I ask, my voice sounding far away.

"Kendall made bail," he says, "She was living at her place, but we had her under surveillance. She missed a meeting with her lawyer. He went to check on her and didn't get an answer. She was in the bedroom. Cold."

I struggle to get words out. "How?"

"Best guess is poison. The coroner found a pin prick on her neck. We're waiting on toxicology, but I'll bet that's what it comes back as."

"You think it's Deirdre?"

"She'd be the number one suspect," Street says, "We've got Dustin Felt in custody, Payton Hicks is under surveillance. Chelsea Hollins is in the morgue. Given the sophistication, it would fit Deirdre's M.O." He scrutinizes me. "You really haven't heard from her?"

"I haven't."

Street slips his hands back into his pockets. "You might want to watch your ass. I don't think Deirdre's through with you."

Now a chill runs through me. "Maybe not."

"You hear from her, you call me. Understand. Don't mess with her, Slick. You'll live longer."

Street buttons up his coat and disappears into the darkness. I fall back against the door. Deirdre killed Kendall. No doubt about it. Sure, Skizzy might be a suspect, but he's the kind to set fire to the building and hope for the best. (And probably get the wrong building.) I move inside, not sure what I'm going to tell my friends. As soon as the backdoor closes, my phone rings. Somehow, I know who it is. I answer without a greeting.

"You've heard," Deirdre says.

I step into the bathroom, giving myself some privacy. "Where are you?"

"Close enough to know you talked to Street. What did you tell him?"

"The truth. That I haven't heard from you."

Things are silent, then Deirdre says, "That's good."

I put a hand against the wall. "Why did you kill Kendall?"

"I told you, sweets. I don't like loose ends."

"She wasn't a threat to you."

"She knew about me," Deirdre says, her voice getting cold, "And her tits were in the ringer. Push comes to shove, she was going to tell the cops everything she knew."

I close my eyes, afraid to ask this next question. "What about Skizzy?"

Her voice lightens. I can picture her self-satisfied smirk. "Skizzy's disappeared. He's going to stay that way."

"Unless they find the place you buried him."

Still the light tone. "*Places*, darling. Places."

It's all I can do to keep from throwing up. I manage to choke down the bile. "What about Payton Hicks?"

"He gets a pass," Deirdre says, "He didn't know about me. He didn't know what Kendall was up to. She protected him. In more ways than one."

"What about Dustin?" I ask.

"He doesn't know anything. Not about me, anyway. And he's half-crazy. I don't need to worry about him."

I'm sweating. Thirty-eight degrees outside and I'm sweating. Because I have a question for Deirdre, but I'm not sure how to ask.

"Are, uh…" I say, "are you…?"

Deirdre knows where I'm going and she's nice enough to speed me along. "You're worried about you?"

"You don't like loose ends," I say.

Another pause. "I owe you. That keeps you safe." I don't say anything to that. Deirdre says, "You sound disappointed in me."

"Maybe I didn't really know who I was dealing with."

"You know now," she says.

"I do."

We're quiet. Melting snow drips outside the bathroom window. Soothing, in a strange way. Deirdre's voice comes on the line.

"Thank you for your help," she says, "I don't think we'll be seeing each other again. But who knows?" A beat. "Goodbye, Joe Davis."

"Goodbye, Christina."

There's a faint noise in the background. It might be a gasp. It might be a sob. Before I can figure it out, the line goes dead.

I walk back to the breakfast bar. Everyone stares at me, concerned. I slip my hands into my pockets.

"How much did you hear?" I ask.

"Nothing," Carol says, "But it wasn't hard to figure out who you were talking to. Is everything okay?"

"I think so," I say, "But who knows?"

"You think she'll be back?" Lars asks.

I join them at the breakfast bar. "Hard to say. I don't want to think about it."

We go back to our food, though the whole *family meal* vibe has been shattered. Nobody quite knows what to say. I reach for an eggroll, then stop.

"Okay, who took my eggroll?" I say.

Everyone turns to Mike. He throws up his hands. "Why do you think it was me? Why do you *always* think it's me?"

"Because it's usually you," I say.

Mike frowns. He pushes aside the Tupperware, revealing where he's hidden the eggroll. He returns it to my plate.

"Would it have killed you to give me some food?" he asks.

I stare at Mike as I bite into the eggroll. He promptly backs down, realizing what he's said. You can't threaten me with something that will kill me.

I've been threatened by that thing already.

THE END

Randall J. Funk is the writer of the Joe Davis Mystery series. He is also an actor, director and playwright. His plays include *The Hound of the Baskervilles, The Mudslinger Party*, and *Bring Me the Head of Dominic Papatola*. He lives in St. Louis Park, MN, with his son Ben.